THE SCREAM BEHIND HER SMILE

ATHENA DANIELS

SUNSET COAST PUBLISHING

THE SCREAM BEHIND HER SMILE

An emotionally gripping story of love, marriage, deception and...murder.

It's one thing to realize the man you married is not who you believe him to be. It's another thing entirely to prove it. After all, who is going to take the word of an unstable woman who's never fully recovered from the heartbreak of losing her child?

The only question now, is how far he will go to protect his secrets.

PRAISE FOR ATHENA DANIELS

The Seer's Daughter

"...the perfect culmination of paranormal mystery with steamy and sensual romance and just enough suspense and intrigue to guarantee a chilling, goose bump-invoking, story line... *The Seer's Daughter* would be a brilliant option for adaption to screen—there's a television series/movie in here for absolute certain." —*AusRom Today*

"...as chilling as it is sexy... This is much more than a romance. The paranormal aspects along with the secondary characters really make the story. The descriptions, language, emotions, dialogue... are all cleverly written to keep you engaged and the pages turning, while the suspense will make sure you read this story with all the lights on." —5-star Top Pick, *The Romance Reviews*

"If you are looking for a book to give you goose bumps and keep you watching over your shoulder, then I can recommend this one! ... I got dragged away from this book late in the evening by my husband, as I had an exceedingly early start the next day. This didn't stop me from thinking about the book and what I had read for well over an hour after the lights went out, as well as dreaming about it!"
    —Archaeolibrarian, 5 stars, Amazon review

"What a rush! One of my most favorite reads this year! ... It's almost like Stephen King meets Christina Dodd... I loved it; can't wait for book two!" —5 stars, Amazon review

"...a perfect blend of paranormal fiction and romantic suspense that had me completely captivated to the very last page... flawlessly delivered." — Faridah, 5 stars, *Readers Favorite*

The Alchemist's Son

"...go the hell out and buy both of these books now because they are freaking FANTASTIC. I am not exaggerating when I say this is some of the best romantic suspense I have ever read, paranormal or otherwise; I literally couldn't put down *The Alchemist's Son* until I got to the final, thrilling climax."
    —5 stars, Amazon review

"This book is as good as the first, with twists and turns! You get the good ol' creepy feels! You may be wanting to look behind you, or not go in your attic or basement anytime soon! I wish this author could write as fast as I can read; I would never put her books down!" —5 stars, Amazon review

"This book had my hair standing on end and gave me chills from start to finish. Once again I could not put it down and loved how, no matter how hard I tried, I just couldn't guess ahead what was going to happen next." —5 stars, Amazon review

Girl Unseen

"For paranormal fans, *Girl Unseen* can't be beat! The depth of emotion with which Athena Daniels fills her characters provides such intensity that you feel their pain and heartache... Just make sure to leave the lights on! Fabulous read! I couldn't put this down and can't wait for more!"
    —5 stars, *Readers Favorite*

"A wonderful, spooky story with lots of action. A murder mystery to solve and a scorching hot romance. It has everything and will keep you guessing all the way through. I loved it." —5 stars, Amazon review

"I loved it so much! For me, this book covers a lot of ground when it comes to romance + something else. You like a little bit of scary? You've got ghosts and spirits. You like a little bit of detective work? You've got a badass PI trying to solve the mystery... You want romance? Well, you have one amazing medium falling for the PI, while trying to help out a lost soul. Oh, and maybe, just maybe, you want all these with nice writing? You've got author Athena Daniels. Congratulations for your future book to read!"

—5 stars, *Lilly's Book World*

When Darkness Follows

"...heart-stopping, explosive tale of the paranormal...This is a masterpiece, written in exactly the right tone to send shivers down the spine; a combination of strong romance, horror and the paranormal all wound up in a neat bundle and then spread out in a web that draws the reader in."

—5 stars, *Readers Favorite*

"When Darkness Follows leaves no question in my mind as to why Athena Daniels' series is so wildly popular. It takes off from the first line and just doesn't ever slow down. I'd recommend When Darkness Follows to readers who adore an intense paranormal thriller with a healthy side of sizzle by an author who is as skilled at crafting a story as the list of accolades she's acquired say she is."

—5 stars, *Readers Favorite*

"This book had it all: a suspenseful paranormal mystery, a heroine who's fighting forces she can't defeat alone, and a strong, sexy hero. This was also a true page-turner for me, because I couldn't stop reading. I was literally angry that I had to put this down to take a shower and get ready for work :) I devoured it in less than one day, and I'm now left sad and bereft that it's over."

—5 stars, Amazon Review

"Wow! This book kept me sat at the edge of my seat and turning pages till well after I should have been asleep but being bleary eyed the next day was well worth it. I was hooked from page one and couldn't put it down, it was that gripping."

—5 stars, Amazon Review

Desperate

"What can I say other than I absolutely loved this book from the start, and the prologue really set the pace for a fast-paced plot with lots of suspense and the right touch of romance. The plot was strong and progressed well and I loved the flirty banter between Eric and Ivy, which added to the growing relationship between the pair and provided a few good sex scenes illustrating their intense chemistry... the author has done an amazing job of penning this novel and I can't wait to read more of their work in the future."

—*The Romance Studio* (TRS)

"Suspense and steamy romance line the pages of this fast-paced thriller, with action and drama from start to finish.... If Athena Daniels keeps it up with writing like this, I have no doubts that she will establish her place among the most well-known authors of erotic literature.... If you're a fan of romantic thrillers, I would definitely recommend giving this one a read."

—Official Review, *Online Book Club*, 4 out of 4 stars

ALSO BY ATHENA DANIELS

BEYOND THE GRAVE SERIES

The Seer's Daughter (Book One)
The Alchemist's Son (Book Two)
Girl Unseen (Book Three)
When Darkness Follows (Book Four)

DESPERATE SERIES

Desperate (Book One)

NOVELS

The Scream Behind Her Smile

PART I

One lie is enough to question all truths.

PROLOGUE

*S*ix feet under, and I continue to fall.

Hurtling out of control in downward spirals into an inky dark pit of pain, sorrow, despair. And regret.

As I lie here in my front hallway, in the place where it all began, I wonder what would have happened if I'd never opened the door that Tuesday afternoon?

Would she have gone somewhere else? Would she have swept off in another direction, an alternative reality where our lives would never have crossed paths?

It's called a pivotal moment, isn't it? When you can pinpoint the precise moment that changed your life. The moment I realized the life I'd been living was nothing but an illusion, my heart ripped in two. Shredded would be more accurate. But then, there never were any half measures in any of this mess.

And now I'm lying here, blood pooling beneath my body, deep crimson smears on cold white tiles, remembering every sordid moment in vivid detail.

I'm curled into a ball, my arms wrapped tightly around my stomach, but I can't stem the flow of blood seeping through my fingers, warm and sticky.

I can't breathe.

I cry out but can't hear if I've made a sound through the roar of blood rushing past my ears.

There's a shadow standing over me.

"I want you to die here, slowly and alone." Her voice is cold, emotionless. "And I want you to use the time you're bleeding out on the floor to think about what you did. And when you take your last breath, I want you to fully realize the extent of the damage you've caused. It's all your fault. *All* of it!"

I drift in and out of consciousness and wonder if I had my chance to do it over again, if I had the choice, would I choose not to open the door that day?

Even after everything, I know that I would.

I'd go through it all again, and then some, if it meant I had the chance to be with Zach just one more time…

CHAPTER 1

Three months earlier.

The high-pitched chime of our doorbell grates across my nerves. An uninvited visitor is *not* a welcome distraction.

Straightening, I rub at the back of my neck and run a critical eye over the expanse of exquisite imported Italian fabric that fans across my workspace. Rebecca's engagement dress. The extra detail in my best friend's project means time is tight.

The doorbell rings again.

Is it too much to ask that Derek answer the door?

He knows I don't like to be disturbed when I'm working. Reluctantly, I leave my unfinished project and make my way down the hallway, the white tiles smooth and cold beneath my bare feet. I open the door and squint against the harsh afternoon sunlight.

"Hello." The woman on my doorstep is holding a suitcase. "You must be Claire." She assesses me from head to toe, and the intensity with which she does so causes me to do the same to her. She's around my age, maybe two or three years older than my twenty-eight. *Derek's age.*

She's shorter than my five-foot-nine by a few inches with long and glossy dark brown hair that falls in soft designer waves to her shoulders.

Her tailored shirt is slightly sheer, revealing seductive glimpses of a lacy black bra.

My comfy tracksuit pants suddenly feel shabby, and I run a hand over my hastily tied-back hair that is several weeks overdue for a trip to the salon. "Yes, I'm Claire. I'm sorry, I don't know who you—"

"Jasmine," she interrupts, smiling brightly. "Derek didn't tell you I was coming?"

A fixed smile hides my irritation that he hadn't.

Even if I hadn't heard my husband coming up behind me, I would have known because Jasmine's expression changes instantly, eyes softening, lashes fluttering as she looks over my shoulder.

"Jazzy! You're here." Derek's shoulder bumps mine as he rushes past me to grab her suitcase. I stumble slightly, placing my palm on the wall for balance. "Let me take that," Derek says. "Come in, come in."

Jasmine embraces my husband in a cloud of exotic scent.

"Thanks, Hardty," she says, adding a "y" on the end of his—our—surname, Hardt. "Thank you for taking me in."

"Think nothing of it. I'm only too glad to help."

Derek takes a step back so that his gaze includes both of us. "Jasmine, this is my wife, Claire. Claire, this is Jasmine Ravendish. We went to school together. I'm sure you remember me talking about her."

"Of course," I reply automatically, but I don't. Derek and I have been together ten years, since I was eighteen. I'd heard stories of his school friends so often I could recite them by heart, but not one of them included a Jasmine or *Jazzy*.

"Nice to meet you, and please forgive my surprise." I let my gaze settle on Derek. "My husband didn't let me know to expect you."

"You were working." There's a familiar edge to Derek's voice. "I didn't want to disturb you. I know how much you hate that." Our eyes meet, and the space between us shifts, the atmosphere turning chilly. A sharp retort freezes on my tongue. I will not argue with my husband in front of a guest.

Our marriage is going through a rough patch, if three years can still be referred to as a patch. Small arguments can result in days, even weeks, of stone-cold silence. We don't resolve anything; we just allow enough time to pass so that neither of us can remember what it was we'd disagreed about in the first place. There are no passionate arguments, no earth-shattering make-up sex. Just a quiet resuming of married life and daily conversation.

"Jazzy needs a place to stay," Derek says. "And I told her she could stay here."

"You don't mind, do you, Claire?" Jasmine asks, eyes wide as though afraid I'll say no.

"Of course, I don't mind." I ignore the strange premonition trickling down my spine. I find my reaction to her unfounded and more than a little unsettling.

But I am unhinged. Derek would be the first one to tell you that. He reminds me constantly of how unstable I am. You'd think he'd have a little more compassion. After all, what happened to me happened to him, too.

"Well, then!" Derek's voice is a touch too loud. "What are we doing standing in the hallway? Come in, let me get you a drink."

Their footsteps fade, and I stand in the resulting silence for a moment, thinking about the way Derek's hand so easily fell to rest on the small of her back and the natural way she leant into him as they walked. Isn't that overly familiar for an old friend my husband has never mentioned? But it's too late for concerns; the decision has been made.

My husband and I have a house guest.

There is absolutely no reason whatsoever for me to have a problem with an old school friend staying a night or even two. Lord knows we have the room.

It's just something about her…

I'm sure it's nothing.

I'll relax once I get to know her better.

I shift my focus back to work and the need to finish Bec's engagement dress in time.

Several hours later, I look up from my sewing machine in time to see the sun disappear over Nedlands into Western Australia's horizon. Through the floor-to-ceiling windows of my sewing room, the sky is painted in a stunning array of pastels—pink, lilac and yellow—across the ocean. The view is spectacular.

I stretch my neck and run a critical eye over the finished gown, the silky fabric sparkling with Swarovski crystals. I smile, satisfied I've done the best job I can. Rebecca is getting married to Rob Stanton Jr., the son of the managing partner in the accountancy firm Derek works for, and the last thing I want to do is disappoint her.

I set off in search of Derek and Jasmine, but before I leave the room, my hand hesitates over the door handle, my gaze invariably drawn to the picture of our beautiful girl with bright blue eyes and bouncy blonde curls on her fourth birthday. A year before we found out.

A lump lodges in my throat. *Katie.* Placing a hand on the large timber dresser anchors me, keeps me from sinking into my demons.

Three years... When will missing you stop hurting so much?

I blink back the hot sting of tears and, with practiced long, deep, breaths, fight the seductive lure of numbing darkness.

No pills. Not tonight. Not anymore.

I've got this.

Without the numbing influence of the pills, my thoughts may be a painfully discordant jumble of shattered glass, but at least, they're my thoughts. I hug my arms around my stomach. Despite the lingering warmth from the sunny autumn day, fingers of ice crystalize inside my veins.

Life goes on, they tell me. God, how I hate those words. *Claire, you need to find your spark again. Claire, you need to engage in life again. Claire, it's not healthy taking all those pills. Claire, when was the last time you cut your hair? Claire... Claire... Claire!*

But how do you continue to live after you've already died on the inside? I exist as a walking corpse with an exterior that only resembles the woman I used to be.

Three years.

Three years, and it still hurts just as much today as it did that day, Mother's Day, three years ago. *Katie...*

Two things helped get me through each day: medication and design. To avoid thinking, to avoid feeling, I'd lose myself for longer and longer stretches of time in work, bringing creation after creation to life. From simple high-tea dresses to elaborate ball gowns. The relief, however, was only temporary. Reality was always waiting for me when I came up for air.

Of course, what happened to Katie was hard on Derek, too, but he handled his grief differently—drinking and taking up activities that took him away for days, even weeks, at a time. We avoided life, and we avoided each other. We both escaped this new world we were forced to live in.

The distant sound of laughter brings me out of my reverie. Before I move away from Katie's picture, I let my fingers touch my lips then trace them across my daughter's sweet, smiling face in the white-gold frame.

Detouring into the bedroom, I change into my favorite pair of comfy jeans and a clean T-shirt and run a quick comb through my light brown, shoulder-length hair.

Something awful must have happened for Jasmine to need a roof over her head for the night. I, of all people, know the curveballs life throws at you. What happened to Jasmine for her to turn up on our doorstep needing a place to stay?

~

Derek and Jasmine are on the balcony watching the sunset. The same sky I'd been admiring from my office window moments ago, except the views of the Swan River are better out here.

In the kitchen, I open the cupboard and reach for a wine glass and watch them a moment through the floor-to-ceiling windows. She's sitting very close to him, her body angled in such a way that their legs are touching. He throws his head back and laughs at something she says.

I tip my head to one side. When was the last time I heard him laugh like that?

Jasmine reaches across and touches his arm. She doesn't immediately withdraw it. He doesn't glance down at it or appear surprised by it in any way. He leans toward her, his face lit up in a smile as he listens to something she says. My stomach clenches uneasily, and I hold my breath.

Jasmine withdraws her hand, and once again, they're just two old friends catching up. I release the breath I'd been holding, but my chest remains tight, my pulse a touch too fast.

I tug at my T-shirt, a thin layer of sweat making it stick to my skin.

I recognize the symptoms. *Anxiety.* Anxiety and depression: two emotions not unfamiliar to me.

Maybe I *should* take the pills?

No. Three years of medication is long enough. Besides, since I've stopped taking them, real life, real emotion, has been bleeding back in. And it feels good not to be numb, despite the pain.

Selecting a bottle of wine, I pull the cork and watch the crimson liquid fill the glass. I focus on the way it clings to the side before pooling in the bottom. I catch the cork before it rolls off the counter and hold it to my nose.

Ripe berries and hints of vanilla, full-bodied and lush, just like your wife, the guy at the Margaret River winery had said to Derek on the wine tour. Was that really six years ago?

Katie had been three then.

We'll take a case, Derek had said, grinning at me. I take a breath and remind myself of the way he'd looked at me that day, the way his eyes had glistened in the setting sun as he said how much he loved us, me and his little Katie-bear. The way the swipe of his tongue had transferred the taste of wine from his mouth to my lips.

I would no longer be described by anyone as full-bodied and lush. I've lost a lot of weight since then, but not because I diet and look after myself.

Back then, we were young parents to a beautiful girl who put the sunshine in each day. We had a home, my husband a successful career, and we were in love. At least, I think we were in love. Either way, we were both very much in love with our little Katie. And that made everything all right.

Until...

You can glue a vase together, but no matter how well you make the repair, the cracks will still be there. Weak points, ready to crumble with the slightest pressure.

I should know. It's the way I feel about myself every single day.

Broken.

I open the glass doors, and a rush of balmy evening air washes over me. I smile at them, and even though they both glance my way, they continue their conversation without pause.

Derek is wearing a white shirt, unbuttoned at the collar, and his favorite pair of jeans. He's handsome; I know that objectively as I watch him from the doorway. Brown hair neatly trimmed, short at the collar and around his ears.

I hold the bottle up. "Would anyone like a glass?"

They both look up at the same time. Derek shifts position, leaning back in his chair. His knees are no longer touching hers. The neck of the bottle is cool and smooth as I wait for their answer.

"Sure," Derek says, immediately taking the bottle to top up Jasmine's glass. I take the seat across from them.

"Thanks, Hardty," Jasmine says, her face flushed, her voice slightly breathless. Is it just from the wine? There *is* an empty bottle on the table. The conversation they were having before I joined them has now stalled.

Derek clears his throat. Jasmine shifts in her seat. Gone is the laughter from a moment ago.

I'm intruding.

I immediately dismiss the thought. This is my house; that is my husband. Maybe it's just because she doesn't know me.

"We didn't get a chance to meet properly earlier," I say. "I understand you need a place to stay. Is everything okay?"

"I—" She blinks a few times, and tears appear in her eyes.

"Jazzy has just left her husband," Derek says.

"I'm sorry to hear that," I say, meaning it.

"Derek said it's all right if I stay here for a while, just until I find myself a new place," Jasmine says, twirling an earring. When she lowers her hand, I notice it's in the shape of a bloom with five slender petals. It's a star jasmine flower. I know that only because Derek asked the gardener to plant some of those bushes in the front yard last year. Was that just coincidence?

"My aunt lives in Perth," Jasmine says. "But she doesn't have much room, and I'd have to sleep on her fold-out couch. Derek said he had a spare room if I ever needed it. I just didn't know it would be under these circumstances. I'll start looking for a job and apartment tomorrow."

"You're staying in Western Australia?" I'm surprised her unplanned marriage breakdown has turned into a permanent move.

"Yes," she says, not volunteering a reason why. I sense there is a lot more to her story, a lot more to her, than meets the eye.

"What do you do?" I ask. "What kind of work are you looking for?"

"Jasmine's a nurse," Derek answers for her. *For her.* And she doesn't pull him up on the annoying trait the way I do.

The sun sinks fully into the horizon, and I turn on the outside light, lighting citronella candles to deter the mosquitoes.

"Don't worry, Claire," Jasmine says. "I won't be a bother. Derek and I realized in February that we like all the same things."

"February?"

"I caught up with Jazzy when I went to Sydney last," Derek says. "I'm sure I told you."

"Of course," I say slowly. "I think you mentioned it."

But he didn't. When he went to Sydney in February, he saw Ben, Jake, and Ryan, their wives, and caught up with his sister and mother. He also caught up with his friend Amelia and her husband and kids. So why wouldn't he mention Jasmine? Especially as he'd clearly spent enough time with her to know her problems and to offer her a place to stay.

"You caught up with her at Amelia's house, didn't you?"

"No. We caught up at The Arms on Friday night," Jasmine says, referring to the hotel I know Derek and his mates favor. "I still can't believe the music they were playing that night. It was nineties night, Claire," she says, "It brought back so many memories for us. Those were the days, weren't they?" She turns to Derek. "Remember when you used to wear that horrible denim jacket?"

Derek laughs out loud, a slight flush of color appearing on his face. "Don't mock it. I loved that jacket."

"But it was just so... *daggy*," she says, placing a hand on his knee as though to soften the blow of her words. "All those tassels across the back."

"It's only daggy now—it wasn't back then. Besides," he adds with a smirk, "I could work it."

I raise my brow, hearing my husband use language and a tone that I'm unaccustomed to hearing from him.

"Yes, you certainly could." Jasmine laughs.

"Don't talk to me about my jacket." Derek's tone is playful. "You used to wear those tight jeans, so painted on I don't know how you even got into them."

"I had to lie down on the bed and thread a coat hanger through the zipper to do them up." She winces at the memory. "I'm sure you did crazy things back when you were young, didn't you, Claire?"

"Of course." Up until I was eighteen and my mother died in a car accident. My childhood home had been fun, full of color and texture and a total contrast to how "proper" my life became after I married Derek. My new husband didn't approve of my relaxed style of upbringing or the carefree, artist's lifestyle I left behind in England.

And now... here he is, laughing and carefree in a way he's never been with me. Remembering times that were fun before I knew him.

They launch into a discussion about nineties fashion, which turns into an hour-long episode of "Remember when..." and "Where are all our friends now?". I smile when they laugh. I even ask the odd question, but it slows down their storytelling, and I sense Derek's impatience when he has to stop and explain in more detail. Their stories always lose something in translation.

"You had to be there," Jasmine keeps saying.

But I wasn't. And she was.

And now she's here.

Several times, I attempt to steer the conversation to the here and now. Offer a plate of food. Each and every time, the conversation turns back to their childhood days. The good old days. I get it. I do.

Who doesn't love to reminisce? But…

But no matter what I tell myself, I can't relax.

And Jasmine looks fun. Even I have to admit that.

When did life get so serious?

May.

Mother's Day.

Three years ago.

My smile becomes forced. My face is going to crack apart and scatter across the floor like a broken china cup, so I excuse myself.

"If you're going to stay, I need to set you up a bed." I stand.

I leave them together on the balcony but take the bottle of wine to bed with me.

Derek comes into the bedroom some hours later. He wobbles from too much wine, sits heavily on the bed, and kicks the jeans from his ankles.

"Derek," I say when he slides into bed next to me. "Why have you never mentioned her before?"

Derek sighs and turns the bedside lamp off. "I'm sure I have. Maybe you just don't remember."

"Why is she here?"

Derek groans. "She explained that earlier, Claire. I know you heard; you were standing right next to her when she was speaking."

"Don't take that tone with me." I keep my voice even, wanting answers, not another fight. "I'm trying to understand why she came *here*. She lives in Sydney. Surely, she has friends and family over there. Why come all the way to Western Australia?"

"Her aunt lives here."

"But she's not staying with her aunt. She's here."

Derek yanks the sheet around him and turns over, the action pulling the blankets away from me. I have the choice of moving closer to him or being cold. I can't decide.

I stare at the crisp white sheets. White sheets. They match the white carpets, the white floor tiles, white kitchen cabinets, and the white walls.

Everything is clean and organized. Clinical. I used to think Derek's minimalist taste was stylish. Classier than my preference for bold colors and textures. But without Katie's bright energy, the house feels cold and empty. The more distant I feel from my husband, the more I crave the lively, organized clutter of my childhood home. My mother.

My chest squeezes. I miss her. I miss them both.

"Why didn't you tell me you saw her in February?" We've been married eight years. Surely, we are past this. Derek's trips to Sydney have increased in frequency the last couple of years. Every few weeks, he is over there for at least five days at a time, sometimes more. But that is only because the accountancy firm is expanding nation-wide, and Derek has been helping set up the Sydney office. Isn't it?

"I saw lots of people in February," he says. "Since when do I need to give you a blow-by-blow account of my every move? It's late, Claire, and I'm tired. Its jealousy that's making you overreact. You wouldn't have a problem if it was Ben or Jake needing a place to stay."

Is that true? Chances are I wouldn't have this uneasy feeling if it were Ben or Jake. But does that make it any less valid?

I've spent the last three years putting myself back together again, but I haven't succeeded. There's a stranger living in my image. I'm alive, but I couldn't tell you who I am anymore.

"I went to school with her," Derek mumbles into the pillow. "I don't want to fight with you. It's not a big deal, so please don't turn it into one. Can you please just trust me and get some sleep?"

His breathing turns heavy and regular as I stare at his back. My eyes sting, and a lump forms in my throat. There's a gaping emptiness inside of me. An endless span of hungry darkness that's threatening to swallow me whole. Can't he see that?

I resent the sudden rush of neediness and resist the urge to wake him. The last thing our marriage needs is another fight. But what about what I need?

Watching him laugh with Jasmine tonight caused me to miss how our relationship used to be in the early days of our marriage.

I want... My throat closes over. I want to tell him that I miss the way he used to smile at me—the way he did years ago—the way he smiled at Jasmine tonight.

I want him to show me that he still cares about how I feel.

Even if it's irrational.

Especially if it's irrational.

Isn't that what married people do for each other?

I can't breathe.

I cross to the window and open it. Warm, humid air enters the room, mixing with the dry air-conditioned air like oil and water. I take a series of deep breaths, but it does little to sort my jumble of discordant thoughts.

Derek and I met in England just prior to my mum's car accident ten years ago. I was only eighteen, and losing my mum so suddenly left me lost and floundering. Derek stepped up and handled arrangements for the funeral and her estate. Mum, an eccentric artist, didn't have anything as morbid as a will, but Derek sorted everything out. After a whirlwind romance, he brought me back here to Australia to live with him. We bought a house, married, had a daughter. We were living the dream. Everything was wonderful.

Until it wasn't.

Through the bright moonlit night, I look back at the bed, at my husband on his side, at the empty side I just slid out of. Derek's snore is loud and irregular. His mouth is open, and a trickle of saliva runs onto the pillow. In this moment, he looks so terribly unattractive to me.

But it wasn't always this way. Derek Hardt is a handsome man. *A clean-cut Jamie Dornan,* Bec once told me.

Does Derek look at me and find me so terribly unattractive too? He's seen the very worst in me, watched me sink as low as it's possible for a person to go. It has to have made a difference, especially in contrast to Jasmine's quick smiles and fun trips down memory lane.

I stare at Derek's prone form, at his head on the pillow. The mess our marriage is in is just as much my fault as his. I just don't know how to get us back to how we were before.

Or if it's even possible.

Despite my resolve not to, I press out two pills. Then press out two more.

I won't sleep without them. I need to sleep. I have work tomorrow.

Back in bed, I lie with my back to my husband and hug my pillow to my chest. I wait for the medication to work, to silence the voices, always so much louder during the quiet stillness of night. I try not to think about my life, try not to force myself to come up with reasons to wake up tomorrow.

I already know I won't come up with any.

And morning will arrive regardless. That relentlessly chirpy bitch always does. And I'll have to live yet another day with the excruciating pain of knowing what I've lost.

Of what I'll never have again.

But Derek...

Derek has somehow found a way to laugh again.

And now, with my conscience as my only witness, I can't help but wonder if that is what upsets me about Jasmine the most.

Derek and I have both suffered. But now, Jasmine appears to be pulling Derek up and out of his nightmare while I'm left still sinking, lost and flailing. Alone.

Grief is the only solid thing left between us.

What do we have if we no longer have that?

CHAPTER 2

*A*t a fashionable hotel overlooking the Swan River in Matilda Bay, the music's low seductive beat pounds relentlessly through my head. Outside, lavish mansions overlook sparkling water the way that inside, the chandeliers reflect their glitter across flowing champagne in crystal glasses.

Everywhere I look, there are couples, laughing, kissing, holding hands. A blinding pain pulses behind one of my eyes, and my jaw aches from holding a smile fixed in place.

No one notices.

They never do.

Instead, they ask polite questions I don't have answers to, like: "How are you Claire?" But the well-worn question is entirely rhetorical; no one really wants the answer.

Not the truth anyway.

But I'm holding up well tonight, my social mask's as good as the best of them. My smile carefully crafted, well-practiced, my outfit appropriate and put together. Not too much cleavage. Smoky eyes with pale lips. My bag matches my shoes.

Glass in hand, I gravitate toward the outside edge of the room, step out on the balcony, and pull the door closed behind me. The sound of music and laughter is muffled, and I breathe deeply, dragging fresh air into my lungs.

The balustrade is cool beneath my hands as I look across the sparkling Swan River. It would make a captivating gown, that deep blue color; the cut on the bias would flow like a river, like cool water trickling down a woman's curves.

The glass door slides open, and the music becomes temporarily louder before fading again. "Claire!" Julia says brightly. "What are you doing out here all by yourself?"

I turn and give my friend the first genuine smile in what feels like hours. "Just getting a little fresh air."

"You look so pretty tonight," Julia says. "And tall!"

I stick out my leg, showing her the red heels I don't normally wear. With heels, I'm taller than Derek, something that irritates him. It makes no difference to me either way. Nicole Kidman is taller than Keith Urban, I'm fond of pointing out, although I can't claim to quite have Nicole's height. To avoid the fight that would inevitably spoil the night, I'd wear the flats Derek insisted on, but I take the opportunity to wear heels every time I go out alone.

"Bec looks beautiful tonight as well," Julia says. "Positively glowing. That dress is stunning on her. It's almost as though it was made especially for her."

"It was."

"So it was!" Julia's laugh becomes a giggle, transformed by a glass too many of bubbly. "Everyone has been commenting on it. You're going to be booked out for the next ten years after this party. Where's Derek?"

"One of his friends from school is staying with us," I say with what I hope is a casual shrug.

"Why didn't he bring him?" Julia asks.

"Her."

"What are you two doing out here?" Bec asks, joining us on the balcony.

"Look how gorgeous you are." I embrace her warmly.

"Where is that gorgeous husband of yours?" Bec asks. "He'd better have a damn good excuse for not being at my engagement party. If not, Rob is going to kick his ass."

My smile slips, and Bec notices immediately.

"What is it? And don't you dare say nothing," she adds before I can say exactly that.

I'm cornered.

"I was just telling Julia that Derek has a friend from Sydney over."

"He could have brought his friend," Bec says. "Who is it? Do I know him?"

"Her," I correct. "An old school friend. Husband troubles apparently, and reconciliation doesn't appear to be in the cards."

"Derek didn't know she was coming?" Bec raises a perfectly sculpted brow.

"He did, but it was all very last minute."

It is almost unthinkable that Derek isn't here celebrating Rob and Bec's engagement.

"I'm sure Derek's reasons for not being here are sound," Bec says, her tone reassuring. And she's right. I shouldn't be critical of Derek's decision to stay home. Earlier tonight, Jasmine had a conversation with her soon to be ex-husband that didn't go well. She was in tears and ripping through a box of Kleenex, so Derek opted to stay home with her. After all, he's a nice guy. He's being a good friend. It wasn't right to abandon Jasmine when she was so upset.

"Are you worried about this woman being left alone with your husband?" Bec asks.

"No." I look out across the river. "I'm not worried about them. I'm just disappointed he isn't here, that's all."

"Of course Rob and I are disappointed," Bec says. "But I'm sure he made the best decision under the circumstances. I'm glad you're not worried about them. It wouldn't be a good look for him. Not when he's so close to making partner. You know how Rob's father is about projecting the family image."

I force a smile. "Our marriage is just fine. The same as it's always been." Comfortable, familiar, like a well-worn pair of slippers. On a scale of fire and ice, Derek is... *tepid*. But he's my husband. And making partner in the firm is important to him.

"What you and Derek went through with Katie—" Bec winces. "I'm sorry to bring it up, but going through a loss like that can damage a couple. And you're still together. What doesn't break you makes you stronger, right?"

But it *did* break us. We're still together, but we're broken. I'm existing, not living. I have Novocain main-veined, and I don't know how to take out the needle.

How to feel alive again.

Because feeling alive means feeling the pain, too.

And it just feels so... wrong to be happy. Parents aren't supposed to bury their kids, and they certainly don't just "move on" after they do. And yet, that is precisely what they tell me I need to do.

It's what I will do tonight.

For Bec.

"What are we all doing standing out here?" I smile brightly. A little too brightly. They don't appear to notice. "Let's get back inside and party!"

Two hours later, I'm rushing through the hotel back to the party with a box of matches to light Bec's engagement cake. A forgotten detail I'm more than happy to help out with. A function down the hall ends, and dresses and suits spill out into the foyer. I'm moving against the flow of people when something catches my dress. I curse out loud when I see the fabric has been caught on the winding mechanism of a man's watch. I shove his hand out of the way, before he does any real damage, and free my dress. There had been a loose stitch at the seam, which had formed a loop where I'd tied off a thread. I'm never as particular on my clothes, especially when in a hurry. I would *never* have left a thread visible on a design for someone else.

What were the chances of that getting caught on someone's watch?

"I'm sorry." The voice is low and deep and sincere with a smooth Australian accent. I look up, my gaze following the tanned arm, the cuffs of the black silk shirt, all the way up to broad shoulders and dark, moody eyes. He studies me, and his intensity is a little unnerving. Like he can see straight through the façade to the real me.

He's tall, six-foot two at a guess, and handsome in that rebellious, aggressively raw, dark, and dangerous way rock stars have about them. Male sexual energy washes over me, making my pulse race. I take an involuntary step back.

He looks familiar. Is he famous? An actor maybe. But before I can place where I'd seen him, Julia appears at my side. "Did you find the matches? They're almost ready to bring out the cake."

"Yes."

"I saw you looking at your dress," she says. "What happened?" She grabs a handful of material. "Oh no. It's ripped."

"No, the seam has just come undone. My fault. I can fix it in a moment."

"You just happen to walk around with a sewing kit in your purse?" The handsome stranger's eyes hold a hint of amusement, and I find myself smiling up at him.

"You never know when a stranger will try to rip off your dress." His eyes darken further as though he'd love to do nothing more than just that. And Lord help me, right here, right now, life melts away, and I want to let him.

What would it feel like to be totally possessed by a man like this? My cheeks flame, and there's no hiding the effect he has on me.

I look away, take another step back. This man is disturbingly sexy, and being in his personal space is unsettling.

"Claire is a famous designer," Julia says proudly.

"It's a pleasure to meet you, Claire, the famous designer." He holds out his hand. "I'm Zach."

Zach.

I take his hand, and heat transfers up my arm and spreads like a current of electricity throughout my body. I stifle a gasp of surprise, and he drops my hand abruptly. I don't know whether to be embarrassed or insulted that my touch seemingly repulses him when his clearly had the opposite effect on me.

"Hey, you're Zach... Zach Argos, aren't you?" Julia stares at him wide-eyed. "You're the famous artist."

Zach Argos. Of course, now I remember where I've seen him. He owns the shop a few doors down from mine in North Beach, but he's hardly ever there. I've walked past it many times but never entered.

"Zach Argos, the famous artist," I say. He gives me the hint of a grin, and something about it makes me want to push him, see if I could get him to break out into a full smile. Smiles, I instinctively know, are rare for this man. But when he does smile, I know his eyes crinkle at the corners. I can see pale lines in his tanned skin as though he spends a lot of time outdoors, squinting into the sunshine.

Julia is talking to him about his art, which lines the walls inside the adjacent function room, then adds, "We're here for our best friend's engagement party. Bec's fiancé works with Claire's husband. They're accountants at Markson, Stanton, and Associates."

And just like that, I'm shoved back into my life. The life where I have a husband at home who sleeps with his back to me. It felt nice, this momentary escape from reality.

Zach's gaze travels to my left hand. My ring finger. A shadow moves across his face, and his eyes shutter, his expression turning cool and businesslike with none of the warmth I'd felt a moment ago.

Zach utters the requisite words required for a polite but immediate departure and disappears into the crowd. Vanishing as abruptly as he appeared.

"Oh, em, gee," Julia says, fanning herself. "Talk about sex on legs. So hot, I bet he'd set your sheets on fire." She slaps a hand across her mouth. "Don't tell Neil I said that! But looking isn't cheating. And he wasn't looking at me anyway." Her eyes rake down my body. "It's a wonder your skin isn't scorched right off."

"Stop it." I laugh. "My skin is still perfectly intact." I hold out an arm to prove it.

"What kind of parents were needed to create a man like that?"

"Come on." I tug her arm. "We'd better get back to Bec and the cutting of the cake."

I don't have time to repair my dress right now, so I cover the tear with my hand and lead Julia back to the function room. And wonder why I feel a little guilty. No matter how bad my fights with Derek have been over the years, no matter how long the periods of silence or how hurt and lonely I've felt, I've always been faithful.

I've never even once crossed the line with another man in a way that would betray Derek's trust. Besides, I didn't approach Zach.

Zach's watch getting caught on my dress was pure coincidence.

Except... There's physical distance between Zach and me, but my body still feels flushed, my heart still skipping along at an accelerated pace. And for the first time in a long time, I'm not numb.

Somehow, the tall, dark, and handsome stranger has managed to remove the Novocain from my arm. In his presence, I'd felt something.

And for once, it wasn't pain.

It was something far more exciting.

Something I hadn't even known I wanted before tonight.

Before meeting Zach Argos.

CHAPTER 3

I wake to an empty bed, and an empty house. Two hours later, I'm in the kitchen, freshly showered and invigorated after a nice long run. The digital numbers on the iPad in the kitchen show me it's just after noon. Flicking the switch on the coffee machine, I reach for my phone. Six messages, four from potential new clients, one from Bec, and one from Julia.

None from my husband letting me know where he is. Letting me know where *they* had gone.

A tightness forms in my chest, and I force myself to relax. Just because Jasmine appears to be a flirty type, it doesn't mean my husband is doing anything inappropriate. Besides, even if Derek did find her attractive, it doesn't mean he would act on it.

My mind immediately turns to meeting Zach Argos last night. Case in point. Just because you feel… an attraction to someone, it doesn't mean you have to act on it. Physical responses aren't intellectual. They are something else entirely. Something that has nothing to do with reason or intellect.

Chemistry is a primary level mystery. Whether or not you act on your physical impulses is a choice. Most certainly an intellectual choice. And Derek is nothing if not smart. Zach Argos walked away last night—ran away to be more accurate—the moment he found out I was married. And he was right to do so.

My coffee cup echoes loudly in the empty room as it lands on the marble counter. Once, the house was never this quiet. The pitter-patter of Katie's footsteps and the sound of her laughter used to fill the halls, along with the scent of cinnamon and vanilla from home-baked cookies.

If only I had known then just how little time I had.

～

The sun is setting when I next emerge from my workroom, and I follow the sound of voices to the lounge room. There's a football rerun on the TV in the background, but they're not watching it.

"Hi, guys. Did you have a good day?" I ask, determined to be happy and upbeat. "Where did you go?"

"We had a wonderful day." Jasmine smiles, her eyes twinkling. "Derek took me to Kings Park for a view of the city, then we had a gorgeous lunch overlooking the beach at Cottesloe."

"That's nice." I force myself to hold the smile. "I'm glad Derek showed you a good time."

"We had a very good time." She smiles up at him.

They're just school friends.

"Who would like wine?"

"Derek just poured me one," Jasmine says.

Of course he did.

"We're fine, Claire," Derek says. "Just look after yourself."

In the kitchen, I "look after" myself.

I pour a glass of wine and try not to think about the way she'd said they had a very good time in a tone that suggested it was something more than a tour.

They're just old school friends.

But telling myself that doesn't stop the voice inside that warns me she either is, or wants to be, so much more. But what can I say? Don't show your friend around Perth because... Why? She's too beautiful? I don't like the way she looks at you?

I don't like the way she looks at *me.*

There's something in her eyes when she speaks. A look reserved just for me. It isn't there when Derek can see it. I tell myself it's just my imagination. But is it?

Technically, we should be showing her around together. Derek and I are married, so she should be a friend of *ours*, not his. Yet there's something in the shrewdness of her gaze that makes me acutely aware she doesn't want to be my friend.

I rub my eyes. Or is it all in my messed-up mind? Remnants of my breakdown still linger tauntingly on the edge of my consciousness like a laughing clown in a horror movie. There were days I barely recognized the reflection staring back at me from the mirror. That couldn't have been easy for Derek. I simply existed, got through the days, the hours, the minutes, because that's what the doctors told me to do. Break it down, moment by moment, keep moving forward.

And that's what I choose to do now.

Keep moving forward. I select a play list on my iPad, and music filters into the kitchen through speakers in the ceiling. Singing to one of my favorite songs, I begin chopping up vegetables for a casserole.

Over my music, her laughter trickles into the room.

And down my spine.

I move to the doorway where I can see straight into the lounge room. My hand on the wall, I watch them a moment, wanting to see something that will ease the tightness in the pit of my stomach.

Derek and I are having problems, but he's still my husband. And she seems like a thief in the night. I hate the way she leans in and touches his leg every time she laughs at something he says. Can't she keep her goddamn hands to herself?

I study them, and it strikes me I'm watching two strangers. There's a familiarity about the one I know to be my husband, a face I see nearly every day. But the expression on his face is new, as is the timbre of his laugh.

He looks like an old friend, someone I used to know.

When did my husband become a stranger?

My hand begins to shake, and the knife slips from my fingers and clatters loudly across the white marble tiles.

"Are you all right?" Derek calls out from the couch. But he doesn't come into the kitchen.

I don't answer, and Jasmine immediately continues her conversation, reclaiming his attention. I pick the knife up off the floor, make the sauce, then put the casserole in the oven.

When I run out of things to do in the kitchen, I walk back into the lounge room. Derek is telling her a story, something from the past. Something from a time before I knew him. They've turned the television off and are now listening to old nineties songs, no doubt selected from the aisles of memory lane.

Since they are both sprawled out on the three-seater couch, I sit across from them in the armchair. She flicks her hair often as she speaks. Her unrestrained happiness grates on my nerves. Unable to help it, I watch her through narrowed eyes. She's laughing at everything he says. *Everything.*

He's not that funny.

I shift in my seat, my grip tightening around my wine glass. I may not be an expert, but this feels more like flirting than friendliness. Is there a proper way to tell her to back off without sounding like a shrew?

"A little closer and you'll be sitting in his lap." Okay, maybe not as subtle as I could have been.

My comment silences them, and for a heartbeat, no one speaks. I raise my chin against the frown on Derek's face. The one that says I'm being rude to our guest. *Tell me I've got nothing to be concerned about.*

But my husband remains silent. It's Jasmine who speaks. "I'm sorry, Claire," she says, her wide, doe eyes directed at Derek. She tucks her legs up beneath her. "I thought we cleared up the fact you have nothing to be jealous about. Derek and I are just good friends." Her voice is contrite, but when she turns to me, the glint in her eye makes me feel as though she'd just won a point in a game I hadn't known I was playing.

"Suggesting I am jealous only makes me think I have reason to be," I say.

"I can't help what you think," Jasmine says dismissively. "We have lots to talk about. As we keep telling you, Derek and I are old friends. We go way back."

"I didn't just meet Derek last week either," I say. "We've been together ten years, *married* for eight." I emphasize *married*. "Over the years, I've managed to meet nearly everyone Derek went to school with, but for such good friends, I don't remember him talking about you much." *At all.*

Derek shrugs. "If I didn't, it wasn't intentional."

"Didn't you tell Claire the fun we used to have? How I warned you the teacher was coming when you were behind the toilet block kissing Donna Langley in sixth grade?" She hits him playfully. Is she touching him deliberately now? To aggravate me? My chest tightens, and a vein in my temple throbs. I try to clear my head, rationalize my thoughts. *Stay calm.*

Am I just imagining the way she looks at me? Are they really only just friends? Am I creating an issue where there isn't one, the way Derek told me I am?

"You still owe me for that," Jasmine says to Derek. "Donna's dad would have killed you if he'd found out you two were dating."

"He nearly killed Dean," Derek says. "Dean was the first boy Donna brought home."

"Dean Whitmore?" Her brows shoot up. "Shut the front door!" She tosses back her silky mane. "I can just imagine how that went."

"Shut the fuck up," I say.

Derek and Jasmine both turn in my direction, Derek with his mouth open.

"It's shut the fuck up," I say. "Not shut the front door. The front door isn't even open."

"There's no excuse to use that kind of language, Claire," Derek grumbles, looking embarrassed. "Sorry, Jasmine. Claire doesn't mean to be rude."

My eye starts to twitch. "Don't speak for me, Derek."

"I saw her a few months ago, did I tell you?" Jasmine says, twisting her body so that she's facing Derek again. Either dismissing me or attempting to diffuse the tension between Derek and me, I can't decide. "Donna, I mean. She's married with three kids. Just think, that could have been you." She laughs again, but this time Derek doesn't laugh with her.

His eyes meet mine.

Kids are a touchy subject.

A grief we still share.

Is that all that's left holding us together? There's no such thing as a perfect life, but is that really the only thing we have left in common?

Jasmine is still talking although now I can't hear what she's saying through the blood rushing past my ears.

I can't be in this room.

My heart is pounding, and a thin sheen of sweat breaks out across my forehead. I need air. The room starts to spin.

"Claire, are you all right?" Jasmine asks. "Maybe I shouldn't stay here. Upsetting you is the last thing I want to do." She blinks wide eyes at Derek.

"Don't be ridiculous," Derek says quickly. "Claire's issues have nothing to do with you. She suffers anxiety. Panic attacks. She had been getting better, but now she's stopped taking her medication."

"Stopping your medication abruptly can be dangerous, Claire," she says. "Trust me when I tell you that. I'm a nurse, remember?"

I bring my hands to my tingling face, pressing fingertips cooled by my wineglass against my heated cheeks.

"You're looking pale," Derek says softly, his expression one of concern. He's seen me sink as low as a person could go. A level of darkness somewhere below rock bottom.

But he makes no move to cross the room to me.

"Why don't you go lie down," he says instead. I try to meet his gaze, but he's speaking into his wine as he twirls the stem around and around in his fingers. *Screw you, Derek.*

Of course, I don't need his help. Grief is a road you travel alone. But still, his response to my need in front of her is a slap in the face. As is the way he rose to her defense. And not mine.

Once, my husband had put me first. Now the distance between me and this stranger I married is a chasm I have no idea how to close. But the blame is not his alone.

My chest tightens. I can't breathe. Exhaustion smothers me like a lead blanket. I'm tired of being sad. Of being lonely. Of being confused. I'm tired of doubting myself.

I want to feel something other than this damned relentless grief.

I want to taste something other than the bitterness of loss.

There are only so many times I can hear what an emotional cyclone I am before I'm forced to believe it myself. When did the world get to be such a confusing place to be?

I'm supposed to be doing better than I am. The professionals tell me that, so it must be true, right?

I force a smile.

It hides the scream.

My earlier resolve to join them for the evening and get to know this friend of Derek's has long gone. I excuse myself, almost running from the room.

To avoid temptation, I take the remainder of my medication and flush it down the toilet.

Knowing sleep will allude me, I head to my office to start work on a new design. With any luck Jasmine will be gone soon, and I won't have to see her for another ten years. And then maybe, just maybe, Derek and I can work out what, if anything, we can do to repair whatever is left of the couple we used to be.

CHAPTER 4

One week later

I stand on the curb and look across the road at my shop. The large front windows reflect the glistening Indian Ocean behind my back, and written in stylish gold script are the words *Designs by Hardt.* It's a small shop in a high visibility position on West Coast Drive.

I've spent more and more time in my shop this last week, working later that I normally would and coming home after dinner to finish work in my home office. Of course, I recognize that I'm avoiding her. Avoiding them. And each day I awoke this past week, I told myself it would be the last day she'd be in our house.

But she's still there.

The times I've seen them, she's been perfectly polite. Too polite. Watching every word as though afraid to provoke the bear. Exaggerated manners, I'd go as far as to say. Although complaining that she is being too polite would only make me look as crazy as Derek thinks I am. So, I do what I do best and avoid this new, unpleasant reality and bury myself in work.

A few doors down from mine is Zach's shop. My heart skips a beat as it does whenever I think of him, ever since I met him at Bec's engagement party. Although I'd been in my shop for a few years, I'd rarely seen Zach. Occasionally, I'd glimpse him coming or going. Then again, I'd hardly been what New Agers would call "fully present" lately.

I'm just about to walk across the road to my shop when I glimpse Zach walking through the laneway to the car park behind our shops. He's walking with a teenager on one side and a young girl on the other. Zach has kids? I guessed his age to be a couple of years older than mine, Derek's age. Maybe thirty, thirty-one. Maybe the kids are his cousins, or a niece and nephew. Zach's head is down, and all three are moving quickly.

The girl drops something. They don't seem to notice.

I race across the road, the gravel causing my heels to slide, and I hope I don't fall right over. Landing on my ass with my legs in the air isn't the impression I wanted to make when I saw him again.

I grab the toy, a small, faded-pink, rather grubby stuffed bear. "Excuse me," I shout, running after them.

Zach stops and turns. I wave the bear in the air. The teenage boy, on closer inspection, appears to be around seventeen. Eighteen? He places his body in front of the girl's in a protective gesture. Zach says something in the boy's ear, and his defensive posture eases. Surprised, I slow down, approaching more cautiously.

I've regulated my breathing by the time I reach them. I smile first at what I assume is the older brother then bend down and smile at the girl, who looks around eight, maybe nine.

The age Katie would be now.

I swallow a lump in my throat. Eyes wide, the girl shrinks behind Zach's leg. Her clothes are ill-fitting, her toes poking so far over her sandals that they touch the ground. There's a red mark across her right cheek, and her eye is breaking out in a bruise. The injury is recent, and I look up into Zach's face. His expression is neutral, unreadable. But his eyes are wary.

"You dropped this," I say softly to the child, putting the tiny object back into her pocket. And it falls straight through!

She blinks up at Zach, and tears well in her eyes. "I'm sorry," she says weakly. "I didn't mean to do a hole."

Zach mutters something under his breath that could be a curse. "Nothing to be sorry about," he says, his voice softer than I've heard it. "It's not your fault."

Zach looks at me as I hold out the bear again. "We have to go." Zach's expression is one of... annoyance?

Is he angry at me for pointing out that the girl had holes in her pockets, or for stopping them, or both?

"Thank you for returning the toy." His tone is brisk, and he turns, urging the kids to follow.

I want to call out. I want to ask him where he's going. Ask what he's doing. What happened to these kids? Why does the girl have a black eye?

I know that whatever happened to these kids, Zach was not the cause of their fear. That was clear in the way the girl clutched his hand, in the way the brother trusted without question whatever Zach said about me.

They disappear into Zach's shop, and I enter mine.

"Hi, Kira," I say, greeting my assistant who takes care of the shop and orders when I'm with a client or working from my home office.

The shop is decorated in high-end, earthy tones and is bright and airy with strategically placed mirrors and lighting to highlight certain pieces to perfection. Everything sparkles and smells of lemon-scented polish, which Kira favors. I am lucky enough to have hired someone who cares for my business almost as much as I do. Kira is wearing a fitted blue and white summer dress that would look stylish at any high tea or corporate lunch.

"That dress looks gorgeous on you," I say with a smile. Kira considers the complimentary wardrobe a perk of working here, but the advertising to me is invaluable. Kira is twenty-three, a stunning natural blonde who can out-surf most of the guys on the coast. Her tanned and toned body showcases my designs to model perfection. I've sold numerous outfits because women have seen them on her. It's win/win for both of us.

"Kira, what do you know about Zach Argos?" I ask, hopefully casually, as I pour myself a coffee. I don't need to ask if Kira would like one. She's holding a large takeaway cup of that green juice from the health food shop she favors.

"Zach?" Kira asks. "He's a great guy. I often see him at the beach where we hang out. Zach and his mate Richard teach kids to surf most weekends. Have you ever seen him on a board?"

I smile and shake my head. Derek doesn't like the beach. Too sandy.

"Did you know he's one of the top surfers in Australia?" Kira asks. "I saw him at the Margaret River Pro championship this year. Do yourself a favor and watch him ride one day. Your eyes will thank you for it." She grins. "Why are you asking about Zach?"

I grab my coffee and walk back to the shop front. "No reason, really.

Just curious. I met him at a function a couple weeks ago and saw him again now in the car park."

"Top bloke," Kira says. "Richard, too. They're a great bunch of guys to hang out with. Here's your schedule for today," Kira says, glancing at the clock on the wall. "Mrs. Rodgers had to postpone her four o'clock appointment."

Mrs. Rogers is the wife of the chief executive of an international mining company, in Australia for a short time while some big deals are sealed. Or so I'm told through the gossip vine. "I rang Sue Bradbury," Kira says, "who was first on the cancellation list. She's wanting you to design her honeymoon wardrobe, so that should be fun." Kira grins playfully. "But we'll have to talk about that later. Your ten o'clock is just pulling up outside."

I glance out the window to see a tall woman get out of a Porsche. Carole Roberts is the wife of one of the partners in Derek's firm. A serious lady who knows exactly what she wants and is not afraid to let you know if she doesn't get it.

"Okay, we're professionals now," I say. Kira pretends to stub out an invisible cigarette and pouts prettily, making me laugh.

At twenty-three, she's only five years behind me but sometimes seems an eternity younger. Still living with her parents in nearby Mullaloo, a trendy suburb, Kira grew up on the beach, spending long, carefree weekends with her surf crew. She sports a year-round tan and an easy smile, and after growing up with the boys at the beach, she can—and does—swear like a drunken sailor, something more than one customer has been shocked by. Kira's fun, sweet. And I love her to pieces.

Carole Roberts, in a business suit and carrying a Gucci handbag, enters the shop.

"Da-a-arling." Carole air-kisses both of my cheeks and nods briefly to Kira.

I take Carole's design out of the garment bag and am inwardly relieved when I see her eyes light up. I took some creative license, which is always a gamble with a woman like Carole. Fortunately, it appears the wager was a winner, and when she reemerges from the changing rooms, Kira's gasp is music to my ears.

"Holy mother of Je—" Kira puts her hand over her mouth before the curse can fall out, but luckily, Mrs. Roberts turns and beams at her.

"I look good, right?"

"Fu—um—far out. You look awesome," Kira gushes.

"Thank you, Claire," Carole says, turning to me, her eyes shining. "It's beautiful. Being so tall, I can never find dresses to fit. This is amazing. You've done a wonderful job once again."

"I'm glad you like it," I say, eyeing the gown critically, placing a couple of pins where I'll make minor adjustments.

"I missed you at the corporate lunch last Friday," she says.

"What lunch?" I mumble around a mouthful of pins.

"You didn't know?" She looks surprised. "When your husband showed up with that other woman, it caused quite a stir. No one likes a scandal. But she's just a friend, right?"

"Of course," I say, but struggle to meet her eyes.

"Good. Derek would be an idiot to lose you—you're his biggest asset. Especially if he wants to make partner one day. The publicity and attention you're getting with your latest work reflects wonderfully on the firm. You're going to be a big star one day," she says. "Especially if you keep designing gowns like this. There's not a chance I can keep you my secret, can I?"

My smile is fixed on my face. "'Fraid not," I manage to reply. Derek hadn't mentioned anything about a corporate lunch, let alone taking Jasmine with him. The fact she went in my place is annoying. The fact he hid the fact, pisses me off.

Did Derek think I'd react badly? He had to know I'd find out eventually, so I can assume he was just looking to avoid a scene in front of Jasmine.

But was that to protect me?

Or her?

❧

Tuesday morning, I'm alone with Derek in the kitchen, making breakfast.

"Coffee?" he asks, and I nod, biting down on a piece of toast and the vegemite I'd grown to love since moving to Australia. This is one of the few times when we weren't sleeping that Derek and I have been alone in the two weeks Jasmine has been here.

"You didn't tell me there was a work function last week." My tone is casual, but Derek tenses as he works the coffee machine.

"You were busy," he says, already anticipating my next question.

"But you didn't even tell me about it," I press. As strained as our marriage has been lately, we still communicated about things like work and our schedules. Didn't we?

"I took Jasmine," Derek says, volunteering the information I already knew. From someone else. Derek places the coffee in front of me, made the way he knows I like: milk with one sugar.

"Why didn't you tell me?" I tug the coffee closer, hug the warmth between my palms. "It was embarrassing hearing about it from Carole Roberts."

"You've been acting so...weird about Jasmine being here, I didn't want to...upset you." But he meant argue. He didn't want to argue with me again. *About her.*

I've been so busy this last week with all the new design work I'd picked up at Bec's engagement party that I'd barely seen them. It's Derek's last day of holiday today, so chances are she'll go somewhere else now she doesn't have my husband to play with all day long. After all, she can't continue to stay here when Derek goes back to work. What will she do with her time? Surely, she's had long enough to work out what she's doing. She'll likely be gone by the time I get back home from work, and we can put this whole situation behind us.

Feeling the need to close the distance between us, I cross to him and embrace him. He stiffens in surprise then, after a heartbeat, he wraps his arms around me.

"We've hardly had any time alone these last two weeks," I say. Maybe once she's gone, Derek and I can reconnect in some way. Discover who we are again as a couple. Without Katie. Not taking the pills has been the best thing for me mentally and emotionally. I can think clearly for the first time in far too long. "Do you want to go away for the weekend?" I ask. "Just the two of us?"

Derek is about to answer when I hear something smash. Derek and I rush to the lounge room where I see Jasmine crouching over something broken.

"It was an accident," she says, eyes filling with tears as she blinks up at Derek.

She's picking up pieces of clay and glass, and my heart stops dead in my chest. I rush to the broken picture frame and sink to my knees. I angrily brush her hands aside.

"Get away!" My voice cracks.

Jasmine rises and rushes to Derek's side as though afraid of how I'll react. Carefully, I begin picking up each delicate piece as tears blur my vision. Derek crosses the room, kneels down next to me.

"It was an accident," he says, but his voice is thick. Our gazes collide, and I watch him draw in a shaky breath. In pieces on the floor is a clay frame made by our daughter at preschool. Behind the shattered glass is a picture of Derek, Katie, and me at Adventure World on our last holiday as a family to Queensland. A treasured gift from our daughter and, behind the glass, a precious family memory.

"We'll get it fixed," Derek says, reaching out to take my hand. My hands are trembling, but his are, too.

"She made it, Derek." I struggle to breathe. We don't have many gifts from our daughter, especially handmade ones. All we have are some drawings and this photo frame. She was only five when she left us.

I hadn't even noticed Jasmine leaving the room when she's back with the handheld vacuum.

"No!" I scream. Jasmine freezes, vacuum in hand.

"I'm just trying to help," she says. "I said I'm sorry. I'll buy you a new frame."

Derek crosses the room to her and, without another word, leads Jasmine from the room, leaving me with the pieces of broken glass and clay on the floor.

I'll painstakingly glue the pieces of the frame together if it takes me the rest of my life. I'll buy a new glass.

But it will never be the same.

My hands are still shaking when I've picked up the final shard, all of the pieces arranged neatly, a broken jigsaw on the coffee table.

How did Jasmine manage to knock down a photo frame that was sitting snugly on a shelf in the floor-to-ceiling wall unit? What was she even doing, touching it? How could that accident possibly have occurred?

With a sinking certainty, I know that this was no accident.

Jasmine had deliberately broken this picture. And with force, judging by how much it shattered.

Can this school friend from Sydney possibly be that cruel?

And if so, why?

CHAPTER 5

*A*t a trendy café in Nedlands, a fashionable suburb on the Stirling Highway, Julia and Bec sit across the table from me. It's lunchtime on Saturday, and Bec has just regaled us with story after story of her escapades during her romantic engagement holiday in Bali with Rob.

I'm happy for Bec. But in listening to her, I'm painfully aware of a vast emptiness inside me. A crippling loneliness from being in a failing marriage. The sense that I am in the wrong house, accidentally living someone else's life. The persistent niggle that I don't belong where I am. What would happen if I got into my car and started to drive without a care about where I was going until I just stopped somewhere and found where I belonged? And when I stepped out of the car, I'd be free to be the person I truly was meant to be.

I drain the last of my second cup of coffee. So much caffeine, and I still feel tired. How is that even possible?

"Did Claire tell you we met Zach Argos the night of your engagement party?" Julia asks. A sudden surge of adrenaline wakes me up. I sit straighter in my chair, and my skin heats.

"Really?" Bec looks surprised.

"Yeah, his watch got caught on Claire's dress."

"Is he as gorgeous in real life as the image on his website?"

"Much more," Julia says. "There's something edgy and… mysterious about him. What do you think, Claire?"

What do I think? The man who sets my blood on fire with the mere mention of his name? "Sure, he's handsome." I try to affect a casual tone. "If bad boys are your type."

Julia lowers her voice to a hushed whisper. "I did a little digging since we met him. Rumors are his artwork and his shop are a front for an illegal business."

My mind immediately conjures up the image of Zach with the two kids. The unkempt appearance of and bruises on the little girl. Zach is definitely up to something secretive. But what?

"Conversations like this are exactly how rumors start," I say, unsure why I'm feeling so defensive of a man I don't know and shouldn't care about.

"We're just having fun," Julia says. "He's a sexy mystery we're trying to solve."

"Look at Claire all flushed," Julia says. "You're all hot and bothered, just like you were around him that night."

Bec's smile fades. "His shop is near yours, isn't it? Stay away from him, Claire. We were joking around just now, but seriously, you don't know who he is or what he's involved in."

I inwardly bristle at the warning I don't feel is warranted.

Bec reaches across the table, places her hand over mine. "We're just looking out for you. You've been through so much already."

I withdraw my hand and take a sip of my coffee.

"How are things with that girl?" Bec asks, clearly thinking she's changing the subject to something lighter. "Is she still staying with you? What was her name again?"

"Jasmine." I set the cup back down on the table and reach for the jug of water. "Her name is Jasmine Ravendish, and yes, she's still here."

Bec leans forward on the table. "Your hair looks nice," she says, twirling the sparkly diamond on her finger.

"Thank you." I run a hand automatically through the blonde highlights I had added this morning.

"You really should get over the Jazzy situation," Julia says with a touch of impatience, and heat rises in my cheeks.

"Get over it?" I stare at her a moment, surprised she would be so blunt. Judging by Bec's expression, so is she. "If simply 'getting over it' was an option—" My tone is cool. "—I would have done it by now."

Julia rips the top off a sachet of sugar and sprinkles it into her cup. "You have it all. You've got a handsome husband with a great job, a big house in a great suburb, and a job you love. You're practically famous. Everyone wants to be seen in a Designs by Hardt dress. Sure, you've suffered through an unimaginable loss, but it's time you put the past behind you and moved on."

My left eye twitches. How is it fair that I get to move on when Katie doesn't?

But being angry isn't bringing Katie back. Nothing is.

"You have it all," Julia repeats, and is it my imagination, or is there a touch of bitterness there? "The way you complain about Jasmine staying with you, the way you're treating her after everything she's going through, doesn't paint you in a positive light."

"Is that so?" *Everything* she's *going through...* I feel my eyes narrow. I haven't been complaining about Jasmine to Julia at all. So that could only mean... "You went to the corporate lunch last week, didn't you?"

"I met her," Julia says, but doesn't meet my eyes.

"You did?" Bec is surprised.

Julia twirls her cup as coffee churns unpleasantly in my stomach. She looks up then. "It was no big deal. Jasmine was telling us all how... difficult things are for you. How much you're struggling to cope on a daily basis." My mouth drops open. How dare she!

"Jasmine really opened up at lunch," Julia says. "She told us that you've stopped taking your medication, and it's made you act... um..."

"Made me act *how?*"

Julia shifts in her seat. "She said you went crazy, like lose-your-mind-insane, when she accidentally broke something. Look, the details don't matter. You've been telling us you were okay, so it came as a bit of a shock to find out you aren't."

"I *am* doing well." My heart is a loud thud in my chest.

"Your business might be going well," Julia says, "but what I didn't know is that behind closed doors, you're still struggling."

"Is that true?" Bec asks me, concerned. "Have I missed something?"

"No," I assure Bec, then turn to Julia. "The incident you're referring to happened this week *after* the corporate lunch." My skin heats. "You've spoken to her since then." *Isn't that against the girlfriend code somewhere?*

Julia's face flushes. "We swapped numbers, that's all. It's no big deal. She was really upset and needed someone to talk to. Besides Derek, she doesn't know anyone in Perth. She's trying to be friends with you. Really trying. But… the truth is, we're all worried about you, especially Jasmine. Maybe if you gave her a chance…?"

Bile rises in my throat. How dare Jasmine go spreading poison to my friends and Derek's work colleagues!

"I'm worried now," Bec says, placing a hand on my arm. "I've been so consumed with my engagement and wedding plans, I've not been there for you. I'm so sorry."

I place my hand on top of Bec's. "I haven't needed anything, I promise. You have nothing to apologize for. I'm feeling better and stronger than I have in years."

I lean back so my gaze includes Julia. "Jasmine is twisting the facts. You asked what my issue is with her. Well, that's it. I told you there's something about her I can't quite put my finger on. And now I find out she's making me sound unstable and trying to undermine me to my friends and Derek's work colleagues."

"I'm sure she's not—" Julia says.

"Clearly, she is," I snap. "Stop defending a woman you've known all of five minutes. We've been friends for years. Have you ever known me to lie?" I demand. Although Julia and Bec's husbands work with Derek, and I met them during corporate functions, they've become my friends over the years. Or so I'd thought. If Derek and I weren't together, would they still be my friends?

Julia looks down, her cheeks bright red. "No, I've never known you to lie."

"I had an emotional breakdown," I say, "three years ago. Sure, I've struggled since then. I won't deny that. But I'm getting better every day. And I'm still the same person I've always been with the same values and integrity. I don't know exactly what Jasmine is up to, but you can be damn sure I'll find out."

Julia looks confused, as though not sure what—or who—to believe, but Bec's forehead is creased in a frown. "I don't like this. I'm going to speak to Rob, find out what his take on her is. Have you spoken to Derek?"

I release a slow breath. "Yes."

"What does he think about your concerns?" Bec presses.

"She's all sugar and sweetness to him," I say, glancing at Julia. "But there's another side to her. I've seen it."

"I'm sorry," Julia says, wincing. "I don't mean to sound like I'm taking her side, but from what I've seen, she just seems so… *nice*."

"I'm here if you need me," Bec says.

"I'm here, too." Julia slides her phone into her bag and stands. "We'd better get going," she adds. "Bec and I are going to Satin Sheets to buy her some sexy new lingerie. Do you want to come?"

"I don't—" I break off. I don't what? Need lingerie?

Derek and I still had sex. Occasionally. Rarely. When Derek and I have sex, it's with the lights out. Passion has never been much of a factor in the bedroom. We share a house, share a bed, occasionally share our bodies.

"Come with us, Claire," Bec says. "It will be fun. And I bet you can find something nice that will make Derek forget he even has a friend named Jasmine."

I follow them in my car to Satin Sheets. It hurt that Julia can so easily be as blinded by Jasmine's charm as Derek is. Why am I the only one able to see through her? I hate that it makes me question my own judgement. But no...I'm right about her. I know I am. And I just have to hope Derek and Julia see Jasmine's true colors before it's too late.

But for now, I'm going to push my fear aside and have some fun with my friends. I'll prove to Julia and Bec that I'm fine. That it's not me they need to worry about. We'll have a fun girls' afternoon like we used to. I'll help Bec choose something sexy to surprise Rob, and I'll even find something to surprise Derek.

He is my husband.

It's time to start mending bridges.

Even if I have to pretend the urge to do so is stronger than it is.

On the drive back to my shop, the little bag from Satin Sheets on the passenger seat, I think about what I'm going to do to surprise Derek. In Satin Sheets, I had browsed the whole shop, trying to get into the mood. I knew what Derek liked. Plain and simple.

What would he say if I took a gamble on something different? Would he laugh or disapprove? I'm certain I can predict his reaction, this man I'm supposed to know better than anyone else in this world. And yet... Jasmine's image rises into my mind. I also feel like I don't know him at all.

After trying on several G-string ensembles, and black leather combos that came with matching whips and cuffs, I eventually settled on a blue lace teddy. When he isn't choosing white, cornflower blue is Derek's favorite color. It's a safe bet. Our marriage can't take too many more mistakes.

With any luck, a night of passion will go some way toward rekindling the spark between us.

And maybe, just maybe, if things are really starting to look up, Jasmine will be gone by the time I get home.

CHAPTER 6

*S*he's still here.

Next Tuesday will be three weeks since Jasmine arrived on my doorstep. How long does it take to find a place? The rental market *is* competitive at the moment with tenants lining up and bidding for houses, but I can't help but think she hasn't been trying as hard as she could be.

I've sat through dinner. It was pleasant enough, and we've adjourned to the lounge room for drinks.

"Do you want a glass of wine?" Derek asks Jasmine, and the question stings. He cares about her wine, yet he hasn't even noticed I changed the color of my hair.

I didn't ask her when I poured my glass just now. I hate that he cares if she wants a wine while I get my own. I hate that my manners are questioned. I would never normally be pulled up on such a thing.

I'm hating the person I'm turning into.

She needs to leave.

I fidget with the stem of my wine glass as she brings up yet another old school friend and something about something that happened way back when. Could they possibly have any stories left to talk about? But I know she's doing it deliberately to exclude me from the conversation.

I visibly yawn, not even bothering to cover my mouth. Nobody notices.

My feet are sore, and I want to sit down, but she's in my spot. The one next to the side table where I can rest my wine. It also has the novel I'm reading beneath the lamp. Can I tell her to move?

If I sit on the other side, it will force Derek to move closer to her. I can't very well plonk myself right in the middle of them.

I hate that I'm even having to consider these things.

I want to cry out in frustration, but that will only make me hate myself more. I hate that this situation makes me feel so weak. The things I've survived in life have helped me grow stronger in so many ways, and yet this situation with Jasmine has left me feeling powerless.

Determined not to let her shake my new resolve to reconnect with my husband, I paste a bright smile on my face, drag a chair in from the kitchen and join in the conversation. I don't know what was said, but I must have said the right things at the appropriate times because they both relax. I still feel like the fifth wheel, but maybe this is a turning point for us all.

Remembering my little package, I excuse myself and take a long, scented bath. I light candles and force myself to remember the time Derek would have sought me out and joined me. Regardless of who was visiting.

He'd have noticed the look in my eye, brought wine and rubbed my shoulders as I sat between his legs. Our relationship might not be filled with fiery passion, but Derek was sweet. Kind. Yes, there were plenty of times I remember us being happy. We can be happy again.

Buoyed by my newfound determination to make things right, I allow my mind to remember every single good time and bring them to the here and now. I dry myself off then rub scented lotion into my skin.

I wipe the steam from the mirror. My naked reflection appears in the rainbow shape left by my hand, and I don't flinch away. I force myself to look. To appreciate me just the way I am.

Jasmine is just a friend. They have a relationship, something they had long before me.

And that is okay.

I slide my hand down my stomach, the muscles flat but soft and marked with tiny silver lines. A reminder of my greatest joy.

My greatest loss.

I push the thoughts away and slip on my new blue teddy.

Covering it with a satin gown, I pad on my bare feet across cool marble tiles to the lounge room and stand in the doorway.

They both stop talking, turning to look at me. Jasmine's eyes narrow as they travel down my body. "I feel like an early night," I say, my gaze on Derek.

"I'm not tired yet."

"Neither am I," I say pointedly. His eyes widen.

Jasmine puts her hand on his leg. "Our movie still has half an hour to go."

Derek looks up. "Give me half an hour?"

I cross the room, lean forward, and kiss him fully on the lips. I pour myself a glass of wine, head to the bedroom, slip between the sheets with my book, and wait.

He comes in a little after midnight.

"That was a long half an hour."

"I couldn't just leave our guest."

"Of course you could." There's an edge to my tone. I can easily turn this into an argument. His choice to stay out there with her instead of coming to me in the bedroom stung. But another fight is not what our marriage needs right now.

I bury the anger, the hurt and disappointment, and, sliding out of bed, cross to the window. The action is less about letting in the cool ocean breeze and more about letting him get a good look at the new, lacy blue teddy. I take some satisfaction from the look of surprise that crosses his face. I move to him, wrap my arms around his neck, and he wraps his arms around me. It feels a little awkward, so I lead him to the bed, jumping on it and facing him, my back against the pillows.

He undresses, and I smile and try to remember a time when seeing my husband naked was as new as my lingerie. A time where I cared more about sex than the way Derek leaves his dirty clothes on the floor for me to pick up.

Derek slides into bed and turns out the light.

I swallow my disappointment. Had I been hoping he would appreciate me, perhaps run his hands over my body, tell me I look nice in the new lingerie? Notice my hair, the effort I've made?

The sheets rustle. He rubs himself hard, then climbs on top. Pushing his weight to one side, he licks his fingers, puts moisture between my legs. The standard foreplay.

"Wait," I say. I move my hand between us, grip his erection. I move my body down, intending to replace my hand with my mouth, but he brushes me away.

He shifts me back up to the pillow and slides his erection inside me.

My eyes cross to the candle flickering in the breeze across the room. Eventually, his tempo increases, and I remember the conversation with the girls this afternoon. How things were supposed to be different.

But they are exactly the same. The sex is the same. The distance between us is still there despite the fact that we are in the midst of one of the most intimate acts between a man and woman.

I drag my gaze from across the room and look at my husband. Really look at him. He has his eyes squeezed shut. Has he always done that?

Was there ever a time we'd looked at each other as we made love?

"Derek?" I whisper. "Derek," I repeat a little louder when it is clear he hadn't heard me.

Derek opens his eyes, a slight frown between his brows. "Do you want me to stop?" Is that impatience in his tone?

"No," I say. "I... I love you."

"Love you, too." But he closes his eyes as he says the words. He doesn't see the tear that escapes between lids I've squeezed shut.

He changes the angle of his thrust. It's only slight, but I recognize it, and I know he is getting close. I can almost tell, to the exact thrust, when he'll climax.

Then he'll roll off me and onto his back. I'll lay my head on his chest and listen to the beat of his heart as it slows. For one minute. Never longer. He'll then roll over, and I'll spoon his back.

His eyes are shut, so he doesn't see the other tear that rolls down my cheek to dampen the hair at the base of my neck. But I'm not even sad.

I don't feel anything at all.

How can I cry when I feel this empty?

How can I feel empty with my husband inside me in the most intimate way possible?

With the final thrust of his hips, like an orchestra conductor's last wave of his staff, Derek finishes.

Without a single glance in my direction, he rolls onto his back.

I didn't even bother to fake an orgasm.

He doesn't seem to care.

This time I roll over, my back toward him.

He doesn't move to hold me as his heart slows. Instead, I listen as his breathing turns to a light snore.

I'm not where I belong. But that can't be right. I'm married. I'm living with my husband. Surely this is where I belong.

Then why do I feel so lost?

And so terribly alone.

Rising up through the darkness, Zach's face appears in my mind. He's wearing the same black shirt he wore when I first met him outside Bec's engagement party. His eyes hold a hint of amusement. He's asking me if I always walk around with a sewing kit in my purse. Warmth floods my body. Takes the chill off the ice in my veins.

In my mind, I'm wearing the black leather ensemble from Satin Sheets, and Zach has the cuffs. His chest is now bare; the top button on his jeans is undone.

My breath hitches, my heart races, and heat pools between my thighs. Zach pushes me back on the bed and, with his knees on either side of my hips, leans over me. He grabs one wrist, cuffs it to the bedpost. Takes the other wrist, cuffs it to the other side.

A lock of hair falls across one of his eyes, and his muscles flex as he moves down my body…

I sit up in bed, my heart racing.

Not helping, Claire.

Leaving Derek snoring, I slip out of bed and head to my workroom.

I sift through bolt after bolt of fabric until I find one just right. I picture the girl, wide-eyed and scared, clinging to Zach's hand as though it were her lifeline, and perhaps it was. Whatever Zach was doing with those kids, he was helping them. I know that deep in my heart. The idea calls at something inside me. I want to help, too. But seeing as I can't just come out and ask him what is going on, I do the only thing I know how.

Estimating the girl's size, I set about designing and cutting out the fabric for a jacket.

The digital clock clicks over to three a.m. by the time I finish with a jacket I'd be proud to give the little girl.

I set the coat down, and suddenly I'm filled with self-doubt. What the hell am I doing? What if it makes things awkward? Would a stranger giving her a coat make her feel better or worse about whatever she's going through? Would Zach be upset by me sticking my nose into something that is not any of my business?

I release a long, calming breath.

I've made the little girl a coat because hers had a hole in it, and I felt bad for pointing it out when she clearly had something far bigger to worry about. I made her a coat. I'm a designer and dressmaker; that's what I do.

I won't think about it. I'll just walk right in tomorrow and give Zach the coat. It will be up to him whether he gives it to her or not.

I carefully fold the coat, wrap it in gold tissue paper, and put it in one of the designer bags I use for my most exclusive clients.

I head back to the bedroom, and as I slide off to sleep, it's Zach's arms I feel wrapped around me. Not Derek's.

CHAPTER 7

*M*y nine o'clock appointment has cancelled, so I don't need to go into the shop until after twelve. But I want to see Zach, so I'm heading in early.

I've just finished pouring a coffee when Jasmine walks into the kitchen. She's wearing a wine-colored, ankle-length sheer lace negligee with a plunging neckline and shoestring straps. She looks like she stepped out of the pages of a magazine. Has she been getting up every morning looking like this?

Just how long does she spend dressed like this with my husband in the mornings?

"Put some clothes on if you're going to be in my house." My tone is cutting.

A glint enters her eye. "Derek doesn't have a problem with it," she says sweetly.

"You might be here as a friend of Derek's, but this is my house. Wear some clothes when you're around my husband."

"You know, Claire." She leans across the counter. "You wouldn't feel so jealous over me if you took some care with your own appearance. What are those things you're wearing?"

I glance down at my faded, worn singlet top and extremely comfy sweat pants.

"These are what you should be wearing in someone else's home if you had any decency at all," I say. "Now go change before I toss you and your suitcase onto the front verge."

One of Jasmine's perfect eyebrows raises, and a smirk follows. "Derek would never let you do that."

"And why exactly is that?" I challenge.

"What I wouldn't give to be able to tell you," she says, a calculating gleam in her eye.

Derek walks in, stills when he sees us. "Everything all right in here?"

Jasmine sniffs, places her hand on her heart, raises her chin slightly. "Claire has a problem with how I dress now as well," she says, affecting a delicate little shake to her voice. How does she do that?

Derek's gaze travels the length of her body. He clears his throat. "You'd better hurry up and get dressed."

"Are you going out?" I ask, surprised.

"Jasmine needs to go to the shop. She wants to cook dinner for us tonight. To say thanks for letting her stay."

It will be three weeks tomorrow.

It's nearly eleven a.m. when Zach pulls his black BMW 4WD into the car park behind the shop. My heart skips, and my pulse starts racing.

Placing her hand on my shoulder, Kira peers through the window next to me. "That man is to die for."

"Really?" I say. "I hadn't noticed."

Kira laughs then heads back to the desk to answer a phone call. I smooth down my skirt, straighten my shirt, and check my reflection in the mirror. There's a flush to my cheeks, and my eyes are glistening. I feel like an excited teenager about to meet her favorite band member. Which is ridiculous.

Before I can change my mind, I take a deep breath and march over to Zach's shop with the bag in my arms. Once I step inside, my lungs are filled with the scent of timber and paint. The space is filled with artwork, on easels and leaning against the walls. The pictures are varied, but most have deep colors that seem rich, moody. Evocative. I'm captivated. I hardly breathe as I walk from piece to piece, tracing my fingers down the carved timber frames.

There's a tall, thin teenage boy at the counter with longish dark hair. Seventeen, perhaps eighteen, but his eyes are world-weary, making him seem much older, as do his piercings and the skull tattoo riding up his neck.

"Can I help you?"

"I'm looking for Zach Argos," I say.

His eyes narrow. "Why?"

I find that curious. "I saw him pull into the car park. I need to see him."

"Why?" the teenager repeats, appearing uneasy.

"I want to talk to him."

"What about?"

"I want him to paint something special for me," I say, and the boy's shoulders relax slightly.

Why is he so cagey? What is he protecting Zach from?

"Who did you think I was just now?" I ask, even more curious about Zach than before.

"Nobody," the boy replies.

At that moment, Zach walks in from a side door. The storeroom? He draws to a stop when he sees me and places some bags on the counter.

The boy reacts to Zach's surprised expression, straightening and standing slightly in front of Zach in a protective gesture. Something I find amusing, and... sweet. Zach exudes confidence and danger. He clearly doesn't need protecting from a teenage boy.

Zach places his arm around the boy, gives him a light pat on the shoulder. "Sam, this is Claire Hardt. She's the famous designer that works in the shop down the street." Zach deliberately emphasizes "famous". "Claire, this is Sam."

Sam gives me a small smile and holds out his hand. "Nice to meet you."

"Nice to meet you, too, Sam." I smile openly and shake his hand.

"Sam, why don't you take your break now? Lunch is in the bag on the counter. Take a walk along the beach and get some fresh air."

Sam looks between Zach and me then grins at Zach in a way that makes it clear he approves of Zach's taste in women.

Zach rolls his eyes, and my stomach flips. "Claire's married."

"Pity," I think I hear Sam mumble as he grabs the bag without looking at what's inside and leaves the shop.

My heart is beating fast, and the shop seems so much smaller now, Zach's presence filling the room to capacity. His sea green eyes lock on mine, and the oxygen is squeezed from my lungs. He's wearing jeans and a fitted T-shirt, and he smells fresh and rugged like the outdoors.

"You've changed your hair."

"Highlights," I say, my hands instantly rising to my hair, which is now more blonde than light brown. I run my fingers through to the ends, averting my gaze to hide how flustered I feel under his attention. How does he do that? A few words, and I'm struggling to merely breathe.

Derek still hasn't noticed the color change, yet with one look, this stranger makes me feel like the center of his whole world.

This stranger who according to Bec and Julia could possibly be a criminal.

"I'm sorry to drop by unannounced," I say, relieved my voice sounds normal and does not betray any of my internal turmoil. "I just want to say sorry. You know, for last week. I think I may have embarrassed the girl with the hole in her pocket."

Zach waves away my words. "I already told you there's no need to apologize." God, his voice is so deep. How can it sound so strong and powerful when he speaks so softly? Men confident in who they are don't raise their voices or throw their weight around. They don't need to.

"I have something for you. For her. Here." He takes the bag, and I can't help but notice how large his hands are, how tanned and strong. Heat radiates off his body and onto mine, and my mouth dries. He's devilishly handsome. I have the sudden urge to either take a step back or strip naked and throw myself at him.

He raises a brow. "What's this?" He opens the bag, glances inside, and I realize he can't see what's wrapped inside the delicate gold paper.

"It's a coat." I feel like an awkward teenager in his presence. Where did my years of experience in adulting just go?

Zach tries to hand back the bag, but I don't take it. "You didn't need to buy her a—"

"I made it," I interrupt. "There's matching gloves and a scarf in there as well."

His eyes meet mine. Something shifts in the air between us, and an emotion I can't quite read flitters across his expression. He thrusts the hand not holding the bag through his hair.

As socially inept as I feel around him, Zach makes me feel alive, my body zinging with electricity that's wreaking havoc on my synapses.

There are a million questions I want to ask him. Who is the girl, and why did she look so terrified when I approached? I want to ask him who he really is and if his shop really is a front for something illegal.

I know Zach isn't doing something revolting, like trafficking kids, because of the way the little girl clung to him. If I'd thought that, I would have stepped in back then. The teenage boy the girl was with looked up to Zach, as does Sam. No, whatever Zach is up to, he isn't hurting the kids.

But one thing is for sure. Zach Argos is definitely up to something. But I can't just come right out and ask. Can I?

As if he'd tell me anyway.

Zach might have an irritating way of making me lose whatever is left of my mind, but I at least know that much.

I just might have a better idea.

CHAPTER 8

*T*his is so not a good idea.

I've officially lost my mind. A twig digs into my knee, and I shift position. Here I am, Claire Hardt, the *not* famous designer, in the rear car park, crouching in the dirt near Zach's parking spot like I have a few kangaroos loose in the top paddock. That's Aussie for I've lost my mind. An ant crawls across my toe, and I'm sure if I looked, I'd see a spider in the bush I'm hiding behind. The one next to the large green rubbish bin that I keep getting a stomach-turning whiff of. Someone clearly had seafood and not so recently.

I don't know what I'd say if someone noticed me here. I'd have to pretend I'd dropped something. I take out an earring and hold it in my hand.

Seconds turn into minutes.

The buzz of my stalker-ish behavior soon wears off, and embarrassment takes its place. It's best not to think about what my therapist would say.

So what am I doing? I'm waiting for Sam to come back from lunch so that I can listen in on their conversation. I want clues as to what Zach is up to. I fantasize they will launch into a discussion about what they're doing, like discuss a deal that will go down at midnight or talk about how much money they just laundered.

But it's likely I'm here because I'm just addicted to this new sensation of feeling alive after spending the last three years as the walking dead.

After a while, I feel less like a detective and more like an idiot. What the hell do I think I'm doing? Seriously. What Zach Argos does is none of my business. What kind of a lunatic hides out in bushes listening in on someone's conversation?

Embarrassment heats my cheeks, and I straighten, brush dirt off my skirt. No harm done. No one needs to know.

I hear a door opening. My heart in my throat, I crouch back down so fast I lose my balance and land on my ass. Scrambling to get up, I slip and land against the bin. Now something sticky is on my palm. Half-chewed pizza. My stomach turns. What idiot puts pineapple on pizza? I scramble onto my knees and peer at Zach through the cover of the branches.

He locks the back door with one key and uses another key to lock the top deadbolts. There's twice the security on his door than there is on mine. I wait until he starts the engine of his shiny black BMW before I scramble back to my car.

In for a penny, in for a pound, as the expression goes. I've come this far...

Tucked under Zach's arm is the bag with the jacket. Where is he taking it?

Surely, the next logical step is to follow him and find out.

What could possibly go wrong?

I've been following Zach for about twenty minutes, hanging right back. Allowing cars to get between us but keeping him in my line of vision. Adrenaline is firing like rockets through my veins. The rush makes me feel alive.

I'm just starting to think I'm the world's best undercover detective and could get a job as top international spy if I ever got tired of designing when he drives down a side street that leads to another back street, and then he disappears out of sight. I press my foot down hard on the accelerator, determined to catch him. I take the street I thought he went down, then down another, then another.

Damn! I've lost him.

I reduce speed, and the beat of my heart slowly returns to normal.

Guess it's too soon to give up my day job.

I look around at the suburban street, which looks like any other. Double brick houses, tiled roofs, front gardens with neat lawns edged with garden beds full of manicured plants and flowers.

Where am I?

I key my home address into my GPS and wait until it finds my location. I follow the directions that will take me back home, and as I'm winding my way through a series of streets, I see Zach's car in a driveway! What are the chances? I drive past, hoping he doesn't see me, then double back around, parking a few houses down.

Blood is rushing past my ears again as I wait for what feels like an eternity for Zach to come out of the house. When he pulls into the street, I follow. This time, I won't lose him.

Fifteen minutes later, I'm again doubting my sanity as we seem to be travelling further north. We travel through a small town and, after a few minutes, take a road that leads us further into the bush. The scrub is thick with tall gum trees, grass trees, and native shrubs. A mob of kangaroos looks up to watch as I drive past. The road narrows, becoming rough with corrugations. My grip on the steering wheel is tight as my tires slide over loose sandy patches. I totally get why Zach would have a 4WD if he drives here often.

What if he doesn't?

What if he knows I'm following him and is leading me out here to…?

I am just about to turn around and go back when Zach slows down and parks next to three older model cars in a clearing defined by a semi-circle of thick tree trunks.

Heart hammering in my chest, I pull up alongside of him. Breathe, I order myself. Stay calm. I watch him open his door then make his way over to me. He raps on my window with his knuckles. I press the button, and the window slowly slides down. He rests his arm on my door and peers in at me.

"What the hell do you think you're doing?"

"I, uh—"

"Let me help," he says. "Finish this sentence: I am following you because…"

My face heats, and I straighten my shoulders. "I am following you because I wanted to know where you were going." I meet his gaze head on. "Isn't that why people usually follow someone?"

His lips twitch, and I can't decide if he's amused or majorly pissed off.

He walks around the car, opens the passenger side door, and gets in. "So," he says slowly. "Tell me if I have this right. For no apparent reason, you follow a man you don't know, one who leads you down a series of back streets. A man who is now in your car." He makes a show of looking around him. "There are no witnesses, and you are now alone with a man who is much stronger and could overpower you at any given moment."

The emotion swirling in his eyes is anger. I shrink back against the door but hold his gaze.

"Stop trying to scare me." He's only trying to scare me. Point out the potential danger I could have put myself in. Right?

"What the hell were you thinking?" His voice is a low growl. "What if you'd followed the wrong man? Hell, I *am* the wrong man."

"You left with the bag I gave you for the child. I thought you might be taking it to her."

He narrows his eyes. "Why? What exactly did you think I was doing?"

"I wanted to make sure she was okay."

"You think I might have intended to cause her harm?" His eyes darken.

"How do I know?" I snap. "I'm the one who's supposed to be asking the questions."

Zach is a formidable presence at the best of times, and being so closely scrutinized by him is not a pleasant experience.

"I'll admit to not thinking this through much, or at all, but I know there were two kids with you in the car park. A teenage boy and a young girl. Both looked tired and scared out of their wits, and the girl appeared to have been recently hurt. Beaten, even. Perhaps I should have called the cops then and there, but I didn't. I hope that wasn't a mistake. As an adult, it is my responsibility, *my duty*, to make sure kids are protected and not being harmed in any way. Where are they, Zach? Are they okay?"

Had the girl been Katie, I would have hoped an adult would've stepped forward and done the same for her. And if it turns out there is nothing to worry about, all the better.

"And if I am hurting the kids?"

"I'll find a way to kill you myself. If there is anything left after the authorities have finished with you. Are you hurting the kids, Zach?"

He doesn't answer, but his eyes continue their relentless assessment of me. I resist fidgeting under the intense scrutiny, and I'd give anything to know what he's thinking. He reaches a hand toward me, and I involuntarily flinch. He stills. "Despite your sassy attitude, you *are* scared of me."

"I am not." My heart is racing, but it has nothing to do with fear.

Slowing his movements, he reaches forward and pulls something from my hair. He holds it up between his fingers, trying to work out what it is.

My cheeks heat. "It's pizza."

"Really?" He looks surprised.

"Look," I say as he flicks what I now see is a saucy piece of ham out of the car. "I should have just asked you outright what you were doing when I saw you at the car park. But I didn't, and now I'm here. So you may as well show me the kids. Once I see that they're okay, I'll leave."

Zach's up to something. But what? I've come this far, I'm not leaving without at least some answers.

"Let me see the girl," I say. "And if you don't, I'll call the police right now, and you can prove to *them* she's okay." I pull out my phone and unlock it with my thumbprint.

He makes a low growl in the back of his throat.

"Go home, Claire," he says. "You have my word that the children are in no danger."

"Prove it." I dial triple zero, the emergency number, into my phone. "We're in the bush a long way from the nearest town. What am I supposed to think? I'm not leaving until I know she's okay." My finger hovers above the green call symbol.

"Bloody stubborn woman," he mumbles.

His apparent displeasure only strengthens my resolve. Clearly, this is a man not used to being told what to do, and I can't say I'm not enjoying this moment.

"Look, I'm here," I cajole. "Wherever this place is, it's no longer secret. At least not to me. One way or another, I'm going to find out what is going on here. So you may as well show me, or the next time I come back, it will be with the authorities."

He reaches across, takes the phone out of my hand, yanks the keys out of the ignition.

"What are you doing?"

"You want to see what I'm up to, follow me." He walks to my side of the car and opens the door.

I clutch the steering wheel, my head spinning. What did I expect? That he'd just suddenly materialize the kids in front of me?

"You started this," he says. "Now follow through. You want to see if the kids are safe? Come with me."

Slowly, I get out of the car. He presses the remote to lock my car then slides my keys and my phone into his pocket. He walks to his car, grabs the bag I gave him out from the back seat, along with a khaki backpack that he slings over his shoulder.

He walks to the edge of the clearing without a word. I glance once back at my car and follow him. I'm running on sheer instinct. And adrenaline. Zach is danger and excitement.

And I'm enjoying every second of it.

As we start to walk, I see the first cracks in his veneer. There's a few second's delay before he takes the barely visible path as though he, too, is wondering what the hell he is doing. That whatever reaction we are provoking in each other is as strange for him as it is for me.

"Do you make a habit of making threats to strangers and sticking your nose into other people's business?" he growls as he slips on dark sunglasses.

"Nope. You're the first."

I'm not sure, but I think I see his lips twitch.

"Where are we going?" I ask as the track winds deeper into the bush.

"You demanded to see Mandy."

My throat closes over. "The little girl's name is Mandy?"

"Yeah. And Claire?" He glances over at me. "If you ever do anything as foolishly dangerous as this again, I *will* kill you."

I should be nervous. What does it say about me that I'm not? Who does that? Follow a man I know nothing about, except that he's not who he says he is, into the bush. He could be the next Christopher Worrell or James William Miller, the Truro murderers, for all I know.

I should have called or texted Bec or Julia…no, Kira…when I had the chance, and told her where I was and what I was doing. At least then the police will have an idea where to start looking.

"Does your husband know where you are?" Zach asks as though reading my mind.

Why hadn't it even occurred to me to tell Derek?

I don't answer Zach's question, finding myself unwilling to talk about my husband. Zach slants a curious glance my way. But whatever he's reading into my reactions has nothing to do with being scared of him and everything to do with the effect this man has on me.

Hell, yes, this man may very well be dangerous.

But he isn't dangerous to me.

"How much farther?" I ask, maybe just to fill the silence. "If you're going to kill me, can you at least make it quick?"

"Now where's the fun in that?" His voice is soft, but his appearance as wild and rough as the surrounding landscape. And still, there's something about his presence that soothes my nerves.

"I probably should have asked if you were a serial killer before now, right?"

"Might have been smart. So would have staying the hell out of my business in the first place." His jaw is clenched, and the lines on his face are hard. I decide against provoking him further.

Pink and gray cockatoos screech as they fly from tree to tree, and somewhere in the near distance, a kookaburra laughs. Zach is silent but sticks and twigs snap and crunch beneath our feet as we walk.

The track leads us up a small hill with a steep decline on the other side. I trip on an exposed tree root, and Zach thrusts out an arm to catch me.

"Careful." He's surefooted and easily supports me as I find my balance. A little farther along, he stops abruptly, and since I've been concentrating on where to put my feet, I collide with him, my body flush against his hard one. His breath hitches. I'm engulfed in his heat. His scent. His presence.

"You should wear more sensible shoes," he says gruffly.

"They are sensible," I argue, glancing down at my wedges. "At least they were in my shop. I didn't exactly know I was going to go hiking through the Aussie outback today. Where exactly are you taking me?"

"We're almost there."

The path is wider here, and when I hear other voices in the distance, my tension eases slightly. We've been walking for only about five minutes, but thanks to my racing thoughts and overactive imagination, it seemed much longer.

We've only just started to walk again when Zach comes to another abrupt stop, wraps an arm around my shoulder, and pulls me against his side. "Don't move. It's a western brown." He's completely still. Taken by surprise, I immediately follow his command and try not to be over-whelmingly aware of being so close to him.

Zach points to the ground. Just in front of us to the left, a snake slithers past. Although it's the first deadly snake I've seen outside a glass cage, I'm not scared. Much.

"I'm surprised you didn't pull out your big knife."

"You think I'm Crocodile Dundee?" Zach's grin makes my heart skip. "You know there are no crocodiles in this part of Australia, right?"

"I knew that," I say quickly. I'm fairly sure I knew that.

"The snakes won't bother you if you don't bother them," Zach says when the snake is out of sight. I'd never seen a western brown in the wild before. Derek doesn't like the bush. The closest he's ever gotten to camping or hiking is watching it on-screen in a five-star hotel.

Zach's fingers brush down my arm as he takes my hand. My heart is pounding, but it has nothing to do with the snake. I have the sudden urge to follow Zach anywhere. I want him to take me far away from here, deep into the bush and away from my life. It would just be me and him. I'd be safe from anything. There'd be nothing to worry about. None of life's stress and pressure, no grief, no worry.

Except, there was only one problem with running away from problems; you take yourself with you when you go, as the saying goes. And my demons are scratching around in my head. The brief distance from my everyday routine has given me perspective though, makes me determined to clean up the mess my life has spiraled into.

It's time for me to get real.

Decide what's truly important.

Zach's grip tightens on my hand as we continue to walk. Though he wasn't concerned when he saw the snake, I sense a slight tension in him now.

Does he regret bringing me here? Not that I'd left him much choice.

My body is still tingling from where it landed hard against his. My head is spinning, and I have the wild thought that I don't even care if he is a serial killer. I'm fully alive and full of Zach. Even if I'm headed to certain death, I'm happier than I've been in a long time.

He's still holding my hand in his much larger one, and its effect on me is significant. His strong, warm grip makes it impossible not to wonder what it would feel like if he touched me elsewhere. Somewhere more intimate.

I want him to touch me with purpose.

With passion.

For a shameful moment, I wish things were different. What would it be like to live free from the constraints of society?

"What are you thinking about?" Zach asks.

In all my years with Derek, he's never once asked me that question. Had he never cared enough to want to know?

I avert my gaze from this man who sees too much.

"Do you ever wish life could have dealt you a different hand?" I ask softly, surprised I would ask such a personal question.

"All. The. Time."

At the fierceness in his tone, I look up and see dark shadows in his eyes I hadn't noticed before. As though my question too-easily conjured memories that cause him pain. I'm struck with an urgent desire to learn everything possible about this man. Uncover his deepest darkest secrets. To understand what he's all about. So I can appreciate him for all his depth and color. I'm certain his paintings are an outward representation of what's inside him.

Zach has an innate ability to see right through me. To the real me, the one I keep buried deep inside.

I want to see all of Zach.

In a few more steps, the trees thin, and we come to a clearing. Down a slight descent are six or more timber cabins built among the trees.

The little girl I saw the other day, Mandy, runs up to us and throws her arms around Zach. She has short brown hair and is around the age Katie would be now. I can't help but imagine what Katie would be like today. Would she prefer her long blonde curls to be cut short?

"Mandy," Zach says, lowering himself to her level. "This is Mrs. Hardt."

"Claire. It's just Claire."

"I remember," Mandy says, her wide dark blue eyes looking into Zach's.

"She's a friend." Zach's words are chosen carefully, and my throat closes over at the level of trust Zach has given me.

Mandy looks at me then, a slow smile lighting up her face. There's something so vulnerable in her expression that it touches me deeply.

Zach hands me the bag. "Claire has something for you."

I give it to Mandy, and she peers inside.

Her eyes light up. "Is this for me?"

"Yes." I smile. "Open it."

She drops to the ground and sits cross-legged in the dirt. Wiping her hands on her jacket first, she gingerly reaches inside and tears into the delicate gold tissue paper. She pulls out the red coat and gasps. She blinks at it, almost reverently, as though she can't quite believe what she's seeing.

"There are a matching scarf and gloves in there, too," I say. I'm more nervous than when I'm waiting for my fussiest client to give her opinion.

I hold my breath as Mandy's fingers run softly across the material. "This is the most beautiful coat I've ever seen."

My eyes glisten. Her joy is pure and sweet. She rises to her feet, hands the coat back to me, takes off her old jacket, the thin, grubby one with holes in the pocket, but she doesn't drop it on the ground. She carefully folds it and hands it to Zach. The coat I've made for her is a winter coat, not suitable for this balmy autumn afternoon, but the weather will cool down soon, and I hope she'll get more wear out of it then.

She wipes her hands on her sides, looks at her palms and wipes them again. There's a brick in my throat and, unable to speak, I hold the coat up behind her so that she can slide her arms through the sleeves. Large bruises mottle her skin in various shades from purple to faded yellow. Who has hurt this sweet child? Is that why she wears a jacket even on a warm afternoon like this one? To hide her bruises? But I pretend not to notice, keep my questions to myself and my expression even.

Mandy wraps the coat around her body, hugging herself. She hugs Zach, then hugs me, then runs off toward what looks like a playground. There's an A frame made out of timber logs, a seesaw, and swings hanging from tree branches, surrounding a large sandpit. Walking tracks zigzag through the cabins and weave in and out of the surrounding trees. Two boys about fourteen or fifteen are on skateboards, and three others are on bikes. They all stop and stare in our direction as Mandy runs up to them to show off the coat.

"I trust you're satisfied now?" Zach asks, but there is no heat in his tone.

"I had to be sure," I say. "I'm sorry."

"No need to be," he says. "If only more adults took such risks to make sure of a child's safety."

"I didn't really think you were hurting the kids," I admit.

"But you weren't going to leave, either, were you?"

"No."

"Lizzy and Kim dumped some spare clothes here when they left, but —" Zach turns his gaze to me "—Mandy has never had anything brand-new before. She told me that after I said I'd take her shopping for new clothes. And when you came in to the shop with a coat today, made especially for her..." Zach shrugs. "It was just such a damn nice thing to do for a kid you don't even know."

I rub at the ache in my chest. It is impossible to not be moved by this.

"What is this place?" I ask. This village hidden in the woods. I doubt that Zach is some charismatic cult leader. There are no signs of submission or cowering to him, just respect and gratitude.

He starts to walk, and I keep pace beside him. He doesn't take my hand again, but I wish he would.

"To most of these kids," Zach says, "it's home. However temporary."

"But how?" I've already pieced together that these kids are running away from something terrible, but I'm still trying to fit Zach into the puzzle.

He shrugs. "The how is relatively easy. The why is far more important."

"What happened to Mandy?" I ask softly. "I saw the bruises."

Zach's features harden. "Mandy's brother, Aidan, had been living here. Aidan is the teen you met in the car park. He's nearly nineteen and has just gotten his first place. He's in the process of applying for legal guardianship for his sister. Aidan had been living rough for five months before I met him two years ago, but Mandy was still living at home with her mother and abusive stepfather. Aidan has been worried sick about her. I have, too," Zach adds. He glances at me, his eyes flickering across my face.

"What happened?

"Mandy's mother died of an overdose. The night before you saw us. Her stepfather, an addict himself, is a violent drunk. When Aidan heard he was intending to pimp Mandy out for his next fix—"

I gasp. Oh my God! Zach has put a face, a story, to a world that feels like it's on a different continent.

Zach's hands are clenched into fists at his sides. "We removed Mandy and brought her here. It's what Aidan had wanted all along, but Mandy hadn't wanted to leave her mother. Mandy had been caring for her, and sadly, she was the one who found her body after she'd overdosed."

"Oh, Zach, that's awful." The words feel grossly insufficient.

"Mandy's parents had sold everything they owned to feed their habit, the few toys the kids had, even their beds."

"What about child services? Wasn't there something she could do? Go to a teacher, someone for help?"

"Mandy had seen how that hadn't worked for her brother. She'd seen the beating Aidan had received when he'd opened up to a school friend, who told his parents, who reported it to the authorities. There was a brief investigation at the time, but the kids weren't removed. I don't know how their parents hid the abuse, but they somehow managed to. Besides, Mandy didn't want to be taken away from her mother. Kids are loyal, and

Mandy loved her mum despite her flaws, and her mother loved Mandy deeply."

"But not enough to give up drugs."

Zach looks at me. "You don't understand the power of addiction."

"You're right, I don't. I'm sorry." It's just difficult to imagine that kind of influence. There is not a single thing I wouldn't have done for Katie.

"At any stage, either before or after her mother's death, Mandy could have gone into the system. Like I did."

"You were in the system?" I can't hide my surprise.

"Not for long," Zach says. His tone suggests that was the reason why he didn't insist on that path for Mandy.

"It might have worked out better for her than it did for me," Zach says with a shrug. "I'm not saying there aren't some wonderful people in the foster-care system. I know some of them personally, and they provide a much-needed service. I'm only saying that human beings are complex, and what some of these kids have lived through is—" Zach breaks off and clears his throat. "Not every child is a perfect fit for the caregiver they get matched up with. But," Zach says, pride evident in his tone, "Aidan has his first job now. Mandy is enrolled in a new school, and it's only a matter of time before guardianship is approved and they can start a fresh chapter in their lives."

"So Mandy isn't living here?"

"No, she's just visiting with Aidan as he catches up with his mates."

We stop at a cabin at the far end, and Zach introduces me to two boys, Mason and Cooper, who both appear to be about sixteen, maybe seventeen. I step back and watch Zach talk to them. They're showing him a wooden table they've made. The boys look at Zach with reverence, the way they'd look at an idol. The respect they have for him is unmistakable, and again, I'm filled with so much emotion I can't process it.

Zach ruffles Mason's hair affectionately, and then we continue to walk.

"Mason has learnt so much being here. In nine months, he built that cabin we just walked past. During the day, he goes to Tafe—he's just got his first job as a gardener while he gets a trade as a landscape designer."

"But why the secrecy?" I ask. "You're not doing anything wrong, are you?"

"Depends on who you talk to. None of this is approved through any government agency. If I'm found out, this whole place would be shut down."

I can't see how what Zach is doing is wrong, but then again, I know nothing about the laws or the penalties for breaking them.

A cool breeze washes over me, and I hug my arms around my body. Zach shrugs out of his black jacket and places it around my shoulders. The leather is worn and soft and still warm from his body heat. His earthy scent wraps around me, and my body reacts, my nipples hardening instantly. I keep my eyes averted, embarrassed at my internal response.

"What about these other kids?" I ask, deliberately shifting my focus. "How did they get here?"

"Each of them had run away and were living rough. I found them on the streets, offered them an alternative."

What horrors had these kids had to endure to make them prefer living on the streets instead of their home?

"It's harder to place older kids in foster care," Zach says. "Not impossible but harder. The issues are complex. If you lived it for a while, you'd understand what I'm talking about."

Zach has been carefully watching my face, no doubt gauging whether I disapprove of what he's doing, whether I'll report him.

"I give these kids another option," Zach says. "Somewhere to dry out, stay if they choose, for as long as they need. Kids helping kids. It's very effective. No one is forced to be here—they can come and go as they please. They all know I won't tolerate drugs or alcohol here...the rules on that are absolute. The boys have built these houses themselves. Mostly. Of course, there's guidance from me, and the older ones help the new ones. It gives them a sense of self-worth. Of community."

Zach's sea-green eyes glisten in the dappled sunlight filtering through the gum trees.

"Are there many girls?" I ask. Other than Mandy, I've only seen boys so far.

"Mostly boys, but we've had a few girls along the way. And some girl-friends, as well."

He glances at me for a moment then waves to a man, a lot older than the boys I've seen, taking to a tree stump with a saw. The man pauses and waves back.

"Who's that?"

"Richard. He's a qualified carpenter now. Runs his own business. Married, one kid, another on the way. He comes back for group get-togethers and to help mentor the new kids."

"So why don't you apply to—"

"You ask a lot of questions for someone who just wanted to check the welfare of a little girl."

I suppose I do, but how can I not be intrigued when I find this amazing setup in the middle of nowhere.

I watch three boys working together, building a roof. Their easy-going banter, the way they help each other. It's plain to see that whatever their beginnings, they're a family now.

"Log by log," Zach says, his tone wistful. "These kids start to believe in themselves, and they begin to see what their future can hold. It's amazing what happens when you tell a child you can, instead of you can't. These aren't bad kids. They just need more options than the ones they were born into." After a moment, Zach adds quietly, "With my past, I wouldn't be approved to serve these kids meals, let alone get approvals to do what I'm doing."

"Your past?"

"I lived on the streets, Claire. You don't survive a life like mine without a record." Zach's expression is unreadable. "You don't belong here," he says. "I'll walk you back to your car."

A rush of panic wells up inside of me, and I grab his arm. He stills, looks down at my fingers digging into his skin. I remove my hand, but I don't want to leave.

I have so many more questions. About the Village. About Zach. About the difference he's making... His future plans. What he's doing is so...*meaningful*. Something that is seriously lacking in my own life.

But I bite back on my need for answers, fearing any more questions will shut him down further. Or become suspicious.

I can't imagine what Zach could have done that wouldn't make him fit to run this place, but then I remember a friend who looked into adopting and how hard it was for her to pass all the testing to be a fit and proper parent. And she didn't have a record.

"Your criminal history," I can't stop myself from asking, "was years ago, right?"

"Are you still worried I'm going to snap and chop you up into tiny pieces?"

My heart skips, not from his words, but the intensity of the look he's giving me. "I was referring to the kids. Surely you could argue circumstances. Show them what you've done. The difference you've made."

"When you dig for dirt, you're going to find it," Zach says. "Let's just say if they started digging with me, they'd find enough to bury a small city. But more to the point is that I have no intention of putting myself through all that in the first place. The paperwork, the forms. The begging for permission to do what's right from stuffy suits I don't respect. Plus, the visits by officials would bring attention, maybe even a journalist. What would happen if word about the Village got out and I wasn't approved? I'd be forced to close down, and then what would happen to these kids? There's too much at stake."

"But surely—"

"Claire," Zach says, irritation clear in his tone. "I've already told you too much. You're from a different world than me. I do things my way. I don't ask permission from anyone. Never have. And I'm not going to start now."

"But—"

"Claire," he says, twisting toward me, his body heat radiating out like an open fire. "I don't expect you to understand. You and I are very different people. There are those who conform to society, follow the rules, and there are those who don't care so much. Or at all." He shrugs, his gaze switching back to two boys doing jumps on skateboards. "No prize for guessing which one I am."

Envy tightens my insides, and I'm hit again with a rush of longing for such freedom.

"You exist in both these worlds," I point out, unable to forget how sexy he looked in his black suit when I'd met him the first time.

Zach shrugs. "I do what needs to be done."

He doesn't need to say it; selling his artwork is how he gets the money to help support this little venture of his.

"You make me forget myself, Claire," he says, a fleeting look that could be confusion, or even concern, crossing his face. "Come."

We continue walking back to the car, and I slow my pace down, drawing my time here out as long as I can. I may never get another opportunity, and there is so much I still want to know.

And...I may never get the chance to talk to Zach like this again after today.

"The fences are beautiful," I comment, drawing to a stop in front of them. "I love how you've used branches and not square pieces of timber."

"The imperfections are what make it perfect."

Zach is talking about fences, but I am thinking about him.

His eyes connect with mine. "Who wants cookie-cutter when you can have original, unique, and interesting?"

"Like you." *Shit.* I didn't mean to say that out loud.

Zach's expression shutters, and he crosses his arms.

"Don't look at me like that," he says roughly.

"Like what?" I avert my gaze. What can he see in my expression? Respect? Admiration? The powerful desire I keep trying to ignore?

"Whatever that look is," Zach says, "I'm not worthy of it."

I think you are.

"You don't know me, Claire."

I turn away and tug his jacket closed tight around me. That may be true, but I *want* to know him. Right now, I want that more than anything else in my life.

"Are you coming to the campfire on Saturday night?" Mandy asks, running back to us, her cheeks pink and her hands clutching her coat.

"I...uh..."

"No, Mandy," Zach tells her softly but firmly. "Claire has places she needs to be."

"I have nothing on, on Saturday night," I say, ignoring Zach and returning his glare with one of my own. Mandy has given me the chance to come back here again. To learn more. There's no way I'm going to turn that down. Besides, maybe there is something I can do at the Village to help?

"I'd love to come." I look from Mandy's youthful face into Zach's deep, moody, sea-green eyes. "But only if Zach says it's okay," I add, not wanting to undermine his authority.

The intensity in his gaze burns right through me, and I hold my breath for his reply.

When he answers, his voice is deep and rough with an edginess that excites me. "If she wants to." He might be able to say no to me, but he can't say no to Mandy.

Mandy throws her arms around Zach then me, and I laugh as I hug her back.

"Thank you, Zachy," she says. "Yay! I'll wear my new coat. We'll be toasting marshmallows. You won't forget to come will you, Miss Claire?"

Zach's gaze clashes with mine, but neither of us correct Mandy's misunderstanding about my marital status.

"I'll be there," I promise.

CHAPTER 9

*I*t's Tuesday. Jasmine has officially been in our house for three weeks now. I arrive home around five o'clock. It's been an unseasonably hot autumn day, and the forecast is for a warm, humid night.

I toss my keys on the kitchen counter and follow the laughter. What is Derek doing home already? Has Jasmine been here all day by herself? Or did Derek take time off work to be with her?

At the sliding door, I watch Jasmine toss her hair back and laugh at something Derek says. She's sitting on the edge of the pool, kicking the water playfully.

Time slows down. I find myself moving forward until I'm standing over her. I want to push her in the water. No, I want to scream at her until she leaves and never comes back. She has no right to be there.

"Want to go for a swim?" Jasmine asks.

"No," I snap.

"Sure." Derek shrugs.

My hand rushes to my racing heart. "You're going for a swim?" My mouth is dry, my tongue thick.

"Oh, Claire." Jasmine clucks her tongue. "You can't swim?"

Of course, I can swim, you imbecile. "It's just that we don't."

"Well, that's just dumb," Jasmine says. "It's a great pool. No sense letting it go to waste. Good thing I'm here."

Derek and I haven't swum in the pool for three years. Couldn't. Not when she can't. Katie loved this pool, took every chance she had to swim. We spent the money to get it gas heated so she could swim all year round. It was one of the things that helped ease her pain when she got sick.

"Oh, Claire," Jasmine says with exaggerated concern, her hand covering her heart. "It will mean changing into my swimmers."

"So?" I'm distracted, trying to not let memories tear me apart.

"You've had such an issue with how I dress. I thought I'd check if it was okay for me to be wearing a swimsuit."

Derek looks at me in surprise.

She's making a reference to the negligée she was wearing yesterday.

"Unless you want to let me borrow one of your swimsuits," she says silkily. "I'm sure yours would be much more conservative than mine. Oh," she says clucking her tongue again, and shakes her head. "Forget I said anything. Yours would be far too big."

I should push the bitch into the water. But even she can't cut through the ice crystalizing in my veins. I don't want her in the pool, tarnishing the memories of Katie swimming in it.

The moment she leaves, I round on Derek.

"Are you going for a swim?" My stomach is filled with churning knives.

His eyes don't meet mine. "Sure. Why not?" Derek says, but I know by the tightness in his voice this hurts him, too.

"But Derek. How can you do her favorite thing…"

…*Without her?*

"Goddamn it, Claire!" He looks at me then, his face flushed. "Don't make me feel guilty about this. She's not coming back. She's *never* coming back. We've been left behind to carry on without her, and somehow we need to work out how to do that."

The weight of his words hits me with the force of a boulder. Heavy tears roll down my cheeks, splash on my chest. I've cried tears to fill the pool several times over, and yet they still keep coming. How can I continue to cry when there's nothing left inside me?

I just can't…

Then I think of the kids at the Village, their strength, their resilience, and I stand a little straighter.

Somehow, I have to find the strength to let her go.

Jasmine is back, wearing a skimpy red bikini that reveals her perfect body, her smooth, tanned skin unblemished by the marks of motherhood.

"Come on, Hardty!" Jasmine stands on the edge of the pool and raises her arms, ready to dive in. I glance at Derek. Will he go for a swim? His gaze is on her ass, showcased in a G-string bikini bottom.

I head back inside.

Of course, he'll go for a swim.

He'll follow her all around the pool like the disgusting dog he is.

In the kitchen, I splash some cool water on my face. Derek starts walking past, on his way to get changed into his swim shorts no doubt. He stops, and I look up at him from the sink, water dripping from my face down my shirt.

"We have to move on," Derek repeats.

Who's he trying to convince? Me or him?

"Is that what this is about?" I demand, my chest tight. "Moving on?"

"This isn't easy for me, either," he says, his voice strained.

And I do know that.

Derek holds my gaze, and for a short moment, we share in the sadness. He crosses the kitchen, kisses my forehead, and leaves the room.

There's a whooshing sound rushing past my ears.

Oh, Katie! When will the pain become bearable?

I close my eyes, my mind drifting back through the years to just before she was diagnosed, back to one of my last truly happy memories…

"Mummy, Mummy, look at me! Wheeeeee!"

A lump lodges in my throat, and my chest swells, becoming impossibly full. *Derek is holding Katie's hands and swinging her around and around in a circle before the "helicopter" comes to a gentle landing on the lush green lawn.*

I'm on the sun lounge, with my drink and book, where they'd sat me down earlier to give Mummy a little "rest."

"Mummy's going to need to save some energy for later," Derek had said quietly and winked as he'd handed me my oversized sun hat. I'd slapped him on the rear with my hat, and he'd grinned as he'd leaned down and kissed my forehead.

Derek's brown hair is neatly cut, short at the back, his cornflower blue eyes a mirror image of our daughter's.

Tiny beads of sweat prickle my skin, but the gentle breeze keeps me cool. I sip my iced tea. Katie's delighted squeals fill the air, and I wonder how I ever managed to get so lucky.

"Daddy, Katie wants to go for another swim." I press my fingers to my lips to disguise my chuckle. Katie has an amusing habit of referring to herself in the third person.

"Does Katie?" Derek asks, pretending to consider.

"Yes. She does." For a three and a half-year-old, she has strong opinions as to what Katie does and doesn't like.

"Well, then, it's a good thing we bought a pool," Derek laughs. "Just for you."

"Katie's pool."

Derek ruffles her blonde curls. "Katie-bear's pool."

"Let's get in." Her expression turns serious. "But don't splash Mummy this time," Katie warns her father sternly.

"Who, me?" Derek asks, placing his hand on his heart. "Would I do that?" He lunges off the side, curling into a ball and doing a "bommie," sending water spraying everywhere.

"Daddy!" Katie admonishes him, but her smile is brighter than the midday sun, and she claps her hands in delight, the tiny nails I painted pink last night shining.

I brush the droplets off my book. It certainly isn't the first time my book has been wet today, the pages wrinkling and sticking together. I sigh and make a note to do a Google search for waterproof novel covers. Surely someone has thought to invent them. I imagine tiny little book umbrellas for those who like to read poolside and chuckle at the image of books lazing around on little sun couches.

"Mummy, watch me!" Katie jumps off the edge in a move more reminiscent of a belly flop than the dive she'd intended.

I clap as though she'd done a swan dive from twenty feet. She beams at me, joining in my cheers and clapping her hands at her own effort.

A high-pitched trill of feminine laughter, Jasmine's laughter, interrupts my memory, and I glance out the kitchen window. Derek is chasing her through the water, and she doesn't seem to be trying too hard to stay out of his reach.

I can't watch them. I leave them in the pool, waiting until I am in the shower before I let the real tears fall. I stay in the water for as long as I can stand. As I step out of the cubicle, droplets run down my naked body in snaky rivulets. Catching a glance of myself at the mirror, I pause. My eyes look tired. I haven't been tanned in ages, not like I was back then.

I place a hand over my stomach. The stretch marks have faded but are still visible if you know where to look. There were complications with the last miscarriage, and the doctors had said it would be unlikely I'd ever fall pregnant again. The loss had been tempered by the knowledge we had Katie. Derek always said she made up for a dozen children. And he was right. Katie was pure sunshine. She was the center of our world.

And then…

I squeeze my eyes shut and try to conjure that feeling of happiness in my body, of how it felt to watch my husband and daughter in the pool. Just a little warmth to replace the icy emptiness. But it doesn't come. Memories of how we used to be are now one step removed. Like a story belonging to someone else.

Derek and I were happy once. I know that only because when I remember back, we were smiling.

I just can't *feel* it anymore.

I hug my arms around my stomach, icy shards of loss and loneliness starting uncontrollable shivers. Changing into my warmest pajamas does little to ward off the bone-deep chill. At the back of the cupboard, rolled into a ball behind my T-shirts, is Zach's black leather jacket, the one he placed around my shoulders when I was with him at the Village.

I don't think about why, but I grab the soft worn leather and take it into bed with me. I hug it against my chest until the tremors subside. Right or wrong, it calms me, breathing in Zach's earthy scent of timber and the Australian outback. Zach's quiet reserve and strength make a soothing balm for my racing heart.

His deep, moody, sea-green eyes stare intensely into mine, and he tells me I don't know him. What are his secrets? I imagine unravelling them one by one.

And I imagine him letting me.

Through the window, the moon is high in the sky, and I wonder what Zach is doing right now. Is he at the Village? Under the same moon, painting? Or is he with a woman…? Does he have a girlfriend? Just because I haven't seen him with one doesn't mean he doesn't have someone special…

Hours must have passed before Jasmine's irritating voice in the hallway permeates through the walls. I hear Derek say something low that causes her to laugh that high-pitched trill again. Is she leaning in, touching his arm? Is she embracing him to say goodnight?

I've had enough. It's time for the truth, or it's time for Derek to allay my fears.

He opens the bedroom door and heads into the bathroom to brush his teeth. Placing Zach's jacket on the floor under the bed, I turn on the light and wait.

"Are you sleeping with her?" I demand, the moment he reenters the bedroom.

"Excuse me?" He doesn't look at me when he speaks to me. How long has it been like this?

"Just answer the question, Derek."

"Have you been taking your pills? Because it certainly doesn't seem like you have." Derek sits on the bed, takes his shoes off. I stare at him. Always the same question every time I confront him about something. Does he prefer his wife docile, compliant, and drugged?

"You didn't answer the question."

"I shouldn't have to!"

"I need you to answer the question." I sit up. "Look me in the eyes, Derek, and tell me the truth. Are you sleeping with her?"

"No!" He meets my eyes, his bloodshot ones full of anger, resentment, and even, I think, disgust. He leans in close, too close, and alcohol fumes waft into my face. "I am not sleeping with her. Don't ask me that again."

He says it with such conviction I almost believe him. Almost. Maybe he hasn't crossed the line.

And maybe it doesn't matter anyway.

Derek turns his back to me as he kicks his jeans across the floor where he'll step over them every day until eventually I get tired of looking at them and pick them up. He slides into crisp navy sleep pants and a white shirt.

"You always rush to defend her."

"You're always on the attack when it comes to her."

My hands are shaking, and my right eye begins to twitch. I drag in a breath, determined to appear calm.

"Claire, if you'll take a step back for a minute, you'll realize how this looks to anyone but us. Not swimming in a perfectly good pool must appear very strange to Jazzy."

"Quite frankly, I don't give a rat's ass how anything looks to *Jazzy*."

"I won't talk to you when you're being like this."

"How long is she staying? She's been here three weeks now, Derek. Three weeks."

"What difference does it make if it's six weeks?" he asks. "It's not like we don't have the space. There's a perfectly good spare room just sitting there not being used. There's no reason for her not to use it."

"Except for the way it makes me feel."

"The way *you* feel." Derek looks at me, releases a long breath. "You aren't a good judge of anything at the moment, so you're going to have to trust mine."

Tension builds, making my head throb. "So, I'm to let you do all the thinking for me, is that right? The way you have been for three years."

"Look," Derek says in an irritatingly calm voice, "she applied for a small flat this morning. It's a great little place, perfect for what she needs, and the chances are extremely good she'll get it."

"Let's hope."

"You need to stop taking your anger out on Jazzy. I know she's an easy target, but she's not to blame for what happened with Katie."

The anger and frustration I'd been trying so hard to keep contained comes rushing to the surface. "So what if I'm angry? I'm fucking furious!"

Unable to contain the heated rush of adrenaline flowing through my veins, I jump out of bed and begin to pace around the room. His black rubber-soled business shoes in the middle of the floor are the straw that breaks me. I snatch them off the floor and throw them into his walk-in closet. They bounce off the wall, only to land back at my feet. I scream in frustration as I scoop them up again.

"How can you just leave your clothes all over the floor when you're so anal about everything else being so neat and orderly? It makes no sense, Derek! No fucking sense at all."

Opening the window, I shove the screen out, and it lands on the concrete below with his shoes.

I turn, hands on my hips. Derek is staring at me.

"Was that really necessary?" he asks coldly.

"Abso-fucking-lutely."

"Stop swearing, and calm down."

"No!" I'm sick of trying to be calm and removed from what I'm feeling. "I'm angry. And so fucking what? Despite what you say, drugging myself to the point of numbness hasn't helped me get over her. It's just prolonged my grief. And what is the time limit on grief anyway?" I demand. "What is the correct and proper amount of time I'm allowed to miss her, Derek?"

His lower lip starts to tremble.

I lower my voice, and the next words come out choked. Broken.

"It's not right that a five-year-old dies from a brain tumor, Derek. It's just not fucking right." My tears begin to flow in earnest. She was only five... My knees are weak, and I lower myself onto the bed. "It's not right."

Derek rubs his eyes, his hand shaking. "I know. But anger isn't going to bring her back."

"Nothing is going to bring her back, but it doesn't mean I can't be angry about it."

"It still hurts me, too. But what happened to Katie doesn't excuse the scene you made when the picture frame was accidentally broken or when Jazzy wanted to swim in the pool. You can't act out like that anymore, or I'm going to call your psychologist. I'm worried about you. Are you sure you're still taking your pills?"

"Yes," I lie. I don't want him to blame how I feel on little pills. I feel this way. Without the pills, *I feel*. I need to push through the darkness, or I'll never find the light on the other side.

"None of this is Jazzy's fault. She's done nothing to you. You're coming across as a bunny boiler."

"Bunny boiler?" Like the crazy mistress in *Fatal Attraction*? "I can't be the bunny boiler. I'm the wife!"

"All I mean is that you're being irrational where Jazzy is concerned. When she's around, you turn into a jealous fishwife. It's embarrassing. And it has to stop." Derek's gaze hardens. "The Claire I used to know would never treat someone like this. The way you've been acting lately is… It's ugly."

"If I'm acting ugly, it's because you're making me this way. You dismiss anything I have to say about her—"

"That's because you're irrational!" he snaps, uncharacteristically raising his voice.

"You did it again. Irrational or not, it's how I feel," I say, crossing my arms. "And you should care about how I feel. And why aren't you even concerned that I had to ask if you were sleeping with her?"

"I just file it away with all the other crazy things you say." He slides into bed, turns his back. "I'm going to sleep now, Claire. Take your pills. They'll help you calm down. A good night's sleep will do you good."

The pills are no longer in the drawer, but I wouldn't take them anyway. I'm not tired, and the thought of getting in bed next to him churns my stomach.

"Take your damn pills, Claire," he repeats wearily. "I put a new box in there. You should have told me you'd run out."

His cool dismissal makes me furious. I want to shout at him, throw some more things around the room. I want to scream and pound his chest until he has no choice but to listen to me.

But I know that it won't make any difference.

I could throw his whole wardrobe out the window, and he'd just look at me with those accusatory eyes: case in point. He'd say, *Claire, take a good look at yourself. You've really lost your mind now.* He'd be so convincing he'd make me believe it myself. I'd look in the mirror and see my reflection, wild and emotional. And I'd think because he was so calm that he was the one who had it all worked out.

That I was being overemotional. Overemotional!

I'm so sick of being called that. Why is that even an insult? Derek is *under*-emotional!

Why is the way I feel always wrong?

The regular sound of his breathing fills the room. How can he do that? Go to sleep so quickly? How can he just fall asleep when I'm so torn up inside?

Because he doesn't care, Claire. Not in the way you need him to.

I look at him in our bed on the pristine white sheets. His head on the crisp white pillow. I listen to his regular breathing turn into a light snore.

I try to feel something for him.

I stare, long and hard.

Me. Claire Marie Hardt. What is it that I feel for my husband?

I try to find love but only find it in memories. When Katie died, she took all of the happiness with her. But I have to pick up the pieces of whatever is left of my life. I have to find a way to move forward.

The only question now is whether Derek is going to be one of the pieces I take. Or leave behind.

CHAPTER 10

J look through the back window of the shop into the car park. Zach's car isn't there. I wonder what he's doing, what he does when he's not in his shop. There are so many things I want to know about him, and the questions are piling up on top of one another.

He calls to me, this colorful man with wild rock star looks and so many layers. Nothing about him is predictable. He's a free spirit, living in society, yet apart.

"Okay, what's up?" Kira asks, coming up to stand behind me.

"Nothing." I turn from the window, ashamed to be caught thinking of a man not my husband. But it's exhausting trying to continually unravel the problems in my marriage. I'm angry, hurt, and not sleeping. I can't seem to find a single thread I can hold onto to pull me out of the abyss and give me hope.

Kira stands in front of me. "I know you, Claire," she says. "I can see what you hide behind your smile."

I sigh and look over her shoulder across West Coast Drive to the ocean. I don't want to open up to yet another person, only to be told I am being silly or jealous or whatever my two best friends think.

But the look on Kira's face tells me she's not going to let it drop.

"That school friend who is staying with us is still there. It's been just over three weeks now."

"The one you were surprised to hear Carole Roberts mention when she told you Derek took someone else to the lunch."

"That's the one."

"She's staying at your house," Kira says, "flirting with your husband, and you don't like it."

"I didn't say she was flirting."

"And you didn't deny it."

"I don't know if she's flirting. It might be just the way she is. Derek said she's friendly like that to everyone." I shrug my shoulders. "I can't be sure." Especially when everyone around me is telling me I'm crazy for thinking she's anything other than 'lovely'. To be unable to trust your own instincts is its own special brand of torture, forcing me to analyze every action, looking to find even the smallest piece of evidence to justify the way I'm feeling. To prove it's not all in my head.

Kira walks over to the kitchenette and makes a fruit juice drink with a dash of courage, as she calls it, and places it in my hands. I take a large gulp of the tasty juice spiked with vodka, walk to the large shop-front window, and look across the street to the ocean.

"If she's upsetting you and you don't want her there anymore," Kira says, "then the bitch has to go."

I choke on a mouthful of juice. Wiping my lips with the back of my hand, I grin at her. "As much as I'd love to kick her out, I can't do that. She's his old school friend. She's looking for a place to stay, and apparently she applied for one and could leave any day now. What grounds do I have to object?"

"You don't need grounds," Kira scoffs. "Life isn't a court of law."

"But I've told him how I feel about her staying, and he doesn't listen. He just says I'm being selfish or jealous or something. After all, logically, we do have the room. And I have no evidence they're doing anything wrong... There's something about her that I don't trust. She's manipulative, and I don't trust her motives." I shrug. "What does it matter? Nobody believes me. I have no proof."

"You don't need proof," Kira says. "Go home tonight and tell Derek straight up she has to go. Whether she's doing anything sly or not is irrelevant. You've been nice enough letting her stay, and now she has to get the fuck out. Derek is your husband—that is your house. Stop dicking around being nice, and get in there and take back control."

I feel my eyes widen. "Is that what you'd do?"

"Hell, yes! You've been miserable these last few weeks. If it were me, the bitch wouldn't have lasted this long."

I weigh up Kira's words. She has a point. But she's never been married, never had her life intricately entwined with another's. When you're married, things are more complicated than that.

And it's certainly not the advice Bec has given me, but Bec is married to the son of Derek's boss. Rob would no doubt have heard Derek's version of events, and that would have had to color Bec's perspective.

I need to sit down and have a serious discussion with Derek about our marriage. And whatever the outcome, Jasmine can't be there when we do it. And I can't just wait around indefinitely while she fluffs around house-hunting. Who knows how long that might still take?

Kira is right. Tick tock. Time's up. The bitch has to go.

I grin. "This is why I love you, Kira." She's lit a spark of fire inside me whereas the other people in my life seem determined to snuff it out. And considering my life has been one emotional roller coaster of destruction for far too long, it's been way too easy for me to lose sight of the fact that I'm entitled to feel however I do. Right or wrong.

I lean in and give Kira a big hug.

"Your husband should have your back, Claire. Always. If you're not comfortable, that should be his number one priority. It isn't even a question. I'm pissed he's even putting you in the position to have to justify how you feel. He should have read you long ago. He needs to say, 'Look old school friend, time's up. Great to see you, nice to catch up. You're upsetting my wife, now off you go.'"

I laugh, and it feels good. I feel stronger, stronger than I've felt in a long time. Years.

A car pulls into the car park in front of the shop. It's our ten o'clock appointment.

Tonight, I'm going to tell Derek that Jasmine has got to go.

CHAPTER 11

They're on the couch.

I toss my bag onto the kitchen counter and grab a bottle of wine. They've stopped talking, but Jasmine's cheeks are flushed. Derek has shifted now, is sitting more upright in his seat.

"You're late," Derek says. I'd stayed at the shop for a couple of hours after closing to finish a design for a new client. "How's your day?" He reaches for the remote and, finding the news channel, turns up the volume before I've even answered.

I pour myself a glass of wine and take a long sip, letting it thaw the ice that has once again formed in my stomach. I used to love coming home. Now I dread it. The stranger in my house, my husband's friend, is still here. The chasm between Derek and me grows wider by the hour.

"Derek, can I have a word?" It would be so much easier to have this conversation without her in the house, but I have no choice. With Kira's words still fresh in my mind, I wait until Derek is in the kitchen.

"What is it?" He frowns at me. "Is there a problem?"

"Yes," I say, setting down my glass of wine. "It's about Jasmine."

Derek's face closes over, and he crosses his arms. "Not again."

"Please, Derek. Hear me out." Perhaps if I explain how this is making me feel, he'll understand and not just write off my feelings as jealousy. I need to at least give that a try. For me. To know for sure…

"I hate that you think my feelings about Jasmine are irrational. Regardless of your opinion, I am your wife. I want you to put me first. To take my side even if you don't understand it. For no other reason than because I need you to."

Derek narrows his eyes.

"I want you to ask her to leave."

"Why should she leave? She's applied for a few places. She could be approved any day now. What you want me to do? Hurt my friend for no reason?"

"Derek, this is hurting *me*."

"Then you need to get over it."

Get over it?

Whatever is left of our marriage scatters in fragments across the floor.

Jasmine walks into the kitchen. "Oh, sorry. Were you two having a private conversation?"

"Yes." *Now fuck off.*

"Would you mind giving us a moment?" Derek asks her.

I roll my eyes. I've told Derek how I feel, and he dismisses me. Every time. What are my options?

I take my wine and head outside onto the balcony. The breeze is cool against my heated skin. I want to scream at her, kick her out of our house myself. But if there is any hope left for our marriage, her removal needs to come from Derek. So much is riding on his decision to do so.

But he's standing in the doorway, his face creased with anger.

I look past his shoulder, through the glass doors. The lounge room is empty.

"She's gone to have a shower," Derek says, answering my unasked question. "We already went through this last night. Why are you being such a bitch again tonight?"

"Excuse me?"

My heart is pounding on my ribcage like a beast trying to escape.

"Jazzy is a nice girl," Derek says, seemingly unaware of the slippery slope he's walking down. I've made my position clear. Now it's up to him. "And you'd see that too if you took the time to get to know her."

The "nice girl" comment is the final straw. That, and the fact he has the audacity to go into battle for her. All the fucking time.

"She is not nice to me," I snap. "And you'd see that if you took the time to notice." I throw his words back at him, but they appear to bounce straight off. "Do my feelings matter to you at all?" I demand, my cheeks burning as though someone had taken to them with a blowtorch. "Hers do, but do mine? As irrational as you think I'm being or not, they should matter. I'm your *wife*."

"It's embarrassing that my wife isn't behaving better toward a guest."

I shake my head slowly. "What is it with her? I tell you I'm struggling with this, and not once do you make any attempt at alleviating my concerns. You're—"

"That's because you're being irrational."

"Am I really? Whenever I walk in, you're cosied up in some conversation that I feel like I'm interrupting. I've tried—"

"You haven't tried," he spits. "You've done nothing but make her feel unwelcome since the moment she arrived, and I have to say it's not an attractive look."

I try to put my whirring thoughts into words. I'm sick of battling over her.

"I no longer feel like your wife, Derek." My hands start to tremble slightly, so I hide them behind my back. It's not easy admitting that.

"What are you on about now?"

Whether he deserves it or not, I won't give up without knowing I tried. "The way you look at her," I say, cracking myself open, "is how I want you to look at me. You speak to her, laugh with her, your eyes light up around her. When you're with her, it makes me feel as though you're married to her, and I'm the guest."

"You're being ridiculous."

"Stop disregarding my feelings!" I didn't mean to shout quite so loud. I bend at the waist, drag in a full breath before standing back up. "I'm telling you how I feel," I say, keeping my voice steady. "I want you to hear me. Really hear me." A single tear rolls down my cheek. "Look at me. Why can't you look at me?"

He does look at me then, and instead of what I want to see there—love, compassion, understanding—he's looking at me with something akin to pity. Disgust. A choked sound escapes from my throat.

"You make it very hard for me to look at you when you're carrying on like this. I expect more from my wife."

"I'm opening my fucking *heart* to you. I'm trying to decide if there's anything left of our marriage to save. If we can get any semblance of what we once had back."

"For three years, I've stood by you through your breakdown. How dare you say I haven't been a good husband."

My head spins. "I didn't say you weren't a good husband." I press my fingers into my temples. How do I get through to him? How do I make him understand? "I'm standing before you as your wife, telling you something is hurting me, fucking *hurting* me, Derek. Can you hear me? I know you see me speaking, but can you really hear me?" My voice is calm, belying the volcano of emotion surging inside me.

I try to take his hand, but he pulls away. "You haven't exactly been the easiest person to live with," Derek says.

"I agree. Would you like me to apologize for that? I'm sorry. I'm sorry that we lost our little girl, and I didn't know how to cope. I'm sorry that catapulted me into a hole so deep and dark I felt I was in Hell. I'm sorry that I prayed to Satan himself to take my very soul if he would only bring Katie back!" Silent tears roll down my cheeks. "And I'm sorry if during all that, I forgot to be a wife."

I bare my soul, lay my heart wide open for him to see. My pain, my suffering. I'm waiting for him to crumble, to take me in his arms. I'm waiting for him to start crying, to say he's sorry, too. For turning away from me the first few weeks when I needed his arms the most. For holding the bottle instead of me while I cried, as he sat by the pool until the sun came up and staggered into bed with his shoes on.

I'm waiting for him to own his part in this, in the separation of us. We both fell apart, and we've been healing separately and on our own. Without each other.

I accept my part.

Will he accept his?

But he's standing there, not saying a word. Finally, he speaks.

"None of that is Jasmine's fault."

My heart sinks.

"I slice my goddamn heart open for you, and the first thing you can talk about is *her?*"

"Have you listened to yourself?" Derek asks. "Actually taken a step back and listened to how you sound?"

"Like a wife, who feels as though she has lost her husband?"

"You haven't lost me," he says. "I'm right here." He opens his arms wide as though to ask, *what is this?* My vision darkens, red spots flash in my eyes.

"I don't mean physically; I mean emotionally."

Derek stares at me for a long moment as though not quite sure how to deal with me.

"Do you love me?" I ask, my voice breaking on the words.

Derek frowns. "Of course, I love you."

"But are you *in love* with me?" I demand. "Like you used to be? Like Rob loves Bec? He looks at her like he's the luckiest man in the world."

"Claire," Derek says, with forced patience. "We've been married for eight years. Rob and Bec won't continue to act so foolishly over each other for long. Marriage is about two people merging lives. A mutually beneficial joining."

A what? "You think marriage is a business merger?"

"Of sorts. We have a lot that works in our marriage, Claire. You're just choosing not to see it."

"Like?"

"Like the fact that I run your business for you. Manage your accounts, handle all the finances, so you can just work and enjoy what you do. And you help me with my career. The partners love you, as do the wives. You're something of a celebrity at work, and that flows onto me. We have a nice house, nice cars. It's time you pulled yourself together and realized how lucky you are. How lucky *we* are. Together. This drama over Jazzy is complicating a perfectly good arrangement. Get over yourself, and stop being so emotional and dramatic."

My heart is pounding. I struggle to find the right words to make him understand how empty I feel in our marriage/merger.

Julia had said I didn't appreciate how lucky I was when I saw her last. If that's true, then why didn't it feel that way? How do I explain the gaping loneliness threatening to swallow me whole?

"Marriage is not a merger to me," I say, struggling to find the words to make him understand. "I want fire, I want passion. I want…"

I want a reason to stay.

"The kind of relationship you're talking about doesn't exist," Derek snaps. "Not for the long run. The passion you're talking about is only there at the beginning. The marriages that only have passion fail…the ones that have something more substantial last longer."

"You can keep passion alive if you both work at it."

"Life isn't a fairy tale, Claire, and it sure as hell isn't one of those corny romance books you need to stop reading. Get your head out of the clouds. You're confusing fiction with reality."

I'm too stunned to speak. I need a moment to process my husband's idea of marriage. How is it I haven't known this? *After ten years.*

"Look," Derek lowers his tone, his voice even, cajoling. "We need each other, Claire. You're just putting far too much emphasis on romance. When you're not acting all jealous and irrational, we actually get along very well together." He reaches out, touches my arm. "That's how a marriage survives, lasts the distance."

"So, you're happy with how we've been living these last three years?"

He rubs his eyes. "Not with respect to losing Katie, but overall, our marriage works fine. I'm sure if you'll just go back on your medication, your confusion will go away."

"*Everything* goes away when I take those pills." Tears of frustration sting my eyes. The distance between us is insurmountable.

"You're just not thinking clearly right now."

I'm thinking clearer now than I have in years. And one thought is louder and clearer than all the others. "Tell Jasmine to leave."

Derek's expression hardens. "I will not. I have a right to have my friend stay in my house."

"This is *our* house, Derek."

"I pay for it."

"I pay for it, too," I argue.

"What you make pays for the toilet," he says derisively. "Running a business is a lot more than making a few pretty dresses. You wouldn't have that business without me."

My heart pounds violently. Derek handles the accounts from my shop. I've never had to ask about the financials before. But now I'm wondering if that was a mistake. Should I have paid closer attention?

"Regardless of how much you say I contribute financially, this is my house too. And this is Jasmine's last day. She's to find somewhere else to sleep tomorrow night."

Derek's face contorts. He looks ugly, the waves of anger rolling off him, chilling me to my bones. "I don't even know who you are anymore."

"Trust me, the feeling goes both ways."

We stare at each other for long, painful moments. Then he turns and walks away. The door slams shut behind him.

I grip the balcony railing tight, look out over the river. Delusional or not, I'm not going to settle for less than what I believe a relationship to be. Romance books aside, I'm a red-blooded woman. I have hopes, dreams. I desire. And I need love. Passion. *I crave it.*

A heavy knowing settles inside me. Instead of our conversation being the start of an improvement, it's the beginning of the end. Despite his clinical outlook on marriage, I know Derek still feels desire. It's in his eyes every time he looks at Jasmine.

I'm on the balcony, the Swan River sprawling out in front of me, yet it feels as though the walls are closing in.

CHAPTER 12

I arrive home the following night to silence. No background television noise, no nineties music, no annoying giggle from an unwanted guest.

Derek is standing in the kitchen, his body stiff, his expression sullen. I place my keys and my phone on the marble countertop and step around him. I reach into the cupboard and pull out two glasses.

"Are you happy?" he snaps, and I can smell alcohol on his breath from two feet away. "You got what you wanted. Jasmine is staying with her aunt. On a fold-out lounge." He waves his hand around in front of him. "When we have all this room."

I put one glass back in the cupboard and release a breath. Derek steps in front of me, his eyes cold. "Do you have any idea what it felt like to have to tell her she can't stay here? For no reason. Just, sorry, you can't stay here anymore. My wife has lost her goddamned mind. I'm not a child, Claire. And you're not my mother. You don't just get to decide."

"Neither do you."

We glare at each other.

"Derek," I say evenly. "I can't keep going on like this." I say the words I've been thinking out loud for the first time. "I can't talk to you with her always around. I want to talk to you about our marriage, our expectations, and where we go from here."

Without Jasmine hanging around, maybe he'll say he wants to put in some effort, see if we can find a way to move forward. Together. *We've been married eight years, I need to be sure...*

Derek picks up his car keys. "There's nothing to discuss. I made my position clear last night. And since I can't have my friends over here, I'm going out."

I jump at the sound of the front door slamming shut in the otherwise silent house. A moment later, his car's engine revs hard, and the tires squeal as he reverses out of the driveway. With the amount of alcohol in his system, he shouldn't be driving. But there's nothing I can do to stop him.

He's going out to be with her. It wouldn't even matter if he wasn't. He left instead of being here with me.

He walked away. After knowing how I feel.

His words last night weren't spoken in the heat of the moment. He meant them. There was no apology. His views are just as clear in the cold light of day.

I take my wine and lower myself onto the empty couch. My spot. Next to the table and lamp.

At what point do you decide enough is enough?

Do we live like this for another year? Another two? A lifetime? Until we make ourselves so miserable that the very sight of each other causes us to be sick to the stomach?

What would happen if we divorced? What would that be like?

After everything our marriage has been through, I can't believe it has come to this. But losing Katie has taught me one thing.

If I'm forced to continue to live it without her, then goddamn it, I am going to live it to the fullest.

There's just one thing...

I'd have to leave this house. From what Derek said, I won't be able to afford it on my own. Not that the house itself is special. A house is just a house.

But this house has a certain room that is irreplaceable.

I rise up off the couch and walk down the hallway.

I pass the cupboard that inside has her growth chart. Tiny marks and dates carved into timber. Physical reminders that keep the memories alive. Sometimes she seems so far away I wonder if she was even real at all. Then I see the mark on the wall where she rode her trike inside and the handlebars scratched the plaster off.

I brought my baby home to this house.

I pause, my hand hovering over the doorknob to her room.

It's been three years.

Three long, unbearable years.

It's time.

If I have to leave, I have to find a way to say goodbye.

My heart is pounding. My eyes are already stinging.

I can do this.

I need to do this.

To move on, I have to be able to let go of the memories this house holds.

A sound of anguish rises from somewhere deep inside me. It bounces off the walls and echoes in the empty rooms of this empty house. Somewhere inside me, I find the strength to turn the handle.

In this room, time stands still.

It still smells like her. Strawberries and vanilla. My knees go weak, and I grip the door to keep myself upright. Her bed is made up, pretty pink ruffles sitting atop a white timber bed. Her favorite teddy bear sits next to her hospital bag. I placed the bag on the bed on the day they sent us home for the last time. *Without her.*

On the day we finally had to accept she would never be coming home again.

The day God stole our little girl from us.

The day I lost my faith in a higher power entirely.

I closed this door behind me that day and never opened it again.

The air leaves my lungs, the pain as raw and ragged as when I first lost her.

My legs must have finally given way because I'm on the floor. The tiles just outside her room are cold, but they're not frozen like my insides.

I place my shaking hand over my mouth and start to sob. "Katie," I wail. "My beautiful little girl. Mummy misses you so much. Still. Even now."

I crawl into her room, knees now on soft white carpet. My arms reach out, cradling the air as though I'm holding the daughter I'll never hold again. Tears stream down my face, and there's no stemming the torrent now that they've started.

"You'd be eight next month," I say to the room that shouldn't be empty. "I wonder what you'd want for your birthday. Would you still like pale pink, or would you prefer purple or blue now?"

Her little ballet shoes are just in front of me. I could reach out and touch them. But I don't. I can't.

She never got to wear them to a class.

But I can see her excited little face as she picked them out. She wanted to be a ballerina. Her blue eyes were alight, and she twirled and twirled around the house, bumping into walls and chairs when she got too dizzy. She was supposed to start lessons the week after we received the diagnosis.

"Brain tumor," the doctor had said. "We need to operate right away."

She's going to be all right, she's going to be all right became my new mantra. I repeated the words through surgery, through recovery, through radiation, through the agonizing chemotherapy treatments.

But she wasn't all right.

And then the doctors tell you they're sorry. They send you home, without her, and somehow expect you to continue to live when the very reason you take your next breath has been ripped away.

And then life becomes an illusion, your body an empty shell.

It isn't right.

Life isn't supposed to be this way.

A mother isn't supposed to pack away her daughter's things forever.

A mother isn't supposed to bury her little girl.

I slept on her grave that first night. I was convinced she'd be cold. It was winter, and the ground was freezing. I slept there the second night, too. And the next.

Someone, not Derek, dragged me away. I screamed at and hit them, but I can't remember who it was now, to apologize.

The months after that are a blur. I couldn't tell you how I lived, how I ate. But then one day, I woke up to find that damn sun relentlessly shining. And Derek staring at me through the bottom of a bottle of gin. I crossed the room to him, but I never crossed the distance that had come between us.

I pick myself up off the floor. I'm not ready to pack up Katie's room even now. Perhaps I'll never be. I kick off my shoes, padding in my bare feet across the room. I place her hospital bag on her pink sheepskin rug, lie down on her bed.

My head sinks into her soft lacy pillow, and I breathe in her scent. Strawberries and vanilla. Always, strawberries and vanilla. I curl up into a ball, clutch her plush teddy tight in my arms. I kiss its head and imagine I'm kissing Katie's soft blonde curls.

"Sweetheart, can you hear me?" My tears are streaming into her pillow, and my words are choked out between broken sobs.

"I hope that wherever you are now, you're happy. They say I have to learn how to create a new life, one where you aren't at the center. I never thought I'd have to do that. Never thought I could. But you know what, sweetheart? I think maybe they're right after all. I can't keep going on like this. It's give up or fight. I've chosen to fight.

"I've had to do lots of things I'd never have imagined I'd have to do these last three years. Burying you was one. Continuing to breathe, eat and sleep without you was another. But darling?

"It's time. Mummy has to let you go now. Your place in my heart will always be there; nothing can ever take that away. But it's Mummy's time to find a way to be happy again.

"You won't ever come back to me. I've had to accept that now. Just like I've had to accept I'll never watch you grow up, never watch you become a ballerina and marry your Prince Charming. There is a lifetime of being with you I'll never get the opportunity to share. But nothing I do is going to bring you back."

And maybe that's a good thing because you'll never know the pain of watching your mummy and daddy divorce.

"In this lifetime, I'll never stop loving you. It's just that…"

I swallow hard. "Sweetheart? I've got to let you go now because Mummy has to move on."

I feel her tiny fingers run through my hair. I feel her tiny wet kiss on my cheek.

"Goodbye, sweet Katie," I choke out. "Mummy loves you, too."

I don't need her room anymore because I finally realize she's no longer there.

She's living inside my heart.

CHAPTER 13

*T*he scent of smoke and the sound of laughter greet me as I step out of my car. The sun is low in the sky, casting long shadows. I sling my bag over my shoulder and grab three huge buckets of popcorn out of the back seat.

Unlike last time I'd been to the Village, this time I'm dressed appropriately, in jeans, sneakers, my favorite John Lennon "Imagine" fitted T-shirt... and Zach's leather jacket.

I've spent a lot of time thinking these last couple of days, waiting for the doubt about ending my marriage to kick in. It hasn't. And Derek hasn't come home. I rang him, and we've arranged to talk tomorrow night.

I can't keep going on like this with the distance, the cold war, between us. I'm the same person I used to be, but I'm looking at the world through new eyes. I'd spent so long gliding through each day, unseeing, unhearing, unfeeling... Where everything was gray.

I've been more excited about the campfire tonight with Zach and some ex-street kids than any cocktail party or fancy function I'd ever been invited to.

Derek would hate it here. All the dirt and bugs.

Balancing the popcorn in my arms, I turn on my torch even though I don't quite need it yet. Trekking through the bush is exciting, but I don't want to run into a spider's web. Although I'm loving what is a new experience for me, I'm not that comfortable with everything that lives and breathes in nature yet, especially the deadly western brown snakes. Do they come out at night? A shiver rolls down my spine. I don't want to find out.

When I get to the clearing, my eyes find him immediately. *Zach.* His back is to me, but he turns the moment I arrive. This strange connection between us probably should be disconcerting, yet I find it comforting to connect with another human being after feeling alone for so long. Tension eases from my body and is replaced by warmth. A sense of belonging. Of coming home.

Smiling, Zach closes the distance between us. When he reaches me, there's an awkward moment as though he wanted to pull me into his arms, kiss me hello. But he takes the popcorn instead.

I smile awkwardly and tell my stupid heart it has no right being disappointed. I am, at the moment, a married woman.

Mandy rushes up to me. "Claire! I made something for you." She hands me a folded piece of paper then steps backward, looking down at her shuffling feet.

Carefully, I open the fragile page to discover a picture of a girl wearing a red coat. Around the picture are hearts with my name in the center of each one. Clearly, Mandy spent a lot of time on the drawing.

I'm blinking back tears as she looks up at me. "I'm sorry," she says quickly. "I'm not a very good drawer."

"Yes, you are!" I kneel down, hug her to me tightly. I can barely speak, but somehow I manage to choke out, "I love it. Thank you." Katie was drawing stick figures and houses when she died. Is this what her drawings would look like now?

"Claire is crying happy tears," Zach explains from somewhere above us.

I pull back so Mandy can see my smile through my tears. "Zach is right. I'm happy. Thank you, sweetheart. I think this is the nicest thing anyone has ever done for me."

Mandy beams at me, her smile lighting up her face.

"Come and see the fire!"

I stand, and she tugs on my hand. Zach is smiling at me, something unreadable in his expression. I laugh as I let Mandy pull me along.

The fire is well ablaze, and about a dozen boys are sitting around it in a circle. The benches are trunks of trees. Mandy chooses a log next to her brother, Aidan, and Zach and I sit next to her.

The smell of barbequed sausages and steak lingers in the air. My large buckets of popcorn are being eagerly eaten. All around us is happy talk and laughter. One of the kids–I find out his name is Levi—is playing a guitar, strumming the same few chords over and over, but people are singing along as though he's Keith Urban himself.

I'm still wearing Zach's jacket, and he has yet to comment. He's sitting next to me, and I'm hyperaware of his presence. I take in the jumping flames and the kids poking marshmallows on sticks into the fire.

Tears escape out of the corner of my eyes. My past and my unhappiness are so distant they have no place here.

Although the only light is the glow from the campfire, Zach notices the tears immediately. "Are you okay?" His voice is soft, laced with concern, and my chest tightens painfully.

"I can't help thinking about where they'd be, what they'd be doing if they weren't here. You're doing a wonderful thing here, Zach," I say. "Making such a difference to so many lives."

Zach looks around the campfire. "It's not like I had a grand plan or anything. This started with one kid, Richard." He shrugs. "It is constantly on my mind that if I screw up, this place gets shut down."

"That can't happen," I say, surprised at the fierceness in my tone. Already, I'd risk anything to keep these kids here, safe, with likely the only security and home they'd ever known.

I don't care what happened to Zach in the past. Whatever it was—no matter how awful—it made him into the man he is today.

It would be so much simpler if I felt for my husband what I feel for Zach. I've never cared this intensely for Derek, and my stomach twists with this knowledge.

Derek never made my heart race or filled me with pride at some unselfish act of his. Derek turned away charity collectors when they knocked on the door. He even went so far as to put up a sign telling them to stay away.

Watch your pennies, and the pounds take care of themselves, he'd say over and over. It had seemed like such sound financial advice when he said it, but after being here, after seeing what those pennies could really be used for, the difference they could make...

"Zach, Zach, my marshmallow keeps sliding off!" Mandy walks back to us from the fire, holding her charred stick out in front of her.

Zach wipes off the gooey marshmallow with a serviette and shows her how to pierce the soft confection in the center. "You hold it here, on the coals, not directly in the flames."

Mandy follows his instructions and ends up with a perfectly toasted marshmallow. She pops it into her mouth and groans out loud with delight. "Thanks, Zachy," she says and runs off.

Zach's eyes catch mine. His grin fades, and intensity flares in his gaze, a connection that I feel soul deep inside me.

He blinks then looks down at his hands, which are fisted in his lap. He opens his palms and rubs them on his jeans. When he next looks at me, his expression is neutral.

My heart is pounding with a heavy sense of loss. As though something I really, really wanted has just been taken away.

There are some who would say I shouldn't be feeling things like this for a man who isn't my husband.

But what do you do if the passion just isn't there? How do you make yourself feel something you don't? An emotion isn't something you can pick up and place somewhere else. Zach affects me in ways he shouldn't, yet reason and logic play no part in this.

My right thumb rubs the ring on my commitment finger. Reminding me I have something that needs to be resolved first.

Maybe to put distance between us, Zach walks away, across the circle, and picks up the guitar Levi has just put down. There's a coldness in the place he left, but when he returns a moment later with the guitar, all is right in my world again. Zach's fingers pick across the strings, and a haunting melody floats around the campfire. Conversation dies down, and Zach's music fills the air.

My throat closes over. He's playing the hell out of that guitar, clearly gifted in more than one area. Zach creates music in the same style as his paintings. Slightly dark and haunting, the notes spark an ache in my heart.

The song is familiar, but I can't place it. Then he switches to something upbeat. A Keith Urban song.

And then he starts to sing...

Zach's voice is beautiful. Dark, husky, and velvety smooth. A few people join in, but I can hear only Zach.

My body heats, a slow burn like straight whisky warming my blood on a cold winter's night.

Zach flicks the occasional glance my way as he continues to play. His eyes are soft. His dark hair is long and messy. A little wild. A lot untamable. A little Michael Hutchence, a little Kurt Cobain, and a whole lot of Zach Argos.

And oh so sexy.

I want this man.

I want him so bad desire burns like fire inside me.

My wedding ring digs into my skin. The symbol of my vows burns my flesh.

"Come on, Claire. Sing along."

I hadn't even noticed Mandy at my side until she slips her hand into mine. Smiling through the tears burning my eyes, I join my voice with hers. Zach looks over at us. A gentle smile lights his eyes.

I am happy.

Truly happy for the first time in a very long time.

Since Katie.

The moon is full and high. The kids are all safely in their respective cottages, Aidan has driven Mandy back to their new apartment, and the only two left by the fire are Zach and me. We have dragged our log closer to the dying flames, the woody smoke filling my lungs.

I don't want the night to end.

Zach is sitting next to me, poking the last of the coals, his body heat radiating up my arm and spreading through me. It's too dark to read my watch, but it's well after midnight. The hours since I arrived have seemingly vanished. My voice is hoarse from the smoke, from singing and talking so much.

The most pleasant surprise of the evening is how easy it is to talk to Zach. To my surprise, I've told him all about my childhood, how I never knew who my father was, what it was like living with my mother, who was so passionate about art and love and life.

I don't watch my words the way I normally would with strangers. Nor do I wonder if I'm talking too much. Am I being too personal? am I being too loud? Is there food between my teeth? Do I need a mint? Do I sound crazy?

Zach is just so damn comfortable to be around...except for the powerful attraction I feel for him. If only he wasn't so damn sexy!

"Are you where you thought you'd be in life?" Zach asks, staring into the flames. "I mean, if you could be doing anything at all, are you doing what you'd want to be doing?"

If you mean being right here, right now, with you? Yes.

I don't say that. Such a deep question surprises me. It would almost be considered rude in my circle, at the very least, far too personal. But something tells me Zach spends a lot of time thinking out here in the bush while staring into a campfire or writing music.

"Are *you* doing what you want to be doing?" I ask him his own question to give me time to think about my reply.

"Yeah." Zach tosses a stick into the fire and it crackles, sending sparks spiraling upward. "There was a time I thought I'd live out my adult life behind bars, so my life the way it is now is pretty damn good, all things considered."

"You're a famous artist," I remind him with a smile.

Zach turns to me, his eyes glistening in the last glow of the firelight. His lips curve in a way I feel all the way to my toes.

"Not just in Australia," I add, "but overseas as well. Rumor has it you're known as quite the artist in London, my hometown."

Zach runs a hand through his hair and stretches out his long legs. "I've been lucky. The money gives me the opportunity to spend time at the Village and teach the kids to surf." Zach looks at me then. "Now it's your turn. Answer the question."

He's asked me twice now. What does he want to hear? "I never even realized there was a choice until very recently."

Zach looks at me. "It's your life, Claire. You only get one. It's always your choice."

"Not always," I say defensively. Zach didn't intend to end up with the Village the way it is, and I didn't intend to end up getting married and pregnant at nineteen, losing my only child at twenty-five, and being in a loveless marriage by twenty-eight.

Sometimes shit just happens.

I rub my eyes, and I'm suddenly exhausted.

Zach's strong fingers link with mine. "I didn't mean to upset you."

I glance down to where our hands are resting side by side. His palm still flat on the log, his fingers have tangled with mine.

His touch.

It captures and holds all my attention.

That tiny connection between us is as powerful as anything I've ever felt.

He notices me staring and moves his hand away. "Sorry."

I feel the loss of his touch, a severed connection.

"Isn't your husband wondering where you are?" Zach's voice is rough and he clears his throat.

It's long after midnight on Saturday night. I can't imagine Derek being home; he hasn't been there all week.

"I doubt it."

Zach raises his eyebrows in surprise but doesn't press me for details.

It hits me then, the contrast between us. The way Zach lives so free, so true to himself.

My life is as fake as the people who fill it. I close my eyes against the threatening tears.

"Damn," he says. "I didn't mean to upset you again. Will he be angry?"

"Can you not?" I snap, then pause. "Please stop talking about him."

Zach looks at me then, intensely. A frown creases his forehead. "I'm sorry."

The emotion leaves me in a rush. None of this is Zach's fault. He just asked a simple question. One that should have been easy to answer.

"I'm the one who's sorry," I say, releasing a deliberately slow and calming breath. "It's the anniversary of my little girl's death in a couple weeks. Three years ago, this coming Mother's Day. It always hits me hard."

"That's fucked."

There's anger in his tone, and I like it.

"Yes," I agree. "That *is* fucked."

I can't help but smile. I'm so used to people being uncomfortable when I bring up Katie, telling me it's God's plan, that she was too good for this world, or the kicker, it happened for a reason... As though there would ever be a reason to justify a parent suffering the loss of their child.

There was no reason, no silver lining to all the pain. Zach was right. It was fucked. Plain and simple.

He stands, wipes his hands on his jeans, and then extends one to me. There's a charge as our skin touches, an awareness as he tugs me to my feet. His masculinity, his strength, his pure maleness, makes me feel all the more feminine.

The effect is heady.

"I'd better get you home." *Back to your life, to your husband.* Zach doesn't say the words, but they hang in the air between us anyway.

He leads us up the path back to the cars by torchlight.

I scrounge in my bag for my keys. He flicks his torch on my bag. For an instant, the light is blinding, and when he flicks it off, the world is totally black. My eyes struggling to adjust, I thrust out my arm to press the remote and accidentally punch him in the stomach.

"Sorry," I rush to say, whipping my arm back too fast, my feet slipping on the rocks. Zach grabs my shoulders, stopping my fall.

He doesn't immediately release me, and my heart misses a beat. Then one of his hands skims down my arm, and he takes the keys from my fingers.

He unlocks the car and opens the door, and once again, I can see by the interior light.

I don't want to leave.

God help me, I don't want to leave.

Don't want to see the cold, white tiles in the empty house that waits for me.

"I'm keeping your jacket," I say.

Zach's eyes are swirling with emotions I want him to articulate. Because I sure as hell can't define exactly what this is between us. His eyes fall to my mouth, and I instinctively draw my bottom lip between my teeth.

His gaze darkens. The air between us is charged, crackling.

"Zach." His name is a breathless whisper on my tongue.

What would it be like to kiss him? Just once?

His throat moves as he swallows. "Yes?" His voice is low. Husky.

When I breathe you in, it fills the emptiness...

"I have to go."

His lips curve into a sexy half-smile. "You realize I'm not keeping you here, right?"

Something is.

Something inexpressible.

I thumb the gold band circling my wedding finger.

I have unfinished business to attend to.

CHAPTER 14

Sunday evening, the night after the campfire, the night Derek is supposed to meet me at the house, I pull into the driveway past my white picket fence. All my life I wanted a white picket fence, but it feels clichéd now.

As does my life.

I turn the lock, and the sound of my keys jangling echoes in the large empty space. The place is so quiet. So cold. I rub my palms up and down my arms. No giggling, flirting Jasmine. No tinkle of wine glasses on marble counters.

No Derek.

I see dishes on the sink that weren't there this morning, so I know he's been home at some point. In the stack of dishes, there are two cups, one with a faint lipstick mark on the rim. I hate that I even think to look.

I hate that it pisses me off even as I tell myself I no longer care.

I move through the house, packing everything I can into two large suitcases. I've filled my car and boot with my sewing equipment, designs, and materials. Only the essentials. I don't know how the meeting with Derek will play out, but either way, I need some time away by myself. To put distance between us. To think.

If we can't find a way to move forward, I'll arrange to collect the rest of my things at a later date. Leaving Katie's room, her memories, will be the hardest thing of all, but maybe it will be better to start fresh, regardless. Memories keep you tied to the past.

My throat closes over, and I blink to clear my eyes. I must stay strong.

Maybe Derek will surprise me and do the decent thing, move out and let me stay in the house. But I can't rely on that. I have to be prepared for all outcomes. I can no longer predict how my husband will react.

There's a knock at the door.

It's five p.m., the time Derek had agreed to meet me here. But Derek wouldn't knock, so it's not hard to guess who's at the door. Telling him I needed to talk should have implied "alone." The fact that she's here is confirmation my marriage is over.

I open the door and glare at her. "I was expecting Derek. Not you."

Jasmine gives me the look she seems to reserve just for me. The one that reflects the real her before she slips on the pretty mask she wears around Derek.

"Derek said you had something important you needed to speak to him about, and since he and I are going out together later, he said to meet him here in an hour. But I thought it was a good idea to come early, you know, in case you freaked out or went psycho or something and he needed moral support. Or a witness."

My inner crazy pricks up her ears, but I hold her in check. My conversation with Derek is long overdue, and I'm not going to let Jasmine interfere with that.

I turn my back, and Jasmine follows me inside. "I didn't invite you in."

"Derek said to come on in and make myself comfortable. I just finished talking to him—he won't be long."

In the kitchen, she wriggles onto a barstool. I give her a withering stare that bounces right off her.

"Did Derek tell you I'm pregnant?" she asks.

Shock silences me for a moment while my mind races to catch up. *Jasmine is pregnant?*

"No, he hasn't told me that."

Time slows down, my movements taking an eternity. I set my bag on the counter between her and me. I pour myself some wine and set the bottle on the counter.

"Guess you can't have wine then," I say then add, not wanting to be a complete bitch, "Congratulations, by the way."

"It's good news, right?" Her smile lights up her face.

"Does your husband know?" I ask.

"Yes."

"Are you going back to him now?"

I briefly wonder if that in any way alters the decision I've come to. Decide it doesn't.

As much as Jasmine pisses me off, this isn't about her.

"It's not my husband's." Her eyes remain on me, cool, piercing, calculating. There's something more behind them, and it sends a chill down my spine.

"Do you know whose it is?"

She narrows her eyes at that comment.

Keys jiggle in the lock, and Derek walks in the door.

"Sorry I'm late," he says, acknowledging me with a nod.

"You're not the only one who's late. Jasmine was just telling me she's pregnant."

Derek fumbles his wallet and shoots her a look. My stomach knots.

"How far along are you?" I ask.

"She's three months," Derek replies. *Derek* replies for her.

My face freezes into what I'm sure is a grimace, or worse. Three months ago, Derek was in Sydney.

I grip the counter.

"Who's the father?" I ask through clenched teeth.

"Claire," Derek snaps. "That's rude. Surely that is Jasmine's business." Was that a warning glance Derek just gave her?

"Whose is it?" I demand, looking directly at Jasmine. My heart is pounding, and she smiles this "I have a saucy little secret" smile and stretches back in her chair, enjoying having the upper hand. But she doesn't. Not anymore.

Still, I want to wipe that smug look off her pretty little face.

"Is it yours?" I ask Derek directly.

"No!"

The look Jasmine gives him says otherwise.

Pain is a jagged piece of glass through my heart.

"Oh for God's sake. Stop. Lying. To. Me." My voice breaks, damn it. I thought he no longer had the power to hurt me.

I can deal with their affair. But a baby...?

I grip the counter, two of my nails bending back and breaking. The pain mixes with the ache squeezing my chest, making it hard to breathe. She's having the baby I can never have.

Knowing that I'd planned to tell Derek tonight I want a divorce doesn't lessen the pain.

Knowing I've been lied to for at least three months stings. But I refuse to feel like a fool. I wasn't wrong to trust my husband. Wasn't that what you were supposed to do?

I think of all the time I wasted agonizing over the details of their relationship, of Derek's and my relationship. The arguments, the accusations. His constant and vehement denials.

I was right to trust my intuition about her.

Inwardly, I cringe, thinking of how I bought new lingerie, of how I cried myself to sleep, finding myself lacking. Believing that somehow the problems in our marriage were my fault. If they were in the beginning, they stopped being my fault a long time ago.

Two people are responsible for a relationship.

And he left ours months ago and didn't bother to tell me.

"You screwed that dirty whore without using protection! You bastard. I should cut off your balls," I spit angrily, but I'm thinking much, much worse.

"*What* did you call me?" Jasmine sneers.

"Jazzy, leave us a minute, will you?" Derek says, shifting his feet uncomfortably.

"Hardty?"

"Go wait in the car," he growls in a tone I've never heard him take with her before.

Her mouth drops open. Then she gives me one of her signature smug looks. One that says she won.

But *I* am the one who won.

She may have Derek, but I found *me*.

Jasmine flounces out the front door, but I can't focus on anything but Derek. On what a bastard he truly is.

"Claire," Derek says, his wide eyes watching me warily. "Let me explain—"

"Spare me. I asked you here to tell you that I'm leaving. I want a divorce." He blinks slowly as though he's in shock. "Claire, please, you don't mean that," Derek says after a long pause.

"You're free. I'm not holding you back. I just wish you'd shown me some respect and told me when you started screwing her. Why'd you even bother to lie? Why not have the decency to be honest, especially when I asked you outright?"

"Because I was worried about your state of mind," he says, and I feel a small measure of vindication that at least he's stopped denying it. "I knew you'd be upset," he says, "and judging by your reaction right now, clearly I was right. You've been so unstable lately."

"Fuck you," I hiss. "I have every right to be upset. Don't even fucking think of trying to minimize the gravity of your infidelity."

"Stop swearing, Claire. It's not ladylike."

"Fuck being ladylike!" I shout. "You're a piece of work, you know that?" I lean forward. "And do you know something else? I don't even care that you cheated. Not now. Not anymore. What hurts the most is that you lied about it. That you thought so little of me you carried on together right in front of me, not even bothering to cover it up. Made me think I was crazy when I questioned you about her. Your *friend*," I scoff. "And your ruse was so good you convinced other people I was crazy too, even my friends!" What would Julia say when she found out the truth? She'd believed their lies, too. "You, of all people, know how hard these last few years have been, and to use my emotional breakdown against me is the lowest of lows."

He looks at the large bag packed at my side. Everything else I thought I'd need for the immediate future is crammed into my car. "You're not leaving, Claire."

"Then *you* leave."

"Never. The only way you'll get me out of here is in a pine box."

My breathing grows harsh as this plays out the way I'd suspected it would. Derek, with all his faults, will not leave what we have left of Katie. Despite his apparent inability to love me the way a man should love his wife, Derek's love for his daughter is indisputable.

His expression turns from concern to anger. "You won't leave," he says confidently. "You're nothing without me."

"Then I'll be nothing," I say easily. "But I'll have something more valuable than money and a house. I'll have my self-respect. Just so you know, I was planning to leave you tonight even before you admitted to screwing around. You think I haven't thought about cheating on you? The difference between you and me, Derek, is that I respect our vows. I have the decency to wait until I separate from you before I go ahead and sleep with someone else."

"You want to sleep with someone else?" Derek asks, and I can almost see the cogs turning in his mind. "Okay... yeah... I can be cool with that. As long as you're discreet and my work never finds out."

"*That* is what you're taking from what I just said?" It's using all my willpower to not use my shredded nails to make him bleed.

"Claire, I was your first lover and, to my knowledge, your only lover."

To his knowledge! "Fuck you, Derek. I just told you I never cheated on you."

"Okay, so I'm your only lover. Do you want to spend your whole life only sleeping with one man?"

"Well," I drawl. "That was kind of the take-home message I got from our marriage vows. But what you're really saying is that you don't want to spend the rest of your life only sleeping with me."

Just when I thought this man no longer had the power to hurt me, the blows keep coming.

"That's a little harsh, don't you think? Only sleep with the same person for another—" He pauses while he calculates how long he could potentially live. "Fifty years."

"So you expect to live to eighty one?" I ask. "Then I'd shut up now because if you keep talking the way you are, you won't make it past the next five minutes."

"Claire." Derek sighs. "Men need sex in a different way than women do. It doesn't mean they stop loving their wives."

"Oh my God." Bile rises into my throat. "How many were there before her?"

"It doesn't matter," Derek says, waving his hand dismissively. "Stay on topic. I still love you, Claire. I married you, not anyone else. We've been through so much together. Sex is just sex to a man. If there's a beautiful willing woman, a man will take it. *All* men. You're fooling yourself if you think otherwise. Whether it's in one of the rooms out in back of a strip joint his wife knows he's going to or the office girl on his lunch break his wife doesn't know about. Any woman who thinks her man isn't screwing around on her is fooling herself."

"All men cheat?" I blink incredulously. "Really? Are you sure you don't just think that because your dad screwed around on your mother?"

"This has nothing to do with my parents. I'm a man, and men talk. I'm telling you this is across the board. All. Men."

"So Rob will screw around on Bec?" I ask, heat burning my cheeks.

"We're talking about us," Derek says, clearly not wanting to break whatever bro code he lives by. "Despite what you think, I love you, Claire. I'm certainly not leaving, and I won't let you leave. Aside from this hiccup with Jasmine, our marriage has been working fine. Better than most."

"It's not enough for me."

"Claire," Derek says with forced patience, "you're overreacting about all of this. Please sit down so we can talk this through properly."

"No."

"Okay, then, we'll stand. The way I see it, for us to make our marriage continue to work, I'm willing to turn a blind eye to you sleeping with someone else if that's what you want. After all, fair is fair. And you show me the same courtesy."

"Courtesy?" My mouth is hanging open, but I don't care. He's not trying to be rude or insulting. He's actually trying to negotiate infidelity into the terms of our marriage! "You think it's showing me courtesy to bring your whore into our home and try to pass her off as a friend?"

"That—" Derek releases a slow breath "—was different. Jazzy was—is —a friend. I didn't sleep with her under our roof. I wouldn't do that to you."

"You wouldn't—?" I blink, stunned. "So your moral code doesn't extend to sleeping around, only to not doing it under the same roof you share with your wife. Should I be flattered?"

"Yes." He seems pleased that I understand. "Now, if you're willing to be reasonable, we can negotiate—"

"Oh my God!" I shout. "If you tell me to be reasonable one more time, I don't know what I'm capable of doing."

"I'm trying to work this out with you," Derek says, frowning. "To come to a mutually satisfactory arrangement."

"A *what*? This is a marriage, Derek. Not a fucking business deal."

"Claire, this is a win-win for both of us. I'm trying to keep us together here. Find some common ground so we can both move forward. We're married, and I'd like to stay that way. As I said, I love you. We've been through a lot together. And we lost a lot. Together."

He clears his throat. Finally, some emotion.

"You need me as much as I need you. A divorce would not bode well for either of us," Derek continues. "In fact, it would be an outright disaster, one you would be wise to avoid." I am acutely aware of the shift in his tone. The plea turning to a threat.

I struggle to make sense of his reaction. Whichever way I thought this conversation would go, this is not it. If Jasmine is pregnant with his baby, why isn't he jumping at the chance to start a life with her? Why does he want to continue to tie himself to me?

"Help me understand. What's your plan, Derek?" I ask, curious to see how he thinks this will play out if he has his way. "You think I'll look the other way and play good little wifey while you screw your whore...*not* in our house? Why not just leave and be with her?"

"You get to choose who you want to sleep with, too," he says patiently. "It's not one-sided. I'm being fair. And Jasmine is not a whore, so please stop talking about her like that. A filthy mouth is not attractive."

"Oh, I can talk a lot dirtier than that," I say. "But you'll never get to hear it. Because I'll be whispering those words into my next lover's ear."

"So you're happy to negotiate, then?"

"No, Derek!" I feel stronger and more confident than I have in years. "There's no doubt about it. If you won't leave, then I will. Our marriage is over. You can stick your terms up your ass. There's no coming back from this for me. My only regret is that you weren't man enough to make your views on marriage clear at the time you said, 'I do.'"

"All women have an idealized view of marriage in the beginning," Derek says, talking faster, a spark of fear in his eyes. "Men let them believe the fairy tale in the beginning until it gets to that time in their marriage that they need to reassess, revise, and move forward with more realistic expectations."

Oh God! Is he for real?

"All men think this way?"

"All men, Claire." His tone is absolute. "All men."

I refuse to believe that. I rack my brain, trying to think of examples where that isn't the case. My mum never married, just took lovers, so hers isn't a good example. I shake my head to clear it. Derek's theory can't be true. Why even bother with marriage vows if this is the norm?

"So, you always intended to have this conversation with me?" I ask. "Our whole marriage has been a lie, then? Every conversation, every time we made love."

I am the world's biggest fool. "The thing that hurts the most is that you let me believe this was all my fault. I thought it was my breakdown that had broken us. I stupidly believed if I'd tried harder, not made a scene over Jasmine until she left of her own accord, we could get back to how we used to be when we had Katie. But even that was a lie, wasn't it?"

"I loved Katie just as much as you," Derek says, and when he squeezes his eyes shut briefly, I see the cracks in his veneer. "Katie was the center of my—our—universe." Derek's voice breaks on Katie's name, and his eyes well with tears. The only genuine thing I believe is my husband's love for our daughter.

"Claire," he says softly, his voice low. Pleading. He reaches out to touch my arm, but when I sharply withdraw it, he returns his hand to his side. "I want what we had with Katie again, too. I want that so much it hurts."

And then I get it.

A freight train crashes through my chest.

His face crumples in a rare display of emotion. "I want another baby. And you…"

"I can't give you one," I finish for him. Tears blur my vision, and my hand covers my stomach. My empty, desolate womb.

"How can you be this cruel?" I wipe hot, stinging tears away with the back of my hand. Damn him. We can talk about the state of our marriage, even about infidelity, with relative calm, but the only thing that truly gets to either one of us is talking about Katie.

"Claire, I didn't intend for that to happen the way you think. Jazzy and I…it was an accident."

"I bet." I'd bet any amount that Jasmine knew exactly what she was doing when she got pregnant.

"When Jazzy said she was pregnant, at first I was worried. It was a complication I hadn't considered. And then I thought…what if this is God giving me—us—a second chance? You can't get pregnant, and now I have a second chance at being a father."

A small, strangled sound rises up and out of my chest.

Again, Derek tries to reach for me, but I push him back.

"I'm not going to give you a divorce," Derek says. "So that is off the table. Everything else is negotiable. We are married, Claire. Remember? Until death do us part?"

"Oh, that vow you want to stick with."

Ignoring my sarcasm, he continues, "We can share this. If you open your mind, if you can just get over your irrational jealousy toward Jazzy, you'll see this baby as a gift. One I want to share with you."

I can't swallow, and emotion is choking me so hard I can't breathe. I'm going to be sick. I cover my mouth with my hand and back away.

"Don't just dismiss this," Derek says. "You always do that. You shut me down and make up your mind without giving my opinion any thought."

"You want to know what I'm thinking?" I demand. "You disgust me." There are a million words in my head, but those three sum up what I'm feeling pretty well, so I run with them.

"I want a divorce. You're free to marry Jasmine or whoever else you want," I say. I know that open marriages work for some people. Each to their own, I'm not judging. It won't work for me.

"There is no way I can live looking the other way while you screw that whore," I say. "And if you think I'll ever be friends with *Jasmine*—" I spit her name. "—then you are the one who's lost his mind."

I pull my car keys out of my handbag and pick up my large bag. I'm glad I had the foresight to be prepared. I'd hate to have to start packing now that it's clear Derek has no intention of leaving. I can't stay in the same room with him for one minute longer.

Derek's eyes widen. "You can't do this." He grabs my arm, his fingers digging into my skin.

"Get your hands off me." This man, this stranger in the body of my husband, will never touch me again. "What is your problem with me leaving? You want to screw around? Marry *her*. Fuck around on *her*. I'm giving you your freedom."

I go to move around him, but he blocks my path. He grabs me, and as he lunges, he knocks a glass off the counter. It lands on the white tiles and shatters.

I tug my hand out of his grip and try to pass. I slip on the broken glass and land on the floor. He's standing above me, looking down. He stares at me as though he's in shock. As though he can't believe we've come to this.

As though he can't believe I'm really leaving.

I struggle to stand, and my hand lands on the jagged shards of glass.

I don't feel the sting.

Hot tears still blur my vision, but they don't fall. They clear quickly, revealing drops of blood on the white tiled floor.

White.

As long as I live, nothing I own will ever be white again.

Derek moves then, helping me up. Holding my arm, he steers me to the sink and runs water gently over my palm. Tenderly, he picks out three pieces of glass and wraps my hand with a clean white tea towel from the drawer. I don't know why I let him tend to me. Ten years of being with this man, believing he cares. Truly cares, in the way I needed him to. Why is nothing ever black and white? It would be so much easier if he was a complete asshole with no redeeming features. Tenderly, he brings my wrapped palm to his lips, kisses it gently.

"I love you, Claire."

Somewhere deep inside, I know this is the last tender moment we will share. It saddens me that after ten years it has come to this. Perhaps what happened with Katie killed something vital inside him. I went to therapy. I got counseling, but Derek chose to forge on, numbing the pain with a bottle. He is a confused and broken man. My heart shatters wide open. For him.

For us.

For the unrecognizable people this tragedy has turned us both into.

Derek tries to pull me into his arms, but I avert my gaze and step around him and move toward the door. Again, Derek blocks my path. His eyes are wide with panic or fear. "Claire! Don't do this. Don't leave me."

I hold his gaze, let him see my resolve.

We've both suffered these last three years, and it's time to let it go. It's time to move on. To live again instead of merely existing.

His eyes harden, his expression turning this familiar man into a stranger. "You'll never get the house," he says, anger sparking like fire in his gaze. "You'll have to give up Katie's room."

"I've made my peace with that." But still, his words are bullets to my heart.

"You have? I doubt that. I will *never* let this house go, so I can't imagine how you could."

My heart is heavy. My emotions over Katie tangling with what I feel for Derek. Does he do that deliberately?

"Please, Derek. Don't make this harder than it needs to be."

"You want me to make this easy for you?"

"Don't tell me spousal abuse was in the fine print of our wedding vows, too."

Derek looks shocked. "I would never hurt you."

And yet he has. The emotional pain is perhaps more acute and lasting than any heat-of-the-moment physical pain.

My bag brushes against Derek as I push past him, and my handbag slaps against my back as I toss it over my shoulder.

"Claire, wait!"

I pause on the doorstep, standing in the same position Jasmine stood almost four weeks ago.

I could have saved myself a whole lot of heartache if I had realized then what I know now. This is not a competition between me and her. It never was.

This is about me.

I don't want to win a battle for affection from a partner.

I want a partner who'd never even consider it a contest in the first place.

I want a partner who doesn't see anyone else the way he sees me.

Who'll have my back if I come to him with my fears and concerns. Who'll comfort me, reassure me. And I'll do the same for him in return. That is what a relationship should be. And I'll no longer settle for anything less.

The door closes softly against the jam, and I walk past where Jasmine is waiting in Derek's car to my own.

Leaving a marriage, no matter how in tatters, doesn't make you happy, but it makes you eligible to be happy. I read that somewhere. It gives me hope in this moment.

It's all I have for now.

I begin to reverse out of the driveway.

"You bitch!" Startling me, Derek jumps on the car and pounds on the windscreen. His sudden burst of anger frightens me. I slam on the brakes, and he slides off. "You'll regret this!" His eyes are wild again. Desperate.

There's a… strange madness in his eyes as he pounds on the car with his fists. He's acting way out of character. Derek is not a wild and passionate man, and his frantic expression suggests that our separation has deeper implications than I'm aware of.

But what? Will us separating ruin his chance at promotion or of him ever making partner? Frankly, I just can't see myself as being that imperative to his life or career. Certainly nothing that can't be overcome in time. This is not the sixties. Successful businessmen and women divorce all the time.

But still… there's something very wrong about the way he's acting.

I continue to back out, and when I reach the street, I pull the car to a stop while I shift the gearstick into drive. I'll stay in a hotel tonight and maybe tomorrow night as well, give myself a little space to think. Hopefully by then, Derek will have calmed down enough to want to meet again and talk reasonably. I've been mentally and emotionally preparing for the marriage to be over for a while now, but to Derek, this seems to have come as a shock. Perhaps that explains his reaction.

That has to be it. Give him a couple of days to get used to the idea, and he'll agree it's for the best. Surely, he couldn't have really believed I'd agree to his terms and stay in his mutually beneficial business arrangement. That must have been an impulsive, last-ditch attempt to keep the marriage together.

I press my foot on the accelerator, and the car begins to move. I've just begun to pick up speed when I see a flash of movement and hear a loud thud, and Derek's body lands on the hood. I stomp on the brake.

Is he all right?

Did he just throw himself onto my car? I open the door to get out, to check to see if he's okay. His eyes light up as he slides off, and I realize that he's not hurt badly, just mad as hell. He limps toward me, and I quickly shut and lock the door. At the driver's side window, he raises his fist. His face is deep red, and for the first time in our marriage, I truly believe he might be capable of causing me physical harm.

My heart is racing, and my legs are shaking. I need a minute to be sure I'm steady enough to drive.

"You won't get away with this!" he shouts.

What the hell?

Of all his possible reactions, this was not at all what I'd expected. I'd expected him to be cold, maybe indifferent, to tell me I know where the door is. Or even relieved now that he doesn't have to sneak around with Jasmine.

"You owe me, Claire!" Spittle lands on the window. "You *owe* me!"

But what do I possibly have to give that he needs?

He punches the window and blood springs up on his knuckles.

How quickly love can turn to hate.

Derek's hair is a mess, his face is red, and he's wearing a stranger's smile.

The world comes sharply into focus as though I've adjusted the lens on a camera. I see the dirt on the road, the litter that lines the street. Whatever Derek's problem is with me leaving, it's not about being in love. I know that for sure.

I've been a fraud, living a false reality.

All this time, I really *was* in love with the idea of being in love.

Our whole marriage had been an elaborate illusion, centered around our mutual love for Katie.

There's nothing left to say but goodbye.

I drive away from my home and my sham of a marriage. I look in my rearview mirror at his reddened face, his outrage.

I know this is not over.

My gut twists painfully.

As I drive away, I tell myself tomorrow will be the first day of the rest of my life.

But something about Derek and his reaction is off. A chill rolls down my spine.

The first day of the rest of my life may not turn out quite the way I want it to.

PART II

CHAPTER 15

I park my Audi behind Designs by Hardt. It's still early, and mine is the only vehicle in the car park. Kira doesn't start until nine, so I have a full ninety minutes to unload the equipment I took out of the house last night and transfer and reorganize all the work I'd been doing at home to the shop.

I walk down the laneway between my shop and the yoga place next door. I cross the road and stare out across the ocean, breathing in the crisp ocean air. The morning is still, not a breath of wind. I feel free and in control of my life. As though I've finally left the passenger seat and slipped behind the wheel. I've never been on my own. Meeting Derek at eighteen, I've never known my own power or had a chance to prove to myself what I'm capable of.

But even though I've made the right decision, a knot of tension persists in the pit of my stomach. Derek's reaction when I said I was leaving seemed extreme. It was almost as though us separating had never crossed his mind.

Did he really believe he had such absolute control over me? That I really was nothing without him? Could he be that arrogant? He'd almost panicked when I said I was leaving. I'd replayed the scene over and over in my mind last night, trying to reconcile his overreaction with the one I'd expected.

From the husband I thought I knew.

I'd believed that our separation would be amicable, the details handled in the same cool, slightly detached way Derek handled everything else.

Something is really wrong.

But what?

Determined not to spend the first day of my new life dwelling on Derek, I cross the road to the front of my shop. I slide the key into the lock...

It doesn't turn.

Adjusting the heavy bag on my back, I fumble with the keys, checking I have the right one. I try it again. Still doesn't fit.

Confused, I force it, jiggle it in the lock. It's only when I step back that I see the notice taped to the front door.

Notice of intention to vacate.

There's a handwritten note taped beneath it.

Think about what you're doing.

I step back, my heart racing in my chest as I realize what he's done.

He can't lock me out of my own shop! Can he? This is *my* shop!

The name of the real estate company is on the notice, and a quick Google search turns up a mobile number. Ten minutes later, I find out he can. Derek is listed as the lessor of the lease agreement, and as such, he's removed the right for Designs by Hardt to trade on the premises. Despite the fact that Designs by Hardt is my business, I have no rights whatsoever as my name is not on the lease. I can't even enter the property to get my gowns without Derek's permission. He can just change the locks, and there is nothing I can do about it. The real estate agent suggested I make an application through the courts. But how long will that take?

I can't wait weeks or even months for that. I have dresses in the shop that I need today. Everything I need to run the business is behind those doors. Clients are booked to come in for fittings. There are expensive dresses that aren't even mine inside. Clients have given me their own designer gowns for alterations.

My blood runs hot and cold. With shaking fingers, I dial Derek's number.

"Claire." His voice is thick and rough as though he's been up all night drinking.

"What the hell do you think you're doing?" I demand.

"Trying to get you to see reason."

"This is my shop. I'm going to get a locksmith to let me in."

"I wouldn't do that if I were you."

"Why not?" The words are choked as anger rises in my chest and lodges in my throat.

"If you could even find one who would let you in," Derek says coldly. "Which I doubt as you are not on the lease, and the landlord is fully apprised of the matter. If you do get inside, I'll have you arrested for breaking and entering. Come back home, and we'll talk."

"You're insane. There is nothing left for us to talk about except how we can both move on from here."

"I'm not going to let you leave."

"How are you going to stop me?"

My heart skips a beat. This is how. A cold, calculated demonstration of power. So typical of the way he ruled our marriage for the last eight years. I was just too young, too deeply involved, then later, too enveloped by grief to see it.

"Screw you, Derek!" I shout, but he's already disconnected the call.

I fire back a text:

There will be no further negotiation, esp while you're being so heavy-handed. The marriage is over. Has been for a long time. My decision is final. Do the right thing. Give me access to my shop. Then stay away. Let me move on with my life. Move on with yours.

I wait a full fifteen minutes, but he doesn't reply.

I'm going to need a lawyer. A damn good one. I can no longer assume he'll be amicable when it comes to negotiating.

Who would have thought it would come to this?

Just when I think he's not going to reply, I get his message:

.   .   .

Come back to me, Claire.

I question everything I thought I knew. About life. About my marriage. There's a stranger now masquerading as my husband.

It's as though I never knew him at all.

After leaving a message for a law firm which, according to its website, claims to be the best in Perth, I begin to pace along the sidewalk, scaring a flock of seagulls and sending them screeching into the sky. It's 8:30 a.m., still thirty minutes before official business hours. I hope they get back to me soon. My first appointment is scheduled for ten.

Think, Claire, think.

Derek had said our marriage had been beneficial to both parties. How was I helping him? It has to be more than being an aid to his promotion at work. I know he desperately wants to be partner one day, but it's more than that. His reaction was just too...intense.

Well, screw him. He can't intimidate me to go back to him. Who the hell does that? But now that I'm thinking clearly enough to see the truth, I realize he's been doing that for years. I'd felt powerless when Katie died, devastated that there was nothing I could do to save my daughter. And Derek, day by day, pill by pill, kept me in that vulnerable state of mind. I'd thought he'd been helping me cope. Numbing the pain.

Now, I wonder if there wasn't a more nefarious reason for him to do so. What didn't he want me to notice?

Her?

But he hadn't really been ruffled about my discovering the affair or even the baby. He's hiding something else.

Somehow, I need to outsmart him. I need to do what he wouldn't expect.

And somehow, I need to keep my business running. Some of the clients have paid in full; if I can't get their dresses, I'll need to give them full refunds. But how will I tell Mrs. Taylor that her dress won't be ready for her daughter's wedding on Saturday? One of the most important days of her life.

Fuck you, Derek! Fuck you to hell and back for putting me in this position.

Red tinges the edges of my vision, anger a throbbing pulse behind my eyes. At the same time, the fine grains of cool sand feel like quicksand beneath my feet.

Was this something I could have foreseen? I should have protected myself from this. But never in a million years would I think my husband would do something like this to me.

Fury wells inside me, and I cross the road to the shop. Maybe I can get in through the back door? I storm to the rear entrance, finding new padlocks installed. I pound my fist against the timber frame, the pain jarring my arm. Beating up the door turns out to be nowhere near as satisfying as I thought it would be. I glance up at the newly installed security camera above my head and give it the middle finger.

Nursing my aching wrist, I walk to my car and lean against it. I refuse to let Derek still make me feel powerless. I have to get inside. Those things belong to me!

I stomp back to the camera. "This is my shop!" I shout. "You have no right to do this, you goddamn asshole! You vindictive piece of shit!"

A vehicle pulls into the car park behind me. When I look over my shoulder, Zach is staring at me from his car. I freeze, my hands in the air, then bring them down to my sides.

He gets out of his 4WD and walks a determined path directly to me.

I straighten my skirt and run a hand over my hair to remove the outward appearance of crazy woman. Nothing I can do about the crazy woman on the inside.

"Are you all right?" he asks, standing in front of me. My eyes travel over his faded denim jeans, all the way up his toned torso in a black V-neck T-shirt, to his concerned expression. Despite my emotional chaos, the tingling thrill I get from seeing him is, as always, there. It smooths away some of the rougher edges of my temper.

"Yes," I reply automatically. His eyes are stormy, and he doesn't appear to be convinced.

"Do you always shout like that when you're okay?"

"I've been known to," I say, trying to make it into a joke. He doesn't smile.

I exhale heavily. "I wasn't okay. Just now. What you saw. But I will be. Okay, I mean. I'm just mad as hell. But I'll work it out." I let out a wry laugh. "Did you understand any of that?"

"Strangely, yes." Zach's gaze follows mine to the shop, and he sees the official notice sticking to the door. There are notices on the front and back doors. *Nice.* Guess Derek really wanted to make sure I didn't miss them. Zach moves to the door, reads it.

I lean back against my car, watching him.

"Didn't pay your rent?" Zach asks, making his way back to me. There is no judgment in his tone, just a question, and my chest tightens. A sea breeze picks up his scent and bathes me in it. He smells so good—raw, masculine, and earthy.

"This is not about rent." I shake my head, dragging my mind back to my situation. "This is about me being naïve and not taking proper action to make sure my business was protected." Was it so wrong to trust your husband? "I was an idiot."

Zach growls. "Don't talk about yourself like that." He's all business now. "Tell me what happened."

"My husband is what happened. My soon to be ex-husband."

"What did he do?" Zach is still, his hands clenched at his sides as though he'd go into battle for me. And looking at him right now, all aggrieved for me, I'm certain he would.

Here is this wonderful man I've known for such a short time, ready to fight for me when the man I pledged to spend my whole life with deliberately put me in this position of weakness.

"I left him, and as he is listed as the lessor on the lease agreement of my shop, he has decided I can no longer work here."

"Why would he do that?"

"Leverage," I reply.

"He doesn't want you to leave." Zach nods. As though he, too, would be upset if I were leaving him. However, I could never see Zach doing something like this. But then, what do I know? I never thought Derek would either.

"He wants me to stay, but not for the reasons you think." I wish I could say it's because he loves me so much it's made him crazy. It hurts that the reason he wants me back has nothing to do with love. It's hard not to feel small, to have your marriage reduced to dollars and cents and mutual benefits that have nothing to do with love.

I shake away the negative thoughts. My self-esteem has nothing to do with Derek any longer. Those days are gone.

I stand, straightening, steeling my nerve.

"Are you going to change your mind?" Zach asks, eyeing me carefully. "Is this usual for you? Fighting so passionately, I mean. Will you go back to him?"

"When hell freezes over," I say then look him directly in his eyes. "Never. Ever. Absolutely not, no way."

Zach's lips curve slightly. "That sounds like a no. But you're pretty emotional right now. Maybe things will settle down after you both cool off a bit?"

"We haven't just had an argument, and this isn't the desperate act of a passionate lover. We don't fight like this. In fact, we don't really fight at all. We just shut down and freeze each other out. Ice-age style. Trust me when I say there's no coming back from this." I don't tell him about Derek's infidelity, about his new baby. I feel like the world's biggest idiot already.

Oh, Claire, but you did know. They just did a great job of convincing you that you're crazy.

Zach nods, but his frown tells me he's still uncertain. As though he's wondering whether he should be here, in the middle of a husband and wife tiff.

"There really is no coming back from this," I say with confidence. "It isn't just about today. The marriage has been over for a long time. It's just taken me longer than it should have to realize it."

I walk to the shop's back window and peer in. Zach follows.

"Do you see that apricot dress on the mannequin there?" I say, and Zach nods. "That belongs to Mrs. Taylor. She'll be here at ten for the final fitting. It's her dress for her daughter's wedding on Saturday."

Fuck my husband. *Ex-husband.* He is not just inconveniencing and hurting me. I know in the scheme of things, these are only dresses, not life-saving medical equipment, but people invest a lot of money and emotion in special dresses for special occasions. Mrs. Taylor will be broken-hearted.

"I don't seem to have a legal foot to stand on."

"You're shaking," Zach said. "You should probably sit down or something."

"I don't have *time* to sit down," I snap. "Sorry," I add quickly. "I don't mean to be rude. I'm just frustrated. If you'll excuse me, I need to make a few calls." I press Bec's name and wait three long rings until she answers.

"Hi, Claire!" I can hear the smile in her voice.

I take a breath, almost decide not to burden the bride-to-be with my drama. But she's my best friend, and I really need her right now. I'm also conscious that even though I've walked a short distance away for privacy, Zach hasn't left. He's still waiting by the shop.

My story comes out in a rush. I tell her the shorthand version of what happened when I left Derek last night and how I spent the night in a hotel. I tell her that I found out that Jasmine and Derek have been having an affair for at least three months, and she's pregnant with his child.

"I'm so sorry you're going through this," Bec says, releasing a long breath. "I can't believe Derek is treating you this way. What an asshole. I mean, I knew you had suspicions about Jasmine all along…but an affair? A baby? Locking you out of your shop? It doesn't sound like the Derek I know. It's as if you're talking about someone else. A total stranger."

I squeeze my eyes shut. "It's hard for me to believe myself."

"Why were you the one to leave?" Bec asks. "Shouldn't you have kicked him out? Why should you have had to spend the night in a hotel if he's the one who had an affair?"

"He refused to leave. He was acting so irrationally, who knows how far things would have escalated if I had stayed?" Derek told me, in no uncertain terms, he wasn't leaving. Hell, he told me, in no uncertain terms, I wasn't leaving.

"None of this sounds like Derek," Bec says slowly. "It sounds very strange…"

"You don't believe me?"

"Of course, I believe you," Bec says. "It's just that—"

The vein behind my eye throbs while I wait on the line. "It's just that, what?"

"Claire, can I call you back?" she says finally. "I'm going to talk to Rob, ask him to call Derek. I'll see what I can find out and call you back."

We hang up, and I make my way back to Zach, hoping Bec will call me back soon with good news. Maybe Rob's phone call will embarrass Derek into doing the right thing and letting me into my shop.

"Is there something I can do to help?" Zach asks, his voice soft, but there's steel underneath.

"Thanks, but I'm sure Derek will come to his senses soon. At least I hope so."

A white Volvo sedan, Derek's car, slowly cruises past. His window is down, and he's glaring at me through the gap. He's talking on the phone. Is Rob on the other end, pleading for him to be reasonable?

"That's him." Zach says, and I glance at him sharply. It didn't sound like a question. "Are you okay?" he asks.

"I think so. Yes," I say more strongly. I can't describe the weird feeling I have, a sense of eerie uncertainty I can't shake with any amount of self-talk. A dark cloud crosses the sun, turning the air cool. Heavy drops of rain begin to fall, landing on my face and the ground around me.

Usually, I love the fresh smell of rain, listening to the sound as it lands on dry earth. But not today. At this moment, there's no peace to be found in it.

My feet are on unstable ground, and everything I'd once considered familiar is now strange. Even the Indian Ocean seems different in this moment. As though the waves crashing against the shore are issuing a warning.

Well, I'll be damned if I'm going to let Derek get away with treating me like this.

Zach's fingers trace down my arm, and my breath hitches. "You're cold. I'd give you my jacket, but—" He lets his voice trail off.

"But I still have it." I glance up at Zach, at his cool dark looks and brooding eyes.

"Do you intend on ever giving it back?"

"Will you make me?"

"No."

I wonder if I'll ever tell him that it was his jacket that gave me comfort when nothing else could. But I'm not cold right now. There might be a chill in the wind, but there's a fiery rage burning through my veins.

"Do you have a good lawyer?" Zach asks.

"I will have soon." I glance at my watch. A quarter to nine. Not long to wait now.

Zach nods. "Can I take you somewhere then?" he suggests. "Get you a hot coffee? Have some breakfast while you wait for them to return your call?"

"Thanks, but no. I'll go back to my hotel," I say, feeling stronger. I just need a minute to think things through. I'll feel better after I get some good legal advice. And who knows...maybe Rob can talk some sense into Derek.

"Let me know if there's anything I can do to help. But why don't you at least let me get you a coffee? I can't leave you like this."

I glance at Zach's profile out of the corner of my eye, his strong jawline softened by strands of hair blowing around his face in the ocean breeze.

Right or wrong, there's nowhere I'd rather be than with Zach Argos. Absorbing his quiet strength and confidence, his rebellious way of looking at the world.

In this moment, I simply don't want to be alone. If it's wrong to want to be with Zach right now...well...sue me.

"A coffee would be great," I say, and although his lips don't move, his eyes smile when he looks at me.

"This might be rough for a while, but it's all going to turn out okay in the end."

I slip my phone into my bag and glare at the window of the shop I'd always believed was mine. "I'd just like it better if I could skip straight to the okay part though."

Zach's lips curve this time. "But just think of how much stronger you'll be at the end of this. Nothing is better for the soul than a challenge. And when you get out on the other side, you'll remember this and never give your power away to anyone again."

Something tells me this wouldn't have happened if I'd trusted Zach instead of Derek, but the value of hindsight isn't going to help me now.

"I was horribly naïve, wasn't I?" The heat of embarrassment rises within me. Especially because Zach seems to have his life so together.

"You trusted your husband to look after you. This is on him, not you."

That is true. I honestly did believe Derek had my best interests at heart. *He was my husband.*

"My illusion of marriage may be temporarily shattered," I say, "but I refuse to believe there aren't people in this world who I can trust."

Zach looks at me for the longest moment, and I wonder what thoughts are behind his intense gaze. "I used to believe that, too," he says. "Let's go."

On the way to his car, I text Kira and let her know I don't need her to come in this morning, that I'll call her later. I then call Mrs. Taylor and tell her I need to reschedule her final fitting for tomorrow. Not very professional, cancelling at such late notice, but I'm left with little choice. With any luck, this situation with Derek will get sorted out today so I can be back to normal business tomorrow.

Bec's name flashes on my screen, and I swipe to answer her call.

"Claire, Rob has just spoken to Derek." Her voice is strained, her tone awkward. "How are you, Claire? Are you doing okay?"

"No!" What kind of a question is that? I lower my tone; this isn't Bec's fault. "I'm pissed off, but I'm otherwise okay."

Bec releases a breath into the phone. "Do you want me to come and get you?"

"Get me?" I ask as we stop at Zach's car. "Why would you need to get me? Where would we go?"

"Derek says you flipped out and attacked him last night."

I blink as surprise washes through me. "I didn't attack him." I look at my hand, remembering how I slipped and fell on broken glass on the floor. Is he trying to suggest we fought? After he tenderly picked out the shards of glass and wrapped the towel around my hand?

"I don't understand what you're implying."

"Derek told Rob that you've stopped taking your medication. That you lost control when you found out Jasmine was pregnant, that you accused him of cheating, that you were convinced it was his—"

"It *is* his," I interrupt. "He admitted it." My heart is hammering in my chest. "Oh God. You don't believe me, do you?"

Bec clears her throat. "I want to," she says. "I really do. I didn't want to believe the things Julia was telling me. But... Derek told Rob he was so worried about you last night, said that you were in no condition to drive." She lowers her voice. "He told Rob you tried to run him over when he raced after you."

What the hell? "I did not!"

"Derek is really worried about you," Bec says gently. "We all are. Derek says that the combination of not taking your medication and Mother's Day coming up, it's all gotten to be too much for you. Maybe if you just go back home, talk to Derek. He was really upset when Rob spoke to him. He's worried that you'll hurt yourself. You won't hurt yourself, will you?" Bec's concern is clear in her voice.

My head is pounding, and I squeeze my eyes shut to block out the blinding sun. I feel Zach's hand on my arm, and when I open my eyes, I realize I've been swaying.

"I'm not going to hurt myself," I say through clenched teeth. "I need him to take the locks off my shop and allow me access so that I can continue to work."

"He did it to protect you," Bec says. "And to protect your business. He doesn't think you're in a fit state of mind to be seeing clients. He says you'll thank him for it when you're thinking clearly again."

He thinks I'll fucking thank him? "You've got to be kidding."

"Claire, I have to say I agree. If you say or do wrong things, or act in ways that are inappropriate and not like you, it will affect your business and also reflect poorly on the firm."

Ah, so that's how Derek has managed to sway Rob to his side. The son of the managing partner, Rob wouldn't want anything affecting the company's reputation.

"He's protecting you," Bec says. "Just until you're back to feeling like yourself again."

"He's not protecting me," I bite out. "He's protecting himself. And yes, I'm angry. I just want access to what is rightfully mine."

"But if you're not careful, you could lose everything. He's doing this for you, Claire. Because he loves you. We all do. Listen, why not give him a call or go back home to see him?"

"I've tried talking to him! He's being unreasonable." Frustration makes my voice louder than I intended it to be.

Bec is silent for a moment. "What about counseling? Or mediation or something. Perhaps having a trained professional in the room while you talk things through would—"

"I'm hanging up now." I disconnect the phone before I say something I'll regret. I know Bec only wants to help, but Derek has twisted the facts, and it's all too easy for people to believe the level-headed accountant. Who would believe the crazy wife who never fully recovered from her emotional breakdown after the death of her daughter? Bitter acid churns in the pit of my stomach.

My phone rings again. What now?

I recognize the number of the local police station. It's Detective Sergeant Martin Price's private line. I made his wife a dress a few months ago. Is he ringing to book another appointment? Where would I see new clients?

"Hi, Martin." I picture his face, lined with memories from the hardships he's witnessed throughout his career.

He clears his throat. "Uh, Claire," he says. "I thought I'd give you a heads-up. When I saw the report come through, I must admit to being surprised. But I'm sure if you come into the station, we can sort this out."

My heartbeat has slowed. "What report?"

"There's been a complaint made against you this morning. For assault."

"You've got to be kidding."

Zach's hand on my arm tightens. His touch is firm, heating my skin. I focus on his hand, anchoring me in place while my head spins.

"Derek claims you ran him over."

I hear a knock through the line. "Come in. Sit down." Martin's voice is muffled as though he'd taken the phone away from his mouth for a moment. "Claire, I have to go. It will be better for everyone if you can just come into the station as soon as you can. The sooner we sort this out, the better."

He disconnects the call. My hand is shaking as I drop the phone into my bag. My heart is pounding loudly in my chest.

I didn't deliberately run Derek over! He threw himself at my car! I glance at my hand. Is he going to claim that we fought and I got physical with him? Would anyone believe me that we didn't?

"Claire?"

"I have to go to the police station." My mouth is dry. "Derek is charging me with assault."

Zach's eyes narrow. He scans the road, the footpaths, as though Derek is right there watching. And perhaps he is.

"Claire?" Zach asks. "Did you assault him?" Again, there's no judgment in his tone, just a simple question. Like he wouldn't think less of me if I had.

"No… Well, maybe it might look that way. I'm sorry, I'll have to take a rain check on the coffee."

Vehicles are pulling into the car park, and I begin to walk back to my car.

"Claire, wait!"

"I'm sorry you've had to listen to all my mess," I say, pausing. I glance at Zach. "Thanks for being here for me. I appreciate it."

He looks at me intensely. "Do you want me to leave?" He's stepped closer, and his clean fresh scent washes over me.

I don't want him to, but… "This is something I need to handle myself."

"Look, Claire. I'm not going to railroad you. It seems you're already getting an unfair dose of that. But unless you're going to insist right now that I leave, I'm driving you to the station."

"I can drive."

Zach is tense like he's fighting against a natural impulse to step in, take over. Take care of things. For me. And for a brief moment, I want to let him.

"For all your fire and determination to handle this your way, you're pale and shaking. You need a minute to get yourself together before you go in and give a statement to the police. You don't want to say the wrong thing. Trust me," he adds. "Let me drive you. It will give you the time to clear your head."

I release a breath. He's right. Going in there looking like a crazy woman won't help my case. "Thank you, Zach."

"We'll sort this assault charge out first," he says. "Then we'll have that coffee while you make some calls and work out how to get back in business."

We walk back to his car, and he opens the door for me to get in.

As we pull out onto West Coast Drive, Derek's Volvo pulls out into traffic two cars behind us. What is he doing? A shiver rolls down my spine and my hands twist restlessly in my lap. I can't shake the uncomfortable feeling there's still more to come. But what else can he do to me? I no longer have my marriage and can never have children. He's taken away my shop, the only thing I've found to live for these last three years. He's turning my friends against me, convincing them I'm unstable and not to be trusted. He's made a police report for assault, making sure his version of events is the official one on file.

What else is left that he could possibly do to me?

Something tells me I'm about to find out.

CHAPTER 16

*A*t the police station, Zach sits on a plastic chair in the waiting room while I give my name at the front desk. It's surprisingly busy for the morning of a workday, I assume. It's not like I've actually spent much, or any, time in a police station. I sneak a peek around the room as I wait for my name to come up on their system. The woman at the counter next to me is giving her version of events involving a car accident, her young daughter rocking what appears to be her baby sister in a pram.

The young man on my left is reporting his car stolen. There's a teenager with a black eye and swollen face sitting next to a furious mother and a woman in a business suit holding a piece of paper. A speeding fine perhaps?

"The complaint has been dropped," the female officer says briskly.

"I'm sorry?"

"Most people are relieved to hear that."

"I'm just surprised," I say, stammering slightly. "I received a call less than an hour ago."

"It's quite common," the woman says. "Especially in cases of domestic violence. One partner makes a report in the heat of the moment then, after they've cooled off, considers the implications for their partner and changes their mind."

"I'm not..." Heat prickles across my face. "This is not a case of domestic violence."

"Okay." She glances over my shoulder at the packed room. "Can I help you with something else?"

"No."

I storm out of the station, Zach easily keeping up. When we reach his car, he unlocks my door, and I slide in.

"I'm taking you for coffee and something to eat," he says, putting the car into gear and pulling out into the traffic.

"I'm too worked up to eat," I say. "Please take me back to my car."

"We're going to have something to eat," he says. "If you still want to leave after that, you can go."

I slump back into my seat. I want to feel anger over what on the surface appears to be yet another male making decisions for me, but I can't.

Zach's eyes are on the road, his hands vise-like grips on the steering wheel, his jaw clenched tight. I don't have the luxury to work out Mr. Tall, Dark and Rebellious right now, so I take my glare and point it out the window, allowing the engine's vibrations to roll through me, order my tumultuous thoughts.

What is Derek playing at? Why would he make a police report for assault and then drop it so fast?

Unless...he wanted me known to be violent on record.

Was he creating an official picture of me being crazy? He knows about my psych history, my medication. On paper, am I now criminally violent as well?

I rub at my eyes. This situation with Derek is going to get a whole lot worse before it gets better.

But fuck you, Derek. I'm not going down without a fight.

CHAPTER 17

"I'm sorry, ma'am, your credit card has been declined."

At a coffee shop on West Coast Drive, not far from Designs by Hardt, Zach sits across the table from me. I keep my expression neutral and businesslike as I talk to the receptionist from the hotel I stayed at last night. I read off the numbers from a different card. I already suspect that is going to come back declined as well. This time when the receptionist confirms it, she's a little more impatient, a little snootier. There's not the same respect in her tone she'd had moments ago.

"Do you have another form of payment?" Her voice prickles down my spine.

I use plastic to pay for just about everything. I have about twenty dollars in my purse, in change, for parking meters, but that's it. Even those machines take cards as payment these days.

"Wonderful, thank you," I say into the phone with a smile. For a reason I can't define, I feel especially embarrassed letting Zach witness this latest development. "I'll be in later to pick up the folder I left there."

"I'm sorry? Ma'am, your credit cards were declined. We're going to need another form of payment."

"Yes," I say, flicking a glance at Zach across the table. "Thank you. Please keep it at the front desk. I'll come in later today to collect it. Good-bye. I'll see you later on today," I emphasize so she doesn't call the cops on me, and I hang up before she can argue further.

Not surprisingly, the phone starts to ring again immediately, and I turn it to silent as I slide it into my bag.

"Everything okay?" Zach asks.

"Derek continues to be a jerk," I say, my cheeks heating. I don't tell Zach that Derek has cancelled my cards. It seems to me that it's something I should have been smart enough to avoid. How did I let Derek get such absolute control over me, my shop, and bank accounts? How did I not know to be careful when setting these things up?

"I'm going up to order," Zach says. "What would you like?"

My stomach rumbles. The mouth-watering smells in the coffee shop have made me hungry. I'm about to ask him to order my favorite toasted ham, cheese, and tomato sandwich and coffee, but the words cling to my tongue.

I have no money. It's too embarrassing to ask Zach to lend me money for lunch.

"Nothing for me," I say. "I'm too wound up to eat. I'll get something later."

"Claire," he says, frowning, "you should eat. Even if it's just a few bites." I'm touched this man worries over whether I eat when my lowlife soon to be ex-husband seemingly doesn't care if I ever eat again.

Oh, that's right. Unless I go back to him like a good little girl.

Well, screw you, Derek.

I've uttered those words so often these last few hours I consider getting a T-shirt made with them.

Except... No money.

Zach is looking at me expectantly. I swallow the lump in my throat. "I'm fine," I say. "Really."

I know Zach would pay for lunch, and yesterday, I would have let him without a second thought. But that was when I had money. How ironic is that?

But knowing all I have to my name is the loose change in my purse, money is suddenly precious. Those few coins have become my lifeline. Who knows when Derek will disconnect my phone? I'm surprised he hasn't already. But then again, how could I ring him, begging to come back, if I didn't have a phone?

I should get a new one. *But, no money.*

Things run through my brain like how much fuel is in my tank? I never had to worry about that before. I just pulled into a service station whenever I had to and used my card to pay.

I feel stupidly privileged and embarrassingly naïve now.

Zach moves to the counter to place his order, and I take a moment to compose myself before he gets back.

What am I going to do? I'd never once considered whose name was on the lease of my shop or whose name was on my credit cards. I'm confident I'm listed on the mortgage of the house because I remember signing those documents. After all, it was the inheritance from my mother's estate that we used as the deposit.

Outside the café window, the ocean is choppy. Whitecaps dot the blue all the way to the horizon. Wind whips salt spray onto the large windows.

A white Volvo sedan drives past...

I narrow my gaze, but my hands tangle and twist against each other.

He both frightens and angers me now, the man who until very recently shared my bed.

Zach takes a seat across from me, looks at me with concern. "Are you all right?" His hand moves across the table to clear the space between us, his fingers briefly grazing my arm. Electricity races across my skin and steals my breath. He quickly withdraws his hand, but not before I see a flash of awareness in his eyes.

His hand rests in front of him on the table. So large, tanned, and capable. I know that if I touched him with my cold fingers, his skin would be warm. .

"Derek's playing games," I say. "He's cancelled my credit cards now as well."

Zach's face is hard lines. "I can lend you money. Whatever you want. Tell me what you need, Claire."

I smile, filled with gratitude. "Thank you, Zach. That's very generous. But I'm not exactly sure what it is I need yet myself. I'll talk again to my lawyer, get a better picture of my situation. With any luck, just like the false police report, he'll reinstate the cards and stop being so petty."

We aren't taught to think about how a marriage would end. Although now, I think it should be an essential part of marital preparation.

Especially now that I know what the opposite of love tastes like.

"Here you are." The waitress places a steaming toasted ham and cheese and tomato sandwich in front of me along with a hot mug of coffee. "Are you waiting on anything else?" she asks before taking away our table number.

I look at Zach in surprise. "All I did was ask what you usually ordered," he explains. "I hope that's okay. You really should try to eat something."

My throat closes over. I have never been so grateful for a toasted sandwich before. Not knowing where my next meal will come from, I chew slowly. Savor every deliciously juicy bite of tomato and melted cheese.

"Have you thought about what you're going to do about your shop?"

The mouthful I am chewing is suddenly hard to swallow. I shake my head. When I spoke to the lawyer on the phone earlier, he confirmed what the real estate agent told me. "Apparently Derek is legally entitled to be an asshole."

Zach's eyes are hard.

The lawyer spoke to me over the phone, but the earliest appointment I could make with the lawyer is Friday morning. I've booked the appointment, but now I'm a little concerned over how I'll pay him.

I could take Zach up on his generous offer to lend me money, but that doesn't feel right. I barely know him. And I'm barely more than a stranger to him.

Besides, I'm entitled to the money in my bank accounts. I'll call the lawyer and work out how to go about accessing it. Beneath the table, I pull off my rings, slide them into my bag. I should get a decent amount for them should I need to. Whatever happens, Derek will not beat me.

"What would you do if you were in my situation?" I ask.

Zach raises a brow. "I'd walk right into the shop and take my shit back."

I grin. It amuses me the way Zach says that as though there weren't deadlocks on the doors or a monitored alarm system. "It's locked."

He shrugs. "You asked what *I'd* do." Those sea-green eyes meet mine. "But what you're really asking is what I think *you* should do."

Unable to stop myself, I ask, "Okay, what do you think I should do?"

"Walk right in and take your shit back."

I laugh, and he smiles. His eyes crinkle at the corners, and my heart jumps into my throat. "You're not serious?"

Zach nods. "I am."

"But I'd be breaking the law if I entered the shop."

"Claire, just because something is legal, that doesn't mean it's right. Otherwise, you'd have your stuff, and your husband would be paying the lease on an empty shop."

There's logic to what Zach is saying, but still, knowing my luck at the moment, the alarm would go off, and I'd be arrested before I take the first step.

Was that what Derek wanted? Alongside the assault charge he'd filed and then dropped, did he want to add a breaking and entering charge? Would he use an arrest to further discredit me? Or perhaps he really does believe I'm crazy, and he thinks this will send me over the edge.

Derek knows how not being able to work will affect me. He, of all people, knows how seriously I take my job. On many occasions, I've pulled all-nighters to get a dress finished in time for a client.

I've rescheduled today's appointments for tomorrow, which means I'll need to work through the night once again to make up for today.

And that's providing I can even get my garments and equipment back today. It's not as though my clients can reschedule their events, and I'll be ruined if I don't finish their outfits in time. How could anyone trust me with the most special events in their life in the future if I let them down even once?

And Kira…it's her payday on Friday. I have to get some money together by then for her wages.

Frustration twists my insides, and this time, Zach does cover my hand with his. It feels every bit like I thought it would. And more.

"Claire?"

"I'll be fine," I say. "I have a good lawyer. I'm sure this will be sorted out with a few phone calls and a cleverly written letter. I'm sure I could sue for loss of business or something…?" But if I don't get some money together soon, I won't have a good lawyer. I won't even have a bad one.

But that is not Zach's problem.

It's mine.

"Well, if you're sure…"

The smile is on my face, the one practiced and honed from many years of living in society. "Of course, I'm sure. Thank you for lunch. Next time, it will be my shout."

And I can only pray for that to be true.

CHAPTER 18

*I*n the car park out the back of my shop, I sit in my car and, through the windscreen, watch clouds attempt to smother the moon. Right now, the moon is in the lead, shining defiantly bright and full. But it will only be a matter of time before another cloud snuffs out its light, plunging the night back into darkness. I may also be losing my mind... But watching clouds is preferable to actually sleeping in my car.

The leather seat is as far back as it can go, and I've moved to the passenger side for more room. My head is resting on a rolled-up jumper against the door, and I'm wearing Zach's leather jacket with the collar turned up.

I didn't get a chance to sell my rings before the pawnshop closed. By the time I finished phoning around and talking to lawyers, it was after five p.m., and it was too late. I briefly considered going to Bec's or Julia's house but couldn't face the inevitable discussion about my situation. I know they'd do their best to convince me to go back to Derek, and I just can't face that conversation right now.

Something moves in the shadows outside the window. The hammering beat of my heart fills the enclosed space inside the car. I sink down lower in the seat. Maybe it's just a stray cat or dog? But I sense from the subtle sounds of movement that whatever it is, it's much larger than that. It's human. Peering through the window, I search the darkness.

A beam of torchlight hits the window, and I instinctively shield my eyes from the brightness. My pulse is racing, and I regret shifting from the driver's seat. How can I make a quick getaway from here?

Knuckles rap on the window. The figure is dressed in black, wearing a hooded jacket. Fear lodges in my throat, and I jump, landing painfully on something hard in the center console. The torch light shifts to a face.

Zach!

Relief floods my body, turning it to jelly. With trembling fingers, I turn the key in the ignition, press the button, and the window slowly glides down. I use the few seconds to compose myself and still my racing pulse.

"What are you doing here?" I ask.

"That's my question." His voice is a low growl. "Don't you know how dangerous it is being alone here?"

I hear the sound of an engine approaching, and Zach opens my door. "Hurry," he says. "Come with me." He reaches for my hand, and I take his. Before I lock the door, I grab my small suitcase, which Zach immediately takes, and sling my backpack over my shoulder. The engine I hear continues past us on West Coast Drive.

Is that relief I see wash over Zach? Why? His surprise at seeing me tells me he didn't know I was here. What is Zach doing dressed in black in a dark car park at two a.m.?

Zach opens the passenger side door of his BMW, and I climb inside. He doesn't turn the headlights on until we hit the main road. For long moments, he doesn't speak, but I'm highly aware of each time he slants that moody glance in my direction. Heat is rolling off him in almost tangible waves. But I know his anger is over my situation and not directed toward me.

"Just like old times," he says, breaking the silence. And some of the tension.

"I'm not sure what you mean."

"Living on the edge, baby," he says. "Me breaking and entering, you sleeping in your car. The only difference is this time I'm not stoned, and the girl is much prettier."

I twist to face him. "You broke into my shop, didn't you?"

He broke in to get my designs so that I can continue to work. Tears spring to my eyes.

"That is possibly the nicest thing anyone has ever done for me," I say, struggling to speak past the lump in my throat. "But what if someone saw you? What would the kids in the Village do if you got yourself arrested and sent to jail? Why would you take a risk like that?"

"Your first thought is to worry about me?" He shakes his head in disbelief. "No one saw me," he says. "It was just like riding a bike."

"Which tells me that even if you've broken into someplace before, you haven't done it for a very long time." Now I understand his concern over the car we heard. Did he think it was the police? Security? I glance in the side mirror, half-expecting to see a dozen cop cars chasing us.

"Not since I was sixteen."

"Wow," I say, careful to make sure there's no pity in my tone. He wouldn't like that. "At sixteen, I was living with my mother and worrying about exams."

"You'd be surprised at what you're capable of doing when no other options are available to you," he says.

What must his childhood have been like? I hope one day, he'll open up and tell me his story.

"I can't believe you were sleeping in your car in a deserted car park," he says. "Why didn't you call me?" He sounds hurt.

"I...uh..."

"I told you what would happen if you did anything so foolish again," he growls.

"You said you'd kill me, if I recall correctly." I can't help but smile. "Which seems to me decidedly more dangerous than sleeping in my car."

"Damn it, Claire. This is not a joke. You could have been hurt." His hands are clenching and unclenching on the steering wheel. "I've seen firsthand what can happen on the street. I never want you to experience that kind of horror."

"I know what I did may appear reckless," I say, my smile disappearing. "But I didn't get a chance to sell my rings before the pawnshop closed."

"You should have called me," he says softly. "It hurts that you didn't."

I glance at him, surprised. "I'm sorry, Zach. I didn't think my situation through very well. I'm taking it moment by moment. When I missed the shops, I simply decided I'd sleep in my car and, in the morning, sell the rings and continue work on my situation with Derek."

"Don't do something like that again," he grumbles. Then, "Aren't you going to ask me whether I managed to get Mrs. Taylor's dress for you?"

Is it too much to hope that he did?

"If it was the one on the mannequin," he says. "Then yes. Although I have to say the women I'm used to undressing are not cold and hard. Each to their own of course, but necrophilia is not my thing." His lips curve into a gorgeous half-smile. "And while I was there, I filled up my Santa sacks with anything else I thought might help you. Paperwork, half-finished work, something covered in pins on a workbench. If you see any blood on anything, that's where it's from. It was like picking up an echidna. I grabbed what looked like your order book and your address book. Basically—" He gives me a smile I feel all the way down to my toes. "—I cleaned you out."

My throat closes over, and I'm speechless for a moment over what Zach did for me. The risk he took. To help me.

"Thank you, Zach."

He shrugs. "No big deal."

But it is. To me.

That he took such a risk for someone he barely knows.

Zach changes to a lower gear for a roundabout, then powers out. The engine sounds deep and throaty in the stillness of the night.

We follow the coast and, twenty minutes later, arrive at Zach's house. The sun is still a few hours from coming up, but the clouds have disappeared, giving the full moon center stage. It illuminates the sky and ground like a streetlight in the clouds.

While Zach parks the car in the garage, I move to the unbelievable view he has of the Indian Ocean from the balcony out back. I take a deep breath of fresh salty air and listen to the low rumble of the waves crashing to shore.

Although my shop faces the same ocean as Zach's house, West Coast Drive runs in between the shop and the beach. But here, farther north along the Sunset Coast, Zach's house is nestled on top of the dunes with no road separating his home from the water.

I sense Zach approaching before I see him. He stands at my back on the balcony and looks over the ocean with me.

"I love it here," he says, his voice low and deep in my ear.

"I can see why." The price tag for the land alone would be astronomical. I had no idea Zach had this kind of money; he certainly isn't the type to flaunt his wealth.

"Derek is going to be furious when he realizes I have the designs from my shop." But what can he possibly do that he hasn't done already?

Zach leans forward, covers my hand gripping the railing with his much larger and warmer one. His chest is a wall of solid muscle against my back, and it steals my breath.

"You can handle anything he throws at you and then some. Believe it. I do."

For so long, I've been made to believe I'm irrational, bordering on crazy. Certainly not stable enough to handle this thing called life. Tears sting my eyes, and I shut them, hoping he can't see. He might think I'm overreacting, but it's overwhelming to hear the absolute faith he has in me.

"Hey," he says gently, his breath a whisper in my ear. "I didn't mean to upset you."

"It's not you. Derek always made me feel incapable, as though if something were left to me, I would find a way to mess it up. Looking back now, I can see how he eroded my confidence, comment by comment, but at the time, I couldn't see what he was doing."

The hardest thing I have to do now is untangle myself from the web of marriage and work out what was Derek and what was me.

"I met Derek in England," I find myself saying after we're silent for a while. "I met Derek by chance. He was a few years older, in England on holiday with some friends. I was still only eighteen when I lost my mother. I'd never lived on my own, never got the chance to find out who I was as an adult. My mother passed suddenly, and I was adrift, confused."

Derek had been so nice, so charming back then.

"Ours was a whirlwind romance," I say as a gentle sea breeze kicks in. "The way it happens when you have limited time together. He helped me make the funeral arrangements, and since he was an accountant, he handled all the financial stuff. There was no will. I was emotionally overwrought...it was all so overwhelming at the time. But Derek sorted it all out, put the house on the market. He was there like a knight in shining armor, and at the time, it made sense to just let him do what seemed to come so naturally to him."

He'd been so attentive, so loving. I'd thought he was perfect. Our relationship had started out as everything a marriage should be.

"Derek swept me off my feet and then back to Australia with him," I continue, condensing ten years into a few sentences for Zach. "We bought a house, got married, and I became pregnant. Katie was born when I was twenty, and after that, my life became all about her. When she fell ill, getting her better became my sole focus." I took a breath, let it out. "And the last three years have been simply about surviving, learning how to live again without her."

"I'm sorry about your daughter," Zach says softly. "And your mum."

Thinking about Mum makes me smile. "You know she was an artist. A painter, just like you."

Zach has moved to stand next to me, leaning against the railing, his arm pressed against mine.

"What was she like?"

"She was very passionate," I say, searching for the best words to describe her. "Our house was full of color and smelled of oil paint. All the time. Her lifestyle was what you'd call alternative. Her friends were artsy, as colorful as her work. Growing up in that environment was wonderful."

Derek disagreed. He was fond of reminding me what happened to my mother, especially in the beginning, telling me over and over how that free-loving hippie lifestyle killed her even though I never saw it that way. I was happy with how I grew up, how we lived. Except for the never knowing my dad part. I wished that was different.

At the time, I took Derek's criticism as a show of how much he loved me and didn't want to lose me to the same fate. *He just wants to protect me,* I thought. *Because he loves me so much.*

It wasn't long before I believed that white walls, marble floors, and a serious outlook were the proper way to live. Especially once you became a parent.

"Do you mind if I ask how she died?"

"She was killed in a car accident. She was with her lover, a French painter as passionate as she was. She'd been drinking, and so had he. It was raining. They had argued. She took off in her car, and he took off in his, chasing after her. According to the police report, he'd been over-taking her, trying to get her to pull over. She lost control of her car on a corner less than fifteen minutes from where we lived. She was trapped in the car for almost an hour before they could cut her out. She died on the way to the hospital."

Perhaps Mum's death contributed to why I'd agreed to marry Derek at the time. Fear of such a passionate and powerful love. But there has always been a secret part of me that has envied my mother for having someone willing to risk everything for you. Even if it ended in tragedy.

Zach's hand entwines with mine.

"Ever since then, storms have always felt ominous to me like they carry with them a sense of foreboding or doom. I'd stood outside our house that day, listening to sirens race down the road, somehow knowing who they were for. It was still storming when uniformed officers pulled up at our house a few hours later."

Zach slants a glance at me. "I love a good storm," he says. "Love watching it roll in from the ocean, all that power, all that intensity and violence."

Something in his tone makes me shiver, reminding me that despite his kindness, there's something dangerous about this man.

"Thank you for helping me get my dresses and paperwork back, Zach," I say, my voice thick with emotion. "And for giving me a place to stay tonight."

He shrugs as though it were nothing.

"I won't become a burden though. I'll sort everything out tomorrow."

A sudden gust of chilly ocean breeze washes over me, and I shiver. Zach puts an arm around me. "Let's get you inside."

The house smells like Zach: raw timber, paint, and rugged outdoors. The tables are rich dark wood and covered in sculptures and shells from the ocean. There is a modernity to the place in the floor-to-ceiling windows that open to a balcony and give a perfect view of the ocean, but this isn't some designer showplace.

Zach's furniture is eclectic. Like everything in here has been chosen because he likes it, not because it fits a particular vision. A large black leather chair is positioned to look out across the view instead of being arranged with the rest of the pieces in the lounge, and books litter coffee tables. His oversized timber dining table is covered in paintbrushes, half-finished artwork, and an open laptop. It should feel cluttered and messy, but somehow it works. Everything looks as though it belongs. It looks luxurious, artsy, and reminds me of my mum and our house when I was growing up.

Derek would hate it.

I'm drawn to the artwork lining the walls. Some I immediately recognize as fitting Zach's trademark style of wild landscapes and heartbreaking portraits, but I'm certain not all the pieces are his. I'm far from an art connoisseur, but some are definitely childish.

"There's so much more to you than meets the eye," I comment. He tenses, and I immediately regret the comment. "I only meant to say that you intrigue me."

"The truth can be disappointing."

"You can tell me. Not that you have to, of course. But you know so much about my mess of a life and that I'm a long way from perfect. Yet, I know next to nothing about you." For a moment, I wish he'd tell me something personal. I fantasize about him sharing a drink and telling me all about his colorful life.

Zach turns, moves to the artwork I'm standing by. "Some of the boys from the Village made these for me," he says, clearly changing the subject, and I swallow to hide my disappointment.

"This one is by Billy." Zach points out a painting of a cabin against a sunset sky. "He doesn't live at the Village anymore, has his own place now in the city. He gave it to me before he left. As a thank you. That's the cabin he built."

It would be impossible not to be touched by the way he has displayed the artwork next to what are clearly more expensive pieces.

Without warning, a wave of exhaustion washes over me, and I yawn deeply.

"You can use the guest room," Zach offers. He opens a nearby bedroom door and turns on the light. It's a very large room full of art supplies and paintings resting against the far wall, and he picks up some books and what appears to be the suit jacket he wore to the function where I'd first met him off the bed.

"Sorry," he says. "I put it there to remind me to take it to the dry cleaners." He gestures around. "The room might be a mess, but the sheets are clean. It's not the Hyatt Regency, but I suspect it will be more comfortable than your car."

"Thank you. I appreciate it although as tired as I am, I won't be able to sleep tonight. I need to go through the bags you retrieved from the shop and make sure Mrs. Taylor's dress is ready for her tomorrow." I am utterly relieved that I won't have to cancel her appointment.

Although, since I'm unable to see her at the shop, where will our appointment be?

I'll turn my shop into a temporary mobile business, I decide. I'll see her at her place. With the sewing machine and the other pieces in my car, along with what Zach managed to get back for me tonight, I am in reasonable shape. Zach managed to get Mrs. Taylor's dress, but he didn't grab the dressmaker's mannequin. I can survive without it since her dress will need only minor adjustments, but I'll need one to be able to continue to work on other designs.

"You're welcome to stay here as long as you like," Zach says.

Tomorrow morning, first thing, I need to turn my jewelry into cash. And I'll need to arrange to go back to the house, collect as many of my belongings as possible. I have more jewelry there that I can sell, but hopefully Derek will be reasonable and release money to me. After all, it is mine, too.

"Claire," Zach says, his voice soft. "I don't want to see you sleep in your car again. Not ever. I can lend you money, whatever you need."

My throat closes over. When he offered last time, I'd thought I couldn't take money from a relative stranger. But after tonight, after everything he's done for me... Zach no longer feels like a stranger. He's quickly become something far from it.

"You've already been far too kind. The lawyer I spoke to today said I can apply to the Family Courts for mediation," I say. "If Derek wants to keep the house, he'll need to pay me out."

"That might take a while. How about I give you whatever you need to see you through for now, and you can pay me back when your settlement comes through or whenever you can afford to. Lawyers can be expensive."

"You'd do that for me?"

"Of course," Zach says easily. "I'd even go as far as to insist."

Our eyes catch and hold. My body heats with desire, and I'm painfully conscious I'm standing in a bedroom with him.

What the hell is wrong with me that I'm thinking these thoughts about Zach when I should be concerning myself with far more pressing issues? But I'm not alone in the attraction between us. I see it in the way his eyes darken, the vein pulsing on the side of his neck.

"I'll get your things from the car," Zach says. And then he's gone.

Alone, I do my best to slow my racing heart and catch my ragged breath. No matter what happens from here, I'll be eternally grateful to Zach, not only for what he did for me tonight, but for sharing his strength. His *I don't give a fuck* attitude is something I can adopt more of.

On top of everything, Zach has eased my immediate financial worries. I'll still sell my jewelry, but it's a relief to know I'll have money available to pay for the lawyer should I need it.

I can't imagine what it would be like to be in this situation without him. What if I'd still had Katie to care for?

Zach comes in with my bags.

I unpack Mrs. Taylor's dress and get to work. The best revenge is success. And to show Derek he won't beat me.

CHAPTER 19

I'd worked all night, cataloguing what I had for my business to function correctly and what I needed to purchase. I seem to be in pretty good shape. Mrs. Taylor's dress is finished and pressed and ready for her final fitting. I've just had a shower, and smelling coffee, I throw on the comfiest clothes I'd packed in my bag and head to the kitchen.

Zach is sitting at the table and looks up as I enter. I think I see his breath hitch. Or maybe it's just mine.

I'm wearing sleep pants and a thin white singlet top.

Zach clears his throat. "I've made fresh coffee. Have a seat. I'll get you one."

"No. I'll get it," I say quickly, not wanting him to wait on me. He's done too much already. He slides his chair out as I'm about to rush past. I stumble, falling heavily into his back just as he is about to stand, knocking him off balance and onto the floor.

"I'm sorry!" Heat rushes to my cheeks. Zach rolls over and into a sitting position in one swift move. Feeling the need to redeem myself, I lunge forward with the intention of offering my hand to help him up, but I trip instead, catching my toe on the leg of the overturned chair. I fall in an ungainly sprawl of limbs directly on top of him.

He's completely still. The first thing I notice is the long, hard length of his body. The next, his warmth, the scent of freshly showered male, the feel of his arms wrapped around me, holding me in place.

He doesn't let go.

I don't want him to.

We are trapped in the moment. An accident neither of us try to rectify.

I can't breathe.

My mouth is dry.

The pound of Zach's heartbeat is loud between us.

His lids are lowered, his eyes dark. I'm highly conscious of there being almost nothing between us.

Abruptly he stands, bringing me up with him. To keep my balance, I grab him on the shoulders with both hands. My nipples are painfully hard, and I know they must be clearly visible through the thin fabric.

He pulls away. "I said I've got it." His voice is deep and rough, and he clears it. What is he talking about?

That's right. The coffee I'd needed so badly.

He's turned away from me, and I take the moment to calm my racing heart. I can't take my eyes off his strong back and shoulders, the muscles working in his arms as he pours the coffee, adds milk and one sugar. He remembered that from that one time in the coffee shop. He turns, hands me the coffee without meeting my eye.

"Thank you." My face feels hot, my skin still on fire from his touch. "I'll, uh, go and get dressed."

As I leave the room, I feel his gaze scorching across my skin.

"Derek's name is on the lease of your shop," Zack says after we'd finished eating the large bacon and eggs breakfast he made for us. I'm dressed for business, wearing a fitted black skirt, silky blouse and, as always, Mum's diamond earrings.

I'm focused and determined.

Zach turns his laptop around, showing me what appears to be something like a commercial lease database. I have no idea if that's a site readily available to average humans. But I doubt it.

"He arranged the lease," I say a little defensively. I didn't even question Derek doing something like that. An accountant, he handled all our financial decisions.

Zach nods, his expression serious and unreadable.

"Is the business in your name, his, or both?" He taps on the keyboard, and another screen opens.

"Mine," I say quickly. "I went into town to fill out the paperwork for the business name. It was only my name." I've at least done that right. I don't admit that was only because Derek was interstate that day, so I went alone. Of course, now I remember how he argued that I should wait until he got back...

"Good. But your business bank account was in both names?"

"Must have been," I say. "He handled the accounts, tax returns, paid the bills. My lawyer has advised me to go to the bank and see the manager. I intend on doing that first thing after my appointment this morning."

"Do you mind if I ask how the business is doing?" Zach looks up quickly. "I don't mean that to sound rude. The only reason I ask is to establish if your business is financially able to pay for a lease. You don't have to give me figures, but are you making enough to pay for a reasonable lease and make a wage you can live off?"

"I... I have no idea." My face heats, and I look away.

"You don't?" This time, Zach doesn't keep the surprise from showing on his face. "You don't know if your business is profitable?"

"No." My face is hot. I'm so damned ashamed that I allowed Derek to take such total control of my life. Regret is a very bitter pill to swallow. I twirl my coffee cup. I should have paid more attention. It seems almost absurd that I didn't now.

"I don't mean to make you uncomfortable by asking these questions, I'm simply trying to establish your position so I know what type of lease you can afford. Unless I'm wrong, finding you a new shop to work out of is paramount. But I don't mean to take over. Seems to me you've had your fill of that. Tell me to back off, and I will."

It warms me that Zach sees and recognizes that. He's right, this is something I have to do myself. Except... I sit up in my chair. "Why?" I lean forward on my elbows. "Not that I don't appreciate everything you've done for me, but what I want to know is why. Why are you helping me?"

Zach keeps his eyes on mine. Intense, they bore into me and through me. "Claire. There are no strings attached." He pauses. "Never were. Nor are you under any obligation to accept my help or my advice for that matter. What happened to you is wrong. Plain and simple. And I'm not the type of person to stand around doing nothing when I see someone being treated badly. It's a...I guess you could say it's a sore point for me."

I can see that's Zach's nature, helping the underdog. Just one look at what he's doing at the Village proves that.

"You think I could look the other way when I see you locked out of your shop and sleeping in your car? I'm not that man, Claire."

No, he's not. I don't know if I'm relieved or disappointed to hear him blatantly admit he'd do this for anyone. I need to be careful not to read too much into his help. Zach is the quintessential bad boy with a heart of gold.

"Look," Zach says. "What Derek is doing to you is disgusting. You could have been seriously hurt last night. He's using money as a weapon, a tool to control you, and that pisses me off."

Oh, it pisses me off, too. I just have to decide how to handle it. Right now, it seems Derek's holding all the cards, a perfect hand in a carefully stacked deck. But I'm not folding just yet.

"If I know how much rent you can afford, there's an empty shop a few streets back from ours. It's not oceanfront, but the owner is a mate of mine."

My heart leaps. "Do you think he'd let me use it?"

"And because he's a mate," Zach continues, "I need to make sure that you can pay the rent. I'm not going to recommend you as a tenant to my friend if you can't."

"Of course. I'm sorry."

"Claire." I look up to find Zach's lips curving. "I know you're going to pay your rent. I know that you're smart enough to run the shop so that you do. You just need an opportunity to prove that to yourself."

Tears sting my eyes, and I cover them with my hand. Will I ever get used to people believing in me?

Zach places a hand on my arm resting on the table, his touch warm, comforting. "I keep upsetting you."

I shake my head. "You didn't upset me. I just hate not being able to answer your questions about my business. It seems ludicrous now that I can't. Finances were something I never had to worry about. And yes, I know how spoilt and entitled that makes me sound." I peek at him through my fingers. "I know what you must think of me."

"No, you don't."

I'd love to ask what he does think of me, but I'm afraid of his answer. I am not the woman who was married to Derek. This woman will not make those same mistakes.

"So, first thing is getting access to my business records," I decide.

"I might be able to help. I'm not an accountant, but I know a thing or two about business. Certainly enough to look at your financials and get a picture of how well you're doing. Were your business records with the stuff I collected from the shop? I can go back in tonight if I've missed anything."

"No," I say quickly. "No more risk. You've done enough. Besides, my financial records weren't at the shop. They'll be in Derek's home office."

Rather than show me how, Derek simply ran the accounting side of the business from his home office. I considered that perfectly reasonable at the time. After all, if I married a mechanic, I certainly wouldn't feel obliged to learn how to service my own car. I'd leave it to my husband, right?

"You do make money though, right?" Zach presses. "The business. You're making a decent profit?"

My shoulders sag slightly. "I honestly don't know. After Katie was diagnosed, I stopped working and cared for her. Then after she...she died, I focused back on my work. It was never about the money. It was about finding something—anything—to live for."

Recently, the clients have been more high profile, the designs are more extravagant, and the prices have increased to reflect that. Clients want to pay a lot of money for a custom design; they want to make an impression. Stand out. And the hours I put into each design have increased exponentially. But I love it, even though I used it to avoid thinking about, well, everything. Katie, my marriage.

"I thought I was doing all right." I clear my throat, remembering how Derek said that what I make wouldn't pay for the toilet. It was one of the reasons I thought I couldn't stay in the house. How would I be able to afford such a grand place without him?

"But?"

"But I don't really know."

My name is Claire Hardt, and I know nothing about money.

That all changes now.

"I have time to go back to the house before my appointment with Mrs. Taylor. I'll pick up some more of my belongings while I'm there. I'll see if I can cram in the dressmaker's mannequin as well so I don't need to buy another."

Zach grabs his keys. "We'll go in my car. I'll drop you off at your old shop so that you can drive your car back here."

Your old shop. I'm making a fresh start...with everything.

Then I remember the crazed look in Derek's eye when I last saw him. What will he do if I turn up at the house with Zach?

He puts a hand on my arm. "What is it?"

"Nothing." My voice is strong. Determined. I force down the image of Derek throwing himself at my car, the memory of him subsequently reporting me for assault. At least Zach will be with me as a witness if necessary. It's sad that I no longer know my husband or what he's capable of.

I throw my bag over my shoulder.

"Let's do this."

CHAPTER 20

*F*rom the passenger seat of Zach's car, I stare at the place I used to call home. Once, it had been my sanctuary, my retreat from the world. I'd loved the large front room I'd used for my work. It overlooked the rose garden.

But now, the house represents pain, tragedy, loss, and deception.

I tell Zach to wait in the car.

I can't see Derek's car in the driveway, but if for some reason he didn't go into work today and is here drinking, his mood will be unpredictable. I don't want Zach to get into trouble. What if the police have to be called, and that shines a light on Zach? What if they find out he was the one who broke into my shop?

Zach is at my side of the car before I've even picked up my empty backpack. Why did I think for a single moment that he would listen when I told him to stay in the car?

He walks with me to the front door. His expression is unreadable, his eyes narrowed with intensity. His hand on the small of my back is possessive. His muscles tensed with unleashed power. I have no doubt Zach could be deadly if you got on the wrong side of him. And Derek is already on the wrong side of him. Over what he's done to me.

What if Derek does something more to antagonize Zach today? My anxiety ratchets up a notch. Zach has plenty of reason to be cautious when it comes to the law. With his responsibility to the kids at the Village, Zach is already mixed up in this far more than I'm comfortable with.

At the front door, I discover my key no longer fits the lock.

I drop my hand and stare at it. *Oh, you can't be serious!* The shop and now the house? *How dare he!* This is still my home; my name is on the mortgage. At least, I think it is. How can I be sure of anything anymore?

I ring my lawyer on his mobile, and he tells me that Derek can't legally lock me out of my marital house. I hardly notice Zach disappearing out of sight. The lawyer is telling me to call a locksmith when the front door springs open.

My breath lodges in my throat as I half expected to find Derek standing there only to see Zach. I hastily end the call with the lawyer then turn to Zach. "How did you get inside?"

"It's your house, too, Claire."

I smile and shake my head. Have to love Zach's outlook on life. Don't ask permission. Take what's rightfully yours.

"You just hung up with your lawyer. Surely he told you Derek can't lock you out, didn't he?

"Yes. But the lawyer also advised me to ring a locksmith."

Zach shrugs. "Why wait? Here." He tosses me a key. I look down at the tag labelled "spare key."

"He's such a tool," Zach says. "Who would hang the spare key to their house on the key rack and label it?"

Derek would. A place for everything and everything in its place. It might not be smart, but in Derek's mind, he'd at least know where the spare key was.

"I can't just take this."

"Keep it," Zach says. "It's yours."

A white car is traveling down the street, and for a heart-stopping moment, I fear it's Derek. "Let's make this quick."

The house is silent, echoing back every noise we make, and when I reach the master bedroom, I take the opportunity to empty my jewelry box into my bag. I'm not sure how much I'm going to get for my rings, and I don't want to sell my mother's diamond earrings unless I absolutely have to. I'll sell everything Derek gave me first.

In my sewing room, I grab a few more things I need. Zach takes the dressmaker's mannequin from my arms and a bolt of material and carries them out to his car.

"Your house is very neat and...very white," Zach says when he returns. "It doesn't seem like your style."

"It's not."

This whole place bears Derek's stamp. And I realize now his stamp had been all over me, too.

After a quick glance out the window to make sure the next car driving by isn't his pulling into the driveway, I sneak into Derek's office. It's tidy and very minimalist just like the rest of the house. I squash a sense of guilt. I've never invaded Derek's private space. But he's forced my hand through the situation he's imposed on me, and he has no one to blame but himself.

I flick a switch, and the computer monitor fires up to the password screen. I search through Derek's desk drawers, but I suspect he won't have his passwords written anywhere. I try a few combinations, his date of birth, obvious personal numbers.

After several more incorrect answers, I'm about to give up, not wanting to risk locking the screen and giving myself away when I have an idea.

Katie-bear.

The name he called our daughter followed by her date of birth as a six-digit number.

The computer logs into the system, and I gulp in air, trying to shove down what I'm feeling. Zach's warm hand is on my shoulder. "You okay?"

The breath I release is slow and shuddering. "Yes." It shakes me to learn Derek types her name and birthdate every day.

Now that I'm in, I realize that Derek's anal tendencies will make this easy. On the main screen, there's a folder titled *Designs by Hardt*, and inside are more folders, each labelled by year. Derek is nothing if not organized. I hope Zach will see this and realize how easy it was for Derek to assume the role he is clearly good at.

Zach rifles through the top desk drawer until he comes across a USB drive. Stabbing it into the side of the laptop, I right-click the mouse, and my business records begin to transfer across.

Vibrations echo through the house, signaling a car pulling into the driveway. Zach and I exchange glances. The files are in the middle of transfer.

My heart drops into the pit of my stomach.

Zach's car is parked in the driveway. Derek will know someone's inside.

The files are still transferring, the little box on the screen showing the progress bar, the USB flashing red on the side.

I hear the front door open. "Claire?" Derek calls out. "Claire, are you here? Where are you?"

I bite my lip, and my leg jumps up and down impatiently.

Hurry! Why are they taking so long to transfer? Seconds tick by painfully slowly.

I hear Derek's business shoes on the tiled floor as he walks toward us.

Zach positions himself in the open doorway.

"What the fuck are you doing here?" Derek snaps when he sees Zach. "How'd you get in? I changed the locks. Where's my wife?"

Finally! The transfer finishes. I whip out the USB drive, tuck it inside my bra, and slam the laptop screen closed. Zach is filling the doorway, so I squeeze alongside him.

"What are you doing in there?" Derek narrows his eyes menacingly. His hair is mussed as though he'd been running a hand through it. He looks scruffy, smells of bourbon, and the wildness in his eyes makes him look slightly unhinged. Nothing like the put-together husband I once knew.

He'd never recovered fully from losing Katie; had my leaving tipped him over the edge? But why would that be? What, other than love, can make someone so desperate to keep their marriage together?

Zach angles his body in front of mine in a protective gesture. I'm flattered, but as much as I don't recognize this new Derek, I've never known him to be violent. He looks wild and reckless, but I don't think he'd hurt me. Physically, anyway.

I step around Zach and face Derek. "I'm taking what is rightfully mine." I'm relieved to find my voice strong and confident. "You don't have the right to lock me out of my house. You'll be hearing from my lawyer."

"What lawyer?" Derek scoffs. "What are you going to pay him with, buttons?"

"You're an asshole," I say. "But you won't get away with it. I'm not going to stop until I get everything I'm legally entitled to."

"What are you doing here?" Derek says, turning reddened eyes on Zach.

I'm relieved he's seemingly forgotten that I was in his office, but I guess my getting business records wouldn't be the first thing to cross his mind. Especially in his inebriated state. I have no doubt though he'll know once he opens his laptop and sees the folder open to the business.

"This is Zach Argos," I say. "And I invited him in. He's my friend."

"I know who he is," Derek says, and something passes between the two men. "What are you doing here?" His voice slurs and the skin on his face is red and blotchy. He's drunk and confused.

"Derek," I say sharply, snapping his attention back to me. Zach could tear Derek apart limb from limb without breaking a sweat, but I don't want to involve him. Derek filed a police report on a lie; I can only imagine what he'd do if Zach assaulted him. Besides, this is my fight, a battle I need to win. For me.

"We were just leaving," I say.

"You're not leaving," Derek says menacingly. "Not until we talk."

Zach steps forward, towering over Derek. "She said she's leaving." His tone is cold, his voice tight.

Derek opens his mouth to say something, but I interrupt. "What the hell are you doing, Derek? Why did you lock me out of my business? My house! How dare you cancel my cards, leave me without access to my own bank accounts! And what is with charging me with assault? *You* were the one who jumped on my car."

Derek shrugs, his blurry eyes back on me. Zach's hands are clenched into fists at his sides, and a muscle is working along his jaw like it's taking him all his willpower not to pummel Derek.

"I've dropped those charges, but I wanted your erratic behavior on record. You've been so unpredictable lately, ever since you stopped taking your medication. Who knows what you're capable of? You're becoming wild and unstable just like your mother."

"You know nothing about my mother," I hiss.

"Did you expect me to make this easy on you?" Derek sneers. "Come back, and this all goes away."

"Why do you even want that? We can barely tolerate looking at each other."

"I've explained how it will work," Derek says in his best *I'm the competent one, and you're an idiot* voice. "I can write it down for you if you want. I'll write real slow because I know you can't read fast."

"Our marriage is over. Notice how slowly and deliberately I said that. Because it's seems to me that you're the one having problems understanding."

"Then you'll be living in a gutter by sunset."

Zach growls low and deep and takes a step forward.

I rest my hand on Zach's arm firmly to assure him I've got this. His muscles are granite hard.

"I just want you to remember something," Derek says. "I'm the one who's holding all the cards. Every single one of them."

"So you did set this up from the start," I say, sickened. "Everything in your name, even the bank account associated with my business. And that was deliberate so you'd have total control over me. Did you think if you did that, you'd own me?"

Derek glances at Zach and says to him in an undertone, "She's slow to catch on, but eventually she gets it." He turns back to me. "You owe me, Claire!" Derek shouts, spittle landing on my face. "You don't get to leave me."

"You don't get to tell me what to do," I reply with equal force.

"You're finished. Nobody will believe a word you say about anything, what with all your violent attacks on me and with your best friends validating your unstable state of mind."

"You bastard!" My body starts shaking, and I take a deep breath before continuing. "You won't get away with this."

"But you must see, Claire," Derek says, his tone silkily smooth, "I already have. This is your last chance to come to your senses. You're throwing a hell of a lot away. This house, your status in the community, your business. You'll have nothing, not a red cent to your name. Come back, and all this ends. Hell, come back, and I'll even let you fuck him if that's what you want."

Zach lets out a primal growl, and the sound sends a chill through me. He lunges toward Derek, and I throw myself in front of him, forcefully placing my hands on Zach's chest. It's like holding back a mountain. I pierce him with a look. *Please*, I implore frantically with my eyes. *I've got this.*

I'm sure the pounding I can hear in the room is Zach's racing heart. I need to get him out of here. I'm not sure I'll be able to stop him the next time Derek says something stupid.

"Read my lips. I'm not coming back to you. Not ever. You want to start a war? You've got one. If what you say is true, I have nothing to lose anyway. You, on the other hand, have *everything* to lose."

Derek storms into the kitchen. To the cupboard where he keeps his gin. He opens the door so hard, it slams against the wall, the handle sending a chip of plaster skittering across the floor. He pours himself a solid glass, drains it, then pours another, slamming it so hard on the marble counter I jump.

Zach is still predator tense, watching Derek's every move intently.

"Is there anything else you need before we go?" Zach asks softly at my side. If only I knew whether there was any cash hidden anywhere in the house.

I make my way into the lounge and take a framed photo of Katie off the shelves. Derek is watching me from the door to the kitchen. He has that same wild look in his eyes he had when I was in the car before he hurtled himself on top of it. A look that softens slightly when he watches me carefully slide the picture into my bag. I glance at him, and our eyes meet.

I feel an unwanted rush of compassion for him and hope that Katie's death hasn't destroyed everything good in him.

Then his eyes turn cold, and he addresses Zach. "I see the way you look at her. If you're thinking about trying to fuck her, don't bother. She's frigid. It's like fucking a cold, dead, fish."

Zach reacts in an instant. I'm too far away to intervene this time. Before I can blink, Derek is up against the wall, Zach looming over him. Zach is only a few inches taller than Derek, but his power, his energy fills the room, making him seem twice Derek's size. Zach's arm is across Derek's chest, and he peers down at Derek, his whole body straining with tension.

"I warned you twice."

"What are you doing?" Derek wheezes, maybe from the punch I hadn't seen but heard. "This has nothing to do with you. This is between me and her." Derek is coughing, struggling to breathe.

"Wrong again," Zach says, abruptly letting Derek go so that he slides down the wall and slumps into a crumpled heap.

Zach looks down at Derek's prone form. "I've never met a bigger fool in my life. Do you have any idea what you've lost?"

I realize Zach is talking about me, and I cover my mouth with my hand, unwilling to show how much this touches me.

Derek is looking up at Zach with glazed, bloodshot eyes. I hardly recognize the man on the floor.

Fingering the USB I've moved to my pocket, I walk over to Zach and link my arm through his.

"Let's go," I say softly. "We have everything we came for."

As I leave my husband, broken and out of control, I can't help but feel saddened that it has had to come to this.

"This is not over!" Derek's shout is slurred.

And although I can't imagine how much worse this can get, I also know that it will.

CHAPTER 21

One month later…

*D*esigns by Hardt has moved!
    I proudly stick the sign on the door of my old shopfront. I've signed a lease on a place only ten minutes away. It is not on West Coast Drive with ocean views, but it's twenty square meters bigger, and it's half the rent I was paying before. As the owner is a friend of Zach's, my lease is less formal and doesn't require all the checks and rigmarole my current financial situation wouldn't pass. But everything is documented, official and, most importantly, in my name.

My business has a new name: *Simply Claire*.

I've opened brand-new bank accounts and have begun making deposits. I finished Mrs. Taylor's dress on time, working from Zach's front room. I sold my wedding rings and some odd jewelry, and that, along with the final payment on Mrs. Ransom's gown, paid the balance of Kira's wages and the deposit on a short-term rental of a cozy two-bedroom near the beach. Zach loaned me money for the upfront costs of refitting the shop and the initial rent and although he says there's no rush, I plan on turning a profit and paying him back everything as soon as I can.

The deposits on my new work have paid for the material and stock I needed to complete the gowns. I'm watching every penny, and it's a juggling act, but so far, I'm managing to make it work. It feels strange starting from scratch, but the bonus is that I'm learning how to run the business on my own from the ground up.

Zach has printed out the previous years' financial records, and soon he'll be showing me how to set up and run my accounts on a new software program. There were other files on the USB flash drive that I'd copied over that day in Derek's office, but I'm not sure what they relate to. There were also some large payments being made to an unknown supplier that I haven't been able to account for. But I'm sure with Zach's help, we'll be able to work it out. I can't worry about any of that now.

Today is my official opening day, and I feel younger, lighter, and more in control of my life than I ever have before.

As I pull into the car park of my new shop, I smile at Kira, who's waving at me from the front entrance. Black and silver balloons flank the doorway to match the elegant new signage on the shopfront.

"Claire!" Kira embraces me, and we spin around in a happy dance. "Congratulations, you did it!"

"*We* did it." I smile down at her. "Thanks for standing by me through all this."

"Of course! I wouldn't have missed your transformation for the world."

"My transformation?"

"You've been half alive the past three years, and now look at you! Derek has done you the biggest favor in the world by being such a dickhead."

In the small kitchen in the back, I flick the switch on the new coffee machine, and it springs to life, grinding up fresh beans.

"Look, Claire," Kira calls out excitedly. "Your first customers in the new shop."

I walk to the window, my smile fading when I see the car. Jasmine and Julia step out of Derek's white Volvo, and I meet them at the entrance.

"Claire," Jasmine says, her voice sickly sweet. "You've moved." She makes a show of looking at the mechanic's shop across the street.

Ignoring Jasmine, I let my gaze rest on Julia. "Hi, Jules," I say. "Nice to see you. Where's Bec?" I've hardly spoken to Bec or Julia at all this last month. Bec, I know from our last conversation, is conflicted, torn between wanting to support me but also feeling that if she does, she'll be betraying her fiancé, who strongly believes I shouldn't have left my husband. I think it's easier for her to simply not call and let the dust settle.

It hurts, but to be completely honest, I've been too busy to let it bother me much. And Zach and Kira have been wonderful support, as have Mandy and the boys at the Village, who've been helping with the renovations to the shop. My life is full, and I'm happier than I've been in a long time.

"We've just been at a corporate function, a champagne breakfast for some interstate VIPs," Julia says but doesn't meet my eyes when she speaks. "Derek got a lift back to the office with Rob and Bec, and I left with Jasmine. We were just driving past when Jasmine saw that your new shop is open."

"Yes, it's my first day." There's an awkward pause, and I think Julia expects to be invited in.

"Well, we just wanted to stop by and wish you the very best of luck," Jasmine says sweetly. "Julia is helping me pick out baby clothes and some new furniture for the nursery."

Although it stings that Julia is going baby shopping with Jasmine, I don't let it show.

Julia says goodbye, and I watch her walk with Jasmine back to Derek's car. Before Jasmine opens the door, she rushes back on her own. "Oh, I forgot to tell you," she says, arching her back and rubbing her baby bump. "Derek and I found out yesterday that we're having a girl." Jasmine leans forward for emphasis and adds, "I'm giving Derek another Katie."

I feel the blow, a punch to the gut. I grip the doorframe for balance as the world spins.

Jasmine is having a *girl*? Somehow, knowing that detail makes it feel real. The fact that Derek can be a father again when I can never be a mother seems so terribly cruel. That he's having another girl...?

"Derek always wanted another Katie," Jasmine says smugly. "It's the one thing you can't give him that I can."

I hug my arms around my stomach.

I blink. Time has slowed down.

"You'll never replace Katie," I hiss. "Never!" Kira appears at my side, her hand on my shoulder.

"Who's replacing Katie?"

"I am." Jasmine smiles, rubbing her stomach. "It's a girl."

"What do you think you're doing? Get off our porch, you nasty bitch," Kira snaps angrily. "And don't come back."

At the sound of Kira's raised voice, Julia rushes back to Jasmine's side. "What's going on?"

Jasmine blinks up tears. "I just thought Claire would be happy for me." She sniffs. "I was trying to be nice and offered to share this experience with her. Claire can't have any more kids. I was only trying to—"

"Does Julia know the baby is Derek's?" I interrupt, raising my eyebrows at Jasmine.

Julia's mouth drops open.

"Oh, Claire," Jasmine says, tutting sadly. "Stop imagining things. Derek and I have already had this conversation with you. Please, for heaven's sake, take our advice and get some help. The offer is still there to share this experience with you, but you need to get your head sorted out first. I won't put the baby in danger. Make an appointment with your doctor or go back on your medication. Derek has been so worried about you. Hasn't he, Jules?"

Jasmine looks at Julia who nods solemnly.

"You were told to leave." My fists clench and unclench at my sides. What I wouldn't love to do to this evil woman. "Go!" I yell.

"Bye, Claire," Julia says, springing into action. She tugs on Jasmine's arm. "Good luck with your new shop. I really hope everything works out."

Jasmine allows herself to be led to her—Derek's—car, but not before she shoots me one last self-satisfied smirk.

Back in my shop, Kira thrusts a hot coffee in my direction, and I cup it with both palms, absorbing its warmth.

"She lied just now, didn't she?" Kira asks. "She is having Derek's baby, isn't she?"

My throat has closed over, so I can only nod, yes.

"And Derek won't let her tell anyone because it would expose his affair," Kira says, but it isn't a question. "She loves rubbing that in your face but then makes you look as though you're crazy and jealous if you try to tell anyone else."

While Kira puts it all together, I take a sip of coffee, willing the hot liquid would thaw the chill in my blood from seeing Jasmine.

"What a piece of work," Kira says, her eyes narrowed into hard slits. "I wanted that bastard Derek to get what he deserved after the way he's treated you, and it looks like my wish has already come true. Imagine having to live with that shrew day after day."

But it appears Derek's wish really has come true. Tears burn my eyes, but I don't let them fall. He might be having a girl, but it won't be Katie.

Our beautiful little girl is gone. Nothing can bring her back.

And nothing and no one can ever replace her.

I tell myself that over and over, but it only goes so far in easing the pain. What I wouldn't give to have her back. To hold her in my arms one more time...

"Are you okay?" Kira asks softly, concern reflected in her eyes.

I take a deep breath. It catches in my throat. I drag in another. Better. I place my hand on Kira's arm. "I will be." I summon a small, reassuring smile. It's shaky, but it's a start.

The moment stretches.

"There's nothing you can do," I tell Kira. "There's nothing *I* can do. Except get on with my life. And that is what I intend to do."

"As much as I'd like to see that bitch get what she deserves," Kira says, "you're right. The best revenge is success."

But it's not even about revenge for me. It's still about survival. One day at a time, the way it has been for the last three years.

"This place looks wonderful," Kira says. "Zach did a great job. And, yes, this is a deliberate change of subject."

I look around the shop—the symbol of my future—and forcefully shove the past and Jasmine behind me.

"Yes, it really is beautiful," I say. Zach and some boys from the Village have spent the last week fitting it out with shelves and a beautifully polished timber floor in the display window. Zach somehow transformed this ex-carpet business into a spectacular designer showroom.

"A space fit for a famous designer," he'd told me with a wink that I'd felt all the way to my toes.

Kira is grinning from ear to ear. "Look at you," she says. "One mention of his name, and you're reduced to a puddle on the floor."

"Nothing has actually happened between us yet," I point out. "We're just friends."

"It will," Kira says. "Zach's rare. There aren't many men like him around. He's giving you space. Waiting for you to signal that you're ready."

I'd have to be dead to not be aware of the powerful attraction between us. But I'm not as confident as Kira that Zach is giving me space. What if, after seeing the messy wreckage of my marriage, he's having second thoughts?

What if we've somehow missed that stage and have now slipped into the friend zone? Because he's certainly turned out to be the best friend I've ever had.

"I've invited him out to dinner." I don't know why I lower my voice as though I'm imparting some great secret. Perhaps it's because of the way my body tingles with awareness at the thought of being alone with him in a romantic setting.

"When?" Kira's eyes twinkle, making my blush deepen. God, I feel like a schoolgirl.

"Tonight. To celebrate and thank him for all the help he's given me these last few weeks. Especially with the shop."

Kira laughs. "Look at you, all hot and flustered. Zach, Zach, Zach—"

I swat her away.

"What are you going to wear?"

"I…uh." I frown. "I haven't really thought about it—" I think about what people wear all day long. I guess when it comes to me, I'm over it already.

Kira shakes her head in exasperation and begins to sift through the dresses on display. "What about this?" She holds up a slinky, off-the-rack red dress I designed to be customized.

"Kira! No!"

She frowns at the dress then at me. "Why not?"

"Well," I drawl. "One–it's blood red, and two–it's far too short. It's designed for someone half my height. It will look like a T-shirt on me."

"How dare you call this stunning red dress a T-shirt!" Kira says, hugging the dress to her as though offended on its behalf. "Don't you listen to her," she coos at the dress then thrusts it toward me. "You're wearing this. It's perfect, and it only needs a nip in at the waist and a tweak at the neckline. Wear it with these heels." Kira holds up a pair of the shoes we keep in different sizes for customers so we can get the correct dress length. "They're your size, and they'll look hot."

I look at the dress. And I do like the idea of wearing the matching heels. But—

"Zach will think I'm coming on to him."

"So?"

"I don't want him to think I'm throwing myself at him." There's that niggling doubt again. What if I'm now just another charity case to Zach like the kids in the Village?

"The dress is an invitation, that's all," Kira says.

"That dress is more than just an invitation; it's a flashing neon sign." What if it makes Zach uncomfortable and ruins the relationship? I can just imagine his embarrassed excuses as he backs away. *"Claire, you're a good friend, but I just don't think of you that way..."*

I shake my head. "No, I can't. I think I'll wear the navy dress." I make my way over to a lovely knee-length shift dress. I could wear my comfy flats.

"Bah!" Kira says, ripping the navy dress away. She rolls it in a ball and hides it underneath the counter. "Touch it, and I'll infest your car with a family of tiger snakes. You're wearing the red dress, and that's final."

I groan. "Kira, it might as well have 'fuck me' embroidered across the plunging neckline."

"And I bet that man knows how to fuck—" Kira breaks off and fans herself with exaggerated flare.

I laugh, but I can picture myself with a naked Zach. He's towering over me, taking control. My nipples harden painfully, and my mouth dries. I already have an intense sexual attraction to him; how will I possibly hide it wearing that dress?

Maybe Kira is right. It's time to find out where I stand. If Zach's not interested in a relationship with me, it's better I know now, right? Get that little talk out of the way.

But if he is... I glance down at the dress. How soon is too soon to sleep with someone after you've separated from your husband? What are the rules? My heart races at the thought. I don't know what I'd do with a man like Zach. Derek is the only man I've ever had sex with. And he says I'm a cold fish. I envy Kira's confidence and wish I had more experience to draw upon.

"Seriously," Kira says. "Have you forgotten what you're always saying to clients? A confident woman dresses for herself, not a man. Look hot because you can. Not because you're seeking something from a man. Wear the dress for you."

Wear the dress for me.

I take the dress from Kira, hold it up against my body, and eye myself critically in the mirror. I never wear red.

Derek would think it's trashy. Cheap.

But there is nothing cheap or trashy about this dress. I should know; I designed it. It's both classy *and* super-sexy. I designed it for a woman who is sure of who she is and her place in the world.

A woman with enough courage and self-confidence to pull off wearing a sexy little red dress.

A woman who'd wear it for herself.

"I'll do it."

CHAPTER 22

*Z*ach's sea-green eyes scorch my skin as a waitress escorts me across the dimly lit restaurant to our table. Candle flames flicker and dance in crystal holders on intimate round tables, and a pianist plays a seductive song on the glossy black, baby grand in the corner. I'm conscious of heads turning in my direction as I walk. It's the dress. I resist the urge to tug it down or adjust the plunging neckline, determined to wear the dress and not let it wear me—advice I'm always giving my clients.

Zach stands, and now all I can see is him.

When I reach our table, he embraces me. I breathe him in, his now familiar masculine scent putting me at ease.

"Damn," he says, swallowing hard. "I can barely look at you in that dress."

I smile at what I take to be a compliment. Seeing Zach dressed so formally reminds me of the night we first met. When somehow his watch got caught on a tiny loop of thread on my dress. What were the chances?

That night, he was wearing a black silk shirt with the sleeves rolled up at his wrists, and I'll never forget how dangerously sexy and mysterious he'd appeared to me. Tonight, his six-foot-two frame is encased in a dark, midnight blue suit and a crisp white shirt without a tie, unbuttoned at the collar.

I know him better now. His rock star looks are still raw and dark, but

I interpret them differently now. The dangerous edges have been smoothed by the kindness in his heart. Appearance aside, the effect of being in his presence, as always, is immediate and powerful. My mouth is dry, and my pulse is racing. Sexual tension is crackling so loud in the space between us I'm sure everyone can hear.

A waiter appears, and we use the next few moments to decide our choice of wine and meal. When we are alone again, our eyes meet. I let the moment draw out. His lids lower, and his eyes darken with desire.

"Thank you so much for all your help with the shop," I say, to fill the silence. The sentiment, although heartfelt, isn't adequate. But how do I find the words to tell him how much everything he's done means to me? For simply being there. A tower of strength and calm during my personal storm.

"When I see Sam and the boys next, I'll thank them, too," I add. "They've worked really hard this last week. The shop looks beautiful."

"You can come with me to the Village on the weekend if you like," Zach says. His voice seems a little deeper tonight, his Australian accent a little more pronounced. "They'd love to see you."

"I'd like that."

The waiter is back with our wine, and we both reach for our glasses at the same time the moment he leaves. Zach's casual ease is absent tonight. He appears uncomfortable in this setting, but hell, so am I.

"With all my drama, this is kind of like our first official date." I blurt the thought that has been rolling around in my brain all day, and my face immediately heats. What the hell did I say that for? What if he doesn't look at this as a date?

I try to read his face.

Glance away before he can read too much into mine.

"I didn't mean to assume it's a date," I rush to say. "If you think it's just..." Oh God. What is it about this man that gets me so easily flustered?

I take a breath and straighten. "What is this? Between us, I mean." I hold my breath for his answer, mentally preparing myself for a polite rebuff. Either way, I have to know. I might be making a fool of myself over this man, but he's worth the risk.

His eyes travel to my left hand. There's no wedding ring, hasn't been for a while, but there's still a faint indentation of where it had been for eight years. I am right. The trouble with Derek has killed the potential for the spark between us to develop into anything deeper. My baggage is too fresh, too heavy.

My cheeks burn. "I'm sorry. Forget I said anything."

"Claire—" He stops.

I wait for him to say more, but the moment stretches as I watch his fingers move across the table as though pressing invisible strings on the neck of his guitar.

"You don't know me, Claire," he says eventually. His eyes are downcast, his fingers playing a tune only he can hear. He reaches for his wineglass. "Not really. To know me, you'd have to know the man I once was. Know what I have done. What I'm still capable of today... And I can't help but wonder if you would even want this to be a date if you did."

I already know his past has been...colorful, for want of a better word. From the things he's said, the fact he broke into my shop. But his warnings, everything he's done, have been to help me, not hurt me. I know who the man is today. That's all that matters.

"If you don't talk to me, how will you ever know what I will think?"

The challenge hangs, a heavy weight in the space between us. I need him to trust me, to tell me. Only so that I can prove to him that it makes no difference to me.

Zach remains silent, dark eyes swirling with dark intensity, tension pouring off him in almost tangible waves.

It was a mistake to start this conversation here, foolish to think he'd open up just because I demand it. I've ruined what should have been a fun evening. A celebration. Tears blur my vision, but I blink them back.

I won't be blinded by another man who's not what he appears to be.

Who *is* Zach Argos?

Can I trust him?

And how do I turn away if I can't?

"Claire—" He grabs my hand, the one without the ring. "I wish I could be the man you think you see when you look at me." His thumb traces over the indentation. "But I'm not."

I release a shaky breath and entwine my fingers with his. Tight. I can't let go. I won't let go. *Whatever demons haunt you, Zach, they won't scare me away.*

His chest expands with a deep breath, and I'm filled with nerves. What he is about to tell me might change everything.

"You know my father died when I was fourteen." Zach's eyes remain on our joined fingers.

"Yes." He told me that at the Village.

"What I didn't tell you was that it was me who killed him." Zach's eyes meet mine, and the pain reflected in them stops my heart.

Stunned, I squeeze his hand, momentarily at a loss for words.

"I'll tell you what happened, but it's not going to make that okay. There's no atonement for something like that. I'm going to hell, plain and simple. But over the years, I've made my peace with that.

His expression is pained, his jaw set, but behind his eyes are the remnants of a lost and broken boy.

Our meals arrive. But the aroma of expensive fish and creamy white wine sauce churns my stomach. I push my plate aside, watching Zach do the same with his.

"Both my parents were addicts. Anger and violence were a part of that life. As it does, it became a way of life for me, too. By the time I was eleven, twelve, I was already on a path of self-destruction. I rebelled at the life fate handed me, rebelled at the abusive hand of my father.

"My mother and father never married, but they lived together as though they were. My mother was only sixteen when she gave birth to me in a public toilet block in North Beach. My eighteen-year-old father was high as a kite at the time and bolted when the ambulance came. I was born addicted to the drug Ice."

I made a small noise in the back of my throat, and Zach turns his faraway gaze in my direction.

"I'm sorry," I say, my throat tight.

"It was a long time ago," Zach says. But his breathing is slightly labored, and his hands are clenching and unclenching around his glass.

"It wasn't until I was about nine that I fully realized what that addiction meant financially, emotionally and psychically for their capacity to be parents. It was also around that time that I started standing up to my father. I could no longer sit back while he abused my mother. I was young, but I was tough and reckless in that way angry young boys are. But it only made things worse."

Zach takes a sip of his drink, and I watch his throat work as he swallows.

"One afternoon in August after I'd turned fourteen, I came home from school to find mum cowering in a corner. Her arms were wrapped around herself in the way she did when he broke her ribs. Both eyes were black, and her lip was cut. She told me to leave, to go down the park and play footy with my mates. But there was something different in her voice that day. Despite the way she was huddled, she didn't seem scared. Her eyes were vacant, her voice hollow. She'd given up.

"The place was trashed, tables overturned, chairs broken. Something had snapped in Dad. I rushed to tackle him, but he broke a chair over my head. Before I could stand, he picked Mum up by her hair, held her against the wall with one hand, and with the other, he punched her in the stomach. It seemed as though his fist went right through her and connected with the wall behind her. Her eyes rolled back in her head, and when he let go, she slumped to the floor like a ragdoll. I knew this time, she wouldn't pull through."

A muscle along Zach's jaw was twitching, his eyes hard.

"The last word she ever said to me was run. *Run*," Zach sneers. "As if. Dad was strung out, but he had the abnormal strength of an addict. But I was tall, and I'd been working out on the playground equipment at the park. He pulled out his blade, and the next thing I knew, it was in my hand. And he wasn't moving."

At fourteen, Zach had killed his biological father. How do you even begin to reconcile that? Carry the weight of that around with you into adulthood?

"Mum died of massive internal bleeding. Gus died of knife wounds inflicted by me. I was told there were twelve of them."

His gaze, dark, hard, and frighteningly cold, meets mine. "I only remember the first two."

A shiver trickles down my spine.

Zach blinks, and his gaze clears.

I start to breathe again.

"My biggest regret is that I didn't do something soon enough to save my mother. Maybe I could have gotten her some help. Maybe I could have found a job, shown her a better way of life."

"You were fourteen. It wasn't your responsibility to get a job and fix your mum."

Zach's childhood was filled with neglect and abuse. And he's the one to feel guilty? Anger replaces the horror of what Zach endured.

"Your father got what he deserved," I say fiercely.

Zach shrugs. "Maybe. Who's to say what is reasonable? What is justice?"

"But surely—"

"I can still remember bouncing on his knee when I was three." Zach's voice is thick and tight. "Dad taught me to play footy, and he taught me to fight. Dad bought me my first ice cream and he gave me my first beer. I was eight. It was the same year he gave me my first guitar. It was stolen, but he was so damn proud when I learned to play it. I worked hard to be good at it. Even through the violence, the abuse, to me, to my mother, I was still the boy who wanted his father to love him. To be proud of him. Nothing is black and white."

Except that Zach killed his father.

He is staring out the window. A flash of lightning briefly lights up the street in front of the restaurant, illuminating a patch of tumultuous Indian Ocean just behind.

I should say something. But all I can see is the image of Zach as a young boy, his perfect features, softer and more innocent, and the horror he endured at such a young age.

"There's something you also need to know," Zach says, not looking at me.

Another flash of lightning. I feel uneasy, but I tell myself it's just the storm. "What is it?" My voice catches in my throat, and it's barely a whisper.

Zach turns those dark eyes on me, storm clouds rivaling those outside, but concentrated like a mini cyclone.

"I blacked out at the time I killed him. I remember the knife in my hand, and I remember stabbing him twice. I don't remember the other ten times."

The restaurant fades away, and all I can hear is the pounding of my heart.

"I stabbed someone ten times and don't remember," Zach repeats with emphasis. "What if I'm capable of doing it again?"

The words are a challenge. They hang, a menacing specter in the space between us.

I fully understand now that this is what he meant when he said I didn't know the man he really was. What he was truly capable of.

But aren't we all capable of murder, faced with the right situation? I would have killed for Katie. Without thinking twice. It's not so difficult to imagine a son killing to protect his mother, even if he was too late.

Zach may have killed someone, but do I believe Zach's a murderer?

Am I afraid he'll kill again or be a danger to me?

I've seen the man he's grown into. The boys at the Village are proof of the way he's transformed his life.

"I'll take you home now." He looks out the window as he speaks as though he isn't prepared for whatever he thinks he'll see. Does he think I'm disgusted by his story? His actions?

The realization hits me like a blow to the chest.

I love Zach Argos. With a power I never thought possible.

But the words don't leave my mouth.

The walls are closing in on me. The restaurant, so beautiful when I walked in less than an hour ago, now feels like a concrete cage.

"I don't want to be here anymore," I say, and his shoulders fall slightly forward. "But I don't want you to take me home," I whisper. "Unless it's your home. And you want me there."

Zach turns to me, studies my face intently, slowly. I don't know what he expects to find there, but I feel nothing but admiration for the self-made man seated across the table from me who has overcome such odds.

He shakes his head in disbelief.

"If I were you, I'd be making a land speed record through that door right now," he says. "Never to return."

"Would you?" I raise my eyebrows. "I doubt that. I've seen what you're like when you fight for something you want."

"Am I, Claire?" he asks, his voice low and deep. "Am I what you want?"

"I've never wanted something more."

He squeezes his eyes shut, and when he opens them, what I see in his expression stops my heart. The ever-present electricity crackles between us, a life force of its own.

Whatever is between Zach and me, it's raw.

It's real.

It's frightening in its intensity.

But…it's also new, and very fragile.

Zach stands and, taking my hand in his much larger one, helps me stand. "Come with me," he says. "I have something I want to show you."

Zach takes me to a secluded lookout only a ten-minute drive along the coast from the restaurant. A short walk through the sand dunes, and we come to a run-down shelter overgrown with shrubs and hidden by trees.

"What is this place?" I ask.

"It's where I come to hide away from the world."

From our position high in the dunes, I can only imagine what it would be like to watch a sunrise or sunset from here on a clear day. There's not even a breeze, but directly above us, black clouds swirl and tumble through the sky. There's a magical quality about this spot. Or maybe it's Zach.

It starts raining. The nice type of rain where there's no wind, and the drops are heavy and fall straight down. The smell of rain on the warm sand and timber shelter rises around us, the sound of the drops a loud drumming on the tin roof above us. I can breathe easily now, having left the nightmare of Zach's story back at the restaurant. Out here in the elements, with the vast ocean spread out before us, it feels as though nothing can touch us.

Zach shrugs out of his jacket and places it around my shoulders.

"You know, this is the second jacket I'm giving you," he says. "You'll have my whole wardrobe soon."

"I'll give you *this* jacket back," I tell him. "But so you know, I'm keeping your other one."

A smile plays at his lips. "It's yours. I like that you have it."

"What happened after," I ask. "How did you get from there to where you are today?"

"I lost my best friend, Matt—Matthew Bagnall—to an overdose, the following year. We were fifteen. It had been a hellish twelve months. The police investigation, court appearances, counseling." His jaw hardens. "I was the one who found Matt with the needle still in his arm. I stared at him for the longest time, seeing myself. My future. I even resented him because he'd found a way to escape. And he'd left me behind."

Oh, Zach!

"I met Matt's uncle, Chris, at his funeral. Two months at his bush property, and I was clean and sober. He taught me how to live off the land, how to build a cabin, and how to surf. I owe him my life."

"Is Chris still at the village? I don't' remember seeing him."

Zach shakes his head. "He died of lung cancer a few years back. He said helping me eased the guilt he felt over not being able to save his nephew." Zach clears his throat.

"But he saved far more than just me. I met Richard not long after that. I didn't go looking for him. I'm not a martyr. Meeting Richard was an accident... I tripped over his goddamn boots as he lay in an alley. For a moment, I thought he was dead, just like Matt. I swore at him, at the senselessness, the hopelessness of it all. I kicked him, and he sat up. I had startled him, and when I looked into his eyes, I couldn't walk away.

"So that night, I took him back to my house then out to the bush, gave him an axe, and pointed to the trees. He looked at me like I'd lost my mind. I remembered that look—must have been the same one that had been on my face when Chris gave me the axe. But Richard swung at the tree, swing after swing. Every hurt, all the anger at the circumstances of his life pouring out."

I struggle to swallow past the lump in my throat.

"There's a certain feeling when the first tree comes down. It's cathartic. Richard lay down next to that tree and cried. After that tree there was another, but his energy was different. His anger transformed into something productive. Using only what materials we had, we built a timber cabin. His house. And that's how the Village got started."

"Why don't you turn what you do legal?" I ask. "Surely if the authorities see what you did, the difference you make..."

"It won't happen." Zach's jaw tightens.

"But—"

"I won't get the licenses, Claire. Besides, I won't say I'm sorry or beg forgiveness from a society that pretended I never existed. I won't play in bureaucracy's sandbox. Not my style."

Zach shrugs.

"Besides, there are plenty of people who do good shit legally. I'm not the only one doing what I can to help kids from living rough. There are lots of organizations, church groups...even government departments, in their own way, are doing what they can. In the grand scheme of things, I'm not making much of a difference at all. There are plenty of others who do more. But if I can help one person not go through what I went through, then it's worth it. To me."

I move closer to Zach, and he puts his arm around me. The barriers between us have fallen away. I've never felt so close to someone.

"You're an amazing man, Zach."

He looks at me for a moment. "There are many people who will disagree with that. But your opinion is the only one that matters to me." His expression softens as he leans in, his full, warm lips touching mine.

He looks into my eyes, and as the moment stretches, I wonder if he sees the question he avoided in the restaurant. A question independent of his past. *What is this between us?*

He frowns as though trying to put into words the intensity of emotion that is flowing through and around us.

From the start.

Even before it should have.

I love you. I want to say the words. I want *him* to say the words.

The silence draws out...

"Shut up," I say with a smile to let him off the hook. "You talk too much."

He crushes his mouth to mine, and I'm instantly on fire. I kiss him back. He's rough, but I'm rough with him, too. He wraps his arm around my waist and pulls me flush against him. He runs his hand up the bare skin of my neck before his hands tangle in the up-do style of my hair, making strands start to spill down, hairpins falling at our feet.

"I've ruined your hair," he says, his lips brushing against mine as he speaks.

"You're a bad boy, Zach."

"You have no idea."

"Show me," I challenge, and his eyes darken dangerously.

"Careful what you wish for," he says. But I want him. All of him. Not just the parts he thinks I can handle.

His fingers tangle through my hair as he pulls out the remainder of the pins.

"Why are there so many?" he grumbles after struggling for a few minutes, and it makes me laugh.

"There's always something hidden behind the veneer." I was talking about hair, fashion, but Zach stills. Looks at me for more than a heartbeat. I get the sense that he is still holding something back. After admitting he killed his father, what could he possibly not be able to share?

I shove aside an unwanted rush of unease and shake my hair until it's loose and tumbling down my back.

"You are so fucking beautiful." His voice is thick and hoarse with need.

The rain is coming down harder now, a light sea breeze kicking in, covering us with a fine mist.

"Will you come back to my place?"

I bite my bottom lip and nod.

He pulls me roughly against him, and I feel the hardness of his body against my soft curves. "I want to hear you say it."

"I want you to take me back to your house," I say. "And into your arms and into your bed."

He scoops me off the ground, pushing my back against the timber wall. His lips press against mine, and I wrap my hands around his neck. My grip is tight, my nails biting into his skin. I arch my back, pressing myself harder against him, not breaking the kiss. He traces his fingers down my neck, across my shoulders.

It's not enough.

It'll never be enough.

I break the kiss. I'm breathing heavily, but so is he.

"Let's make a dash for the car," he says. His voice is rough and oh, so sexy.

"Okay then. Ready?"

The downpour intensifies, and a brilliant flash of lightning illuminates the sky above us, followed almost immediately by a loud crack of thunder.

It startles me, and I dig my nails into Zach's arm. Even after all these years, storms still scare me. When the whole sky lights up above us and thunder shakes the ground beneath our feet, I lunge at him, jumping up and wrapping my legs around his waist. Reflexively, he takes a step back, adjusts my weight in his arms as I bury my face in his neck.

He laughs, but I don't regret overreacting because now I'm in his arms. He crushes his lips to mine. My blood is pumping wildly. With my legs wrapped around his waist, he steps back under the cover, sheltering my body with his. The wind has kicked up now. Zach's back must be getting wet, but he doesn't appear to mind. Or notice. He's kissing me hard. My hands are on the back of his head, his neck, tangled in his damp hair. Now they're at the front of his shirt, and I'm fumbling with the buttons. Then, with both hands, I rip it open.

He pulls back, watching my hands as they explore his chest. Even in the dim light, I can see his skin lined with scars. I trace the larger scars with my fingertips. Evidence of the journey of his life carved into skin. Overwhelmed, tears rise unbidden to burn my lids.

I feel a tear roll down my cheek, but I don't let him see. I lean in to kiss him.

"Claire—?" He pulls back, concern creasing his forehead. "Are you crying?""

"No."

The tenderness in his expression causes another tear to roll down my cheek. He looks at me quizzically for a moment, and I try to put into words what is welling up inside of me. "Will you do something for me?"

"Anything." His eyes search mine.

My fingers feather down his stomach and begin working on his button and fly. "I want you to fuck me. Right here. Right now. Here. In the wind and the rain with the storm and ocean raging around us." I've never done anything as adventurous or sexy in my life. But right now, I need that–need Zach–more than I need my next breath.

I unzip his fly and wrap my hand around his erection. He groans, low and deep.

He nips my neck with his teeth–hard–and any hope of rational thought disappears. He unwraps my fingers from his straining cock and places my arms around his shoulders.

"I want you, Zach." My demand is breathless. "Now." I arch my back and rub my body against his. "I have to know what you feel like inside me."

The rain is bucketing down around us, hammering on the tin roof. But we are surprisingly dry, the sudden downpour a temporary cocoon. It feels as though we're the only two people in the world. A trickle of rain drips off the tips of his hair. I lean forward to lick the droplets off his neck, enjoying the salty taste on my tongue.

The low rumble of thunder is background noise, melding with the blood rushing past my ears as my need for him climbs to an explosive level. He kisses me with a fervor that matches my own.

He slides my dress down off my shoulders, takes a moment to appreciate my breasts before cupping one in his palm, squeezing my nipple between his thumb and finger.

"I want to learn every erogenous zone on your body," he says. "But that will have to wait until next time. And there will be a next time. And one after that. You're under my skin now. *Mine!*" My body reacts to the rough possessive growl in his tone.

I tangle the fingers of one hand in his hair, and the other grips his back, sure my nails are biting into his skin. He doesn't appear to mind. I breathe him in, his scent, intoxicatingly sensual, mixing with the clean, crisp wind and rain of the storm echoing around us.

He traces a palm up my thigh, beneath my dress, and with a quick flick of his wrist, rips my panties away. I part my legs for him, and he traces a finger back and forth, circling my clit before plunging inside of me. I cry out and enjoy the low possessive growl that rises from somewhere deep inside of him. I have never felt like this before. Never felt so overcome. So deliciously overwhelmed.

He's exquisite torture. A knife's edge from being too much.

"I don't want to hurt you," he murmurs, his fingers massaging me. He lowers his head and traces his tongue along the long column of my neck.

He sucks hard then, using his teeth, bites down. I scream, and my breath comes in short pants. He chuckles as he continues his relentless assault on my body.

"Zach!" I beg when the need for release becomes too much. "I can't wait any longer. Please."

He reaches into his pocket, fumbles with his wallet. He rips the package open with his teeth and rolls it on. He lifts me up, and I wrap my legs around him. His erection is a hard, demanding thickness between us.

He grabs both my wrists in one hand and pins them above my head. Holding my gaze, he positions himself then thrusts into me. I cry out.

"Look at me," he demands. "I don't want you to close your eyes, not for one second."

He thrusts inside me, and I become painfully aware that I will never be able to get enough of him. The powerful way he takes control makes me hunger for him even more. Now that I've had this taste of Zach, I will crave him for eternity.

Holding me against the wall of the shelter, he alters his angle to penetrate deeper...harder...faster... I cry out his name, thrashing my head from side to side, my need for more making me wild. He's watching my face as though drinking in each nuance in my expression as I writhe beneath him, as much as his restraints will allow.

"Zach! Oh God, Zach!" I scream, and a crack of thunder shatters the sky above us.

My whole body shivers, and my orgasm explodes over his cock in tremor after tremor. Zach finds his own release as he continues to thrust inside me, drawing out the last of my climax.

My body trembles, turning limp in his arms.

He holds me close, pulling me off the wall and against his chest. He tugs my dress up over my breasts and back down over my thighs and wraps his jacket around me. He yanks his trousers back into place then scoops me up into his arms.

The rain has subsided to a gentle mist, droplets landing on his face as he contemplates me with an expression I can't read.

My heart slams an irregular beat against my ribcage as he walks me through the sand dunes back to his car. He lowers me into the seat and buckles me in.

The ride back to his house is silent. The motor's deep rumble is soothing, and I glance in the side mirror.

A white Volvo sedan is trailing us.

CHAPTER 23

Zach pulls into his driveway, and I check the side mirror again, half expecting to see Derek pull in behind us. What would he do? What is he capable of?

But it's mercifully dark. No headlights. I hope he's continued on and hasn't killed the engine to stay out of sight.

I've caught him numerous times, driving slowly past my shop, even my new apartment. That, I can understand. He's keeping an eye on what I'm up to with the business, where I'm living. But would he go to such great lengths to follow me at night, during a storm, to watch a private moment?

It sickens me that Derek may have seen, however distantly, my first time with Zach.

Zach has been taking no chances. Sam, Aidan, Richard, and Zach have been taking shifts watching my place for the last month.

Despite my protests that it isn't necessary.

Derek won't hurt me.

Not physically, anyway.

Or would he?

The brutal truth is I really have no idea how desperate Derek is.

And what lengths he will go to get me back

"Are you okay?" The sound of Zach's voice sends warmth through my body. I blow out a breath and smile. "Yes."

"I can take you back to your house if you want me to?"

"No." I lean across and kiss him. Hard. The electricity that's always between us sparks, and all thoughts of Derek blank from my mind. No sooner does Zach break away and slip out of the car than my door opens, and he pulls me out. He sweeps me off my feet and into his arms. Until tonight, I've never been carried before. I'm tall, far from a petite bundle. Derek never even attempted to pick me up. But in Zach's arms, I feel light and feminine.

A woman being conquered by her man.

It's an addictive, heady feeling.

Zach puts me down to unlock the front door, and once inside, he kicks the door shut behind us. He kisses me as he walks me backwards. My legs brush up against something, and his arms lift me onto the rich timber of his kitchen table.

He shrugs out of his ripped shirt and tosses it aside. I throw my head back, and his lips trace and nip down my neck, across my shoulders, while his hands release the zipper that runs down the back of my dress. The material falls open, and he stops as my breasts are exposed, and he can see them clearly for the first time. I search his eyes. Please let him like what he sees.

"My God, Claire. You're even more beautiful than I imagined." Relief washes over me the same time his mouth reaches my breast. He cups one breast with his hand, then draws the other into his mouth and sucks hard.

I cry out as a rush of desire floods my body. Need, urgent and hot, pools between my thighs. I squirm beneath him, unable to keep still. His mouth is exquisite torture. I'm back on the edge of orgasm, desperate for release. As addictive as Zach's mouth is, I need to feel him inside me. I need him to fill me again.

My palms on his chest, I push him back and slide off the table. My dress falls to the floor. I undo the button on his pants, and then his hands take over, removing the remainder of his clothes until he is naked in front of me.

I barely have time to appreciate his perfect frame, his wide shoulders and chest, the defined abs on his stomach, before we are back in each other's arms. His skin is tanned from the Australian sun, his body fit from outdoor work, not pull-ups in a gym. He's ripped, and he's one hundred percent pure male.

And right now, he's all mine.

Our bodies are coated in a layer of sweat. I run my fingers down his back to cup his high, round ass. He groans as I squeeze his perfect firmness.

"Turn around." Zach's voice is deep and rough.

"What?" I blink up at him, my mind having difficulty forming the most basic thoughts.

He turns me around roughly, bends me over. The timber is cool against my stomach, my nipples pebbling against the hard wood. His breath is against the skin on my neck. Then he kisses a trail down my back, my hips, my thighs. He spreads me wide and slides his fingers inside me.

"Do you like that?"

I only realize I'm gasping when I try to say yes. Incapable of speech, I push back against him.

He withdraws his fingers, and I hear foil tearing. I feel his solid hardness at my entrance, hear Zach take a breath before he plunges in hard. I cry out, pleasure stealing my breath.

Zach is large and so different than Derek. Zach's power and sheer presence surround and swallow me.

"Sorry," Zach rasps. "Do you need me to be more gentle?"

I hear the tension in his voice.

"Take me the way you want me," I say. "The way you've fantasized."

"Fuck, Claire."

He drives into me, but after the initial burn, my body adjusts to accommodate his size, and the heat turns into pleasure. Zach's body slaps against mine as he thrusts.

He leans over me, grabs a handful of hair, and yanks my head back, then kisses my neck, gently nipping my skin. He's rough, he's tender, and the combination is exquisite. His cock fills me completely. His hands and mouth are all over me, and I can't get enough.

His damp hair brushes my shoulder, my back, as he kisses and licks my skin, murmuring words I can't make out, but that doesn't matter. The sound of his voice alone is as sexy as hell.

Before this, I'd only ever had sex in a bed. And now I've had sex at the beach during a storm and bent over a table in the same night. It doesn't feel real. I don't recognize this strange, wanton woman. But I like her much more than I ever liked the other one.

Zach grabs my hips firmly between his large hands, and I cry out at each blinding thrust. He reaches between my legs, and his fingers rub my clit.

Already on the edge, the single touch sends me spiraling over. My scream surprises me as I'm usually silent during sex. But I'm gasping and calling out as Zach reaches his own climax, stimulating mine and drawing it out.

He roars my name, and it stops my heart.

It is the sexiest thing I've ever heard.

And already, I want to hear it again.

But my knees are weak, and Zach tenderly lifts my boneless body off the table and into his arms. He kisses me on the forehead, eyelids, cheeks, and then lips.

"Claire, you still with me?"

I part my eyelids a crack, just enough to see his stormy green eyes staring into mine. His dark hair is in damp curls around his face, and his tongue swipes across his lower lip and gorgeous teeth.

It's too much.

He's too much.

Is any of this even real?

I had no idea that sex could be like this, that *I* could feel like this. That such passion, such intense emotion was possible. If my life hadn't taken an abrupt turn, I would have died not knowing.

My heart is full, pounding out of my chest. My body is heavy, and I can't keep my eyes open, but when I shut them, a smile takes over my face.

I feel like I'm falling off the edge of a cliff into something unknown.

Is this what it feels like to fall in love?

Sure, I'd been in love before with Derek. But I'd never had this sense of ambiguity before, of floating and falling at the same time.

I never intended for this to happen. The last thing I wanted was to fall in love so soon. But is it really too soon? How long have I been living married but no longer in love?

Maybe I've been too starved for affection to really know what love is like.

Or maybe it just feels different because, this time around, I've found the right man.

CHAPTER 24

The following morning, I wake in Zach's bed, the scent of us all over the tangled sheets. The sun streams in through the white shutters, and I close my eyes and stretch out my deliciously sore body.

A kiss on my forehead.

A kiss on one eyelid then the other.

A kiss on my cheek.

Then softly, tenderly, a kiss on my lips.

I open my eyes and meet Zach's heavy-lidded gaze.

"Crayfish for lunch?"

I lick my lips. "Mmm, sounds delicious."

He places an arm beneath me, lifts me onto his lap, then stands up and puts me on the floor.

"Hey!" I protest. "Didn't you mean lunch in bed?"

"We can." He grins. "But we have to catch it first."

"What?"

Zach tosses me a pair of my shorts from my bag and a bikini top. "You don't think crays are born in restaurants, do you?"

"Of course not." I hold up the tiny black and green triangles. "You bought this for me?" I ask, hoping he says yes and not that this belonged to someone before me. Then I spot the tag still on it and tear it off.

"I hoped to take you with me when I went surfing one day, and I didn't want the lack of a bikini to be a reason for you to say no."

I turn so that he can tie the strings at the back. I watch him slide on very cool Ripcurl board shorts and run his fingers through his hair. I know this is going to be the extent of his getting ready routine. "Ready?" he asks.

I haven't had a shower, brushed my hair, or even had a coffee yet. "Yes."

He grins, grabs his board with one hand and takes my hand with his other. I expect him to head down to the beach in front of his place, but he surprises me by taking me to his car.

We travel north along the coast to a spot near Two Rocks, on the ocean near the Village. The water is choppy with frothy whitecaps. But the clear blue water within the shelter of the surrounding reef is calm.

He leaves his board in the car, and I comment on it. "The surf's no good here," Zach says. "I'll take you to the Margaret River Pro with me. I'm competing again this year."

I'd love to see Zach riding the waves. In all the time I've lived in Australia, I can't believe I've never gone to watch the World Championship Tour in Margaret River. Now, I find it hard to think of much I'd rather do than watch Zach, chest bare, muscles rippling as he rides a wave...

I must have groaned out loud because Zach looks my way. I smile, but his eyes take in the blush I know is across my face and chest.

"Keep looking at me like that, and we'll have sandwiches for lunch instead."

I consider sacrificing the cray for sex on the beach, but Zach slaps me on the ass.

"Hey!" I protest, surprised at the pleasant way my body responds to the sting of his hand.

He kisses me hard on the lips. But instead of throwing me onto the sand as I want him to, he grabs a long pole with a loop at one end. He slides the snorkel and goggles over his eyes and walks into the ocean, heading through the lagoon to the drop off behind the reef.

He moves with confidence and ease, his powerful muscles rippling across his body like waves onto the shore. He is at one with the water, as powerful and untamed as the ocean itself.

He disappears into the deep blue sea like he never was.

I'm alone on the beach, the ocean's relentless drive sending waves crashing along the shoreline. I breathe deeply, drawing the salty air as deep into my lungs as I can, then exhale, long and hard. I imagine the waves taking the insecurities and fears that belonged to the old Claire and washing them far out to sea.

I could live forever with Zach, no matter where we were. On the beach, in the bush. It doesn't matter as long as I'm with him.

My phone chimes with the message sound. Surprised, I realize Zach must have packed them in our bag. I scrounge through the sunscreen, towels, water bottles, and thongs until I find it, and when I do, I see twelve missed calls.

From Derek.

The outside world seeps in like toxic gas through cracks in a wall.

I check the voicemail, deleting all the messages after the first without listening to them. The first abusive message was enough.

Derek had seen us.

Perhaps crawled behind a bush and watched us.

A shiver of disgust ripples over me.

Damn you, Derek. When am I going to be able to live a day without having to think about you?

There was a time I would have never thought he'd hurt me, but now, after everything he's done, I can no longer say that. It worries me, not knowing what he's capable of. How far he'll go to continue to hurt me. Especially now that he would have received the Family Court application my lawyer filed. That I can't predict the actions of a man I lived with for ten years is a scary prospect.

Enjoy this moment, Claire. This minute.

I use the phone's camera to take a photo of the ocean, of the view from where I'm sitting with my toes buried in the cool sand, the taste of salt on my lips. I want to remember how peaceful this place is.

Slowly, a form rises from the waves. Water rolls down Zach's muscular body in glistening rivulets. It catches the light, clinging to his skin as though not wanting to let go.

In one hand, Zach has the pole. The other hand grips the bodies of two large, wriggling crayfish. His eyes scan the beach briefly before fixing on me.

He grins, and my heart stops dead in my chest. Then it kicks back to life, misfiring and beating in an irregular rhythm.

I can feel the smile on my face stretching a mile wide, using tiny muscles that haven't been used in a long time. I am overwhelmed with happiness. I can't believe this prime specimen of male is heading toward me.

Smiling at me in *that way.*

I dust the sand from my legs and rush into the water to meet him. In contrast to the way Zach glides through the water, I feel like a gangly giraffe, water splashing all around me. A cold wave crashes over me, and I let out a high-pitched shriek.

He laughs, a low throaty rumble. I jump through the waves, throw my arms around his neck, and he braces himself, digging his feet into the sand as he absorbs the impact. He's as solid as the rocks on the beach. I kiss his lips. He tastes salty and fresh like a mouthful of ocean.

"Next time, you'll come out with me." His voice is rough and scratchy from the saltwater and oh, so sexy.

"I'd love that."

"You would?" His eyes search mine.

I'd follow him to the ends of the earth. "Absolutely."

"Let's put these babies to sleep," Zach says, holding up the crays. "I've got some wine that will go perfectly."

I'll do whatever it takes to hold onto this.

Whatever it takes to hold onto him.

And the happiness I never thought I'd find in this lifetime again.

CHAPTER 25

*M*onday morning, I wake to the warmth of sunshine on my cheeks. I open my eyes to find myself in Zach's arms. He's awake, his lips curved into a smile as he watches me.

"Hi." His voice is deep and husky, thick with the remnants of sleep... and fresh desire. He smells so good, and my body instantly responds.

"How is it that you're even more beautiful in the morning than you were in that red dress," he asks, his hand cupping my breast. I groan as his thumb traces over the pebbled nipple.

I can't imagine that to be anywhere near the truth. I've seen myself in the mirror when I've first woken up, it's not a pretty sight. But the conviction in Zach's tone, the tender way he is looking at me now, fills me with warmth.

"I keep waiting to stop wanting you so much," he says. "It never happens. And every moment finds me wanting you even more."

His fingers move in circles on my shoulders then trail down my arms. Softly, gently. I wrap my arms around his neck, pull him down, kiss his lips. He kisses me back. Harder. Letting me instigate, but quickly taking control. His hand cups the back of my head, holding me in place. I surrender.

It feels so right, waking up in Zach's arms. Sleeping in his bed, beneath his fluffy, black-and-red quilt. He's already become familiar, as though I haven't had a life before him. And in a very significant way, I haven't. I might have been existing, but I certainly hadn't been truly alive.

To think, I could have lived that way until the day I died. Experiencing only the grey in a kaleidoscope of color. Safe. *Bland*.

Zach's lips trace along my jaw, slowly down my neck. It takes all my willpower, but I pull away. Despite how many times Zach satisfied me last night, my body is tingling anew, every nerve awake and buzzing, hyper-aware of his every movement.,

"I bet I could change your mind," Zach says with a look that could singe the sheets.

Without a doubt. "I can't," I manage to say, my voice weak. Another kiss...a flick of his tongue...another touch of those long, talented fingers... I could reschedule my appointment.

"Rain check!" I gasp, sitting up. With a low growl, Zach rolls onto his back. I watch his chest expand with each inhale. "You make me forget there's anything else but us," he says. "I don't believe in fairytales, or happy endings." His eyelids are heavy. "But you make me wish I did."

He looks thoughtful a moment, moves his lips as though he is about to say something. But he changes his mind.

I want to ask what he was just about to say, but behind the swirl of desire, so familiar to me now, is something else.

"You don't think we'll have a happy ending?" I tug the sheets, wrapping them tight around my shoulders. It does little to ease the sudden chill enveloping my body.

The weekend is over, and Monday's sunrise has brought with it everything I'd all too easily pretended didn't exist. There's a sense of loss, painful and hollow in the pit of my stomach, making me long for the carefree weekend we'd just shared.

Saturday night, we'd gone to the weekly bonfire at the Village. Mandy's wounds are barely visible now, and her shyness is slowly but surely being replaced by a newfound confidence and zest for life.

Yesterday, Zach and I spent the day alternating between long leisurely walks along the beach and making love on his balcony and in front of the fire, the taste of crayfish and wine on our tongues.

"In my experience," Zach says, "there are only endings. Happiness is short, fleeting moments along the way."

"I don't believe that."

Zach moves across the bed, wraps his arms around me, his chest warm against my back.

"That's one of the things I love about you," he says. "Your eternal optimism." He traces the back of a finger down my cheek, kisses my neck. "I've never felt as though I belonged anywhere," he says, his voice a whisper against my ear. "But being with you, Claire, feels like home."

My heart flutters, but a strange melancholy in his tone keeps me from replying.

Zach's fingers trail down my arm to my elbow and back in long strokes. "I don't want there to be any secrets between us."

A sense of trepidation runs down my spine. "That makes me think there's still something significant you haven't told me." I try to laugh as though he's going to laugh back.

Zach's body tenses.

"I mean, of course we don't know everything about each other, how could we? But... Zach...is there something I should know?"

"Claire—"

"You can tell me anything," I say, bracing myself. Why is he struggling? What could be worse than confessing you killed your own father?

His silence, this strange reaction tells me more than words ever can.

Words can lie. But body language rarely does.

I'm in over my head with this man.

I stare at him, so impossibly gorgeous, sunlight throwing shadows across his face. I want to tell him whatever he has to say doesn't matter.

But it does.

I'd be a fool to forget.

Blind trust—that's for the young, the naive.

I am neither.

Not anymore.

"If there's something you need to share, now's the time." Before I... before I what? Fall in love with him? Too late for that.

Damn him. Only a fool keeps repeating the same mistakes.

Throwing my legs over the side of the bed, I reach for my T-shirt and slip it over my head. I don't look at him, not because it hurts, even if it does, but because I don't want him to see the vulnerability in my eyes.

On shaky legs, I stand. Collect my belongings. "Never mind," I say. "You don't have to answer me. I'm going to have a shower. At my place."

"Claire!" I stop at the door, my shoes tangled in the outfit I was wearing yesterday. "Claire. Please." His voice cracks, and I look back at him.

Zach's dark hair is mussed, and he looks so sexy on the rumpled sheets. I look away.

"I have a client coming to the shop at ten," I say, hating the tremble in my voice. "I have to go."

I clear my throat, determined to be strong. Goddamn, I haven't learnt a single thing about not giving men the power to hurt me.

Zach curses and gets out of bed.

He grabs a clean pair of jeans out of a drawer and slides them on. I put my jeans on as well, and it feels as though not just clothes are coming between us; they are solid walls.

"That's not…you've taken this all wrong."

"Taken what wrong Zach?" I demand. He thrusts his hands through his hair.

"I had no idea that it would be like this between us," he says.

Is that men speak for he wants to slow things down?

"I wasn't prepared either, Zach," I say, my hurt hiding behind a sudden rush of anger. "But you don't have to worry, I'm not looking for another husband. I don't need a man to complete me. I'm not asking anything of you."

"Claire… That's not… *Fuck!*"

He snatches up yesterday's dirty jeans from the floor and stalks out the door, presumably to the laundry. In Zach's rustic house with its artistic clutter, he takes his clothes to the laundry. The random comparison with Derek strikes me as ironic.

The silence in the room is deafening. I finish getting dressed and hug my bag to my stomach.

The contrast from the warmth and passion of mere moments ago is stark. A reminder of how little I know about the man I spent the most incredible weekend of my life with.

The complex man I've fallen in love with.

Zach walks back into the room, and I realize I haven't moved.

He stills in front of me, his presence filling the room.

It is his bedroom, but he looks lost.

Broken.

My heart is scattered into tiny fragments across the floor-space between us.

I can't be here. I need to get out.

Zach's gaze meets mine, but just when I think he'll open up, he averts his gaze. His body is as still as his surfboard against the wall.

I smile.

It's fake.

The sensation of stretched skin bunching my cheeks.

I let my lips fall.

I'm not going to hide behind a mask. Not anymore.

I didn't know the real Derek after ten years, and I don't know the real Zach even after the intense weekend we just shared.

"I don't want to lose you, Claire," he says. "I've never met anyone who's made me feel it's possible for me to have what comes so naturally to others." He's talking about love. About family. He's looking so sad. Like he, too, doesn't like the distance between us but doesn't know how to fix it.

I want to move to him, wrap my arms around his rigid torso. I want to erase these last awful minutes, turn back time to how we were before.

But I don't close the distance between us.

And neither does he.

"I have to go. I'm already late."

He's completely still, his unseeing eyes staring at a point in the past I can't reach. He's told me time and again, he doesn't know how to do relationships. He's said he will fail, and I told him I would be patient. Have I set the bar too high?

This time, I do move to him, place my palm on his jaw, physically turn his face to me.

"Zach." *Come back to me.* Slowly, he turns his head, his pained gaze meets mine.

"Meeting you was not supposed to be by accident," he says. "I've known Derek for years."

He's saying something else, but I can't hear past the roar in my ears. The room spins.

I can't feel anything but the blinding pain of Zach's betrayal.

"Claire, let me explain." Zach reaches for me, but I use both hands on his chest to shove him back. Hard. It is as effective as kicking a brick wall, but he lets me go.

I turn my back. Force my legs to move. One foot after the other, until I'm out the door and into my car.

It is only then,

Only then, that I allow the tears to fall.

CHAPTER 26

"Oh my God," Kira says as I walk in the door of Simply Claire. "You had sex. And not just hot sex, you had blast-yourself-off-the-planet sex."

"How the hell can you tell that from one glance?" I grumble.

Kira smiles proudly. "It's my superpower." She flicks the switch on the coffee machine. "But what's with the frown? What did he do to stuff it up?"

I get two mugs out of the cupboard, place them on the counter. Kira holds up her green juice, and I put one cup back.

"I don't want to talk about it."

"Oh, hon," Kira says.

The bitter fragrance of coffee made from freshly ground beans fills the air.

"Your ten o'clock cancelled," Kira says carefully. I pour the coffee, then, while I'm waiting for it to cool, blow the steam off the top of the mug, watching patterns form and swirl on the surface.

"Never mind," I say with forced brightness. I can use a few more moments to gather myself after Zach's bombshell. "Where's the appointment book?" It's not by the phone where it normally is. I look at Kira in question.

She grabs a cloth and begins to wipe the counter. "There were a few cancellations this morning."

"How many?"

"Eight."

My stomach plummets. "Eight?" I run through the list in my head. "That's every job we had booked in this week so far."

Kira nods. "I came in this morning to a phone full of messages."

"Did they say why?" I can't believe this. My new shop opened on Friday, and here we are Monday morning, and I suddenly have no clients. How will I pay the rent to Zach's mate if I don't have any work?

The door opens, and Bec and Julia walk in. Something in their expressions freezes the smile of welcome on my face.

"Claire," Bec says, standing in front of me. "We need to talk."

I show Bec and Julia to the lunchroom. Although it's a small room that doubles as a kitchen at the back of the shop, it is twice as large as the one in my old place.

"You're looking well." I smile at Bec, hope it hides the devastation I'm feeling.

I make Bec a coffee and Julia a tea, just the way they like it.

"Is everything okay?" I ask, regretting the strain my separation with Derek has caused in our friendship. You learn who your true friends are when the chips are down. Bec and Julia were there for me when I lost Katie, so it saddens me that Julia, and now maybe even Bec, have sided with Derek during our separation.

But I try not to judge them too harshly, knowing how convincing Derek has been, how he's carefully orchestrated events so that the "facts" are on his side and my credibility has been questioned at every turn.

"I don't know how to say this, so I'm just going to come out with it. Derek has received the documents from your lawyer. He's very angry about it," Bec says.

"I can't imagine why." I make sure my tone is even.

"Everyone thought you would have gone back to him by now," Bec says, waving a slender hand around, indicating the room, her shiny new engagement ring glistening in the light coming through the windows. "Instead, you've opened a new shop, complete with a new name."

"I was locked out of my old one," I remind her. "And my new business deserves a new name. Derek ruined Designs by Hardt by not letting me take care of business and not giving me access to my clients' property.

He's tried to destroy everything I've worked to build, so his name no longer belongs on the door." I look between them both, their cool expressions hurting and disappointing me.

"Did Derek ask you to come and see me?" There's a lump in my throat, and I want so bad for them to deny it.

"He did," Julia says, shifting uncomfortably in her seat. "This new shop is sending the message that you aren't going back to your husband, not ever."

"That's because I'm not."

"Claire," Bec says. "I'm not happy that he's doing this, but Derek has been telling everyone at work about what's happening to you."

I narrow my gaze. "What is happening to me?"

"He's telling them you're having another breakdown. That giving you work will make your recovery take longer."

"My recovery." I raise my brows. "You can thank Derek for his concern and tell him I've never been better." Lies! I remember Zach's admission that he knows Derek this morning. Has the whole world been deceiving me? Is there one single person I can trust? There's a painful throb in my temples.

"It was Derek who got your first customers after Katie," Julia reminds me. "He asked for help in supporting your business to take your mind off what happened," she continues. "He found a great shop, set everything up for you. The reason you had customers from the start was because everyone who came to you believed they were doing Derek a favor. You know nothing about running a business," Julia says. "And if it fails, Derek is worried it will come back on him. Affect the company."

I lean back in my seat, finally understanding why Bec agreed to come. Rob would have pressured her to make sure this doesn't affect his father's firm, the family business she's going to marry into, a lucrative business her children will inherit one day.

"My business is not going to fail," I assure Bec. "Nothing I do will come back on Rob or affect anyone else. I'm out on my own. I've changed my business name. Derek may have helped me get some clients in the beginning…I can't prove otherwise. But they came back because I'm good at what I do. My designs get in the paper, the society pages, alongside all the top Australian and international designers."

"Derek has a lot of friends," Julia says. "A lot of powerful business contacts not only in Perth but in Melbourne and Sydney. The firm has offices all over Australia. Every client, every business contact he meets, he gives your card to, gets them to send their wives to you. He's been your greatest advocate, and now you treat him like this…"

"You really do believe I am to blame here, don't you?" Tears blur my vision, and I blink them back.

"No," Bec says, frowning. "You've done nothing wrong." Bec gives a pointed look at Julia. "Claire, I have to admit you're looking good. Sounding strong." Bec chews on a fingernail, struggling with her loyalties. Me or her fiancé. Two versions of events, and she can't be sure where the truth lies.

"Derek is worried about your state of mind," Julia says, her tone cool, seemingly not conflicted like Bec. "He's told everyone to stop coming to you and that if they do, they're enabling you in your breakdown."

The blood whooshes past my ears.

"And, Claire, I really do believe he has your best interest at heart. He said you're in denial but you need to get professional help. He'll pay for it," Bec says. "Even after everything, he still loves you. He just wants you to get better, Claire. We all do."

"I'd be better if he stayed out of my life."

"Derek pointed out that a drug addict or an alcoholic can't see they have a problem," Julia says. "That's why they do interventions. To get them help."

"Is that what this is?" I ask, incredulous. "An intervention?"

Bec says "no" at the precise moment Julia says "yes."

"You're flaunting your affair with that artist guy right in his face," Julia says.

I sit up in my chair. Now I know what triggered this. Derek's jealousy over watching me and Zach Friday night. "This has nothing to do with Zach." For the first time since they arrived, my tone is cold.

"Derek knows things about Zach," Julia says. "He has a criminal record as long as your arm. He's told everyone to stop buying Zach's paintings because they're supporting something illegal."

If Derek and Zach really do know each other, I can't see Zach being in cahoots with him now. I think back to when we were in my old house, how Zach lunged at Derek and dropped him on the floor over the way he spoke to me. Zach has done too much for me that has hindered Derek and his attempts to control me. Not the other way around. If they were in cahoots at one stage, and Zach has since decided to side with me, how badly would Derek take that. And how much worse will this get if they go to war with one another?

"Derek says Zach is wanted by the cops. That it's only a matter of time before he's caught. Derek says—"

"*Derek says!*" I shout. "If I hear what Derek says one more time, I don't know what I'll be capable of." I stand so abruptly that my chair falls loudly behind me. Bec and Julia's eyes widen in alarm. I don't care. Anger is firing through my veins. *Don't shoot the messenger,* I remind myself, but I'm too angry to heed my own advice.

I might not understand yet how Derek and Zach know one another, but I do know what Zach does with the money from his paintings. Of course, I can't say anything to compromise the safety of the kids at the Village.

My hands clench and unclench at my sides.

"Get. Out." I tell Julia, seething. "You are not a friend of mine. I'm not even sure you ever were." I've had as much as I can take of her. My head is pounding. I've been being blindsided by everyone. Derek, Julia, Bec, and now…even Zach. And that hurts worst of all. I blink back stinging tears.

I won't cry. I won't cry.

"Oh, Claire," Bec says, choking on a sob. "I'm so sorry."

"So am I, Bec. You have been put in a difficult spot. I see that. I know you don't know what to believe right now, but in the end, the truth will come out." I let my gaze zero in on Julia. "You'll see what Derek has done to me, the lengths he has gone to take away everything I love—my career, and, sadly, even my friends."

Bec stands, leans in and gives me a hug. "I really want this to work out for you," she says, pulling back, tears welling in her eyes. "I'm here for you, but I'm just so torn about what to do to help."

"Nothing," I say, mustering something that may or may not resemble a smile. "There's nothing you need to do. I've got it all under control. But Bec?"

"Yes?"

"Tell Derek the next time he has anything to say to me to have the balls to come here and say it himself."

I watch Bec and Julia leave, and only when they drive away do I let my tears fall.

I think back to Derek's reaction when I went to the house with Zach to get my business records. Derek was furious, his eyes wild, glassy with anger. Desperation. But his anger with me that day wasn't really about me turning up with Zach. It was about something else.

This entire time, Derek has been showing me his hand, and I've barely noticed. Sending Bec and Julia in to see me, alienating my customers, in the hope that his schemes would intimidate me into going back to him.

Why would he want me to?

Why this desperate push—still—to get me back? The wannabe designer who lost her child then lost her mind.

It must have something to do with money. Despite his insistence otherwise, I must be financially beneficial to him in some way. It's the only thing that makes sense. Money is what motivates Derek.

Kira is standing next to me, and she places her arms around my shoulders. "You don't believe any of that stuff about your business, do you?"

"There's some truth to it. Derek is responsible for my more high-profile clients."

"I didn't mean to eavesdrop," she says. "The shop isn't that big. It was hard not to overhear."

"It's fine," I reply absently. Derek would know that having Julia and Bec deliver his veiled threats would effectively get under my skin. Is he hoping I'd overreact? Lash out? Do something to validate his claims I am unstable?

And yet...there's enough truth in his claim to make me question myself. Isn't that the hallmark of a great con artist? Mix in just the right amount of truth to seed doubt? What Derek says could be true. It is possible that he knows all my clients. Is he the only reason I have a business at all? The cancellations this morning prove he has a lot of influence.

"He is trying to manipulate your clients," Kira says, "and, by extension, you. But it's because everyone likes you, Claire, that they want to do the right thing by you, not because they don't."

I summon a small smile. "Thank you, Kira."

If only that were my only problem. I wish I could tell Kira everything. But I can't. There's too much at stake. Too much I still don't understand. The least being Zach's involvement in all of this.

I'm suddenly tired, like someone has sliced open a vein and all the blood is draining from my body.

In my chair, I bend forward and touch my toes, take several deep breaths. Then stand. Shoulders back. If there is one thing this experience has taught me, it's resilience. Being on my own, solving my own problems, has given me a belief in myself I couldn't have achieved any other way. I have confidence in my ability to survive.

So what if Derek takes away my existing customers? He may know the elite in Perth society, but he doesn't know everyone in this state. I'll revise my strategy. I'll go online. Set up a website, invest in a social media presence. I'll diversify, branch out across Australia then the world. Why not? What's to stop me?

"Hey, Kira. What do you say we finally do something about that line of swimwear you've been talking about?"

A smile breaks out across her face.

"And while we're going down that avenue," I say, ideas firing like adrenaline through my veins. "We might as well extend to a surfy line of casual wear. Something stylish that can go from the beach to an oceanside bar." I rip out a pad and start sketching strappy dresses and tops.

"We'll attract a whole new clientele," Kira says with a gleam in her eye. "People Derek has no influence over."

"Exactly."

"Maybe I can incorporate some jewelry I've been working on?" Kira asks, her voice uncharacteristically tentative.

"I didn't know you made jewelry." I smile up at her then glance at the beaded bracelets and matching crystal dolphin earrings she's wearing. "Did you make them?"

"Yes."

"They're nice." Really nice. Perfect to match our new line. "Bring in your other designs. I'll take a look and see what we can make work."

I'll always keep a line of evening wear; it is my passion after all. But the only customers I want are the ones who appreciate my work and find me on their own. I don't want anyone who comes to me because of Derek's influence. Clearing out those customers is like clearing out the final pieces of Derek from my life. The bastard will not win. His days of intimidating and controlling me are over.

Filled with determination and fresh enthusiasm, I settle in with Kira and get to work.

At a little after six p.m., Zach's car pulls into the customer bay at the front of the shop. If the synapses in my brain didn't fry every damn time I saw the man, I might have thought it odd that he didn't park in the rear car park near mine. But the instant he gets out of the car, I can see only him. He's wearing faded, ripped denim and a black shirt unbuttoned at the collar. His sleeves are casually rolled up at the cuffs, and the masculine silver pieces in the black plaited leather bands at his wrists catch the sunlight.

I've never been so affected by a man—by anyone—before. He's hurt me, more than I thought possible, but the instant he appears, he's all I can see. All I can think about.

Meeting you was not supposed to be by accident.

What does that even mean? I'd left him this morning without giving him a chance to explain. I wasn't ready to hear him admit he'd lied to me. Been lying to me all along. My experience with Derek is still too raw. Too painful.

And still ongoing.

I needed distance between us, an opportunity to clear my head. Steel myself for a fresh onslaught of disillusionment.

The distraction provided by a busy day at work has given me that. Is there a reasonable explanation? Or has everything between us been a lie?

"I didn't know Zach was a flowers and hearts kind of guy," Kira whispers, her eyes wide. "What the hell have you done to him?"

There's a cocktail of emotion roiling inside of me as I try to sift through what to think. What to feel.

Through the window, I watch him slowly approach the shop door. His usually confident stride now hesitant. His face appears drawn, his eyes reddened, as though he's been rubbing them.

"Oh, Claire," Kira says, placing an arm around my shoulder. "Whatever he's done, tell me you're going to forgive him."

He opens the door.

Time stands still. His eyes search mine as mine search his. He's looking for possibility of forgiveness. I'm looking for honesty. A reason to trust him.

"Please leave," I say, relieved my voice is stronger than I feel.

He winces. "No," he says. "Not until you've given me the chance to explain. After that, if you still don't want anything to do with me, I'll walk away, and you'll never see me again."

Without breaking my gaze, he hands Kira the flowers.

"Uh...I'll see if I can find a vase," she says. "Then I'll head on home. Nice to see you again, Zach. See you tomorrow, Claire, and remember what I just said."

I murmur a distracted goodbye and, after she leaves the room, Zach reaches into his pocket, holds out his palm. "This is for you."

I stare at his palm a moment. I was expecting words; an apology, a justification...

"I never lied to you, Claire. But I did withhold information from you. In your eyes, there may be no difference."

"What is this?" I ask, taking the black USB out of his palm.

"It's proof that what I'm about to tell you is the truth. I won't lie to you, Claire, but you'll need to know that for sure. After everything you've been through, after hearing me admit to knowing Derek, trusting me will be an issue. I get that. But I'm willing to spend the rest of my life making it up to you by being totally transparent in everything I do." He lowers his voice. "I want to be the man you see when you look at me, Claire. I'll never be the man you deserve, but I'll go to my grave trying to be as close as I can be."

My breath catches. He meets my eyes then looks away. But not before I see the vulnerability in them. Did he think if he came to me with just himself, offered an explanation, it wouldn't be enough?

That *he* wouldn't be enough?

"It's everything you need to get Derek to back off and leave you alone for good."

My eyes widen in surprise.

"Claire," Zach says softly, "the information on this USB could get us all killed. You need to be aware of that."

If what Zach is saying is true, he's taking a huge risk giving me these files. To prove I can trust him.

But what could possibly be on them that could risk lives?

CHAPTER 27

*Z*ach and I move to my office in the back of the shop. I fit the USB into the port on the side of my laptop, and an encrypted password screen appears. Zach slides a scrap of paper across the table. "The password."

I type in the complicated series of letters and numbers, and several folders appear on my screen, arranged by financial year, dating back nearly ten years.

"What is it?" But even as I ask, things are becoming clear. Within the files inside one of the folders, I recognize my business records immediately although there are others. Companies I've never heard of, some I have. Interestingly, there are names and contact details of several influential people, celebrities, media moguls, top politicians and even the Prime Minister.

"I suspected *who* the large payments out of your account were for," Zach says. "But I didn't know *what* they were for."

"Why didn't you say anything to me?"

"I hoped you'd never have to find out." Zach leans against the desk and wipes his palms down his jeans. "It was safer for you not to know. Besides, you'd opened your new shop. You were making a fresh start. I hoped that would be enough to distance you from whatever Derek was involved in. But it's clear he won't leave you alone without some...encouragement."

My fingers shake as I click on the file that opens my business records for the most recent financial year. It looks the same as the copy I have—the official file for the tax department—except these ledgers are far more detailed. In this spreadsheet, the payments I haven't been able to decipher have references. *Rydell Industries*. Names, addresses, amounts, dates, times.

"Who is Rydell Industries?"

"It's a shell company owned by Bill Rydell, founder of Dark Ryders Bikers Club," Zach says. "It's one of the companies they use for money laundering."

I'd heard of Dark Ryders Bikers club. I doubt there's a soul alive who hasn't. I still don't quite understand how this relates to me or why Derek was using my business to pay them money, but I have the feeling it's all about to become alarmingly clear.

"How are you connected to all this?" I ask. "You said you know Derek. Do you also know Bill Rydell?"

"Yes," Zach says. "I've known Bill since I grew up on the streets. Derek was my accountant."

Was. "Not now?"

"Of course not," he says. "It hurts that you'll now be questioning everything between us."

I look up from the screen. "What do you expect?"

He runs a hand through his hair. "Everything we've shared, everything I feel for you, is real. What's that saying? People who have nothing to hide, hide nothing." Zach waves a hand to the USB. "This is everything I know. It's me being an open book for you. Nothing more to hide."

I hold his gaze for several moments, searching his eyes, waiting for an instinct, some sixth sense to warn me he's not telling the truth. That he's holding something back, or worse, setting me up in some plan I couldn't possibly imagine. But I find nothing, sense nothing but a certainty that he's telling the truth.

If only relying on instincts alone could be trusted.

"How did you get this information?" I continue to click through the folders, open random files. Although it's impossible for me to make sense of all the figures scrolling down my screen and understand what they all mean, I know enough to be awed by the gravity of what I was seeing. Of the price Zach would pay for imparting if discovered by Bill Rydell, the founder of the most notorious biker's club in Australia.

"Off Derek's computer." He pauses, then adds, "I saw you work out the password to access his computer. Once in, I knew exactly what to look for."

"You broke into Derek's office?" I don't know if I'm surprised, shocked, or something else entirely.

Zach shrugs. "It's still half your house. You needed proof that what I'm telling you is the truth, and I knew Derek had the files to prove it."

I shake my head and decide not to question him further. What difference would the answers make? Zach has proven he's willing to break the law for what he considers right.

For me.

Still...I can't know if I can trust Zach without fully understanding him.

"What's your involvement in this?" I ask.

"I've known Bill Rydell since I was fifteen years old," Zach says. "You couldn't grow up like I did and not have dealings with Dark Ryder Bikers Club. They run the strip clubs, brothels, and are still the biggest suppliers of recreational drugs in Perth. Before you ask, I am not, nor have I ever been, involved in distributing drugs or prostitution, either with the Dark Ryders or otherwise. Other than taking drugs myself for a period of time when I was on the streets. You should know how strong my feelings are about that from my work with the boys at the Village."

"I know that," I say quietly. And I do. Zach may have lied to me about something I am yet to fully understand, but his passion to get the kids off the street, for his work at the Village, is genuine. And started long before he met me.

"The USB contains evidence of Derek's connection to Bill Rydell," Zach says.

"Derek is connected to a bikers gang?" I try to reconcile this with the man I know and lived with for a decade. The straight-laced man who prefers white to color, who sticks to routine and who I'd thought considered starting his own accounting firm his biggest risk.

How do bikers fit into that picture?

How do I?

It's dark outside, the streetlights are on. The world looks so very different to me now.

How can my husband have been involved in criminal activity without my knowledge?

Disappointment—disillusionment—is a lead weight in my stomach.

How could I be such a poor judge of character? Twice. And why is it that Zach's betrayal hurts far more than Derek's ever did.

"I am such a fool." Hot tears prickle my eyes.

"No. Claire..." He places his hand on my shoulder. I jerk away.

"Don't touch me."

He makes a pained sound in the back of his throat but removes his hand and takes a step back.

"Were you working for Derek when you met me?"

"No," Zach says. "I did Derek a favor. There's a difference."

"What were you supposed to do to me?"

"I was only meant to keep tabs on you. Follow you if necessary. Make sure you didn't become a liability. Derek's words, not mine."

"You mean I'd become a liability if I didn't go back to Derek?"

Zach nods. "Yes."

"Why?" Why was—is—Derek so desperate to get me back? Just because of the money he was siphoning from my business?

"What's in this for you?" I ask, feeling my face become uncomfortably hot. "Derek wants money from my business for whatever scheme he's got going on with Rydell. But what is it that you want from me?"

Zach's pained expression deepens. "Only you," he says. "I've only ever wanted you. Everything I've done since knowing you, Claire, has been to help you. You have to see that."

"All I see are lies," I say, tears stinging my lids. "Lies, deception, and people using me. Right now, despite this USB, I don't trust anyone. Not even you."

Zach lowers his eyes. "I can't blame you for feeling that way, Claire. It breaks my heart, but I understand."

My head is pounding.

"From the moment I met you, I knew there was something special about you, the moment my watch got caught on your dress. But you were married. At that time, I didn't realize who to."

Zach leans against the wall, rubs his eyes. "Derek saw me the day you were locked out of your shop. He drove past, and we were standing in the street. Later that day, he called me, asked me to follow you, keep tabs on you. It was clear he had no idea that we'd met previously or that we had been spending time together. I didn't tell him. And I also didn't tell him that I had fallen in love with his wife."

He glances at me briefly, then turns away. "I told him I'd keep tabs on you, report your actions to him. I didn't want him to become suspicious if

I said no, nor did I want him to employ someone else to watch you. So I said yes. It worked in my favor because I wanted to keep you close. I didn't know what he was up to. I saw what he was doing to you, but I didn't understand why. You didn't either. I thought if I kept him close, I'd be able to get you answers. And keep you safe. There was no way I was going to let him hurt you more than he already was.

"It wasn't until Bill Rydell contacted me that I began to understand the full gravity of what you were involved in."

"Me? I wasn't involved in anything."

"At first I was forced to consider the possibility that you were playing me with your innocent routine, even thought there was a possibility you were using me to help you get back at Derek. That day we went to your house for your business records, I looked for signs. But you were genuine. Your split with Derek real. I saw his desperation. Derek was too drunk to see how I felt for you. He probably assumed I was following you by pretending to be your friend. But it was clear you had no idea what was going on. You knew nothing about Derek's debt with the Dark Ryders and nothing about whatever scheme Ryder was using you for."

I stand up so fast my chair falls backward. I hold up my hand. "Wait!" I walk to the window, putting distance between us.

"Now I know you're mistaken," I say. This is a mistake, everything. The USB, Derek's involvement with the bikers. This is not my life. I was a wife, a mother who lost her little girl to a brain tumor who struggled to get her life back on track.

Zach squeezes his eyes shut. "I tried to protect you from this. While I distanced myself from Derek, I kept communication open with Rydell. Bill asked me to break into your shop, make sure there was nothing there that would incriminate him. Derek had become a liability. I agreed to help Bill but only to make sure they didn't see you as a liability as well, Claire."

The room starts to spin, and I suck in a series of deep breaths.

"You didn't break into my shop for me?"

"Of course, I did that for you!" Zach growls. "Those dresses were rightfully yours. I gave you everything you needed. It just so happens I also used the opportunity to convince Rydell that you knew nothing."

"I *don't* know anything!" At least, I didn't.

"It was Rydell that needed to be convinced," Zach says softly. "Not me."

"I don't give a toss what he thinks. What any of you think."

"You need to care what Rydell thinks," Zach says. "He's a very dangerous man."

"This whole situation is screwed up." I cross the room, yank the USB from my laptop and throw it at Zach. It hits his chest and falls to the floor between us. He makes no move to pick it up.

"Take it," I shout. "I don't need it. I didn't ask to know any of this. Take your files, your stories about bikers and whatever criminal shit you and Derek are involved in and leave!"

"Claire—"

"Please go." It's too much to take in. I need a chance to process it all.

I'd thought Zach's big secret was that he'd killed his father. I knew his life on the streets had included criminal activity, but I never would have thought he was still involved now. He's so strict on drugs and crime in the Village. Setting such a great example. Getting kids set on the right path.

I can't reconcile that with Zach associating with the bikers. He said he was no longer involved but, by his own admission now, said he's still in communication with Rydell. How can I just blindly trust the reasons behind him giving me this incriminating evidence? Why would he risk so much to do so?

The two men in my life, both hiding a criminal past with the same bikers club. What were the chances?

Zach picks the USB from the floor, places it on the desk. "You'll need to keep this safe," he says, his voice sad. "Go see Derek. Get him to admit everything I told you. Find out how you are involved with Rydell. You need to know that Claire. To understand your exposure."

I glance out the window as a motorcycle cruises slowly past. Was it a Dark Ryder? Are we being watched? Or has this made me paranoid?

"Come see me after you've spoken to Derek," Zach says. "Please. I'll keep you safe. I won't let anything happen to you. If I thought Derek would tell you with me there, I'd go with you."

"No," I say. "This is something I need to do myself."

"I thought as much. I also know you still don't trust me again yet," Zach says, picking the USB up off the desk and placing it in my hand. "I promised I would never lie to you. And I haven't. This is the truth, Claire. And what's on this USB is your proof of that. The information you will need to get you out of this mess. To save your life."

I turn the offending piece of plastic and metal over in my palm. If only I could erase this new reality as easily as I could erase the data on the USB.

"Giving you this information, Claire, not only gives you the leverage you need to free yourself from Derek; it proves to you that my loyalties are with you. Not Rydell, not Derek. You. And only you."

He steps forward, places his hand briefly on my arm, then allows it to fall away.

His eyes mist. "I'm sorry I ruined what we had. I can only hope you will forgive me and, in time, trust me again. In the meantime, this is proof of how much I love you."

Our eyes meet.

"You now hold everything you need to destroy everyone involved," Zach says. "Including me."

CHAPTER 28

I arranged to meet with Derek at a popular café overlooking the ocean in the northern suburbs. We are sitting on the first-floor balcony, our table in a private corner. Through the clear glass balustrade, I can see that the ocean is calm and sparkling, no one surfing today. While the waitress pours us each a glass of wine, I watch a lady pushing a stroller on the walkway that runs between West Coast Drive and the beach. There are many people walking on this picturesque pathway, especially on such a sunny afternoon. But my eyes follow only the mother with the contented smile on her face and the way her child's feet kick playfully. My chest constricts, and I look away.

The lunch hour rush has passed, leaving only a few people lingering over drinks. Later this evening, a band will play in the inside section, and this upper section will be festive and packed.

I look across the table at the man I'd once promised to spend my life with and see a stranger. Derek's eyes are still cornflower blue, but his face is drawn. He appears to have aged a decade in the last few weeks. He's a lot thinner than he was, his hair cut in his usual military-short style. He's familiar, but I'm struggling to remember feeling comfortable in his presence. Going to this man for comfort, love.

This man I shared a bed with but barely knew.

Never would I have thought I'd ever have reason to be scared of Derek, the mild-mannered accountant. Scared of my own husband.

I feel the outline of the USB safely secured inside my bra.

"I was going through my accounts—"

"You?" Derek cuts me off, his tone derisive. "You can't work out how much change you get from five dollars for a liter of milk."

I stare at this man, memories flooding back. His condescension is jarring now, but I still remember far too clearly how that verbal abuse had been normal. More subtle, but still threaded through every word he said. Slowly, over the course of days, months, years, he'd convinced me I wasn't capable of handling anything important, as if the smallest financial decision would be too much for me.

It strikes me now how hearing the same thing often enough can make you simply believe it. I think of the kids at the Village, at how determined Zach is to instill in them his "can do" attitude and replace negative self-talk the moment he hears it. We all know beliefs formed early on shape the child for life. What I hadn't known was how the reverse could happen as an adult. Confidence could be whittled down like how water can erode a boulder over time.

He picks up a bread roll and twists it between his fingers. Despite his bravado, he's nervous.

"Are you going to say sorry and you want to come back?" Derek asks.

"That, I can assure you, will never happen." There's a quiet confidence in my tone he wouldn't recognize.

Derek makes a show of sighing, shaking his head slowly as though he's forced to summon great amounts of patience. It makes me want to dislodge his head from his shoulders. "Your actions are embarrassing and reflecting badly on the whole firm. Rob Stanton is not at all impressed."

"Don't talk down to me, or I walk."

"You won't walk," he sneers. "You want something from me. That's why you finally agreed to meet with me."

I take a sip of my wine, slowly place my glass back on the table.

"You're right, Derek. I do want something. Two things. The first, is answers. The truth, or don't bother talking at all. And two, I want you to back off and leave me alone to get on with my life without interference. No contact, either directly or indirectly through rumors, or I'll spread some rumors myself, only mine will be true. And they could get you killed."

Caution appears in his eyes, and he sucks in a breath. He stares as though he can look right inside of me and see exactly how much I know.

"I don't mean to be rude," he says carefully. "That wasn't my intention. I really did think you wanted to come back."

"I trust you're suitably aware of how absurd that notion is."

"You're my wife, Claire," he says. "You can't fault me for fighting to get you back at my side."

"Did you think that cutting off access to our bank accounts and locking me out of my shop to keep me from making money to put a roof over my head would force me back?" I demand. "And when that didn't work out, alienating my friends and taking away my support network as well as my clients, past and prospective? Did you think I'd run back to you with my tail between my legs, begging your forgiveness? Just so I could put food in my stomach? Have somewhere to sleep other than my car? Are you that desperate to have me back, Derek, that you don't care if I hated you during the process?" I lean forward, my gaze hard. "But what I really want to know, is why?"

I don't come straight out with the information I have from Zach. The proof on the USB I went through more thoroughly after Zach left. Maybe it's because, sitting across the table from him, seeing through my new perspective, I can't help but wonder how he so easily deceived me. I observe him now, looking for evidence of the duplicity I should have seen.

When I came off the medication, I'd sensed something with Derek was off. I'd attributed that to his affair with Jasmine. Had I been so focused on catching him out in that one lie that it blinded me to what has turned out to be much more vitally important?

"I mean you no disrespect," Derek says in that familiar tone he often took with me, slow and clear. Parent to child. Therapist to patient. "I met you when you were just eighteen. I handled your mother's estate—do you think you would have been capable of that? And after Katie died, you had your breakdown and were a mess. But I was always here for you, picking up the pieces. I can't believe how easy it is for you to forget that. I helped you, Claire. You needed me. Everything I have done has been for you. Don't make me out to be a bad guy."

I'd always thought of abuse as physical. If he'd hit me, it would have been easier for me to see that as wrong. What I'd failed to see was the passive-aggressive emotional abuse and manipulation I was subjected to on a daily basis.

Derek leans back in his chair. There are breadcrumbs on his perfectly pressed navy-blue shirt. I don't flick them off the way I once would have.

"I never thought you were stupid," Derek says, leaning forward. "I've always respected you. You're the best thing that ever happened to me. I love you, Claire." His eyes tear up. "It's been so hard on me since you left. I didn't realize it before, just how much you mean to me."

"Your actions prove otherwise," I say, my voice calm. Emotionless. "People aren't what they say, Derek. They're what they do. And speaking of doing, there are some anomalies in the financial records I'd like you to explain."

"Anomalies?" His tears dry instantly, and he sits up straighter in his chair.

"Some irregularities in expenses," I clarify.

"I know what anomalies are," he snaps, noticing the crumbs on his shirt and picking them off. "I simply have no idea what you're on about." His tone is blasé, but he's on edge. He's looking everywhere but at me.

"There are some large expenses I need you to explain. Regular payments of around twenty-five thousand dollars each, totaling more than three hundred thousand dollars for one financial year."

He shrugs. "How should I remember? It was probably to an overseas material supplier. You have no idea how much the silks you like so much cost."

"Perhaps the name Rydell Industries will jog your memory."

Derek pales, his eyes narrowing to thin slits. "How did you get that information?"

"I want the truth, Derek. No more lies. No more bullshit."

He opens his mouth as though about to say something then changes his mind, leaning back in his chair.

"You've changed," he says. He stares at me for several long moments like I'm a stranger he's trying to figure out. "Have you done something with your hair?"

Now he notices! "No," I say with a shrug. He frowns as though unsure.

"Who is Rydell Industries, Derek? And why were you paying them such large sums out of my account?"

"Your account?" Derek's tone is now on the attack like the cornered rodent he is. "You wouldn't even have that business without me. Don't you—" He breaks off, whatever he reads in my expression causing him to slump forward over the table. He rubs his eyes, his head lowered. He doesn't speak for a very long time. When he does, it's in a low, resigned tone. "You really want to know?"

"But don't say another fucking word unless it's the truth. Got it? Or I walk out of here with what I know and destroy you."

"You don't have to be like that, Claire. I'll tell you everything." He pauses. Takes a deep breath. "After what happened with our Katie-bear, I started drinking. Heavily. Just to deal with the pain, you know?"

My throat closes over as it still does when I think of Katie, the debilitating pain of those first few months still quick to rise to the surface. "I know."

"I drank because of you," he says.

"Me?" I grab a bread roll and start ripping into it.

"I couldn't look at you without seeing her. It was a constant reminder of how much we'd lost. It just seemed so wrong that we continued to live, together, without her."

As much as I now loathe the man I used to be proud to call my husband, I can relate to his words. I still feel guilt during times of happiness like it's somehow wrong to feel any joy in a world without her in it. As though by doing so, that means I didn't love her enough.

Derek wipes away tears with the back of his hand. His eyes are puffy and red. We've never talked about the loss of Katie. In the three years since she left us, this is the first time he's opened up about how it affected him. Unlike me, he refused to see a therapist.

"I even hated you," Derek says. "I hated you for the whole of that first year. Every time I looked at you, it sliced open the wound that just wouldn't heal. I couldn't understand how it was right for a five-year-old girl to be the one to die. I—" He buries his head in his hands. "I was angry it wasn't you instead of her. Or me."

As hurtful as it is to hear your husband to say he wished you'd died, it was the way I'd felt, too. Every day she was sick, I prayed t for her to get better. To take me instead of her. I would have gladly taken her place. She had a full life ahead of her. I couldn't make sense of it.

I still can't.

A parent is not supposed to bury a child.

Derek reaches for my hand, and I yank it out of reach. "Don't touch me."

"So you drank to ease the pain," I say. "How did you go from grieving the loss of your child, drowning your sorrow in alcohol to making payments to Australia's most notorious motorcycle club?"

"I also started using cocaine."

My mouth drops open in shock. "Cocaine?"

Drugs connected him to Bill Rydell? That is something I never would have considered a remote possibility. Embezzling. Misappropriation of funds. Tax evasion. But drugs?

"Keep your voice down," Derek says, looking around us. "Yes, cocaine. I wasn't sleeping. I was drinking way too much, and I needed something to help clear my mind. To think. It doesn't take brains to make clothes, but *I* needed clarity to go through pages of figures and prepare financial statements and complex, corporate tax returns. With the lack of sleep and the alcohol fog, I needed cocaine to function normally again. It was only meant to be temporary."

I let Derek's comment about me not needing brains slide. He will never see who I really am, only the woman he wanted to beat me down to be. But I don't want or need his approval, so his opinion of me no longer has the power to hurt me.

"I'd run up a bit of debt with Rydell, and Bill offered me a way to pay it back, plus make myself a decent amount in return. It needed an initial investment of five hundred thousand for a potential return of one and a half million in the first year alone."

He glances up at me. "I borrowed the money against the house. You remember, you signed the mortgage agreement."

"I don't remember that," I say. But then through the haze of medication Derek had insisted I take daily, I can't say for sure that I didn't sign something.

Derek shrugs. "You know I've always wanted to start my own firm, and I saw that as my opportunity. The investment did well initially," Derek says, "and in the first six months, my investment doubled. Then two of the men I'd invested with went to jail on unrelated trafficking charges, and the whole thing went to shit. The money we invested went missing. Rydell wanted his money, and, Claire, the Dark Ryders don't forgive a debt."

He clears his throat. "Initially, I arranged to pay it off. I borrowed money from some clients' accounts at Stanton and Associates to meet the installments."

I suck in a breath. "You idiot."

"I didn't know what else to do. I needed cash fast. I borrowed as much as I could against the house. The money I'd reinvested paid off, but not at the rate I needed it to. Even with the additional amounts I was drawing from your account, it still wasn't enough." He lets out a breath. "At the same time, Stanton Senior had begun to watch me. Things were getting hot in the office, and it became urgent I pay back the money I'd taken from the clients before Stanton Senior found out and I ended up in jail. I needed another flow of cash. Bill Rydell came up with a more lucrative idea."

I lean forward. So far everything Zach showed me on the USB was proving true. The installments from my account to pay off Derek's debt.

"What was the idea?" I prompt.

"People pay big money for dirt. They pay to keep their secrets from being exposed and even bigger money for something to hold over a rival. To stop a deal going through. To blackmail and force a deal. A private investigator can only gain so much information. Everyone has secrets, Claire," Derek says. "And the more influential you are, the more you have to lose. Turns out a bug sewn into an evening gown could prove lucrative. I'd almost finished paying back my debt to Rydell in full when you left."

Oh, God! I fall back into my chair. *This* is how I was involved?

"Are you telling me what I think you are?" I ask, horrified. I think about my client list: wives of politicians, CEOs, mining bosses. All unsuspecting.

"When you left," Derek says, "Rydell was furious. He had clients lined up, politicians, wealthy businessmen. People you don't fuck with. And all eyes were on me to get you back."

"You bastard."

"What choice did I have? Besides," he adds, desperation bleeding through his tone. "It was for your own safety. Being with me was the only way I could keep you safe."

"If that's true," I say, "then why aren't I dead now?"

Something dark flickers in his expression, and his jaw clenches. There's still something he's not telling me.

"You have to come back," Derek says. "If you don't, you'll become a loose end. A liability. And you know what they do to liabilities, don't you?"

"I'm not coming back to you, Derek. Ever. And this is your mess, not mine."

"You don't have a choice," he says.

"What about Jasmine?" I demand.

"That," he says, thrusting a hand through his hair, "was a complication I could have done without."

"She didn't seem too much of a complication when you were screwing her."

217

"I'll never see her again," Derek says quickly. "Is that your problem? Jealousy? If you don't come back, they'll kill me."

"That's emotional extortion," I say.

"Please, Claire, be reasonable. We'll negotiate terms acceptable to both of us. I won't force you to do anything you aren't comfortable with. Marriage can be a façade only. Everything else, we can decide."

"And Jasmine? How does she fit into your picture? She's *pregnant*, Derek. She is the mother of your child. What would she say if she heard you having this conversation with me?"

Derek releases a breath.

It shakes. Like his hands.

"Wait," I say, "is she involved in this as well?"

Derek rolls his head on his shoulders. "Jasmine was the one sewing the devices into the seams of the gowns," Derek says. "I wouldn't be able to do that and make the bugs invisible."

My jaw drops, and I close it.

"The gowns we needed rigged were the ones I arranged to deliver for you. After Jasmine worked her magic."

"How long has this been going on?" I demand. "Was she doing this before she came to stay with us?"

Derek can't meet my eyes. "A few months before that. We discussed it when she was in Sydney. But, Claire, I won't need her now that you know about it. You can do it. See? This can all work out to everyone's advantage. What do you need me to do, Claire? Beg? Do you want me to get down on my knees?"

I look at Derek with disgust. And pity.

Then, Derek's lips curl into a sneer. "It's because you're with *him*, isn't it? The two-faced asshole. He was supposed to be helping me, not fucking you. Did he tell you he's in bed with the Ryders as well?"

A shiver of unease rolls down my spine. "Who I'm with now is none of your business."

"The hell it's not." Derek's voice lowers, becomes menacing. "If you don't come back to me, you can forget ever seeing Argos again."

"This has nothing to do with anyone else but us." This is the real Derek behind his social veneer. A selfish man with a hollow, desolate heart. "After today, you'll leave me alone and never contact me again. I have everything I need to put you away for a very long time."

"Argos," Derek spits, his face red and flushed. "Did he tell you he was following you? That he broke into your shop?"

My heart pounds, but I keep my voice even. "Yes," I say. "He's told me everything."

Derek eyes me suspiciously. "And you can forgive him, but not your own husband?"

"Ex-husband."

Bill Rydell may have asked him to, but Zach broke into the shop for me. Without my designs, orders and paperwork, it would have been so much harder for me to continue to work. Perhaps impossible. Without Zach's help in finding another shop to work out of, his financial help, his help in getting my financial records back from Derek, teaching me how to set up my accounts, run my business...

The last of my anger towards Zach drains away as I begin to see him in a new light. Unlike Derek, I have no reason to doubt Zach. Everything he has told me as disturbing as it has been, has at least been the truth.

I've been hard on him.

"My relationship with Zach is none of your business," I snap at Derek, eager to get this conversation over with and get back to Zach. Derek is going to have to find another way to pay his debt, and I'll make sure of the integrity of every future piece of clothing that leaves my possession.

"You weren't so pigheaded when you were on the pills," Derek says, seething.

"Argos is going to go down. It must have been him that gave you all this information. You aren't smart enough to piece all this together without help. Besides, the files containing the information you are talking about were encrypted. He's the only one who could have accessed that information or even known where to find it. You bring me down, I'll take you down with me. And forget Argos, he won't even make it to jail. Rydell will kill him first."

"Seems like we're all dead then." I hold his gaze. "And the knowledge of that is still not enough for me to go back to you. Let that sink in."

"Argos killed his own father," Derek says as though he wants to shock me.

"I know." My tone is as casual as if we were discussing ice-cream flavors.

Derek narrows his eyes. "Oh, how the mighty have fallen. You've sunk to an all-time low with him. Just make sure you sleep with one eye open."

Derek drums the tips of his fingers on the table. "You know, I followed you the other day," he says slowly, a calculating gleam in his eyes as he switches tactics. "Saw the little ramshackle caper he has going on in the forest..."

My stomach clenches.

"Did you know he hasn't made one application to the council? Not one building permit. I don't know what kind of sick game he's playing with those kids, but I don't suppose he'd welcome a call to the authorities to report suspected child trafficking..."

It doesn't matter what happens to me, to Derek, or even Zach. We're adults; our choices have consequences. But the boys at the Village are innocent. Mandy is innocent.

I look across at the man who I'd promised to spend eternity with and feel nothing but disgust.

"That's not what's happening, Derek." I want to rip a hole in his chest and tear out his despicable black heart. "If you know Zach as well as you claim to, you'd know that."

"Come back to me, Claire," he says. "And this all ends. You get your clients back, and I'll restore your reputation. I can pay off my debt to Rydell and start making money beyond our wildest dreams. We'll live the lifestyle we always wanted. You'll want for nothing. And Zach's sick secret with the kids will never become public. I'll even let you keep fucking Argos. As long as you're discreet."

I lean forward so there's no mistaking the sincerity of my words. "You so much as think about involving Zach or his project again, I'll go straight to Bill Rydell. I have his address in the files. I'll tell him I'm never going back to you, that you told me of his listening device scam and that it was *you* who gave me the evidence to prove it. It is, after all, the most logical explanation. I'll tell him you don't have the ability to pay him. And that's just for starters. After all, fair is fair. You've been lying about me to anyone who'll listen."

His eyes bulge, veins popping in his neck. "That would sign your death warrant."

I shrug. "Perhaps. But it would surely seal yours. You always said a person with nothing to lose is the most dangerous. Seems to me it's the situation you've put me in."

Derek looks at me differently this time. Like he now sees me as a worthy adversary. I stand.

Leaning over the table, I peer down on the man I hope I never have to see again. Except across the desk at my lawyer's office. During the property settlement.

"Stay away from Zach. If Zach has one single issue relating to the Village, I'll assume it's because of you and my next step will be to go to Rydell. That's a promise."

"You think you're so smart, but you've learned nothing," Derek sneers. "Take your threats and shove them up your ass. You're a fool for not taking this seriously. For rejecting this opportunity to come back. It's a decision you'll come to regret. And that," he says, "is my promise to you."

CHAPTER 29

The horizon is a sinking sunset of burning embers. The air is still, humid, without a breath of wind. Heavy gray clouds cover the earlier bright blue sky, and the eerie, haunting cry of a lone seagull echoes somewhere off in the distance.

It's the calm before the storm.

But there is no peace in the stillness.

I let myself into Zach's house. The space is empty, but at the same time filled with him. I take a deep breath, saturating my lungs with the scent of paints and canvas and, as I walk through the kitchen, freshly poured scotch. I trail my fingers over the thick, smooth glass of the bottle then over a drop spilled on the counter. I bring my fingers to my lips, the taste on my tongue reminiscent of Zach.

I move across the empty balcony, down the stairs to a space at the side of the house that I've only seen through the upstairs window.

I hear him before I see him.

The music is laid-back and sultry. The beat a physical pulse, resounding, thrumming, resonating through my body.

I round the corner, and the sight of him takes my breath away. Guitar resting across his thighs, he's sitting on a timber bench seat, a glass of scotch at his side. His chest is bare, his jeans low on his hips. His eyes are closed, his song in a haunting minor key, the chords, the taps, the beats on his guitar are powerfully emotive. Enthralled, I'm captive to his music, his presence. Sorrow bleeds through his music and fills the space between us.

There's something extraordinary about this man. Charismatic. Listening to him play is surreal, transporting me to a place somewhere other than here.

I watch him for a long moment. When I move closer, he stops and looks up at me. His expression is dark, but when he sees me, his eyes clear.

"Hi."

"I wasn't sure you'd come." He rests his guitar against the bench and stands.

"How could I not?" I am unable to resist the invisible pull between us.

I close the distance, wrapping my arms around him. His skin is soft and warm, but his muscles are tense, unyielding beneath my fingers. He pulls me hard against his chest, winding one hand through my hair to cradle the back of my head.

"Nothing but the truth between us," I warn him straight up.

"I'm truly sorry, Claire."

"I can deal with almost anything else, but not lies. Not anymore. I can't live my life second-guessing everything you say or do. I don't want to be looking for proof you're telling me the truth. Looking for proof you're not. I need to be able to take you at your word. Unconditionally. If you can't promise me this, tell me now."

"You can trust me, Claire. I promise to always tell you the truth," Zach says with a conviction I feel resonate through my whole body.

"Good." I reach my hand between his legs, squeeze firmly. His eyes widen in alarm. "If you ever lie to me, Zach Argos," I say through my teeth. "I'll cut off your balls and feed them to you for breakfast."

Zach swallows. "You can remove your hand any time you're ready."

I give another firm squeeze before I let go.

"Does this mean you've forgiven me?" he asks, hopefully.

"Yes," I say, and he smiles. How can I be angry with him when he looks at me like that? I remember Derek's comment from earlier about me being able to forgive Zach, but not him. It strikes me then, that Derek hasn't apologized at any point. For anything.

Zach's lips meet mine, and I'm filled with a sense of belonging. I understand what Zach meant when he said being with me was the closest thing he'd ever felt to being home.

I feel that with him, too.

Life around us is in turmoil, a storm with no sign of letting up, and only here, in Zach's arms, do I feel at peace. We met through circumstance, but the friendship we formed was genuine and strong. The passion that grew between us is powerful. I didn't know love could feel like this...this startling rollercoaster of emotional lows and dizzying heights.

"I have to apologize to you, too," I say, breaking the kiss. "I think I've made things worse. Much worse."

"What happened?" Zach pulls back, his dark, hooded eyes searching mine.

"Derek knows you gave me the information. He threatened to tell Rydell, said that Rydell would kill you when he found out." Guilt has swallowed my voice, making it hard to speak. But I push through, my words coming out in a somewhat coherent rush.

I tell him what transpired during the meeting; Derek's admission to a cocaine habit, the debt he incurred with Rydell, how he used money from his firm's trust account, how Derek—Jasmine—had been sewing listening devices into dresses. I told him that Derek had followed me to the Village, how he threatened to report Zach to authorities.

"I'm sorry, Zach. I thought the information you gave me would get him to back off. Instead, it has made him even angrier. He seemed wild and reckless when I left him. I have no idea what he'll do next."

I shiver, as though the sea breeze is a chill deep in my bones.

"You have nothing to be sorry about," Zach says. "None of this is your fault."

He cups his hand under my chin, raises my face so that I am looking at him. "Nothing you said or did was wrong. You're not to worry about Rydell," he says. "I'll handle him. I told you I'm not doing any work for him, and I'm not. But we go way back. He trusts me. And I trust you. I gave you the information on the USB because you wanted answers. You're entitled to the truth."

"But what if Derek—"

"I'll take it from here." Zach's tone sends a shiver down my spine. "You've confronted Derek. Warned him to back off. That's the end of this for you. I'll handle anything that arises from the meeting."

"But—"

"It's not open for discussion," he says with a hard kiss on my lips that takes the sting from his words. "I haven't interfered until now. It's taken more willpower than I thought I had, but I watched you rediscover your own power, watched you stand your ground and fight for what is right-fully yours. There's no doubt Derek knows your strength. As do you." He traces the back of his finger down my cheek. "But now it's time to place your trust in me. I'm your man. I need you to promise you'll let me take it from here. Promise me, Claire."

"Okay, I promise."

He crushes his lips to mine, perhaps so I won't continue to argue. If I was able to think while he was kissing me, I may have asked him what he meant to do. How he meant to handle the threat of Derek and Rydell. But I cannot think of anything, my mind blanking as my senses drown from the taste of his mouth. His scent, all earthy and male. The feel of his muscles rippling beneath my fingertips as I claw his back, trying to get him closer.

I pull back long enough to drag my strappy sundress over my head. He groans and reaches behind me to unhook my bra. It falls to our feet, and this time, when my body presses against his, it's skin to skin.

"I love you," I whisper, and he looks at me with something like bewil-derment.

"You're nuts, you know that?"

"Yep. Heard that once or twice before." I grin.

He cups my face in both hands, his thumbs brushing tenderly across my cheeks.

He looks deep into my eyes. "I love you, Claire."

I throw my arms around his neck and hold on tight. He kisses me and wraps an arm around my waist, the other cupping the back of my head, supporting me as his tongue caresses mine. I can't get close enough to him.

I want to climb inside him, place my heart in his chest, right next to his.

He supports my back and, with his leg, sweeps me off my feet. I fall backwards, but he doesn't let go, lowering me onto the soft lawn, taking me with him.

I laugh as he smiles down at me. His dark hair is mussed, blowing around his face in the sea breeze. His body is on top of mine, but his arm supports his weight.

His lips meet mine as heavy drops of rain begin to fall on and around us.

He groans. "Seems we don't have much luck when it comes to the weather."

"I don't care," I say. "I want you, Zach. Now."

His grin feels like a wave of warm chocolate throughout my body.

"You," he says, "and my guitar, both need to go inside out of the rain."

Zach pulls me to my feet, grabs my hand, my sundress, his guitar, and leads me up the stairs and into the loungeroom. Rain lands on his chest, trailing down the sexy contours of his muscular torso in tiny rivulets.

I probably should be cold, but I can't feel anything but a raging fire in my blood. And the furnace-like heat coming from Zach's body.

In the lounge room, Zach hands me my sundress, and I hang it over the back of a chair while Zach lights a fire. "I know it's not winter, but the storm makes me feel as though I can justify one."

When he's finished, he opens the French doors to the balcony. The salty sea air is fresh and crisp, the fire ambient and warm. The storm that was brewing earlier has arrived, flashes of lightning brilliant in the darkening sky.

Naked, I stand by the fire and watch Zach kick off his jeans. Light gusts of wind burst in through the open door, brushing over my heated skin, across my pebbled nipples, the sensation heightening my already highly aroused state.

"Fuck, you're sexy." Zach's eyelids are heavy, his eyes molten pools of fire and desire. Right now, there are no shadows, no walls. No darkness from his past. His expression is open, full of wonder...and love.

He moves to me. His large hands travel across my chest, cup my breasts, he squeezes my nipples. I gasp in pleasure, and he lowers me onto the black sheepskin rug in front of the crackling fire. He straddles me, and I raise my hips, rubbing against him, trying to ease the urgency of my need for him.

He brings his hand between us, his fingers exploring the tender place between my legs.

A low growl rumbles through his chest. "You're ready for me."

"Like, an hour ago already!"

He laughs, his eyes bright. His hair is wet and hanging in sexy curls around his face. Shifting to his knees, he pulls me up onto his lap. I spread my legs, straddling his thighs. I make a choked sound as his erection pushes inside me. His cock is hard and thick, and though I'm stretched wide, he has farther to go. He thrusts up with his hips, and the sensation takes my breath away. Holding himself still, he waits for my body to relax, to accommodate his length.

My arms are around his shoulders, and his hands are on my waist. He begins to thrust upward with long, powerful strokes, and I match his rhythm, rising and falling in time with him. We look into each other's eyes for long moments, desire sweeping us away. Together. There are no barriers between us, no dark secrets left to tear us apart.

I lean down and kiss him as he continues to drive me to heights I've never been to before. He brings his hand between us, plays with my nipple, squeezing and rolling it between his thumb and forefinger, and pleasure, white hot and demanding, sends tiny shivers skittering across my skin.

The storm is above us now, rain driving down outside, the wind carrying a fine mist of salt spray through the open doors. Outside, waves crash heavily onto the shore, and a flash of lightning lights up the horizon. But the world is background music; nothing exists but the feel of Zach's body in mine.

Zach is smiling and it reaches his eyes, crinkling the corners.

God, I love this man.

My pleasure continues to build, Zach's thrusting skilled and controlled, slowly increasing the pace, but not taking us to the peak too fast. Desire burns and coils steadily, relentlessly, toward the ultimate climax. Thunder rumbles in the distance. I've never felt so wild, so free, so passionately entwined with another human.

"God, you feel so fucking good." Zach's voice is gruff, and it's hard to breathe. I tangle my fingers in his damp hair. Our eyes are only for each other as Zach increases the pace, faster, deeper, harder. He lowers his hands, supporting my rear as he quickens his pace. I grip his back, my nails digging into his skin as his thrusts drive us to that exquisite precipice. Just when I think I'll die of wanting, wave after wave of scorching white-hot ecstasy washes over me.

Zach cries out my name as he finds his own release. Tears roll from my eyes, but my hair covers my face, hiding them. As the ripples of pleasure gradually subside, I hold him tight.

"You're shivering," he says. "Let's take a nice warm shower together."

I let him help me up, but I'm not shivering. I'm shaking.

I'm overwhelmed.

His eyes crinkle at the corners as he brushes my hair, damp from rain and sweat, off my face. He kisses me.

"Fuck, I love you, Claire."

I've never felt so happy in all my life. So glad to be alive.

I grin back at him. "Fuck, I love you, too, Zach Argos."

CHAPTER 30

I can't shake off a heavy sense of foreboding. We are on the couch in front of the dying fire, Zach's head in my lap where he drifted off to sleep after the last time we made love.

I run my fingers through his hair, watch the gentle rise and fall of his chest. The lines at the corners of his eyes have relaxed, making him appear younger. He seems more at peace than I've seen him. The last of the walls that have been standing in the way of us have fallen.

But I can't stop thinking this bliss is only temporary.

Derek and his threats toward Zach and the Village have been playing over and over in my mind.

I trace my fingers across Zach's cheek, listening to the soft sound of his breathing, almost drifting off, when his phone starts to ring in the bedroom.

"Zach," I whisper. "That was your phone."

"What time is it?" His voice is a low, sleepy mumble in my ear.

I glance at the digital clock. Quarter past nine.

Zach sits up, scrubs a hand through his hair. "I fell asleep?"

"I think I wore you out."

Giving me a wicked grin, he leans over me, kisses my lips. "Consider me refreshed and ready for the next round." His erection pressing against my thigh is proof of his words.

"Your phone," I remind him.

Zach grumbles.

"It might be important," I say as the phone dings, signaling a message. Zach moves to the bedroom.

What if it's the police? What if Derek has notified the authorities about what Zach is doing?

Derek said Zach would go to jail. Is that true?

Dear God don't let that be true.

Zach walks back into the room, his phone in his hand.

Tension radiates out of him in waves. He dials a number, holding it to his ear as he slides on jeans.

I jump up from the couch to his side.

"I'm on my way," Zach says briskly. "Get everyone out. Make sure they stay out. Do a headcount. No one goes back in. For any reason. I'm on my way." Zach disconnects.

"What is it?" I speak so fast the three words come out as one syllable. I pull Zach's jumper on over my jeans.

Zach's keys are in his hand.

I'm shaking, not from cold but stone-cold fear.

Zach's eyes are swirling with emotion, stormy, dark, and wild.

"Stay here."

I grab my phone, slip it into my back pocket, and chase after him. I catch up to him at the back door as he's grabbing his Maglite torch.

"You're not leaving me behind."

He turns to me, his face creased in lines of worry.

"I'm coming," I say forcefully. Whatever it is, I'm going to help.

He presses the remote to open the garage door. I've never seen it roll up so slowly. Zach grabs the fire extinguisher off the wall, looks over the roof of the car at me. "There's a fire at the Village."

"Shall I call the fire department?"

Uncertainty flashes across his face. Then it dawns on me. That would alert authorities to the Village.

"Hurry!" I shout. "Go! I'll meet you there."

The engine of Zach's BMW roars as he speeds down the driveway. I rush back inside, opening drawers and cupboards, gathering towels, a large first-aid kit, ice packs from the freezer...and water. With shaking hands, I fill as many bottles with water as I can find.

I leave barely minutes after Zach, my car loaded with everything I can think of. I have no idea whether any of it is needed, whether the fire is just a stove fire.

But from Zach's reaction, I know that whatever this is, it's serious.

And that it's also my fault.

CHAPTER 31

I see the golden glow of flames and smell the smoke before I get out of my car. Levi, Cooper, Oliver, and William are in the clearing, and Noah and James are running up the pathway. Zach had likely told them to stay up here.

They're at my car when I park, talking a hundred miles an hour, filling me in on what happened.

"Everything is on fire."

"All the cabins."

"Explosion."

Explosion? "Is anyone hurt?" I ask, getting out bottles of water and thrusting them into their hands. I'm worried about smoke inhalation. Burns. But the boys all appear to be okay and, to a large degree, relatively calm. Concerned, a little bit angry even, but none appear panicked.

"So everyone is okay?"

"I think so."

"Where's Mandy?" Aidan asks, running up to us.

"Mandy is here?" I ask, my heart beginning to pound.

"We were just about to leave when we heard the first explosion," Aiden says.

"Is she with Zach?" Cooper asks.

"I don't know," Aidan says. "There's so much smoke. If no one has seen her here, I'm going back."

"Wait!" I call out, but he's already running. Quickly surveying the group, I can't see any injuries, but I have no idea if anyone is hurt at the cabins.

I fling the back door of my car open. "There are things you might need in here. There's ice in the Esky," I say, using the Aussie term for a portable cooler. "There's a first-aid kit. Whatever you want, help yourselves."

Leaving the ignition on to provide light for them, I grab the smaller first-aid kit and rush down the path toward the burning cabins. Thick smoke fills my lungs and makes me cough.

"Claire! Zach said everyone has to wait in the car park," Mason yells as I pass him moving the other way.

"Have you seen Mandy?"

He shakes his head. "Too much smoke."

"Go wait in the car park like Zach asked you to," I tell him. "Hurry."

The sound of a siren in the distance fills me with dread.

Zach has made the call.

There will be questions. An investigation. If anyone is injured, will Zach be held accountable? Go to jail?

Oh, God. Oh, God.

My mind is racing, and I can't control the myriad competing thoughts as I race toward the glow of flames through the trees. Despite the thick plumes of smoke, I spot Zach straight away. He's with Richard, and they're trying to put out the fire with a garden hose. Zach's voice, loud, clear, and authoritative, easily rises above the commotion. Lucas and Isaac have just left his side and are heading toward the track, and I realize Zach's doing a head count, sending them up to the car park and safety.

Of the six cabins, two are fully ablaze, three are on fire, and the one closest to us is out, the timber charred black. Zach and Richard yank the hose, moving it down to the next cabin. Quickly, I move around to the rear of the property, scanning and listening. The timber on the back of the cabins is well engulfed.

At Zach's side, I place my hand on his shoulder. His muscles are bunching beneath my palm with tension as much as effort.

"Where's Mandy?" I ask.

"Here I am." Mandy appears from behind Zach at my side, and relief floods my body.

Aidan throws his arms around her. "You scared the life out of me," he says.

"Is anyone hurt?" I ask Zach. I have to raise my voice to be heard; whether over the blood rushing past my ears or the fire, I can't be sure.

"Everyone appears to be okay," Zach replies, his voice hard. "Sam's not here, but I think he's out with friends tonight. I haven't seen Levi."

"He's at the car park," I say. "He's fine."

Zach nods, and Richard says something to him from his other side. "Can you take Mandy back to the cars?" Zach asks, turning back to me. "I told her to go with Oliver and Cooper, but for some reason, she's back."

"Of course." I grab Mandy's hand and tell Aidan to go on ahead.

I don't want to leave Zach, but with only one hose, I'm not going to be much use anyway. The sirens are getting louder.

I'm just starting to lead Mandy to the pathway when she darts away. I reach out to grab her, but she's too fast.

It's dark, the thick smoke making it hard to see where she's going.

"Mandy!" I charge after her toward the fire and see her dash inside a cabin, one of the ones that isn't fully engulfed, but the rear wall is lit up.

I run after her, screaming her name as I go. At the entrance to the cabin, I trip and land on something scorching hot. I barely feel my hands and knees, but I know the pain from the inevitable burn will come later.

I'm screaming Mandy's name, my voice hoarse from the smoke. I pull Zach's jumper over my mouth and go inside. The heat is searing my face, my arms, like the worst sunburn I've ever had.

My eyes are stinging, watering so bad that even without the smoke, it's impossible to see. I lower the jumper long enough to scream Mandy's name as loud as I can.

The fire is roaring. A monster gathering intensity.

My vision blurred, I see a shape on the floor. I don't know how I know it's Mandy, but it has to be.

She must have been overcome by smoke, but I'm only seconds behind her. She's going to be okay.

She has to be okay.

Then I realize she's not lying on the floor. She's just picking something up. I scoop her into my arms and make my way back to the door. I cover her head against my chest. She coughs and jerks in my arms, but that means she's okay, and it's the sweetest sound I've ever heard.

"You're going to be fine," I shout as the journey through the small cottage seems to take forever in the dark.

Something heavy smacks into me, and I stumble, barely managing to put Mandy down before I fall.

But I look up, and she's on her feet.

"Run!" I scream, gesturing with my arms. "Run!"

She is outside the cabin in the fresh air. She's coughing, but she's okay. I struggle to stand, confused as to why it's so hard.

My legs are dead weights.

I frantically look behind me and see a large piece of timber covering them.

Mandy is screaming and coughing, shouting at me to "get up, get up" even as I'm shouting at her to run.

The smoke gets thicker, and I can no longer see her.

Then it comes to me. The red coat. She was clutching it to her chest.

She went inside a burning cabin to save her red coat.

Oh, Mandy!

My heart scatters in the wind like sparks from the fire. Tears well behind my stinging eyelids, and it's too painful to keep breathing. My lungs are on fire. That's the only thing I can now feel.

My body is no longer mine.

I am only my thoughts.

And each and every breath that's far too painful to take.

CHAPTER 32

My eyes slowly open to a white room. White ceiling, white walls. There's no smoke, only a faint antiseptic smell. I'm in the hospital.

"Hi."

I turn my head to the voice. *Kira.*

"Hi, Kira," I say. "What are you doing here? Where's Zach?" Images of fire and billowing smoke dance to a sickening tune in my head. I can still see the forest alight, feel the heat and sting of the embers that fell on our skin. I can hear the shouts of panic from the boys...see Mandy run directly into the burning cabin.

"I'm not sure," Kira says, eying me critically. "I'm sure he's fine."

It's an uncomfortable sensation, being in one location full of action and filled with terror, then waking up somewhere else entirely, with no memory of how you got there. No idea of what happened between then and now.

"Is Zach all right?" I ask, ignoring the pain slicing like razorblades down my throat.

Something must have happened. He'd be here otherwise.

"Have you heard from him? And—uh—" I want to ask about Mandy. The boys. But Kira doesn't know about the Village. How does Kira know I'm here?

Kira's hand is firm on my arm. "Richard rang me," she says. "Zach told him to last night. Lucky I'm listed as a contact with the shops after-hours service. Richard told me what happened and what he and Zach were doing to help the kids at the Village. He asked me to be with you at the hospital, but I would have come whether he asked me to or not."

"Thank you," I say. "How's Mandy?" I cough, wincing from the pain. "Is she okay?" I whisper. "Was anyone hurt?"

Kira's face creases more deeply with concern. "Shh. Don't talk. The grumpy-ass nurse that just did her rounds told me you have to rest and tried to make me leave. The hell I was going to. I only managed to get in here in the first place because I lied and said I was your sister. Apparently, their stupid rules say only family is allowed in, and the only other family you have is Derek. I wasn't letting that fucker in here."

In spite of everything, she makes me smile. "Thank you," I tell her again. "For being my sister. You've been a true friend to me."

I struggle to sit up. "But please, I need you to tell me everything you know. What else did Richard say? Is anyone hurt? Does he know where Zach is? Was he arrested?"

"Claire, lie back down, or that nurse will come back in here and tear strips off both of us."

The nurse must be pretty scary for Kira to take notice. She waits until my head is on the pillow before she continues to talk.

"Everyone is fine. Mandy is fine, thanks to you. A log fell on your lower legs, pinning you to the ground. Zach heard Mandy screaming and managed to get to you in time. He freed you and pulled you out. You were overcome by smoke inhalation. You've been sedated and on oxygen or something for most of the night, but you don't have serious injuries. I'm told a doctor will visit you at some point today to explain everything."

My eyes close without any direction from me. Learning no one was seriously hurt in the fire has used up the small amount of energy I had.

"What happened?" I ask. "How did it start?"

But I already know.

"Why am I so tired?" My voice is thick.

"You were sedated," Kira says. "It's wearing off, but slowly. Go back to sleep."

"Where's Zach?" I force my eyes open. "I need to know he's okay."

"I don't know," Kira says.

"Then tell me everything you do know. Talk, Kira. And talk fast."

"Mandy is fine. Like you, she's been on oxygen, but because of her age, I think they will want to monitor her for longer than you. Then Aidan will pick her up and take her back home. His guardianship approval came through a few days ago. As soon as she's released, he's taking her shopping to buy something new for her room. Apparently, she doesn't often get new things."

That's why she risked her life for the red coat. My throat constricts with emotion, and I cough. Aidan has some furniture already and will be preparing everything she needs, but...

"I have something I want to give Mandy. If she wants it, of course." I don't know why I think of this now, why it's suddenly important. Perhaps because it's something I can focus on in the midst of all this tragedy surrounding me that doesn't make me feel powerless. Mandy moving in with Aidan and getting a chance at a better life fills me with much needed hope that the world isn't always such a wicked place. I cling to that with both hands.

I picture the beautiful hand-carved chest of drawers and mirrored dressing table, painted a gloss white with gold trim, matching desk, chair, and four-poster single bed with sheer curtains. The set had cost a small fortune, but Katie wanted it.

My stomach twists, and I wait for the sensation to pass.

For a moment, Mandy's image blurs, and it's Katie's face I see.

A tug on my hand with little fingers, and I teeter between two worlds for a moment.

"Claire?" Kira asks, her voice concerned. "Are you all right? Should I get the nurse?"

The sensation on my fingers is gone.

I blink.

Smile.

"I'm fine. There are still times I feel Katie with me."

Kira squeezes my hand.

"Do you believe that's possible?" I ask.

Kira considers a moment. "Yes," she says, nodding. "I do."

"Please offer Katie's bedroom suite to Mandy. It's not new, but it's really beautiful. If she wants it, it's hers. I'll text Aidan a picture if he wants to show her. Katie would want her to have it."

Derek is in no position to argue with me. Not after what he's done. I'll get my lawyer to make it a nonnegotiable part of the settlement.

"Where is everyone now?" I ask.

"Zach has given Richard the keys to his house, and most of them are there, I think. Richard and his wife have also opened their house up. I've offered my place, but for now, most have gathered at Zach's. Everyone is fine—the details can be worked out later. Go back to sleep. I'm heading over to Zach's house to see if I can offer any assistance. Although, the boys seem very capable."

Yes, adversity makes you strong.

But still, they shouldn't have had everything they've worked so hard for taken away like that. It was cruel and needless. Another hard knock in an already harsh and brutal life.

There was no reason for Derek to do this.

The need to balance the scales crowds my brain, suffocating me.

What happens to the Village now? What will the consequences be for Zach? Zach said he can handle Rydell. But how can he avoid the penalties from the law? Questions from authorities, regulatory departments, the police. Will he go to jail? There's so much I don't know, but one thing is painfully clear.

It's because of me the Village burned down.

In one act of heartless cruelty, my vindictive asshole of an ex-husband has stripped away the only security these kids have ever had. Taken away their homes. Perhaps their last chance at turning their lives around.

My thoughts are a rollercoaster hurtling at top speed around my brain. I'm agitated, and despite the residual effects of a sedative, my feet want to run a marathon.

I'd called Derek's bluff.

I'd stupidly hoped the threat would be enough to get Derek to back off. He didn't believe I was strong enough to go through with it. The fool. The way I'm feeling right now? Visiting an outlaw bikers' club at their club address... Small price to pay.

I can't imagine what could have happened between our talk at the coffee shop and his being desperate enough to start the fire. What happened to make him mad enough to do something as drastic as burn the cabins down? It's time to show Derek who the woman he married really is.

High on coke and at the bottom of the bottle, did he forget the woman who'd faced him in the coffee shop?

The one who'd told him what would happen if he didn't stay away from Zach and the Village?

The woman who was now going to make good on her promise.

CHAPTER 33

I key the address to Rydell Industries into my car's GPS. I don't have a plan. I haven't got some carefully crafted speech for when I see Bill Rydell. I'm numb, driving on autopilot. I try not to think about what will happen when I get there. I only know I made a promise to Derek, and I was seeing it through.

I drive down a dirt track, through metal gates that are open, and pull up to a large shed with two massive metal sliding doors. Perhaps this address is not the Dark Ryders biker clubhouse but, instead, just a warehouse full of stolen goods? What do I know about how an outlaw bikers club runs its business? Anything could be behind those metal doors. I have no idea what I will be walking into.

But I'm not scared.

I'm fully prepared for whatever will happen. To not walk away from here, possibly.

I knock loudly on the door, my knuckles scraping on the rusted steel surface, but I'm sure they're already aware of my presence. Cameras are prominently placed above the door, and two angry Rottweilers bark behind the security mesh fence topped with razor wire.

A burly guy, tatted up, six foot-three perhaps, opens the door and peers down at me. His eyes are narrowed, his expression harsh, and he has a missing tooth. His mouth is swollen, his lip split. The tooth injury must be recent. At first, I think he's angry, but on closer inspection, he looks suspicious, even amused.

"I'm here to see Bill Rydell."

He raises an eyebrow. "What do you want, little lady?"

Well, at five foot ten, no one has ever called me *that* before.

"Please tell him Claire Hardt is here to see him."

He doesn't move, just stares down at me. I force myself to hold his gaze, to not shuffle my feet. He looks like he could knock me down with a single wave of his arm.

"I know who you are," Missing Tooth says. "Or you wouldn't have made it this far. I asked you what you wanted."

"Who are you?" I ask. I really don't want to have this conversation with anyone other than Bill Rydell.

Missing Tooth's frown is like that of a bulldog, and he growls in warning.

"Oh, right. Of course, you're not going to tell me who you are." Do I try to get past him? Even I'm not feeling that reckless. "Can you please pass a message on for me?" I use the same tone and formality I would deploy at any corporate meeting.

Another large man with dark hair and a slight beer belly comes to stand at the door. Every exposed inch of skin is covered in tattoos, and he has a rather impressive snake-winding-through-a-skull image covering one half of his face and neck.

"What do you want?" Skull Tattoo asks. Unlike Missing Tooth, Skull Tattoo appears to have been away when senses of humor were being handed out. There is nothing amused in his expression; in fact, he's looking downright pissed off. If I were of a mind to wager a bet, I'd say that was Bill Rydell.

More men gather around him, and I swallow the lump of nerves that has lodged in my throat.

"I know about your deal with my husband," I say, relieved my voice sounds relatively clear. "Soon to be ex-husband. We've separated. I'm not going back. Not ever."

Missing Tooth glances over my shoulder as though expecting to see law enforcement behind me. Skull Tattoo growls, and my tension ratchets up another notch.

"I'm here alone," I say quickly. "I've told no one I'm coming...or about you. I didn't know about...it. About the money he was paying you. At the time, I mean. But I do now."

Okay, not quite as smooth as I would have liked, but I've made a start. And I'm still here. My feet firmly on the ground.

"I can't keep living with the threat of people hurting those that I love. Derek's done enough." I think of the Village up in flames, the sound of the sirens. Mandy.

Zach.

I square my shoulders, my jaw clenched as tightly as theirs are.

"You've got some serious balls being here, lady," Missing Tooth says."Yeah, well, he gave me no choice. Derek was using my business to pay you the money he owes you." I take a breath, steady my voice. "When Derek and I separated, I reclaimed my business. I'm here to tell you that your *arrangement—*" I hold back on giving details for fear they'll think I know too much "—with Derek has nothing to do with me or my shop. I had no part in the deal, no knowledge of it at the time, and I want no part of it now."

I survey the faces before me. The men are silent, peering down at me like scientists examining a strange new species in a lab.

They don't speak, and it's making me more uncomfortable by the second.

"Derek said you would kill him, and kill me, if payments aren't made on time. What you do to him is not my business. Of course, I'd prefer it if you didn't kill me, either, but I refuse to spend the rest of my life looking over my shoulder. I can't do that. I won't do that. So, do whatever you need to do now. No one knows I'm here. This is not a setup. What would I possibly gain from that? I just want to be free. From Derek. The past. I won't be responsible for anyone else getting hurt because of me. Because of Derek. So, this ends now. Whatever needs to happen? Get it over with."

I squeeze my eyes shut. I don't know what to expect, but it'll be over soon, right? Then I open my eyes, needing to confirm I've been specific. "The thing I want to make clear is that Derek—"

"Can't pay his debt," Skull Tattoo finishes for me.

"I can't know that." I swallow hard, then continue, "All I'm saying is that the way he's been paying you in the past—through my business—isn't going to be the way it will happen any longer."

The two bikers in front of the others glance at each other.

"Money is not the only way we settle debts around here," Skull Tattoo says, rubbing his goatee as he looks me over from head to toe.

I take a step backward.

"Good idea. What do you say we bring the little lady in and have a bit of fun?" Missing Tooth says. Without warning, he lunges forward, grabbing my upper arm. He yanks me hard so that my body is flush against his. I struggle, kneeing him hard between his legs. He growls in my ear, his grip tightening into a bruising crush.

"You said you're ready for whatever needs to happen," he leers in my ear. "And the images that conjured has whet my appetite. I'm known for my...creativity in the bedroom."

"Let go of me!"

He runs the back of his free hand down my face, and I bite down hard, catching his fingers between my teeth and drawing blood. He slaps my face, and my head jerks backward.

"Good thing I like my women with a little spunk in them." His menacing gaze pierces right through me. "A meal is always more satisfying if they put up a fight."

"Get your hands off her!"

Zach!

I don't have time to question what he's doing here, I'm too relieved to see him. To know he's all right and not sitting in some cell somewhere. Zach elbows his way through the bikers to the front door. His face is creased into hard lines, contorted into a steely expression I've never seen before. "I said, let her go."

"What's she to you?" Missing Tooth demands. "Isn't she the accountant's wife?"

"She's mine."

"Let her go," Skull Tattoo orders.

The guy grips my arm for another few seconds before abruptly releasing it. He shoves me backward, and I fall.

"Get out of here, Claire," Zach says. He doesn't help me to my feet, but he is now in between me and the bikers.

"But—"

"I said, *go!*" I flinch at the harshness of the order but am not stupid enough to argue.

"Looks like you got lucky this time, little lady," Skull Tattoo says. "But if you manage to find balls enough to come back, you'll be leaving feet first in a pine box."

I'm frozen to the spot.

What about closure? I need assurances I won't be looking over my shoulder anymore. I want to know why Zach is here. Why he seemingly holds some authority with the bikers. They let me go, but that didn't mean they weren't intending on paying me a future visit.

Did Derek already come and see them? Did he tell them Zach gave me the information on the USB like he threatened? If so, then why did he burn down the Village?

What will happen to Zach after I'm gone?

I walk away and get into my car. Even after I can no longer see them, I still feel their eyes on me as I drive off their property and onto the main road. A glance at the two motorcycles in the rearview mirror confirms my suspicion. It is not until they turn off down a side street that my hands start to shake. I focus on keeping my foot steady on the accelerator as alternating sensations of hot and cold filter through me.

I hadn't remembered before now. Zach had been very definite when he'd said he would handle things from here.

Enraged at what Derek had done, I'd forgotten my promise to Zach.

CHAPTER 34

I've spent the night at Zach's house, in his bed. Waiting for him to walk in the door, my sense of dread increasing with every long minute he doesn't.

The boys from the Village are in remarkably good spirits, considering what happened. Not one of them is moping around as we make bacon and eggs for breakfast on the barbeque. They're talking about rebuilding, about where they go from here. Three of them have just come back from a surf at the beach, last night's storm creating some gnarly waves, or so I'm told. But I can't think about waves, rebuilding, tomorrow, or even the next hour with Zach missing.

Where is he? Surely, he wouldn't still be with the bikers. Not unless... he wasn't able to leave. I can't continue that train of thought.

Has he been arrested? Which option would be worse?

Ten o'clock comes, and still no Zach.

I can't eat. I can't drink. My nails are bitten to the quick. My mind is consumed with worry, with anger, with mind-numbing fear. I just know that when I see Zach, things will be okay.

I will be okay.

I can't breathe.

Thoughts continue to roll through my head like boulders down a mountain. I'm at the bottom of the hill, and I can't stop them.

There's only one thing that can.

Zach walking through that door.

But time ticks by, minutes, hours, days. Who knows how long I've waited now. A second feels like a week without him.

And still no Zach.

I tune out the boys' talk and speculation about who could have lit the fire; Mason is worried his dad might have found him. Lucas thinks it might have been his Uncle Bill.

I don't tell them it was Derek.

My mind's a mess, and a quick glance in the mirror confirms my appearance is no better.

I simply can't find it within myself to care.

A little after two p.m., I get in my car and drive. I can't take another second of waiting. I want to go to the police station, see if he's there. And if he is, tell them what a wonderful man Zach is. But that won't help. The law is the law, and being a good person means nothing if you break the rules.

Fuck the rules.

If Zach goes to jail…

I choke back tears.

When I stop the car, I'm at the Village.

It's time for me to see the full extent of the damage I've caused.

The pungent scent of stale smoke hangs heavy in the air as I walk down the pathway that leads to whatever is left of the Village. The sky is overcast. The day is humid, and the occasional drops of rain splatter against my face.

Devastation is all around me. The fire had spread to the surrounding gum trees, and there is little left of the boys' timber cabins. Bushes that weren't burnt have been crushed by fire trucks. The charred ruins are heartbreaking reminders of what used to be. The boys' meager possessions have been destroyed. Everything gone up in flames.

The silence is deafening, not a single bird call. I walk past the burnt remnants of the timber seesaw and stumble over a blackened skateboard.

The Village did not officially exist; there is no insurance.

Derek followed me here. I should have been more careful.

Tears fall unchecked down my cheeks like the rain on the ash. To my left, a scorched branch falls off a gum tree, the sudden movement sending my heart racing. I look around, the hair on the back of my neck standing on end.

I'm being watched.

I peer through the trees, but there's no one there.

I roll my shoulders to shake off the uneasy feeling and make my way to the cabin I had followed Mandy into that night. The heavy chunk of wood that had landed on my legs, trapping me inside, is still there. The red jacket I had made her could have cost her life. That's how important the few possessions these kids have are.

And now, everything has burned to the ground.

I sink to my knees.

My head is in my hands.

I'll never forgive myself for my part in this. I take some consolation that I haven't let Derek go unpunished for his part, either.

A kookaburra calls in the distance, and a gentle breeze ruffles my hair. I'm hyperaware of each beat of my heart. Thump, thump, thump, against my ribcage.

Slowly, I rise to my feet, rubbing a palm across my chilled skin. The sun peeks through the clouds, and movement catches my eye on the ground to my left. A tail disappears into the bush. A lizard.

Something shiny glimmers in the sunlight. I move to the spot, running my fingers through the dirt, and pick up the small metallic object. A piece of jewelry that must belong to Mandy.

Absently, I wipe the earring on my T-shirt then hold it out in front of me…

A bloom with five petals. A star jasmine flower.

Jasmine's earring, the ones I remember her wearing that day she arrived on my doorstep.

For a long time, I'm unable to move. Then a sense of terrifying calm washes over me. The thin thread that's been holding me together finally snaps.

With the intention of calling Derek one more time, I pull my phone out of my back pocket to see two calls from Sam and twelve from Kira.

I swipe the message to return Kira's call, my heart pounding. Has she heard from Zach? Is he in trouble and needs me? *What has happened?*

"Claire, come quickly!" Kira's panicked voice comes through the phone.

"What is it?" I ask. "Where are you?" I'm already running back to my car.

"Your shop is on fire.

CHAPTER 35

J see the billowing smoke long before I arrive at the shop. The street has been blocked off, so I pull up on the side of the road and run through the crowd of onlookers.

Flashing lights, fire trucks, police, emergency services occupy the space in front of my shop. The fire appears to be mostly out, but the heavy tang of burning plastic fills the air. I see Kira talking to a police officer, and I make my way directly to her. She doesn't appear to be hurt at all, and I'm relieved she mustn't have been in the shop when the fire started.

The officer turns his attention to me. Name, address, yes, I am the owner of the business leasing the shop. No, I wasn't here when the fire started; no, I don't know how the fire started… He's asking the questions slowly, clearly, and I bite down hard on my impatience while I wait for him to record my answers in his notebook. Eventually, he gets called away, and I seize the opportunity to take Kira's arm, pulling her a short distance from the group of people.

"What happened?" I ask.

"Sam called me after he called the emergency services. He was driving past when he thought he saw someone running out the back of your shop, but he couldn't be sure."

Kira's eyes shine bright with tears. "All our work was in there," she says. "Our new designs, our sketches for the new line, my entire jewelry collection…everything was in there. First the Village, and now, this!"

I lean in to hug her, and she grabs me before I can, wrapping her arms around me. She bursts into tears, and I hold her a few moments. She pulls back, wipes her nose on the back of her hand.

"Who the fuck did this?" she demands. "Derek?"

"I thought so," I say. But I can no longer be sure. I reach into my pocket and pull out the jasmine earring. "I found this at the Village. It's Jasmine's."

"That bitch!" Kira shouts, drawing attention from a few people in the nearby crowd.

"I don't know it was her for sure," I rush to say. "Perhaps she was there when Derek lit the fire, perhaps she went there on a different occasion with Derek and had nothing to do with the fire."

"Yeah, and pigs might grow little pink wings and start flying."

But there is another possibility, one I can't share with Kira. What if the bikers set fire to my shop in retaliation for no longer being willing to be part of their blackmail scheme? Or for the visit, a warning to not do anything so stupid again.

I'm becoming more and more concerned for Zach. Where is he?

"I have to go," I say. "I need answers, and there's only one way I can think of to get them. Will you stay here for me? Let me know if there are any developments or if the firemen discover how it started."

"Sure," Kira said. "Go do what you need to do." She gives me another hug. "And, Claire?" Kira calls out after I've taken a few steps. I turn around. "Don't let that fucker get away with this."

CHAPTER 36

I don't remember driving, but I must have because the view through my windshield is of the driveway of my old house. I make my way to the front door. I'm a stranger now, unable to recall a time this place felt like home.

As my key no longer fits in the lock, and I didn't bring the spare key Zach gave me on our last visit, I knock on the door.

When no one answers, I knock louder.

Derek's car is in the driveway, so I make my way around the side of the house. Immediately I'm confronted by the smell of smoke.

Not again!

The side gate is locked with a padlock, and I pound on it in frustration. "Derek!" I shout.

I can hear a series of loud banging noises, like furniture being thrown around. I dart into the garage and bring back the large garbage bin. Pushing it up to the fence, I climb up onto the plastic lid, hoping it's strong enough to hold my weight. Holding on to the top of the fence, I pull myself over, landing in a geranium bush on the other side.

I make my way to the outdoor patio and the sound of all the commotion. When I round the corner, I see the source of smoke.

Katie's bed and bedroom furniture have been dragged outside and are lying haphazard in a pile in the middle of the lawn. Drawers from her dresser are broken and empty, and two large garbage bags gape open...I can see Katie's things crammed inside...her clothes. Her hospital bag is squashed beneath her overturned dressing table, the mirror smashed, and floating in the pool is one of her ballet shoes. The ones she never lived long enough to wear to class...

Jasmine is standing next to the pile of furniture, a match in one hand, the matchbox in the other. Her hair is wild. I can see the whites of her eyes. There's a large tear in her white silk blouse, and there are burns on the back of her hand that continue up her arm.

It *was* her.

"Stop! That belonged to Katie!" I shout as she strikes a match and tries to light the leg of Katie's chest of drawers. But of course, Jasmine already knows that.

I rush to the garden hose and turn it on, spraying water onto the furniture.

"Crap won't light," Jasmine says, striking another match and tossing it onto the bag of clothing.

I'm going to kill her.

After I saturate the clothes to make sure they'll never burn, I turn the hose on Jasmine, hitting her in the face with the full force of the jet.

She screams and jumps back. "What are you doing, you crazy bitch?"

Now that the fire is out, I drop the hose and round on her. I take a step toward her, and whatever she reads in my expression causes her eyes to widen in alarm.

"Do you have any idea what you've done?" I shout into her face. "The damage you've caused."

"Yeah," she spits, her face blotchy and red. "But do you?"

"Me?" I ask, unable to keep the surprise from my voice. "What did I do?"

"They've killed him," she says. "They killed Derek."

She lunges at me, the shock of her words making me slow to react. I fall backward, landing on the limestone coping surrounding the swimming pool. She jumps on top of me, pummeling my face with her fists. I manage to grab her wrist and throw all my weight into a thrust to roll her off me.

We struggle, kicking, punching, biting. My face stings as she gouges my skin with her nails. We continue to reverse positions until she hits me in the back of my head with her fist. She pushes me, and slightly dazed, I land in the pool. Before I can come up for air, she is on top of me, holding me under the water. I thrash, trying to buck her off me.

I almost reach the surface, my lungs burning with the need for air, but she pushes my head down. Somehow, she loses her grip, and I grab onto her shoulder. But she's weighing me down, and I can't break the surface. Seizing the opportunity while she's off balance, I wrap my hands around her neck and squeeze with everything I have. Almost dizzy with needing air, I hold on and don't let go.

Eventually, she releases her grip, and I push to the surface, dragging in huge lungfuls of air. Before I've had enough, she jumps onto my back, pushing me back under. The water is churning, long strands of loose hair mixing with tiny bubbles. Her fingernails dig into my scalp; her grip on my head is relentless.

She intends to kill me.

I pull my knees up to my chest then thrust outward, kicking her with everything I've got as hard as I can. She releases her grip, and again, I make it to the surface, coughing but breathing.

To avoid being caught off guard again, I whip my head around, expecting to see her lunge for me again, but she's not there.

Still blinking and coughing, I look around to find her. She's floating face down in the water.

I swim to her, turn her over, wrap my arm around her shoulder and drag her to the shallow end steps. With effort, I manage to pull her up the steps and onto the lawn. I don't know if she was breathing before I pulled her out, but she is now. I collapse next to her, both of us heaving and choking out the last of the water from our lungs.

"I hate you," she screams.

"You're pregnant, you idiot." Disgust is thick in my tone.

I sit up, and when the world stops spinning, manage to stand. My legs shake for a moment but soon firm. I peer down at Jasmine, at her swollen belly, and reach my hand down to her. She grabs it, and I pull her to her feet.

"Are you all right?" I ask. "Do you need medical attention?"

She places a hand on her stomach. "I'm fine," she says after a while then turns her back and stalks inside.

When I enter the kitchen, she is at the opposite side of the island bench, and on the countertop in front of her is my filleting knife.

"You killed him," Jasmine says, her tone flat.

"Killed who?" I ask. "Derek?"

"Who did you think I was talking about?" Jasmine snaps. "Peter Pan?"

"I didn't kill Derek," I tell her.

"They came and took him," she says.

"Who?" I ask, but I already know.

"The Dark Ryders," she says. "They came last night in a black van and took him away. I haven't seen him since, and his phone is turned off. What did you say to them?" she demands.

"I... uh..."

"Derek told me what happened when he saw you at the coffee shop. He told me he explained about what we were doing with the bugs. And why."

"He threatened Zach and the Village," I say. Jasmine's earring is proof she was there, but either way, after the fire, it is no longer a secret. "I told Derek what I'd do if he brought Zach or the Village into this."

"What do you think he did?" She stares at me, her eyes hard with that familiar vindictive glint.

"Either Derek, you, or both of you lit the fire at the Village the night before last."

"We had nothing to do with that fire," she snaps. "I was with Derek the whole night. He was pissed as hell after he'd met with you and damn near drank himself into a coma. He didn't wake up until lunchtime the following day. We heard about the fire yesterday on the local news the way everyone else did."

I let my gaze travel to her arm. The burns and blisters are red and fresh.

"Let me guess, you burnt your arm making pavlova?"

"I got them burning your shop to the ground!" she shouts, red with anger. Her chest is heaving, and she wraps her fingers around the knife.

I tense and look between her face and her hand.

"You thought it was Derek who lit the fire and you went to Bill Rydell in revenge, didn't you," She asks, but not as a question. She's joined the dots herself.

My mouth is as dry as cotton wool; it's hard to swallow.

"You stupid bitch," Jasmine spits. "I knew you were responsible, and now I know how. Look what you've done!"

How could I have gotten this so wrong?

My head pounds, and the room spins.

If Derek and Jasmine didn't light the fire, then who did?

Maybe that doesn't even matter. I jumped to a conclusion and set off a chain of events that has had dire consequences.

"I found this at the Village," I say, reaching out my hand and handing her the earring. "You were there."

"But not that night," Jasmine says. "I was with Derek the night he followed you. He wanted to see where you went. What you were doing walking off into the bush."

"I—" Blood rushes past my ears, and my knees feel weak. "I'm sorry. I thought he lit the fire."

"It's too late for sorry!" she screams. "When they took Derek away, I knew it was your fault. I told him he shouldn't have told you shit, but he said you wouldn't say anything. He said when push comes to shove, you'd never do anything to intentionally hurt him. Hurt anyone. He said you didn't have it in you. Like you're fucking Mother Teresa or something. I told him he was a fool. Turns out," she says, "I was right."

"I didn't intentionally hurt him," I say. "And don't give me your pity party. This happened because you and Derek got involved with the bikers in the first place."

"Derek wanted to make enough money to take us away from here," she says. "To get away from Bill Rydell and start over. Just him, me, and the baby." She rubs her stomach.

I remember the conversation with Derek at the coffee shop and how easily he said he'd never see Jasmine again as long as I came back to him. Which is the lie?

Does it even matter anymore?

"I'm leaving." I need to find Zach. I turn my back and walk down the hallway.

She lets out an anguished cry. In the reflection of the hallway mirror, I see her rush toward me. I don't have time to react, and before I can turn, a force on the back of my head sends me sprawling onto the floor. My chin lands on the cold tiles, my teeth snapping together painfully.

Pain rockets up my spine and through my body as blows from her fists rain down on my head, my shoulders, my back. I attempt to buck her off, fight back. I flail my arms, struggle with everything I have to roll over, to crawl away. But she's sitting on top of me, her body weight pinning me to the ground. Something heavy—her arm? her knee?—is on the back of my neck, jamming me into the tiles, compressing my windpipe.

I struggle to breathe. I use all my strength to buck against her, to force her weight off me, but unlike earlier by the pool, I'm unable to reverse our positions.

I cover my head to protect myself as blow after blow rains down on my body, her fists connecting with my head, my neck, my back, sending white hot needles of pain through my brain.

Her ragged breathing is in my ear, her nails digging into my scalp as she grabs another handful of hair and yanks.

I quickly become disoriented, my head splitting open from the pain. I can barely think through the agony.

Then it stops.

I crawl as fast as I can across the floor, dragging myself down the hallway toward the front door. I hear her footsteps coming back to me.

I spin over, sliding backwards until I'm in the corner. Knees to my chest, I see a bloody smear across the floor. My blood.

She's back.

Her eyes are tinged red, and she's holding the filleting knife from the bench top. It's razor sharp; I use it for slicing raw chicken.

"I should have let you drown in the pool," I say, spitting blood as I talk.

"A moment of compassion I'll make sure you regret," she says. "You're not walking out of here alive."

Using the wall for support, I slide myself up to a standing position.

I'm not going down without a fight.

She lunges forward with the knife. I jump to the left, and instead of the knife plunging into the middle of my stomach, it enters somewhere near the side of my waist. I don't feel any pain, but warm blood pours down my side.

She holds up the knife, the blade and her fist covered in my blood, but before she can lunge again, I kick out at her, knocking her off balance and onto the floor. The knife flies out of her hand and clatters across the tiles.

I rush to the knife, crouching to retrieve it, when I feel her hand grip my ankle. She yanks hard and is on top of me, two hands on my arm that's holding the knife. She bites my wrist, hard, and I jerk back, the knife clattering away. She's on it before I can blink.

Slowly, slowly she holds the knife above me. Or maybe it's that time has slowed down.

The glint of the blade.

Her glance at my neck.

She's going to slit my throat.

With a desperate kick, I bring my knee up viciously, and she flies forward. I slide backward and pull myself up onto my knees. Before I can stand, she lunges at me with the knife, the blade driving straight into my right shoulder.

Cursing violently, I strike out immediately with my left arm, catching her by surprise. I grab her wrist and twist it hard behind her back. She screams in pain and drops the knife. I watch it skid to a stop under the hallway table. I let go of her arm, and she swings around, her fist connecting with the side of my face.

My vision blurs, and scared of what she will do next, I half run, half drag myself to the front door.

I open the wooden door and scream for help.

But before I can take a step out, I feel something crash over the back of my head. Broken pieces of the vase from the hallway table scatter around me.

I drop to my knees.

I'm at the front door.

At the place we first met, all those weeks ago.

I remember when I first saw her, that strange warning I felt. The ominous premonition. As though a higher part of my consciousness already knew how this would play out even as my rational mind couldn't possibly be aware.

She stands over me.

I look up at her.

Distantly, I think that this is the day I'm going to die. And how strange it is that I didn't know that when I woke up this morning.

She has the knife in her hand, but instead of stabbing me again, she kicks me hard in the stomach. The air whooshes out of my chest, and I cough, spitting up more blood.

"I could gut you like a pig," she says. "But I've decided that's too good for you. I want you to suffer. I want you to die here, slowly and alone." Her voice is cold, emotionless. "And I want you to use the time you're bleeding out on the floor to think about what you did. And when you take your last breath, I want you to fully realize the extent of the damage you've caused. It's all your fault. *All* of it!"

Her heels click down the front steps, and a moment later, I hear the engine of Derek's Volvo reverse out the driveway.

Blood spills, red on the white tiles, pooling beneath my body, spreading out beneath me.

I'm curled into a ball. Through my fingers, the blood is warm, sticky. I can't breathe. My phone is in my pocket. I reach back, pain rocketing from my shoulder up my arm and through my body.

Pushing through the pain, I reach back with my other arm. My fingers are slippery with blood, but I tug the phone out of my pocket, and it slides out of my hand. I grab it again, thumb the home button. There's the Apple symbol and a little progress bar.

Are you fucking kidding me?

It's doing an update?

I'd laugh, but it's painful enough to simply breathe. The phone must have hooked into the Wi-Fi when I arrived.

My vision is blurring at the edges.

It's hard to think. I can't…

What was I trying to remember?

I set the useless phone down. Let my head rest on the cold, white tiles. How ironic that I'll die here in the very doorway where I let Jasmine into our lives all those weeks ago.

If I only knew then what she was truly capable of. But then again, I did, didn't I? More or less. No one would believe me. I was the crazy one.

My head is splitting open from pain. I can't think of anything now through the agony.

Footsteps up the stairs.

She's back…

Then there is nothing.

I'm weightless.

Through the throbbing darkness, my head spins, and I struggle to decipher this new sensation.

Have I passed out?

The world spins, twists and sways.

What is she doing to me now?

Panic floods my body with a new rush of adrenaline, and like a flame to a fuse, anger pumps hot and powerful through my veins.

I struggle—at least, I think I'm struggling—and call out. Maybe I can't move, and I'm not making a sound.

The grip on me tightens. "Shh."

Lips on my forehead.

Lips pressing gently against my cheek.

A voice—so deep, so calm and reassuring—washes over me.

I force open my heavy eyelids. *Zach.*

Am I dreaming? Am I dead?

Something is wrong. His eyes are hard, his jaw tight. Is something wrong with the kids? Is Mandy okay?

"Where have you been?" Something is running down my cheeks. Tears? Blood? "I'm sorry," I say, but I can't tell if my lips are moving and the words are coming out. "I'm so, so sorry."

I don't want Zach to go to jail. I don't want him to die at the hand of the bikers like Derek did.

I've messed everything up. Jasmine's right. This is all because of me.

"I love you." This time I know my words have formed. My voice rattles like I'm gargling water. But the metallic taste on my tongue is blood.

Zach makes a distressed sound in the back of his throat. "Shh, don't talk." A kiss on my forehead. "I love you, too. I'm not going to lose you."

I don't want to lose you, either. But it's too late. The only strength I have is borrowed from being in his arms.

"Who did this to you?"

I try to say her name, but it comes out garbled.

"Jasmine?" How did he understand that? He'd make a good dentist. The thought makes me laugh. Except nothing about this is funny. But I'm laughing again, coughing blood on his shirt.

He holds me hard against his chest, and calm washes over me. Peace.

"You're so cold," he says. "Like ice." He takes my hand in his much larger one.

Now he's speaking in a raised voice, and it takes me a moment to realize he's talking to someone on speaker phone. He doesn't want to let me go.

Don't let me go.

He's giving an address. It's my old one. Why is he giving someone my address?

"No!" I shake my head, trying to unravel my confused thoughts. "That's not my address. I don't live with Derek anymore." He should know that. I try to tell him, but he doesn't hear me.

I'm right here. Why can't he hear me?

I want to tell him I can't feel anything anymore, but I can't form the words.

I try to reach up to touch Zach's cheek. To wipe away his tears, tell him everything will be okay. But my arms are dead weights.

And now I'm looking down on myself from somewhere high above. I'm on the floor, being cradled in Zach's arms, my hand tucked into the warm place between our bodies.

Blood is covering his chest, his arms, as he tenderly brushes hair back from my face. He's crying in earnest now, and his fingers trace feather soft along my jaw. "Claire, wake up." He's trembling. "Please, wake up."

His voice is tender as he says over and over that he loves me, his face creased with fear and concern.

"Don't you dare leave me," he growls, his voice thick with emotion. "The ambulance is on its way. Stay as still as you can, sweetheart."

Sweetheart. I like that. It makes me wish we had more time. I'd like to hear him call me that again.

Please call me sweetheart again.

But he doesn't hear me. I seem to float then fall back into my body. Every time I crash back down, the pain returns. It makes me want to float away and never come back.

Gentle fingers brush over my cheek.

Zach.

I can't leave him. He's talking to me, soothing words over and over. Making promises about our future.

He's talking about our wedding; how beautiful I will look in my dress.

I want the dream that will never be.

I listen to his voice, gentle yet strong, describing our wedding day in vivid detail. Our feet will be bare on the warm sandy beach. The sun, warm on our skin. I see the image, clear in my mind. Zach is wearing a loose white shirt, unbuttoned at the collar and rolled up at the sleeves. I'm wearing a pretty white sundress with thin spaghetti straps. Mandy and Kira are at my side, and Aidan and Richard are with him. Mandy and Kira have flowers in their hair, they match the ones I have in mine. He paints me the picture, but I can see the image in my mind, clearer even than the one he's describing. In front of the celebrant, Zach reads me his vows. He's written them himself. He promises to love me forever. He's written me a song, too, on his guitar, but I'll have to wait until later to hear it.

I miss parts of his story, but I know that it is his voice that is anchoring me. Reminding me he's my reason to stay. To fight.

"Keep your eyes open," he says firmly. "Claire! That's it. Eyes on me."

I try, I really do.

But it's hard. And getting harder.

His kisses touch my cheeks, my forehead. I want to tell him I love him, but my teeth are clenched against the pain.

Images form behind my lids, short movie stills, mini trailers of my life. I see myself as a child, then Katie when she was born. When she first smiled, when she first laughed, her first day at school, the day she was diagnosed with the brain tumor.

I see Derek when he was still the husband I believed him to be, and not the stranger he became. I see Bill Rydell at the bikers' club. I see Jasmine that first day on my doorstep, the place where I now lie in a pool of my own blood.

And how I somehow knew it would come to this.

I see Mandy's smiling face as she puts the red coat on for the first time. I see the kids from the Village.

I see the fire, smell the smoke.

And I see the man I love beyond life itself.

Zach Argos.

And he's looking at me as though he loves me that much, too.

He's living, breathing proof that love can be real, and not just in romance novels.

This broken man, who met this broken woman, and somehow they each made the other whole. Whether I live or die, I know Zach will always be with me. Somehow, we will meet again, and we'll get the chance that was stolen from us.

I'll forever be grateful to him for encouraging me to find out who I really was then loving me enough to stand back as I stumbled my way forward. I've lived a lifetime in the short time I've known Zach.

Only with him, I've felt truly alive.

He taught me how to not fear the darkness and how to fully embrace the light.

Zach.

My love. My life.

My reason.

EPILOGUE

Zach

Six months later...

*A*fter a rocky seventeen-hour flight, I step off the plane at the Perth International Airport and wait impatiently for my bag. Has the damn baggage carousel ever moved so slowly? Since the scandal, I sell the majority of my artwork in London, so overseas trips have become a necessary and frequent part of my life.. I don't consider moving there.

Perth will always be home.

Finally, I leave the airport and drive along West Coast Highway, turning off so I can drive past Claire's old shop, the one that burned down. It's a building site now. I heard it's going to be a wood fired pizza place.

The cops held me for as long as they could after the fire at the Village, questioning me repeatedly about my involvement with the kids. I was continually asked the same questions, framed a different way, until I'd had enough and demanded a lawyer. My only thought was of being back with Claire.

But she wasn't there when I returned.

She'd followed through on her threat to Derek to visit the Dark Ryders clubhouse.

And broke her promise to me.

But I forgave her for that a long time ago.

I'd already forgiven her for everything she could ever do from the moment I first saw her.

And then I nearly fucking lost her. I can still see her body in the doorway. That image will haunt me until the day I die. I unclench my hands from the steering wheel and slow down to the speed limit. The terror, that soul-destroying, body-numbing pain of knowing I was too late sits just under my skin. Ready to send me back to that time when I was powerless. Too late to save my mother. Then, too late to save Claire.

But then she opened her eyes.

And said my name.

I'd have traded my very soul not to lose her.

I pull off the highway onto a side road, then after a while, take an unmarked dirt road. It leads me deeper into the bush, south of Perth this time, to where we have rebuilt the Village.

I park the car. The new entrance is defined by gravel and a timber and rope fence. The sound of laughter reaches my ears the closer I get.

And then I see her.

Claire.

In the strawberry patch at our new Village, she's wearing denim shorts, a faded blue T-shirt. And my favorite baseball cap. I'm drawn to her, moving toward her like a heat-seeking, surface-to-air missile.

She's so fucking beautiful it hurts.

She's taught me so much, this woman who caught my eye even before my watch caught her dress. The sadness I'd observed in her as she'd stared out the window and looked out over the Swan River that night has gone.

She still has nightmares, and I know they're related to the guilt she feels over Derek's murder. But we all have demons.

Those of us with a conscience.

Sunlight catches the sun-streaked highlights in her hair spilling out from the cap as Claire picks up a shovel and starts to dig. Her shoulder surgery went well. I've told her, time and again, to take it easier. But there's no slowing her down. She considers she's been given a second chance at life, and she's not about to waste a single minute of it. She's here with a shovel, planting flowers and picking strawberries with Mandy, who's looking at Claire as though she's the fucking sun itself.

Hell, she's that for me, too.

They haven't seen me yet, so I hang back and watch them for a moment. Although Mandy can never replace the daughter Claire lost, watching them together, I know they're what each other needs.

Claire shouldn't be alive right now. She never knew the full extent of the risk she took visiting Bill Rydell that day. How could she? It's not her world.

Bill had plans for her. She thought she was free, but nothing could have been further from the truth. I was there that day Claire turned up. I heard every word, every plea. Would Rydell have killed her had I not stepped in? Without a doubt. After they'd had their fun.

But I was there fostering my own deal.

My final exit. I knew there would be a price. And I knew it would be steep. Bill doesn't allow loose ends.

It was the moment she arrived that Bill saw my vulnerability. Something I valued higher than my own life.

Claire.

Bill's gift—if you could call it that—is his ability to read human weakness. Everyone has something they're hiding. The price people pay to prevent being exposed is limitless.

My weakness is Claire.

Derek was out the back at the time. I watched as they killed him. I didn't step in. Derek's death was assured the moment Claire arrived. I'd never tell her that. She suffers enough.

Lies, to Claire, are a line you don't cross.

Bill knows Claire would never forgive me for being complicit in Derek's death. And I would never risk losing her again. My silence is assured.

It was my last lie to her.

I will spend the remainder of my life making it up to her.

Claire often says how lucky she is.

Fuck that.

I'm the lucky one.

"Zach!" Keith, a twelve-year-old boy who came to stay with us five weeks ago, bounds up to me. "You're back early. Can we go surfing?"

"Sure. Get the guys together. But I need to see Claire first, okay?" I watch him jog off to get the three new kids Richard picked up last night. Three brothers sleeping in their family car. When they were evicted from their family home, their mother drove into the bush somewhere near Gnangara. She parked the car and connected a hose to the exhaust pipe. Tom, the eldest, realized what was happening and overpowered her, saving his younger brothers. His quick thinking is the only thing that saved their lives.

The fire at the Village had triggered the lengthy investigation I'd been dreading.

Turns out Mason's father started the fire. Mason was disappointed, but sadly, not surprised.

Jasmine was convicted of arson, for the fire at Claire's shop, along with attempted murder and is serving a fourteen-year sentence. She gave birth to a baby girl three months ago.

I was fined—heavily—for building without a permit and charged with a dozen other offenses. A good lawyer and a small fortune ensured I avoided doing time. The boys in the Village were not officially in the foster system, all having fled their homes of their own volition, and were living by their own choice on the streets.

It was fortunate that Aidan's guardianship application for Mandy had been approved before the fire. Mandy's age and circumstances would have been an issue, had she been living at the Village, and likely would have forced a different outcome.

Unable to legally rebuild the Village myself, Richard continued what I had started. But Richard is doing it far better and on a much larger scale than I ever did. He has plans to create many Villages, the difference being his model teaches the kids to work within the system. The boys learn how to work to a blueprint, and they apply for and receive the required council approvals.

Richard has been granted the licenses I never would have been given.

But he calls his venture the Zach Argos Foundation.

I'm forced to acknowledge the small part I played in how it all started, but the truth is the student turned out far greater than the teacher.

Claire glances over at me then, and the distance between us dissolves.

She still has the power to stop my heart then send it racing.

She always will.

I never thought my life would amount to anything. How could a boy who killed his own father ever be worthy of anything good?

But Claire made me believe. After all, if a woman like Claire can love someone like me, I already had the whole fucking world.

And now she's walking to me. *Me!*

She's wiping her hands on her jeans. Her smile gets wider the closer she gets.

I can't fucking move. I'm standing, my feet fixed to the ground, as I drink in everything about her.

The last few steps, she takes at a run. She jumps into my arms, hers wrapping around my neck. I hold her tight and swing her around, her simple joy constricting my throat. She's smiling even as I kiss her.

"You're back early," she says, pulling back breathlessly.

Claire is on a crusade. Instead of avoiding the media attention as I have been, Claire embraced it. Even from her hospital bed, she went public, and she went big. She launched a social media campaign drawing attention to the issue of homelessness, not just for today's youth but, surprisingly, the largest growing group among the homeless in Australia: single women over fifty. She's become an advocate for women in domestic-violence situations and donates a hefty percentage of all her design sales.

Claire found herself, her confidence, and then some

"You taste of strawberries," I tell her, and she grins.

"Mandy and I have been taste-testing."

"Mmm, I love strawberries," I say, but it's her that I love. I kiss her again, hard, possessive.

Mine.

She laughs and pulls back. "Shall we go find lunch? I want to hear all about your show."

I glance over her shoulder. "I'll cook you dinner instead." Three new boys, wearing wetsuits and carrying surfboards, are starting to make their way over to me. This will be their first surfing lesson. Later, I'll teach them how to measure timber and use an axe. Then slowly, over the next few weeks, I'll watch the anger fade from their eyes and their unique personalities rise to the surface. It's aggression that makes them all look the same when they first arrive, and it's so fucking good to watch them become young men, living to their full potential.

"It's a date." She lowers her voice. "I missed you."

Her words, her tone, ignite the need I always have for her. I outwardly groan as my desire for her turns painful.

I place my palms on either side of her waist, keep her tempting curves slightly at a distance, knowing my control where she's concerned is always tenuous.

Her eyes are alight with excitement and mischief.

I swallow, nod at the boys.

"I have to go," I say, my voice thick with emotion.

She smiles at the boys then turns back to me.

"Tonight," she says.

"Tonight," I repeat back to her.

And tomorrow. Next week. Next year…

For the rest of my life.

THE END.

MORE BY ATHENA DANIELS

DESPERATE SERIES
Desperate (Book One)

BEYOND THE GRAVE SERIES
The Seer's Daughter (Book One)
The Alchemist's Son (Book Two)
Girl Unseen (Book Three)
When Darkness Follows (Book Four)
Book Five coming 2019

NOVELS
The Scream Behind Her Smile

ACKNOWLEDGMENTS

Some novels take more of a journey to create than others. This book is one of them. I can say now, that I'm grateful for the challenges, the winding path, and the story's stubborn resistance to be told in any way less than it is today.

Thanks to Victoria Curran for providing the clarity and direction exactly when I needed it, and for editing the final version. It has been fun working with you!

Love and appreciation to Leah Frost for reading the original drafts of this book, and for your feedback and suggestions. My beautiful sister, you're always there for me, and I couldn't imagine life without you.

Special thanks to Claire Louisa Holderness for reading multiple versions of the story and for your feedback, insight, support and friendship.

Thanks and appreciation to Dawn Yacovetta for all of your assistance along the way, including the final proofread of the story.

Special thanks to Dana Delamar for your help, suggestions and editing of the original version of the story.

Thanks to Kimberley Whalen, for the idea that changed it all...

Thanks to Alison Stuart for answering my questions relating to Zach's venture. To Loma Eldridge for your help with my questions regarding commercial leases. Any mistakes are my own.

To Mum and Trev who have provided foster care and respite to more than a hundred children over twenty years. Thanks for your help with questions regarding Zach's venture. Again, any mistakes are my own.

To my husband, my boys, and Ali for your continued support and encouragement. You are my world.

To my readers. I'm so very grateful to everyone who has read one of my books and taken the time to leave a review, send a message, like a post or spread the word. Without you, I wouldn't be able to continue to do what I love. From the bottom of my heart, thank you. xoxo

ABOUT THE AUTHOR

Athena Daniels is the #1 international bestselling author of the award-winning Beyond the Grave paranormal romance series and the romantic thrillers; *The Scream Behind Her Smile* and *Desperate*.

In 2016, Athena was nominated for Author of the Year and Best New Author in *AusRom Today*'s Reader's Choice Awards.

Her novel *Girl Unseen* won the Silver Medal in the 2017 Readers' Favorite® International Book Awards, was awarded a Silver Medal in the 2017 Literary Titan Book Awards and was a finalist in the TopShelf Book Awards 2018. *Girl Unseen* was an "Official Selection" in the New Apple Literary Awards and was also nominated for 2017 Book of the Year in *AusRom Today*'s Reader's Choice Awards. *Girl Unseen* is a 5-star Top Pick at The Romance Reviews.

When Darkness Follows won the Bronze Medal in the 2018 Readers' Favorite® International Book Awards, Silver Medal in the 2018 Literary Titan Book Awards, and has been nominated for an award in the TopShelf Book Awards 2019. *When Darkness follows* was an "Official Selection" in New Apple Literary Awards and was also nominated in the Australian Romance Readers Association (ARRA) 2018 awards for Favorite Paranormal Romance.

The Seer's Daughter was the solo Medalist Winner in the Suspense/Thriller category of the 2016 New Apple Annual Book Awards for Excellence in Independent Publishing. *The Seer's Daughter* was also a finalist in the 11th Annual National Indie Excellence Awards in Suspense and in the 2016 Readers' Favorite® International Book Awards. Additionally, *The Seer's Daughter* was nominated for 2016 Book of the Year and 2016 Cover of the Year in *AusRom Today*'s Reader's Choice Awards. *The Seer's Daughter* is a 5-star Top Pick at The Romance Reviews.

Athena has a natural curiosity about the "more" there is in life and holds several qualifications in metaphysics and natural therapies. She is a euro-linguistic programming (NLP) practitioner and feng shui specialist. Athena lives on the northern beaches of sunny Western Australia.

Find out more about her at www.athenadaniels.com.